Chapter 1

Martha & Mary

Whitechapel – 6 August 1888

Something smelt strongly as the big man walked slowly but positively along the shadows at the side of the High Street. To a close observer it might have seemed that he was looking for something, though there was no indication what that might be. It appeared to suit him to hug the shadows, although he made no attempt to shrink or hide. He had come from the direction of the City of London past the church of St Botolph. It was a bank holiday Monday and the weather had been changeable lately following the miserable chills of recent months.

Purposefully he walked forward, occasionally skirting around something unpleasant that lay in his path. His gait might have suggested a hunter, in control, effortless, relaxed but aware. The smell grew stronger but he ignored it, often enough the Whitechapel streets were unpleasant, littered with all manner of waste and debris. It was late but as always there were people about in the area, many had nowhere to go, nowhere to sleep. Noise came from some of the public houses, alive with the buzz of drink-fuelled gaiety and discordant snatches of song. The man walked on, like someone on business, well dressed, a professional, perhaps.

Martha Tabram had been drinking with Mary Ann Connelly when they picked up two guardsmen, a Corporal and a Private, and drunk with them in several public houses in Whitechapel. When they entered their final pub of the evening, the big man followed them in. Unbeknown to any of them he stood nearby whilst he took a drink, he could hear their chatter but retained little of it other than Martha and Mary, names which caught his attention, and were often interchangeable in his times. He had no interest in the soldiers, understanding full well what they were there for.

Martha and Mary were fallen women, brought to this by the poverty of their circumstances. They both knew the area well and shared some acquaintanceship in the pubs of the district. Mary was taller with a somewhat masculine look, while Martha was shorter, dark haired and rounder in both body and face. They weren't really friends; perhaps colleagues might have better described their relationship. Sometimes they teamed up whilst meeting men, who often seemed to appear in pairs. After a few drinks and having quietly agreed terms with their clients, the two women separated outside the pub. It was around eleven forty-five p.m., and each one left with their chosen soldier.

Mary Connelly and her Corporal made for one of her regular spots in Angel Alley. Martha headed, as she had many times before, towards George Yard, a narrow and gloomy alley between Whitechapel High Street and Wentworth Street which ran parallel to Angel Alley. It was a dangerous and unpleasant area, poorly lit and for that reason, quiet at night. Of course, this suited Martha and her clients as it would ensure a modicum of privacy. Real privacy in Whitechapel was a luxury that few ever actually experienced.

Martha led her man unerringly, if a little drunkenly, to a dark stairwell inside George Yard Buildings. She completed her contract with the Private there, knowing it was a spot where they were unlikely to be disturbed. She had used this particular place before on numerous occasions. Even if someone passed them on the stairs, it was so dark that they would see little and accept that it was two people enjoying some privacy. At the very worst, Martha and her client would be turned out of the building and there were plenty of other such places known to her. The act was quick, functional, and fumbling. Afterwards, the Private made his excuses and went off to look for his Corporal.

Martha slowly rearranged her clothing and descended a few steps down, back towards the entrance to the building. She wasn't in a hurry and swayed a little, knowing that yet again, she had drunk too much. In recent years she had become mired in alcohol, her dependence growing worse since separating from her last partner Henry Turner. Martha now found refuge in a common lodging house in Spitalfields. Sometimes she thought with regret about the past, her two sons and the husband who had left her after bitter rows about her drinking. Drink was the scourge not only of Martha, but of thousands of other people in the east London district of Whitechapel at the time. The likelihood of any individual finding refuge in alcohol was hardly surprising, when a life endured in poverty was so hard, so coarse, so unforgiving.

The big man's eyes had grown accustomed to the extreme darkness of George Yard. After following from the public house and watching the pair enter George Yard Buildings, he waited patiently, leaning against a wall near Wentworth Street. He guessed that the couple would go back the way they had arrived, towards the High Street, from where a little faint light crept through into the yard. Nobody was around. The alley was patrolled regularly by a police constable, as were all the surrounding streets, but that didn't trouble the man at all. If a constable appeared he knew how he would deal with it.

After a few minutes the soldier emerged, his figure only a little darker than the surrounding gloom. Glancing in each direction, though seeing little, he sauntered away wondering if he would find his Corporal nearby. The big man moved closer towards the opening in the brickwork that formed the entrance to the building. When first built it had been quite ornate, the brickwork set back in several receding rows to form a gothic archway. The bricklayer would have taken pride in this doorway, no doubt he had stood back to admire his handiwork.

Soon the man heard steps as Martha approached, and he backed away into the darkness. As he had guessed, swaying gently, she set off in the same direction as that taken by the soldier moments before. Approaching the doorway he went inside, up several steps and waited on the stairwell for a few seconds whilst further acclimatising his eyesight. He then looked around carefully before making his way out of the building, following Martha back towards the High Street.

For the next hour or so he observed Martha calling into several public houses, spending the last of her coppers including the money given to her by the soldier. There was no sign of Mary Ann Connelly to be found. Martha drifted uncertainly in a westerly direction towards Aldgate and St Botolph's church. Approaching the church she seemed to make up her mind and slowly completed a circuit of the road that isolated the building on its own island. She was looking for another client and she wasn't the only one there, several others were doing the same slow circle, keeping their distance from each other but stopping to entice any passer-by. Things were quiet and there were few prospects. The big man hung back watching a while longer, wondering if she might head to her lodgings, but the luckless Martha still needed the price of her bed for the night.

Seeing little chance of a client here on Prostitute Island, as it had become known, she decided to try her luck again on Whitechapel High Street. Retracing her steps, Martha headed east from the church, back the way she had come. The big man followed, faster this time, his mind made up. He closed the gap swiftly. Glancing back just once, he stepped in front of her, forcing her to stop in her tracks. Martha stumbled slightly and cursed, staring up at the man who looked down upon her in the gloom.

'Who are you, what do you want?' said Martha suddenly fearful as she realised there was nobody else nearby.

'It's alright, Martha-Mary, I just want your company for a moment,' said the man.

'Well then,' said Martha. 'How do you know my name?'

'Never mind that, will you?' asked the man, grasping her elbow firmly and walking her onwards down the road. She stated her price and he agreed without argument, so she indicated down Whitechapel High Street and they walked together. The man looked around occasionally out of the corner of his eye, but few people took any notice of them. They looked what they were, a fairly nondescript couple heading somewhere in the early hours.

Soon they had turned into George Yard and were approaching the building of the same name. It was a solid looking structure, still darker inside than the yard outside, and as before, no sound came from within. She wasn't worried; Martha knew what he wanted, and men liked a dark and quiet place for it. He allowed her to lead him up the shallow steps to the stairwell where she and the soldier had recently been. Assuming that he would want the same, she turned to face him. Reaching down she gripped her skirts and raised them, then for a long moment there was silence and he said nothing.

In the darkness she couldn't see his hands clamp themselves firmly around her neck. His elbows pushed her violently against the wall, trapping her arms and stopping her from freeing herself. Martha struggled ineffectively, opening her mouth to scream but no sound came out. As she gurgled and collapsed he half lowered, half dropped her to the floor. Wasting no time he drew his blade, and wielding it underhand, plunged it viciously into her chest. Her feet kicked out vainly connecting with the wall. He kept one hand firmly over Martha's mouth, pressing her head down as he cut her throat violently, blood haemorrhaging onto the stone-flagged floor. The man then stabbed again and again, this time into her chest wall, lungs and heart. He felt, rather than saw, a fine mist of blood spray onto the hairs at the back of his hand. She made no movement now.

Still stooping down beside her he released her mouth, then knelt on one knee transferring his weight. He paused for breath before lifting Martha's skirts and petticoats to expose her lower body and complete his grim task. Now the man stabbed faster and faster into her groin and stomach area. Finally he slowed and stood up as more blood ran gently from the warmth of her body. Breathing heavily he tried to survey the results in the almost impenetrable light.

Glancing either way the man stooped again, this time to draw up Martha's legs and open her knees, presumably to indicate that recent intercourse had occurred, which it had. He wiped his blade and the back of his hands cursorily on her clothing, then pocketed the weapon. Rising to full height he walked swiftly down the few stairs and back towards Whitechapel High Street. It was now two twenty-five a.m.

Chapter 2

A Visit from the Love God

Southampton – Present Day

The young man pushed his trolley around the supermarket, a few streets from his apartment. He shopped like a man, knew exactly what his requirements were; there was no dallying or hesitation during his shopping expeditions. Samuel saw his weekly shop as a necessary, though often pleasant enough, evil. He had to eat and drink, so he bought both what he enjoyed and what he thought might be reasonably healthy. Into his trolley went just enough to fill two bags that he could easily carry back.

As he approached his flat he saw a friend, Dave Knox, walking towards him. Dave looked slightly bored and his face broke into a cheeky grin when he saw Sam approaching.

'Hi Sam, what's happening then? Bernie's been trying to contact you, did she get you yet? She phoned me a half hour ago and asked if I knew where you were, so I said I'd wander down and see you.'

'Thanks, Dave,' said Sam, realising that his friend was at a loose end this morning. 'I'll call her when I get in. How's things with you?'

'I'm fine thanks, got all the shopping done then? Good boy.' Dave teased.

Reaching the entrance Samuel handed his shopping bags to Dave while he found his key and unlocked the large old heavy door to his building. The curved apex of the door fitted snugly into the red brick arch of its surround, and spacious bay windows protruded from all floors. It was a satisfying, substantial building. Solid and expensive when constructed many years ago, it looked comfortable and mature from the road.

'You should come round more often, you could carry my bags and I'll teach you all about shopping. You know, that's where food comes from, pal,' Samuel replied with an innocent voice. Dave, whose understanding of food went a little further than takeaways but not entirely as far as cooking, ignored the remark.

'Anyway, she said she had met someone who would interest you and your Conan Doyle obsession. I said I'd pop round and see if you were in,' said Dave, grinning again with his gentle dig at Samuel's lifelong interest in the creator of the world's most famous detective, Sherlock Holmes.

Samuel grinned back, he had known Dave since school, or as Dave liked to say, 'We went to different schools together.'

In Dave's fantasy world he and Sam were two love gods, holding court nightly in city centre pubs, where hordes of gorgeous women would queue up to chat to them. His fertile imagination had him and Sam selecting several and taking them home. Once there, the girls would do their duty, and then even wash the dishes before obediently departing next morning!

Of course, the reality was slightly more mundane. They did go drinking together often but Sam wasn't really one to chase women and certainly not when he had a girlfriend. Sam had spent the last few months in a relationship, so events never quite lived up to Dave's expectations. They were good mates and the banter was a mainstay of their friendship. The regular jokes about his Doyle fascination didn't bother Sam. It had always been something of a talking point when they were with other people.

After their respective universities they had naturally met up again back in Southampton. Sam now worked on the staff of the Centre for Contemporary Writing at the university, where he lectured regularly on a part-time basis. Since completing his education he had tried a number of jobs before deciding that being a writer was something he couldn't avoid. For much of his time he researched and wrote avidly about the Victorian and Edwardian periods, on which he had become something of an expert, whilst specialising in his real love, the life and works of Sir Arthur Conan Doyle. Sam's lecturing satisfied his desire to stay in touch with people who felt the same way as he did about the written word.

Sam steadfastly refused to own a mobile phone. He maintained, to the chagrin of friends, family and colleagues alike that it disturbed his thought patterns while writing and demanded his attention. He felt it took him away from the quiet, more scholarly times of the Victorian era he was interested in. He did keep a landline and a state of the art desktop computer, acknowledging that he needed the Internet for research and to communicate with his contacts in the writing world. His slightly eccentric approach to modern life – he even lived in a red-brick Victorian building – was part of his attractiveness. That, coupled with a friendly disposition and unruly straw coloured locks, made him a magnet for a range of female friends.

'Am I coming in then?' said Dave quizzically.

'If you've nothing better to do, on condition you make coffee while I phone Bernie.'

They climbed the stairs and entering his apartment, Sam parked the shopping bags on the kitchen worktop. Dave knew where the coffee was and busied himself while Sam walked through to his 'library' as he called the only untidy room in his flat. It was clearly a writer's domain, two walls were almost completely covered with books of all ages. In the corner was his desk and computer, surrounded by files, notes and yet more books on every subject you could imagine, a few of them were Victorian rare editions. There were even piles of books on the floor waiting to be read, shelved or otherwise dealt with.

On one of the few visible pieces of wall hung a picture of his parents and another of his sister Paige, whose wild straw hair marked her out as the female version of Sam. Her piercing grey eyes stared unflinchingly at the camera, indicating someone of perception and strength of character.

There were two messages on his phone. I've only been out for an hour or so, he mused, and it is Saturday morning after all. One was from a friend wanting to discuss a forthcoming book club meeting. The other was from Bernadette McKenna, telling him she had an urgent matter which would be of extreme interest to him, the message dryly adding that she had tried his mobile but for some reason she couldn't get through! Sam smiled at the ongoing joke about his non-existent mobile, and rang her home number.

Bernadette, a senior lecturer at Southampton University, picked up straight away. 'Sammy, thanks for ringing back, it's just that I've had an interesting contact and it's right up your street. It may be nothing but you'd hate me if I didn't let you know right away.'

For the last few years he and Bernadette had stayed fast friends, part of a group of six literary fans titling themselves the Mystery Club. The club included Bernadette's husband Gerry, Dave Knox, and two other crime writing fans Alexa Hussein and James Miles. James now ran a successful rare book enterprise, and was a collector himself. Sam was close to them all and Bernadette in particular who had always been his guru. Apart from Gerry and Bernie there were no relationships in the group, just a shared interest in history and crime writing plus mutual respect and friendship. The club met almost every month for an evening of crime discussion, plot analysis and a considerable amount of real ale.

'So what's it all about then?' said Sam.

'Well,' said Bernadette, 'I was in the British Library yesterday and went in the cafe there, and it was busy, as usual, so I shared a table with a girl who was doing research on Jack the Ripper.'

'Oh yes,' prompted Sam gently, 'A Ripperologist eh? You're keeping good company these days.'

'Of course I am,' said Bernadette. 'Didn't I ever? Anyway, we got talking and when she found out my background she started asking about Sir Arthur Conan Doyle. Naturally I know a bit about him but I'm not in your league. She was asking me where he lived at the time of the Ripper murders and what I knew about his domestic circumstances etc. I wondered if she was trying to link him to the murders and I thought it was all a bit cranky, but then she said something that made me sit up and take notice.'

'What was that?' said Sam.

'She said she had something that linked Sir Arthur with the Ripper or that he knew who the Ripper was and had suppressed it. I still thought it was all rather unlikely but she got to me a little bit. She wasn't totally obsessive, you know, blinded by her own theories. She is a bright girl and seemed to genuinely have something. She wants to pursue the matter and I told her that you were the man.' Bernadette paused at that point and waited for him to respond.

'Bernie, this has to be complete rubbish, you can't think there's any truth in it; these people are just conspiracy theorists. Surely she can't be serious can she?'

'Well, I knew you'd say that of course, but there is something about this girl that made me unsure. Why don't you talk to her? At least you can make your own mind up.'

'What does she want with me of all people? I've heard about Jack the Ripper, but surely there are better sources around.'

'You are an acknowledged expert on Arthur Conan Doyle, it's that that she's after, your expertise,' countered Bernie gently.

'I don't know, Bernie, it all sounds faintly ridiculous to me, Sir Arthur was an upstanding guy who always tried to do the right thing, the idea of him being involved in anything like that is crazy.'

'Yes, well it's up to you, but what have you got to lose by talking?' said Bernie in that slightly offhand way Sam knew very well. It reminded him of her lecturing when she would casually point students in a particular direction with a throwaway remark, then wait to see who had tuned in to the fact that it was actually something crucial to their studies.

'Okay, Bernie, you win.' He smiled down the telephone; she knew he was smiling and a grin spread over her own face. 'How do I contact her?'

'I've already emailed you her mobile number; her name is Annabelle, she lives in Kew or somewhere I think.'

'Bernie?'

'Yes?'

'Thanks for that – see you next week?'

'You surely will,' said Bernie. 'You can tell the Mystery Club all about it then.'

Sam said little about the call to Dave who was sitting in Sam's lounge with coffees ready. He contented himself by giving his friend a few details, then the conversation moved swiftly on.

Samuel Taylor had been born and raised in the New Forest and his parents still lived in Brockenhurst. As a child his family had lived in Minstead for several years and he knew the area well. He had played on the village green, in the churchyard, tormented the staff in the local store and disrupted the infrequent traffic by playing football in the street. During the holidays he spent his days in the New Forest with his sister and friends. It was an idyllic childhood and he looked back on it with contentment. The tracts of open heathland buzzing with insects in summer, the damp and green woodland glades where shy deer were to be found at dawn or dusk, were all part of his personal history. Even in the twenty-first century it seemed little had changed in the forest.

Sam's father was a historian and because of that, for many years Sam had strongly resisted the idea of going the same way, imagining he would do anything but that. His mother read to him extensively as a child and he wanted to write, but had no clear idea what he would write about. All this was to change however, when his interest was sparked by Sir Arthur Conan Doyle's unique adventure stories. Finding out he was buried locally, Sam devoured all of Doyle's work and learned a lot about the man himself and his creation, the world famous private detective, Sherlock Holmes. He discovered along the way that Doyle's passion for reading and writing had also been sparked by his mother. Sam's interest in the Victorian period developed from there, starting with wars, trade and conquest, marvelling at the spread of the Empire and the extraordinary self-belief that had fuelled it. The writings of Doyle had been his portal to the Victorians and reinforced his interest, particularly the tales of daring and adventure. His curiosity about those times had gradually spread back to previous eras, developing his knowledge of many periods in world history. Ruefully, Sam eventually saw that he had turned into his father. Though not a qualified historian, he was at least a seasoned amateur.

Wanting to write today and knowing Dave would be hungry, Sam swiftly produced brie and grape sandwiches for lunch and told his friend he would have to go afterwards. Dave, knowing Sam's habits, had his sandwich, then stealing a beer from Sam's kitchen he obediently departed. Once he had left, Sam locked the door, took the phone off the hook and settled down to his latest project. His sister phoned a few times that afternoon but she also knew his habits, and realising exactly what was happening, she resolved to try again tomorrow. She liked to catch Sam when he least expected it, and usually tuned into his mood in seconds. As it happened she was correct about Sam's mood, she knew his latest relationship was in decline and had been hoping to cheer him a little.

It appeared to Sam that his current affair was all but over. During the last year his relationship with Indira had been the most important thing in his life, then it had suddenly waned as she became distant and uncertain, unable to commit, or so it seemed to Sam. For no apparent reason their meetings had become strained, their conversation stilted, their warmth and intimacy had evaporated. Maddeningly she had avoided making her usual eye contact with Sam. Bewildered, he had finally walked out of the bookshop where she worked.

'You know where I am if you decide you want me,' had been his parting shot, hurt and wounded.

Sam was convinced there was no-one else. Although she was still married he had no doubts about her fidelity, she was such an honest, open and loving person he knew she would have told him instantly had there been another love in her life. He also knew she would never hurt him intentionally, so what was it all about? He missed those soft brown eyes. He missed the way she slipped her hands inside his shirt when she hugged him. He missed her planning a weekend for them. He missed the way her eyes would twinkle at him when she felt frisky. He missed everything about her.

Sam was indeed writing to prevent himself from thinking about Indy any more. Writing was his one way of escaping reality and he was tired of going over things again and again in his mind. Sometimes he would allow himself to wallow in his own self-pity, but had decided this definitely wasn't going to be one of those days. He clicked on his data icon and selected the folder that held the file he wanted.

A low background hum of city traffic murmured through the double glazing behind him as he settled down to write. Gradually the light faded and a lengthening shadow slipped slowly down the wall beside him.

The afternoon had sailed by.

Chapter 3
A Fateful Meeting

London – Present Day

The train from Southampton to London was a fast one, Sam barely had an hour or so in his book before the on-board announcement indicated its impending arrival at Waterloo. He was re-reading an early biography of Sir Arthur Conan Doyle, one of several he had on his bookshelves. Sam's long term thinking was to produce his own biography of the great man, but he recognised this would need more time and research than he was able to give at present. More information would also have to become available before attempting this. It was very much something for the future, he thought.

Today he was on the way to meet Annabelle. Following the talk with Bernie he had made contact and had a brief conversation. Looking back he wasn't sure what to make of it. Annabelle had been quite guarded, implying she had something in her possession which might lead to a great revelation about the Jack the Ripper mystery. That something concerned Sir Arthur Conan Doyle, and she wanted to get more information about him quickly. She had done some research but rapidly realised that it would take her years to find out enough. Annabelle had admitted that she was impatient and felt that by talking to someone who had already spent years studying him, she would save some time. Sam mused that whilst she had been grateful he had called she had also sounded a little cool towards him. This was perhaps because he had made it clear that Conan Doyle should never be regarded as a suspect in the Whitechapel murders, at least in his view.

As the train slowed down, curving gently towards its terminus, he wondered again why he was here. Perhaps he was a bit bored and needed something else to occupy him. No, it had actually been Bernie who convinced him to follow it up.

'Well it's up to you, but what have you got to lose by talking?' He could hear her words now, and after all, there was nothing preventing him from meeting the girl. Bernie had seen something in her and she was a shrewd judge of people. He put the biography back in his shoulder bag and stood up.

They had arranged to meet in one of the cafes upstairs at the station; her email had suggested she would try to bag a table in The Cabin unless it was packed, in which case she would be in another one close by. When Sam had asked how he would recognise her she had replied saying she had dark hair and would wear a bright pink scarf.

Sam rode the escalator and walked along the gallery past the shops, then glancing forward to the cafe he saw a girl sitting alone at the bar. She was watching people at nearby tables while she chattered animatedly on a mobile phone. He took in a hurried impression of her profile, one of dark eyes, high cheekbones and a slightly Roman nose, all surrounded by a jumble of long dark hair.

'Annabelle?' he questioned hesitantly as he approached.

'Yes, you must be Samuel,' she replied, slipping off the bar stool to shake his hand. 'Call me Anna,' she said, 'everybody else does.' For a moment he was enveloped in the widest smile he had ever seen, then, just as suddenly it was gone, and she asked if he would like a coffee.

She ordered a couple of coffees and for a while they sat and talked about generalities, taking stock of each other before they got down to the business in hand. She politely thanked him for coming to London and they gave each other a nutshell about their subjects of interest, in his case Conan Doyle and Sherlock Holmes, and in her case the Whitechapel murders. For a while longer they danced around the issue and it was probably half an hour before Sam asked her what exactly linked Doyle to the Ripper. She nodded, expecting the question.

'Can I ask if this phrase means anything to you,' she said. 'First and last lines contain a Ripping Yarn.'

Sam had heard it before and immediately remembered where. But something in her reticence had made him also want to keep his powder dry. He was usually open with people and wasn't quite sure why he was being guarded. The phrase took him back a few years to a man he had met and admired for his knowledge of all things Sherlock Holmes and Conan Doyle. He decided to be non-committal.

'It rings a bell somewhere, but I can't place it. Where did you see it?'

'I have a sheet of paper that used to belong to Conan Doyle, it's written on that.'

'Oh really? Where did you get it?'

'I'd rather not say.'

Sam felt rebuffed. The degree of fencing that was going on wasn't his style. She noticed the effect her reply had had and tightened her lips. He seemed a nice guy, open and friendly but she wanted any discovery about the Ripper to be hers and hers alone. She had invested too much time researching to want to share her findings with anybody, especially on a first meeting.

'I'm sorry, that sounded very rude. I suppose I feel so close to finding out if this is the truth about the Ripper, that I am worried about anyone stealing my thunder.' She softened her abruptness by flashing the big smile he had briefly seen earlier.

Sam returned the smile. 'Okay, I can understand that, even though you are on the wrong track with this Conan Doyle idea. Shall we go somewhere else? My backside is going to sleep in this chair.' She smiled but didn't make any reply.

Sam had plenty of time and return trains ran frequently so they wandered along the South Bank and across the Millennium Bridge to a pub near St Paul's. They had no idea that a man had followed them from the station, hanging back across the bridge, then entering the busy pub and getting a drink for himself at the bar.

Once in the pub with drinks in their hands, Anna and Sam started to get the measure of each other, arguing fiercely about the likelihood of Conan Doyle being the Ripper. The girl seemed to have the idea firmly embedded in her mind, but Sam scoffed openly at it, telling her repeatedly that Doyle was a gentleman, a champion against injustice, a campaigner and, in his younger days, a doctor sworn to save life, not take it.

Anna didn't like being scoffed at. Her eyes flashed dangerously. She started to broadside him with snippets that could support her case. She made great play of Doyle's fixation with his mother Mary, his bloodlust on board a whaling ship, his propensity for leading a secret life, and the fact he was a Gemini with two very different sides to his character. In addition, she said, he had a lifelong fascination with macabre and grim incidents, crimes and even secret rooms.

Put like that it did make him sound like an unusual man, but Sam saw nothing which would make Doyle a murderer.

'Also,' she went on, 'he was very, very interested in the Ripper murders, he visited the Whitechapel sites, viewed Scotland Yard's Black Museum memorabilia, and he was a member of something called The Murder Club. He couldn't stay away from it,' she ended triumphantly.

Sam shook his head. 'I'm sorry, what you call the 'murder club' came much later in his life and the whaling trip was when he was very young, acting as a ship's surgeon.'

Anna ploughed on regardless. 'He admitted that he was personally involved in the terrible killing of baby seals, and he described it graphically! I read all about it online.'

Anna had obviously been struck by Doyle's acknowledgement of bloodlust, and wouldn't let the subject go. She looked up with a challenge in her eye, her chin pointing obstinately at Sam.

'You couldn't get a clearer description of bloodlust, it's all there, he might be describing a murderer in the making, but he was in fact describing himself!'

Sam had listened silently. Unbeknown to Anna he had studied every aspect of Doyle's life from a number of biographies that sat on his library shelves. He was familiar with this particular period, which, he would be the first to acknowledge, gave a great insight into Doyle's spell on board a whaling ship.

'Look, you have to put all that in context,' Sam began. 'Doyle wrote about many things constantly throughout his life; this is just one period when he was employed as a surgeon on the *Hope*, a whaling vessel. Also, the act of sealing and whaling was hardly controversial back then. It was an industry being conducted by many, many nations. Life wasn't as pink and fluffy as it is nowadays, so people weren't as shocked about the realities of animal deaths as they might be now.'

Anna wasn't budging. She repeated her ideas, mentioning again anything that she saw as bolstering her argument. The debate raged back and forth.

After a couple of drinks, if anything it became more intense as Sam found his lifetime study of Conan Doyle under attack. He instinctively admired Doyle for his achievements and the way he had conducted himself throughout his life.

'I've told you, the whole idea of ACD being a murderer is daft, I've even heard people saying that Sherlock Holmes was Jack the Ripper, it's just preposterous.' Sam laughed.

Anna coloured a little, her eyes blazing. 'I didn't say Sherlock Holmes was the killer did I? Obviously he's a fictional character, but Conan Doyle wasn't was he? He was a real man, and *men* sometimes have weird desires and homicidal tendencies, such as his bloodlust!'

She tossed her hair contemptuously, managing to condemn all men with the tone of her remarks. 'I could remind you that most serial killers have absolutely nothing that marks them out as such to the people around them.' Her voice had risen slightly as she had spoken.

There was an awkward silence between them for some moments. Anna looked unrepentant, and finally to move things on Sam said, 'Look, you'll need more than a bit of paper with a few words on it to convince me. Anyway, where is the paper?'

Anna said she hadn't brought it with her. But she did give him some more information, saying that the rest of the paper was covered with figures in four columns, not monetary figures, just low numbers. She was convinced it was some sort of coded message, but could not go further than that. She continued the afternoon by asking more and more questions about Doyle and his life.

Sam had no difficulty in answering most of them. She asked about Portsmouth, where Doyle had lived at the time of the murders. Sam gave her a quick rundown on the author's time at Bush Villas in Portsmouth and his other dwellings. He mentioned Doyle's houses at Norwood, Undershaw at Hindhead, Windlesham Manor at Crowborough and Bignell Wood in the New Forest, Sam's own part of the world.

At the mention of Bignell Wood the dark eyes glinted for a second but she said nothing.

After another abortive argument about Doyle, Sam decided it was time to leave. They walked slowly back to Waterloo, once again followed by the man in the pub, his hands in his pockets, whistling softly to himself. This time Anna and Sam avoided the subject and talked about other things. There had been some battles between them but despite that they hesitantly agreed to keep in touch. Whilst walking across the bridge the atmosphere between them relaxed a little. Sam said he would try to remember where he had come across the phrase she'd mentioned. Anna said she would like to talk to him about Conan Doyle again, if Sam would do so.

'Why not?' Sam smiled. Anna thanked him again for coming to London and the dazzling smile made another of its brief appearances as they reached his platform. Putting his ticket in the barrier he walked through to the train. When he looked back from the platform she was gone.

Up on the gallery near the cafe they had used earlier another man stood watching Anna. He wore a black fleece and sunglasses. As she disappeared in the direction of the Tube station, he raised a mobile phone to his ear.

Chapter 4

The Southsea Doctor

Portsmouth – 1882

Arthur Conan Doyle's steamer journey from Plymouth had been completely uneventful. He was well used to being at sea, though on this occasion the coastal trip hardly qualified as such in his mind. His first views of Southsea showed it to be a generally pleasant and thriving area. Doyle was a well built, even plump young gentleman, nicely dressed and with the look of a sportsman about him, rugby perhaps, or cricket. It was a warm day and his tweed suit felt oppressive in the sunshine.

Immediately he set about his business plan. After obtaining temporary lodging he purchased a map of the town and walked its length and breadth, checking every street and area for the type of people who lived in the vicinity. In addition, he paid particular attention to the brass plates of businesses that he came across. He was looking for rooms suitable to enable him to set up his practice as a physician. His main concern was to find an area where he would not impinge on other doctors, thus allowing him the chance of building his practice without too much direct competition.

The ambitious young doctor who had jokingly described himself as 'licensed to kill' when he qualified, eventually settled on some chambers at 1 Bush Villas in Elm Grove, Southsea, which appeared to best fit the criteria he had decided upon.

Over the next few months he set out his stall, though right from the start patients proved hard to come by. His new brass plate attracted many lookers, but failed in its duty to bring patients through the door in viable numbers. At times the young man felt despair at his inability to make progress in his chosen path. In common with other physicians, he prescribed and supplied medicines to supplement his income, but there was never enough to give him the standard of living he desired.

The solution to at least one problem soon presented itself. His periods of inactivity became the perfect opportunity to continue with his writing. Always fascinated by books and having been a voracious reader, Doyle never forgot the stories he had been weaned on at his mother's knee. Before settling in Portsmouth he had written a number of stories which he later acknowledged had not been of the first quality. He had always fancied he could do better and settled down to do so for his own amusement. Not only was he a keen storyteller but also a fantasist whose use of imaginary worlds and places lent weight to his portrayals of characters and locations. Doyle wrote quickly and decisively with a pen and ink, very few changes or amendments were made as the stories gushed out of his fertile mind, often too fast for his pen to keep up.

The idea of writing for financial reward didn't occur to him initially, but soon developed as a possibility while his budget remained strained. Earning a reasonable income as a physician was going to be much tougher than he had imagined. For a long time he envisaged his future as one where writing and his medical practice went hand in hand.

In a class controlled society where everyone had a natural position he was conscious that moving in the right circles was important for a doctor who wanted to rise socially. Doyle, ever the optimist, had his eye on a career in its ascendency. Never lonely, once he was joined by his faithful younger brother Innes, he lacked for nothing but two things he considered important – a healthy income and a wife to share his life.

Eventually both were to materialise.

1884 was a busy year for Arthur. He was writing a lot and hobnobbed on the fringes of the successful writing fraternity. Trying to do everything that was in his mind he spread himself thinly and his writing didn't achieve the success he craved. Apart from his surgery hours, which often palled, Doyle led a very active life. He walked, played cricket and joined a football club – under an assumed name – football wasn't quite the sport of gentlemen.

As a means of supplementing his income, during 1885 Doyle took in a paying patient, Jack Hawkins. The young man's closest family member was his sister Louise and she and Doyle had established a friendly rapport from the start. Jack's condition was somewhat worse than his initial assessment implied and unfortunately after a short tenure in Doyle's rooms, his patient expired. It had been a calculated risk. The potential income raised by Jack's stay with Doyle could be easily offset by the possible damage to a doctor's reputation if he lost a patient. It also transpired that Louise was to receive a legacy from her brother, and in the minds of a few, this threw some suspicion on Doyle and his motives.

However, any concerns came to nothing and Doyle quickly moved on. He comforted Louise after the death of her brother and the warmth between them turned to love. After a suitable interval they married, taking up residence at Bush Villas. The doctor's rooms, already well furnished, were only subtly influenced by Louise's touch, and life continued to be good as it entered a new phase in Doyle's life. Louise had an annual income which undoubtedly helped the couple's budget, but Doyle's writing was still not having the impact he wanted, and to be a successful breadwinner was very important to him.

Over the last couple of years he had at least sold a few stories, and in common with most writers he experienced plenty of rejections. Despite his belief that his stories were good it seemed that others didn't share his confidence and he had limited success. However, Doyle thoroughly enjoyed writing, and committed many stories to paper during this period. He continued sending his manuscripts to publishers with indifferent results.

A Study in Scarlet, his first novel about the eccentric Sherlock Holmes was completed in 1886. It featured the character who was to become without question the most famous detective in the world, celebrated in almost any country where books were available. The templates for Holmes and his crucial sidekick Dr John – or occasionally James – Watson were firmly established at this time, though there was little thought then of sequels for the characters.

Holmes was described initially as not a medical student but someone who dabbled in chemistry experiments and amassed knowledge from a wide range of subjects. Watson entered the scene as a military doctor invalided out of the war in Afghanistan. The two were drawn together by their need for reasonably priced chambers in central London.

The novel did the rounds of publishers before he received an offer of twenty-five pounds for it later that year. The proposal was from the publishers Ward Lock, provided he would give up his copyright. This turned out to be the best deal that Doyle could arrange, and though feeling insulted and disappointed, reluctantly he agreed. In the event Ward Lock did not actually publish the book until late in 1887, the following year.

During these years in Portsmouth, Doyle had continued developing his interest in spiritualism, and attended some seances locally. His disappointment with orthodox religion was confirmed after his attendance at a Jesuit school. Though the education had been good, he railed at the dogma of Christianity. The notion of contact with the other side was always with him, dovetailing neatly with his enthusiasm for mystery, the supernatural and secrecy. These elements appealed to him and pleased him; his stories were frequently peppered with references to the spirit world, both during and after this time.

His practice was now working, income more assured and life with Louise was settled and comfortable, though on Doyle's part, very busy. Throughout 1888 his writing was also becoming well established. During May, Louise became pregnant with their daughter who was to be born the following January. Doyle was making good contacts in the literary world and realised the need to exploit them. He visited London often during this period to pursue these contacts and to visit relatives. He liked the compartmentalisation that this brought to his life. It allowed his secretive nature to enjoy free time away from his usual responsibilities. Like everyone else he was well aware of the shocking Whitechapel murders in the East End.

Surprisingly, given his fascination with macabre crimes and criminal notoriety, Doyle was reluctant to discuss the matter at all during this period, even when called upon to do so by a local paper in Portsmouth. His reticence certainly struck some people as very odd given the national furore over the murders and the fact that they made news around the world. There were even whispers in Portsmouth that he knew more than he was prepared to say.

In 1889 when his daughter Mary was a few months old, Arthur left her with Louise in Portsmouth while he spent some time in the New Forest, the beginning of a love affair with that part of the world. It was an area he was to return to much later in his life. Staying near Lyndhurst with some friends he took time getting to know all the villages in the area, including Minstead. It was at Minstead where he was ultimately to be buried for the second and final time, the first being in the grounds of Windlesham Manor at Crowborough.

Doyle's literary career started to take off, though he still thought he would remain a physician as well. He retrained as an eye specialist and Louise accompanied him to Vienna, where some further training took place, while Mary stayed with Louise's mother. Returning home, he moved the family to London where he believed greater financial rewards would be available to him. The riches he envisaged didn't appear however and his consulting room was often more empty than full. This meant that writing was still destined to occupy most of his working hours.

It was only in 1891 that he finally decided he would be a full-time writer. Doyle was believed to have experienced a true eureka moment, realising that he was already more of a writer than a doctor. As a writer he could put all his energies in one direction, and become even more prolific. In addition, he would have no need of expensive chambers in the centre of London, and could work from wherever he chose to live. This turned out to be in the borough of South Norwood.

Coincidentally in February 1891 the very last of the Whitechapel murders occurred. Although the authorities insisted they were long past, the murder of Frances Coles in Swallow Gardens caused fear and concern all over again in the area. Her throat had been cut and although she had no lower body mutilation it was clear that her assailant had been disturbed. Who knew what might have happened if a police constable had not turned up?

A considerable number of police officers and other senior professionals were in no doubt that the infamous Ripper had indeed struck again. With a natural cynicism and antipathy for the authorities many Londoners also felt the same way, some of the old terror was felt once more on the filthy and stinking streets of Whitechapel.

Chapter 5
Policing & Politics

London – 1888

Throughout the summer Sir Charles Warren was not a happy man. He had a number of serious issues on his plate and his job as Commissioner of the Metropolitan Police was proving more demanding than he had ever imagined. London was frenzied over what had become known as the 'Whitechapel murders'. The press were being merciless in their assaults on the Metropolitan Police within whose territory the murders – except for one – were taking place. The city police, by contrast, were largely escaping such criticism.

Sir Charles had a distinguished background. He had been responsible for increasing British knowledge of Palestine through extensive work there for the Palestine Exploration Fund, whilst seconded from the army. The tasks included both surveying and working on archaeological digs in Jerusalem, adjacent to and under the Temple of the Mount. This had been some of the first real archaeological work carried out there in modern times. Warren's achievements in this area laid the foundation for later analysis and understanding of the vicinity.

In the wake of this work Warren returned to his active service with the army and gained considerable military experience in Egypt, often dealing with sensitive and diplomatic matters. It was while he was in Egypt that he was approached and offered the job of Commissioner of the Metropolitan Police, a post usually filled by military men. He could have been forgiven for not knowing what the future might hold in this prestigious new role. Little did he realise that it would prove to be a position in which the occupier could rarely win.

His first main challenge had been the demonstrations in Trafalgar Square which came to be known as Bloody Sunday. Warren had been acutely aware that his predecessor Sir Edmund Henderson's resignation had been forced by similar troubles in 1886. Henderson had been accused of failing to manage the force properly and he had resigned. Amongst other difficulties that Warren encountered was the Match Girls' strike in London's East End, which gave rise to concerns that civil disobedience would spread. He also had problems within the force to worry about, in addition to those of public order and safety. The Government was becoming unnerved and did nothing to ease the pressure on the Metropolitan Police. In fact it tightened the screw on Sir Charles Warren through his political master the Home Secretary.

Sir Charles had also been at loggerheads with James Monro who headed the CID and had demanded complete autonomy over it. This was something that Warren had not felt he could agree to if he was to remain in control of the whole Metropolitan Force. Monro had been secretive and had failed to give information to Warren about the activities of his department. The ongoing battle had led to disagreement with Home Secretary Henry Mathews, whom Warren also did not trust. Mathews was not an easy man to deal with, too clever by half, with a cutting and supercilious exterior. In addition he was a Catholic and his appointment as Home Secretary had been viewed by many, not least in the police force, with great suspicion. In part this was because the Fenians, who sought an independent Ireland, had caused growing unease in the British Government. Home Rule for Ireland was an extremely sensitive issue. Finally, Monro had resigned his position, resolving the issue temporarily, but Henry Mathews had blamed Warren for his departure. Things remained frosty between them.

The Monro incident led Warren's thoughts onwards. He mentally reviewed the rest of his senior policemen. One of the three superintendents currently in post was demonstrating signs of religious extremism, and his occasional displays of outlandish behaviour had caused remarks throughout Scotland Yard's higher echelons. His unabashed comments about Catholics and women, both of whom he seemed to have problems with, had become a byword at senior level in the Yard. Warren had personally intervened, first speaking bluntly to the officer about his outbursts, and then switching him from operational duties to an administrative job in charge of pay and supplies.

The Metropolitan Police's code of silence about brother officers, even when they might be in breach of the law, was instilled in everyone at all levels and Warren wasn't going to change this. It had prompted him to keep the lid on this affair, despite the fact that the man's behaviour was making him quite unsuitable to remain in the service. Warren was uneasy about the fact that there were many within the force who simply shouldn't have been there, but the code was never going to expose those officers for dismissal, at least not the senior ones. Fortunately the outbursts from this Superintendent had dried up, though the matter hadn't stopped there. Nowadays the Superintendent sometimes came in late, had few discussions about anything except work, and looked increasingly unwell. Warren suspected that there might be skeletons in the family cupboard. However, he had not felt able to probe into the officer's personal life along with all the other pressures he was facing.

He turned his thoughts back again to the Whitechapel murders. He had slowly arrived at the possibility that the killer might know more about police activities than he should. The streets had been flooded with police both in plain clothes and uniform, everybody and anybody had been challenged, and walking beats had been changed and reinforced. It felt almost uncanny how the killer managed to slip through the net and walk the streets of Whitechapel with impunity.

Was this luck on his part? Warren didn't believe in luck or coincidence, he was a practical man who felt the murderer would be apprehended through vigilant police work by a well-trained force. Some of his staff felt that Warren was stand-offish, but in truth the welfare of his men was very important to him. His concern that they be issued with suitable boots to pound the streets for many hours a day had been ridiculed by others.

He also wasn't the first to have wondered if the killer actually was a policeman, but had never voiced this and his loyalty to the force made him dismiss it as a hypothesis too far. He flatly refused to consider it further.

Warren's last meeting with the Home Secretary had not been a success.

His passing mention of the Monro affair and his own Superintendent's behaviour had brought the rebuke that he had bigger problems to deal with. Questioned again about the Whitechapel murders he tentatively floated the theory that someone inside the Yard or the civil service was leaking information about police tactics, which was then being used by the murderer to avoid detection.

This brought another icy response from Mathews who said that Warren should look outside the authorities for what he referred to as the 'Whitechapel abomination', and not inside. It was nonsense that a person from the authorities would be leaking information. What possible reason or motive could somebody have for this? The premise was preposterous and the matter was closed. Warren privately agreed, but had felt bound to raise the matter to avoid being accused of failing to keep the Cabinet informed. He knew that it wasn't just politicians who had to be political.

It seemed now that Warren's relationship with Mathews was tainted, back last spring he had resigned but this had not been accepted by the Home Secretary. Warren had agreed to soldier on, at least for the present. If he felt moved to resign again he had privately decided it would be final and he would not take no for an answer.

Mathews, for his part, was concerned that failure to detect the killer might lead to public disorder on a scale approaching the Bloody Sunday riots in Trafalgar Square. Commissioner Warren had contained them eventually, but it hadn't been a good outcome and Mathews had taken some criticism over it. His political instincts told him that continued failure might easily lead to trouble on the streets that could bring down the Government. Of course before things got that far, the Prime Minister would have relieved Mathews of his duties and appointed someone else as Home Secretary in a bid to appease the critics.

The meeting was unsatisfactory on both sides and ended with no firm progress. The suggestion of offering a reward for information was raised again, and rejected yet again. Warren reported that he was drafting more officers onto the streets and reviewing the rosters. He then returned to his office.

Chapter 6
The Mystery Club

Southampton – Present Day

On the train home from Waterloo, Sam trawled back over his day with Anna. He felt aggrieved at her secrecy and sensed she was holding something back. Whilst understanding her need to avoid being scooped by some other Ripper enthusiast, he still found it difficult. He was a naturally open person and knew he didn't present her with any threat of rivalry. Sam certainly wasn't about to get involved in Ripper research, he had enough interests of his own to pursue. The disagreement was not pleasant and it was a shame she seemed to be closed to all scenarios other than her own theory.

All in all she was quite irritating, bossy and controlling in fact, though there was something of his sister in her demeanour. They were quite different but had some common characteristics. Subconsciously he was measuring Anna against Paige. They could both be very assertive and look straight through you. They also shared a willowy figure and were both very attractive women without being obviously pretty.

His sister took after their mother with her grey eyes and almost telepathic mind. Anna had large brown eyes and the widest smile he thought he had ever seen. Paige, Sam felt, was a more sensitive person and was always there for him when things weren't going well. He trusted his big sister implicitly and would go to the ends of the earth for her. But after all, he thought, even Paige could be very irritating at times! His thoughts turned briefly to Indy, how different again she was, nothing like Anna or his sister, but she had found her way into Sam's soul.

The train clattered irritably over some points, jerking his thoughts away from women. Then the phrase Anna quoted came back to his mind:

'First and last lines contain a Ripping Yarn.'

He had heard it some years before at a Sherlock Holmes convention where he had met Richard Lancelyn Green, one of the all-time great Sherlockians. Another speaker had mentioned the phrase during a presentation, saying that it had appeared in a short memorandum signed by Conan Doyle. It seemingly referred to a book or manuscript he had written. A number of delegates had shown interest and were convinced it was a clue to some mystery, but it just hadn't seemed significant to Sam then, and he wasn't sure it was now, either. Richard had asked for Sam's views about it, but Sam hadn't seen any riddle in the memo, it was just some disembodied document. If you found the rest of it things would easily be explained, he thought.

It was probably a reference to a book or story penned by the great man, but it still didn't mean anything to him. Anna had said she had a document which bore the phrase, but that the rest of the sheet was covered in numbers. Whereas from memory, the document discussed at Sam's convention had no numbers, just a few words on it. What exactly the memo had been or where it was now, Sam had absolutely no idea.

He hadn't been particularly interested in the document then, and he wasn't very impressed with Anna's version of it now, she hadn't even brought it with her for god's sake! There were usually mundane answers to most little puzzles in life and Sam wasn't one to foster conspiracy theories or look for cryptic messages where there weren't any.

Thrusting it all from his thoughts, Sam turned his mind back to reality. Tomorrow evening he would meet the Mystery Club, this time at a pub in the village of Cadnam in the New Forest. Bernie and Dave Knox would want to know all about Anna, but he really didn't have much to tell them. Maybe if she contacted him again and was a little more open he might pursue the matter with her. In the meantime he wanted to hear from Gerry, whose turn it was to chair the discussions. Afterwards they would introduce the next mystery for the following month. Sam was looking forward to both the company and the beer.

As he contemplated spending a few minutes with the biography in his bag, the train pulled in to Southampton Airport Parkway. Not worth it now, he decided. Getting off at the next station, Southampton Central,

Sam walked home.

The following evening Dave Knox picked Sam up at his apartment and they drove the few miles out to Cadnam. It had been Dave's turn to drive.

'No booze for you tonight, Dave!' Sam needled him gently.

Dave scowled. 'No, but how about we get a takeaway on the way home?' he suggested.

'Yep, you're on,' said Sam.

The others were already at the pub and had located themselves in a corner that they called the library. The pub had some of those shelves dividing the tables where old books were casually arranged to lend atmosphere. This was where they would conduct their debate. James was deep in conversation with Bernie at the table, arguing about something, while Gerry was at the bar with Alexa getting drinks in. Once the six were settled, Gerry started the proceedings.

The way the group worked was to discuss a mystery or sensational murder story that had been agreed at the last meeting, all speaking was to be conducted through the chair, though the incidence of rude interruptions or jokes was rife. It could be a fictional matter or a real-life story. When the discussion was exhausted, the incoming month's chairman would take over and introduce the subject for the next meeting. That way everyone had a month to get a handle on the story so it could be debated. It usually triggered some frantic research and sometimes led to hilarious conclusions, particularly from Alexa who was an irrepressible comic and couldn't resist looking for the funny side in any mystery. Bernie could always be relied on for the quality of her research and she would often astound them with obscure facts and plausible solutions.

Trying to outdo each other with little known facts was a favourite technique, and occasionally Alexa would keep a straight face and throw in something totally fictitious to wind them all up. The whole thing was chaotic, Sam reflected, but it was an opportunity for some good company with like-minded people. When lots of beer was added into the equation it made for an excellent evening. Actually, of course, the beer was the main reason they were there, but the Mystery Club was a great excuse.

This evening they were trying to solve the puzzle of the *Mary Celeste* which delivered some predictably strange and humorous interludes. Halfway through the evening they came to a natural pause, James was at the bar ordering his round when Bernie took the moment to ask Sam about his contact with Anna. 'How did it go with Anna then, Sam?'

Dave Knox pricked up his ears. The love god didn't know Sam had actually met with Anna. James came back bearing a tray loaded with drinks, causing a small diversion while Sam wondered what he should tell them.

Sam decided he didn't really have much to say. He kept away from mentioning Anna's cryptic phrase and just said that she was convinced she could find evidence that Doyle could either have been Jack the Ripper, or had perhaps known who it was. The Mystery Club members were immediately interested, sensing a forthcoming subject for a meeting. Gerry snorted with disbelief, the others were intrigued and of course Bernie already had some knowledge of the matter, and kept her views to herself.

Dave brought it down to earth.

'What's she like, Sam?'

'Well she's bright, and has spent a long time studying Whitechapel and the murders, she has also profiled the Ripper and some of the suspects. She's no fool, but she's very dogmatic, argumentative.'

Dave looked around the group and raised his eyebrows resignedly.

'Sam, what's she *like*, you know, what does she look like?' he said.

Alexa sniggered and it went quiet as all eyes turned on Sam.

'Well, striking I suppose, tall and dark,' said Sam looking a little uncomfortable.

'Stunning might be a better word,' remarked Bernie dryly, remembering her encounter in the British Library. The enormous eyes and wide smile framed by raven hair came quickly back to her.

Dave immediately wanted more details about Anna, egged on by James but Sam ignored them, explaining that he just couldn't remotely accept the idea of Doyle being associated with the Ripper. Respecting Sam's friendship, Bernie also refused to elaborate on her 'stunning' comment despite much pestering from Dave. The group discussed the idea briefly, arriving at the consensus that it was most unlikely, though theoretically possible. After another beer for some and softies for the drivers, they agreed the arrangements for next month's meeting and made their way home.

The following day Anna's quest was still on Sam's mind. Mid-morning, he telephoned her to ask if she would let him have a copy of the number sheet she had described. He suggested she scan and email it or put a copy in the post. She declined, feeling possessive about her find, but said she would show him a copy in person if they could get together soon. Yet again Sam felt irritated, he thought this was an overreaction and was tempted to forget the whole idea, but in keeping with his temperament he coolly agreed that he would arrange to meet her when possible.

After putting the phone down his first thought was, *she can wait now, I don't need this.* He had been toying with the idea of going to search Richard Lancelyn Green's papers at Portsmouth on her behalf, but now felt no inclination to do so. He was due to be there tomorrow anyway, but would stick firmly to his usual tasks.

Women! Sam was already in turmoil over his relationship with Indy, if indeed it was a relationship, he wondered bitterly. Exhaling loudly he turned back to his work and briskly typed out a few thousand words, putting the subject of the opposite sex right out of his mind.

Later that afternoon he got a call from his sister. She was sad about his affair yet knew that he probably wouldn't talk about it. However, she might just try him again. Paige had done some homework. A chance conversation with Bernie had intrigued her, when Bernie had said this girl Anna was special. Though keen to find out a little about Sam's meeting with Anna she was very aware she needed to let him mention the subject first. If she questioned him he might clam up, or even worse, think she was matchmaking. Paige rummaged through her Sherlock Holmes books looking for a suitable passage. Having found one, she jotted it down and laid it by the telephone.

'Hi Sam, have you got a few moments? I'm just phoning for a catch up.'

'Of course, how are you all?'

They updated on the news about Paige's family and then, deciding to chance it, she asked him how things were with Indy.

'They're not,' was his abrupt response. Saying she was sorry about that,

Paige asked if there was anything else new. Opening up a little, Sam told her about his trip to London and discussions with Anna. He relayed Anna's conviction about Conan Doyle's guilt and how bossy she was. He told Paige they had argued, saying he didn't really know what to make of it all.

His sister listened carefully, asking the occasional question. He wasn't looking for an opinion but knew she would offer any comment if she had something to contribute. Sam had told her a few years ago that if he was Sherlock Holmes, then she would be Mycroft, Sherlock's older and cleverer brother. Mycroft, mentioned in several Holmes stories, had even greater intellectual ability than Sherlock, but was uninterested and incapable of following anything up in a practical sense.

Initially Paige had been infuriated. 'Are you saying I'm the fat and lazy one out of us two?' she had ranted, before coming to the conclusion that she actually liked the idea of being intellectually superior to her little brother. Since those days she had read up on Holmes and enjoyed her telephone exchanges with Sam, often playing Mycroft to the hilt.

Smiling, Paige paraphrased and delivered her Sherlock Holmes quote.

'So about this Anna, now Watson, the fair sex is your department. What was the lady's game? What did she really want?'

He was used to his sister's ways, and the banter cheered him a lot.

'The Adventure of the Second Stain,' Sam smiled down the telephone, correctly identifying the title of the Sherlock Holmes story she alluded to. He had spoken automatically, his mind still turning over Anna's theory.

He couldn't know it but Paige's grey eyes had been boring down the telephone, picking up on every nuance in his voice about his meeting with Anna. She was watching his freckled face in her mind's eye. She sensed a new interest would be good for him and give him space from Indy. Bernie had even said the girl was beautiful. At the end of their chat, her comment was laconic and deliberately casual.

'It sounds really interesting; you should get involved and prove her wrong.'

Chapter 7

Misspent Youth

East London – 1888

The man's mother, Kate, fussed around the small kitchen, wondering if things were going to be like this forever. It was early in the year and she was hopeful, even optimistic that things would improve. Her son had taken to sleeping in through much of the day; he had become morose, erratic and unpredictable. She continued preparing something for him to eat, guessing he would emerge from his attic room shortly. There was no doubt about it, he was a changed man. What he really needed was fresh employment, though that was an easy thing to say and much harder to achieve.

The afternoon light was already fading as the man woke up. After eating and saying nothing to his mother he went back to his room and started reading. He was working his way haphazardly through an assortment of publications – everything from 'penny dreadfuls' to medical books, even issues of *The Lancet*, the journal of choice for doctors. He would flit from one to another in a seemingly random way, sometimes finishing them and sometimes abruptly starting something completely different.

Often the man would draw sketches to picture people he had seen in the street, men and women, and occasionally medical illustrations stimulated by his informal studies. Some of his pictures were of naked women in provocative poses and underneath the picture he would write Mary, and underline it.

Later that evening the man left the house without saying goodbye. Before doing so he roughly folded his drawings and cuttings together in a bundle, concealing them up the chimney in his room. His mother looked at her sister Clara and shook her head in silence. Since his father had gone, she reflected, the young man's life had started to deteriorate. Though still in his twenties he was becoming a stranger to them. Without a father figure present she had over-compensated and mothered him, but this had just made things worse. She was slow to realise it, and when it had become his habit to leave during the evening and return in the early hours, often after dawn, she would remonstrate with him.

Both she and her sister worried about him, pleaded with him to return to a life of normality, but nothing had worked. Sometimes the words would gush out of him, but more often than not, when pushed too far he became monosyllabic and even violent, frightening them. Much of the time however he simply wasn't listening, retreating into his own world, his mind miles and miles away from their prattle.

For some time the man had been in regular employment as a clerk, then as a commercial traveller for the tea trade. Later he had canvassed for another company all over the East End of London. One after the other he had been dismissed from each of his posts, either after an aggressive outburst or simply for failing to do his work. On one occasion a violent assault he committed had made certain he was promptly sacked. Following his last dismissal he had regressed into himself, spending more and more of his time alone and perhaps without realising it, living a stranger and stranger lifestyle. Sometimes he convinced himself that he would find more work, though he wasn't seeking it now and was starting to imagine that his real vocation might lay in a new and very different direction.

Roaming the streets at night he blended in well. The daylight hurt him; it exposed him and sometimes made him angry. His dress, which might charitably be described as shabby gentile, marked him as someone from the lower middle class, where second-hand clothes which had once been good were often worn. He might be going to or coming away from work. He was a man of average build and nothing in particular distinguished him from the crowds in the East End, except perhaps his eyes. A keen observer might have seen that they sometimes burned with frightening intensity, disconcerting to anyone who displeased him in any way.

The man would walk for miles, not just in the East End, but over a large part of London. In recent times he had fallen into this pattern of spending his days asleep or reading, and his nights wandering. He paid little appearance to his dress or grooming and wore the same clothes for long periods before his mother rescued them for the laundry. Occasionally some of his clothes disappeared without trace, and he would produce new ones to wear but he never discussed what he did, or where they came from. Something was happening to his mind, but he wasn't the one to recognise it. His mother and aunt were aware that his behaviour was becoming more erratic along with his personal habits. They were also becoming convinced that he was slipping away from them.

He left the house via the back door, suddenly and seemingly without effort he ran straight at the fence, gripping the top of it and vaulting over. The fence was about five feet high and it caught on his trousers, leaving a short tear in the corded material. A splinter from the fence entered his left hand, driving deep beneath his fingernail. The pain was intense but he paid no heed, careless as he was of any damage to his body. He liked jumping fences and skipped away down the alley that led to the road nearby. Sometimes he would talk to people almost normally, sometimes he would make aggressive remarks to strangers and sometimes he spoke to nobody.

Occasionally, in his more rational moments, the man realised that his behaviour was variable and unpredictable and marvelled at it. A part of his mind also knew that behaviour was the way to reach his objectives, and he found it simple enough to engage with people when they had something he wanted. He could be pleasant, even charming if he wished, a trait that had served him well in his tea travelling days, though often he was angry and prone to rage, which he justified by pinning the fault for anything on other people.

In a strange way he felt superior to them, superior to all of them, his mother and aunt, the various people who had employed him, the neighbours who had commented on his outlandish behaviour. They had spoken about his habits of vaulting fences and verbally abusing complete strangers. Also, they whispered about his nocturnal expeditions when he could come home with his clothes covered in mud, and some said, in blood. The only person he listened to nowadays was his uncle.

Chapter 8
The Trouble with Rubicons

Southampton – Present Day

Sam leaned back in his chair; his mouth setting in a grim line as the bittersweet memories came flooding in. Once again he was going to torment himself and he knew it. He pushed his mind back over the last few months, staring sightlessly at the wall opposite.

At first with Indy it had all gone so right, their initial mutual respect developing eventually into a frighteningly strong physical attraction. She had seemed so perfect, the few close friends who knew them saw them as a couple. Like two violins they had been tuned together, playing the same melody, though not without some discord on the way. Her shy smile had bewitched him, as it did most people who knew her.

It was a year or so ago he had first met her. Sam always spent time in every bookshop in town and Indira had come to work in one which sold both new and second-hand volumes. Borders the bookshop chain had closed, leaving one less bookshop in Southampton. It was a shame; Sam had liked taking his coffee there, and never left without purchasing something. Waterstones were still in town, but as for independents, with the odd exception, you could forget it.

This shop, titled ironically by its owner, was called The Final Chapter and was a rarity today, how could anyone make a living retailing new and second-hand books? But someone did. That person was Clive Johnson, who Sam had come to know through his friendship with other people in the book and writing fraternity. Sam's friend James, who bought and sold rare books, was a close friend of Clive's, doing regular business with him. Clive was older than both Sam and James and had been fortunate in one particular way. His mother had bequeathed him the retail premises he used, so his costs were not unbearable.

Also, Clive ran the show as a labour of love and was quite happy to allow it to tick over and keep his clientele of regular customers. He stocked it with everything from talking books to atlases and had found several niche parts of his business, sometimes less for profit than the social need they filled. A certain loyal section of the public still shunned the Internet and liked to browse real books in a comfortable environment.

Clive had used many students over the years to man the shop while he went searching and buying books. They came and went but this time he employed someone different. Indira was around thirty, married but childless and needing a job for self-satisfaction more than for income. She was shy with strangers, petite and slightly introverted. Having worked for years in the cruise industry she understood she was isolating herself now and in danger of withdrawing. She knew she should have a job dealing directly with people, and wanted to start a new life. Indy liked people and realised it would be good for her, but she really couldn't face the ordeal of a job in a busy high street. Seeing Clive's handwritten sign one day, 'Help Wanted' and guessing a bookshop wouldn't be too busy, she had walked inside on a whim. After ten minutes chatting with Clive she had stepped out with a part-time job. Within a few weeks she was full-time and ran the shop in all but name. She loved books anyway and her thirst for knowledge made her an eclectic and discerning reader.

Indy got to know Sam slowly during his regular visits. Sometimes he would just call in for a chat with Clive and if Clive wasn't around, Indy and Sam would talk. She learned about his interest in the Victorian and Edwardian eras, and would put aside volumes Sam might want. Indy also had a passion, a little of which dovetailed into Sam's Edwardian period. Growing up in Southampton she had joined an international cruise company, working at sea and then subsequently ashore with them. She was very knowledgeable about the industry and became fascinated by the city's maritime past, particularly the age of the great ocean going liners and of course, the *Titanic*. Like so many people before her and so many that are yet to come, the grim pathos of the story gripped her. In her spare time she had amassed a collection of books telling the story of the great liners and in particular, *Titanic*. She shyly revealed her interest to Sam and they found much to talk about on the subject.

Sam had become very friendly with Indy in a brotherly way, knowing from Clive that she was married he had no interest in her other than the fact she was a lovely person to talk to. She was educated and sophisticated yet shy and demure, an unusual and interesting combination. She would look up at him quizzically, her soft brown eyes watching every expression on his face. Sam called into the shop often, to have coffee with her or Clive – whoever was there.

One day Clive had been in the shop alone and announced that Indy's marriage was over and he thought she was contemplating divorce. Sam had had no idea. He had been vaguely aware that she was in an uncomfortable marriage but didn't realise that she had already lived alone for a couple of years or so. Clive said she had taken some time off to deal with her problems, from which he assumed she meant her husband.

With a sad shrug he said, 'She had a few tears the other day; I just hope I don't lose her, Sam. She's so organised, and better than that, she's trustworthy. I don't even check the till any more when she's around. I knew from the first day she came in here that she was a real diamond.'

Sam had agreed. Over the next couple of weeks he hadn't called at the shop, being busy with other things. Once, in the city centre he had caught sight of two women dressed in saris, making them look so elegant. With some surprise he realised that the woman in yellow was Indy, he had never seen her dressed like that before and she looked really good as the two of them disappeared down the street. She hadn't seen him, but the sighting had sparked his interest in her as a woman. Normally she worked in drab clothes, dark jeans and a jumper or something similar; her slight figure so camouflaged that he could barely recall what she usually wore. The saris made the two women look so... feminine. Sam had been intrigued.

Indy was soon back in the shop. She said little about her absence but the soft eyes had a depth of sadness in them that Sam hadn't noticed before. Not wanting to ask her directly Sam had fenced around the issue before she just came out with it and said she was trying to get a divorce. She had looked up at him and grimaced.

Sam nodded his condolences. The following week he had called into the shop and asked her to lunch. It had been a risk as he didn't want to spoil their friendship, but felt if he didn't ask her out he would regret it. She had instantly agreed and when he asked where she wanted to go, to his surprise she nominated a town centre bar. They found a booth and ordered some beers and lunch. Chatting freely Indy told him she didn't go to pubs too often but had visited this one with her sister and liked it. After a couple of hours the shy smile announced that she had better go.

'If Clive turns up he'll think I'm playing truant.'

'I don't think so,' said Sam. 'He appreciates the job you do.'

'I know he does,' she nodded. 'He's a good man, Sam.'

They had then dated for a few weeks and slipped into a pattern of enjoyable evenings at the theatre, restaurants and cinemas. Sam would drop her at her flat but hadn't yet been invited in. He wasn't in a rush, wanting her to set the pace. For that reason he delayed inviting Indy to his own flat. He didn't really know where this was going but was content to go with the flow, he felt totally at ease and just enjoyed being with her. They had kissed quite a few times in the car and the cinema with growing passion, and there had been no reluctance on her part, far from it. His tentatively wandering hands had been very welcome it seemed.

Calling into The Final Chapter one day, Indy had been glad to see him, he bent to kiss her and she came up on tiptoe to meet him halfway. There were no customers in the shop and Indy asked Sam if he would like to come round for a meal one evening that week.

'I would ask you to come to my flat but my husband is always snooping around I'm afraid. I just don't want any unpleasantness,' she said. 'I'm house-sitting my sister's place while she's away, so I thought it might be somewhere we could... be together.' She had looked up at him enquiringly.

Sam's pulse had quickened. He wasn't normally the fastest at picking up signals from women but on this occasion it was so direct that even he understood the message. He accepted quickly, asking when, and they had agreed on the following evening.

'I'll be predictable and make you a curry, shall I?' Her white teeth flashed as she laughed and Sam was excited by the little sparkle in her eyes.

When Sam had arrived at her sister's address Indy had taken his breath away. She greeted him in a sea-green sari, artfully arranged to one side, showing her bare midriff. Her black hair was piled high on her head, and she was covered with costume jewellery. Pendant earrings, arm bangles, several necklaces and a jewel in her navel. She wore light green eye shadow, and her red lipstick matched the bindi on her forehead. Sam was taken aback.

'You look beautiful,' he said.

'So do you,' she said with a smile.

Closing the door behind him and dropping the catch firmly, she reached up on tiptoe to clasp him around the neck, offering her mouth for his kiss.

Leaving the shop earlier that day, Indy had spent much effort creating the right atmosphere. The time, place and context were very important to her. She showed Sam into the lounge where the curtains were already drawn. It was an absolute sea of candles, some of them scented. There must have been twenty or thirty gleaming through the coloured glass jars that held them, on every shelf or flat surface it seemed. Planet Rock played quietly on the radio in the corner. She had beers on the table and the aroma of cooking drifted in from the kitchen.

The meal was good and Indy was sparkling in her conversation, perhaps because she was on home ground, Sam had wondered. The evening flew by and they did the washing-up together, Indy slipping an apron over her sari. They talked about her sister and the house they were in.

'Her name is Priti; she knows you're here, she suggested it.' Indy laughed. 'She'd like you, Sam, she's not only my sister she's my best friend, we're very close. She just doesn't want me to burn her house down, so she insisted I put every candle in a jar.'

Back in the lounge they had sat on the settee, sipping coffee before Indy had taken their cups and placed them on the table. They had kissed deeply and there was eagerness in her embrace. Indy pulled her head away and locked eyes with Sam, studying him intently. The moment was right.

'Would you like to help me off with my sari?' she whispered, managing to look both shy and coquettish at the same time.

'Of course... if you're sure...' Sam had tailed off.

She rose from the settee and showed Sam how the sari was arranged. 'You'll have to unwrap me, off the shoulder first, there's about eight metres of it.' Indy giggled and Sam smiled back.

'Gift wrapped,' he breathed, 'like a beautiful little parcel.'

He soon got the hang of it as she assisted by twirling very slowly to the Bellamy Brothers 'Let Your Love Flow'. Neither of them was listening to the lyrics, but if they had been they were curiously appropriate.

Indy wore no shift and when Sam had fully unwrapped his gift she stood in a matching choli and pants. Both were heavily embellished with lace, and they bore dozens and dozens of tiny silver sequins which shimmered in the rich candlelight. The sea-green of both garments contrasted beautifully with her skin. Indy was confident about her body and had no scruples about displaying it in private to the right man. After bathing earlier she had examined herself in the mirror and whilst she would have liked to have been slightly taller, she knew all her little curves were in the right places. Shy in public, but secure and comfortable in an intimate environment she was a classic Gemini, two different people.

She noted the approval in Sam's eyes. Reaching up she slowly unbuttoned his linen shirt, starting at the top and lingering to examine the silver chain he wore around his neck. Slipping the shirt from his shoulders she stepped back.

'The choli fastens at the front.' She smiled coyly. 'It's not too difficult to undo.'

They sank down to the settee, watching each other, fascinated. Then kissed again, for longer this time and with more urgency. When they parted for air Indy guided Sam's head down to her breasts, his lips brushing a taut dark nipple. Slowly he traced the tip of his tongue around the halo of each breast finding every little goosebump in turn. Indy made tiny noises of contentment, running her hands affectionately through his hair as she nurtured him. Sam slowly slid lower, finding the jewel in her belly button. Surprised and delighted, Indy giggled again as his tongue tickled around her navel.

Looking back on it now Sam knew it had been one of the best nights of his life. They had made love several times, each more slowly and sensuously than the first, Indy was an experienced lover, a little older than Sam, generous and uninhibited. She had led things whilst still allowing him to try anything he wanted, whispering encouragement and appreciation to him. He had eventually left around four in the morning, tired but exhilarated.

Late in the morning on the following day Sam had turned up at the shop bearing two coffees and biscotti from the nearest coffee shop. Indy had been slightly apprehensive about his reaction to the evening. She felt that it had been wonderful for both of them but she couldn't bank on him feeling the same way.

Planting the coffees on the counter he said nothing, just opened his arms to her, not trusting himself to speak. She had come to him and he squeezed her tightly. No words had been necessary; she smiled into his shirt, listening to his heartbeat, allowing him as long as he wanted. Indy was being slowly crushed but was content to wait till he released her; desperately glad she had no customers. Eventually he had let go, kissing the top of her head and murmuring his thanks for the evening. Hand in hand they had crossed a loving Rubicon together and at that moment they had been so happy.

The shop's doorbell rang and some people came in to browse. Sam took their coffees to the low table at the back of the shop to await her when she was free. Customers gone, they sat and talked. Sam wanted to repeat the experience soon, but Indy wisely demurred.

'You need to recover first,' she smiled the shy smile. 'You were a very... busy man last night and you need a few days. Then we'll meet again.' She wagged a finger at him, teasing. 'Anticipation is the finest thing, Sam, it's so important and there's no rush. You must eat well, and drink lots of green tea first.' She had laughed, her voice tinkling like water over pebbles. Sam smiled, just enjoying watching her whilst she talked to him.

Then she added casually, 'Priti's away for another month or so yet.' Sam grinned suddenly; the promise of their next meeting was already feeding his imagination.

'We must think about each other in the next few days – about what we'd like to do,' she added wickedly.

In the weeks that followed they had met regularly, initially at her sister's, then usually at his flat, each time going through a ritual of seduction and courtship before making love intensely and passionately. Sam was at least a competent lover and had slept with a number of different women, though he rarely sought them out, usually waiting for them to find him.

But with this lady, lovemaking was on a much higher plane, somewhere Sam hadn't yet been aware of. He started to become more caring yet adventurous, he began to learn about her holistic approach to lovemaking, to buy her the flowers she loved, and to be responsive to her physical desires.

Indy was fiercely intuitive about men and their sexuality. She instinctively knew, even if they didn't, that for most men to perform at their best they needed the right atmosphere. Their feelings should be gently nourished and they should be able to trust their partner absolutely. Impatience or criticism was never on her agenda. It wasn't pandering to men's egos either, because in her view, when things were right she became the beneficiary of some extraordinary lovemaking. She wasn't interested in quickies and she didn't use the word sex. Love was too spiritual a business, it was to be savoured and enjoyed until the natural end of each interlude.

Indy had been married for ten years or so and would have been the first to admit that her husband was a great lover. He had opened her eyes to so much before his growing indifference seemed to come between them. She didn't know if he had someone else or whether he had business worries. He just wouldn't confide in her. She wanted to care for her man, but it wasn't a one-way street. He had to do the same for her. Eventually she had moved out, hoping that he would make some positive response. So far it hadn't happened but giving up on somebody completely and forever was a tough call.

But then for Sam something had subtly changed, the visits became more infrequent, the eye contact less protracted. Driving by Indy's flat one day, Sam saw her husband's car outside and whilst he wasn't jealous, it occurred to him he had never been there himself. Indy had become indecisive and less approachable lately. Sam tried to talk about it but she didn't seem responsive. He didn't know how to handle things, so did little about it, assuming she must work it out for herself. Finally he stopped calling at the shop to avoid embarrassment, phoning Clive now and then to keep in touch.

Though he didn't know it, Indy for her part had realised she was hurting and confusing Sam and hated herself for it. She felt she had moved too fast with him, crossing their Rubicon and not thinking about the longer term. She had allowed things to develop with Sam and it had been wonderful for her but... Her confidence took a dive again; Sam was younger than her and her childlessness was still at the back of her mind. Her husband was also in her thoughts though nothing had really changed there. She confided only in Priti, who was too sensible to try to advise her, but told her things would work out once she knew what she really wanted to do, and if Sam truly loved her he would still be there.

That was the trouble with Rubicons, Sam reflected bitterly, looking up to the ceiling but finding no comfort. Once you crossed them there was no way back.

Closing his eyes, Sam could see her now. Dimming down the lights in his bedroom, running cool fingers over his body, wordlessly massaging his shoulders, while the soft brown eyes searched him deeply for... who knew what?

'For god's sake,' Sam murmured. He had to stop torturing himself and he knew it, enough was enough. He missed those moments with her so much. Rising from the chair he went to fetch his jacket, needing to get out of the flat and go somewhere, anywhere.

At almost the same time in a quiet bookshop across the city, someone was having very similar thoughts. A single lonely tear ran down her cheek.

Chapter 9
A Proud New Bonnet

Whitechapel – 31 August 1888

It was a Friday evening, and stumbling slightly Mary Nichols made her way down Osborn Street to its junction with Whitechapel Road. She had been drinking quite heavily and despite having had several clients during the last few hours, the money she had earned had already been spent on drink. It was a familiar story. At some point she needed to keep enough money back for her lodgings at the doss house she was living in, but the pull of another drink had so far made this impossible.

Mary was widely known as – and preferred to be called – Polly. She liked its distinctive and cheerful ring. She considered that there were far too many Marys in this world, and that Polly suited her. She had no idea that her real given name might cause her to become singled out for anything, least of all the gruesome attentions of a homicidal stalker.

On the corner she met Helen, an acquaintance with whom she had shared a room in the past and they talked for a few minutes, deciding where each of them might go next. Helen was heading south, so their ways parted. Determined she would get her doss money this time and return to her lodgings, Polly set off again, east along Whitechapel Road heading for another public house. She expected this pub would still have people clustered outside it, even at this late hour, and she hoped to meet a fresh client there. Polly was feeling confident, proudly wearing the new bonnet which she knew added to her visible charms. It was a black bonnet garnished with a dark green velvet band, setting it aside from run-of-the-mill black bonnets. It was getting late now, around half past two, and this time, she resolved, the money would definitely be used to pay for her bed.

The man stood in the shadows near the public house as Polly approached. In the darkness he looked reasonably well to do, a little shabby perhaps, maybe a gentleman and immediately her mind sprang to the possibility of an extra penny or two for her services.

'Hello, Mary,' he said quietly as she approached. She bristled slightly, cocking her head upwards as she spoke.

'I'm Polly not Mary,' she said. 'Do you know me?'

'Never mind.' He nodded as though it were inconsequential.

She slowed down, failing to see the malicious glint in the blue eyes. Falling in beside her he kept pace for a few yards, then, looking up sideways at him, she asked him what he wanted with her. As if she didn't know, Polly thought to herself. Men were all the same. When it came down to it they needed something she could supply, and like most of her compatriots she was philosophical about it. What must be must be, and the circumstances of life must be accepted and survived as best as one could.

They continued slowly eastwards as he agreed her slightly inflated terms. She had guessed he would, adding another tuppence to her claim, convinced that the new bonnet was going to be lucky for her. Polly led the way naturally, her inner compass knowing the streets around them with their share of dark and quiet places. Initially they turned left and then right into the quietness of Bucks Row, a broad and mainly residential street. In Whitechapel Road there had been quite a few people about, including another man who walked in the same direction as them, quite some way behind. In Bucks Row there was no-one, as she had correctly guessed. She headed on to where the street became much narrower and darker at its eastern end. They slowed down as the shadow of the Old Board School, the largest building in the street, loomed over them.

The deed would be done quickly. Spinning her around to face him and looking swiftly in both directions he made it clear this was the time and place. 'This will do.' She glanced around realising they were in a double gateway. A low wall ran along the street from the gates. Though there were houses opposite, all was quiet and it would suffice. There was no-one about so Polly bent down to grasp her skirts. It took just a second. But as she raised them and looked up he made his strike, grasping at her neck with both hands, viciously starting to strangle her, the power and intensity of his grip surprising even himself.

The man's thumbs forced themselves upward into her face as he squeezed and squeezed, harder and harder, compressing her jaw and forcing her mouth closed. Polly could make no sound though she struggled violently to free herself. He moved forward, his body crushing hers, suffocating her against the stout wood of the gates. There was only a slight scuffling noise as the steel tips on the heels of her boots scraped vainly on the ground. Her hands shot up instinctively to grab his wrists but she had no chance of freeing her neck, weary through drink and a long day, she had nowhere to go and precious little strength to resist. The bonnet fell from her head making a dull sound as it hit the ground, rolled, then settled the right way up.

The unequal battle was soon lost. Polly's head was forced back and her eyes bulged as two unyielding blue eyes stared down at her. She didn't see them, it was too dark. Her body sagged. He lowered her tenderly, almost reverently, to the ground. As she lay there her hands relaxed and fell open, one of them touching the gate she had just been standing against. Her eyes, wide open, gazed unseeing up into the night.

Slowly and deliberately the man stared each way down the street. Seeing nothing to disturb him he drew a long knife from his coat, stooped and cut her throat quickly and confidently. He used the knife with exceptional, even unnecessary force, creating a deep and wide incision. Then, as if not satisfied he cut again, an inch or so lower, this time all the way to the right side of her neck making a gash around eight inches in length. The blood ran mainly to one side, away from him, as he had known it would.

Polly lay on her back, head slightly to one side, her skirts fallen to their usual position as she had struggled desperately with the man. Ignoring her upper body now, this time he went straight for her abdomen. He raised her skirt and both petticoats again until they lay over her chest and selecting a spot under her rib cage, began a deep and clean cut downwards towards her groin.

He made the next cut from Polly's left side, a long gash, so deep that it was completed in a jerky sawing motion. He glanced both ways down Bucks Row yet again but saw nothing. Then the man cut once more, across the stomach. Finally, shifting his position, several more incisions were made. A little blood worked its way up the knife handle, but gripping it tightly he continued.

On the other side of the street some fifty yards away, another man had paused and stood unseen in the shadows. Fingering the handle of his own knife in the pocket of his frock coat, he melted into the dark, going back the way he had come.

Finally the murderer finished. Little blood had made its way onto his person. He wiped his blade slowly on the skirts of the dead woman and walked away. At almost the same moment a man entered the eastern end of Bucks Row. Starting early as usual, Charles Cross was on his way to work. A few yards behind him and walking in the same direction was another man, also on the way to his employment. The two were about to discover Polly, though in the poor light they wouldn't witness either the extent or the savagery of her injuries. Uncertain what to do they pulled her skirts back over her legs for decency before splitting up to find a constable. Even the doctor that was called by the police didn't see the abdominal injuries by the light of a bullseye lantern. That terrible revelation was to come much later after she had been moved.

Beside her body, Polly's new bonnet lay forlornly, its proud green band bearing a single drop of crimson blood.

Chapter 10

The Same Old Watson!

Portsmouth – Present Day

Sam parked his car near Southsea Common and sat for a few moments thinking about the strange chain of events that had led to him even being here. Some one hundred and thirty-odd years ago a young man called Arthur Conan Doyle had moved here to make his fortune and establish himself in his chosen career as a physician. In time he had become a world famous novelist, renowned for his creation – and some said alter ego – Sherlock Holmes.

The fascination and, for some, obsession with the first truly original private consulting detective had continued unabated long after Doyle's death. Societies and clubs were formed all around the world to enjoy, debate and study the Holmes phenomenon. Many famous and learned people devoted much of their spare time and efforts to the cause. Amongst these had been Richard Lancelyn Green. His incredible collection of memorabilia and accompanying archive was perhaps the largest ever to be gathered in one place.

Richard's will bequeathed his collection to the city of Portsmouth. After his untimely death the council had decided to catalogue the collection for the central library. In addition, an exhibition was set up in the city museum. Various people were drafted in to help with the project. This was where Sam had come in. As an expert on both Sir Arthur Conan Doyle and Sherlock Holmes, and living in nearby Southampton, he was a natural to join the team. His wider knowledge of the Victorian period was also invaluable to them.

So it really all started here, Sam mused, glancing involuntarily in the direction of Elm Grove where Doyle's medical practice had been established at Bush Villas. He couldn't see Elm Grove from here but knew exactly where it was and had often walked along Kings Road from the museum towards it. Bush Villas had originally stood between a Pentecostal church and a public house. The irony of the doctor's surgery being in the middle had not been lost on Doyle. He had smilingly commented more than once that, being sandwiched by the two, he acted as a buffer between God and the devil of drink.

The area suffered devastating bombing during the Second World War and sadly Bush Villas had been completely destroyed. The subsequent post-war redevelopment of the road had resulted in some dreary blocks of flats, one of which was called Bush House. Now it carried a couple of faded plaques on the wall to mark the spot. Sam pictured in his mind the young Doyle's first arrival here, earnestly pounding these very streets to find the most suitable place for his practice.

Sam's plan was to spend the rest of his day sifting through some of Richard Lancelyn Green's documents and papers, listing and grouping them. It was fascinating work, and for the umpteenth time he marvelled at the single-minded approach Richard had shown in amassing a collection of this size and complexity.

At lunchtime the phone on the table he was working at rang. Sam picked it up automatically and was surprised to find his sister on the line. Well used to Sam's foibles, particularly his having no mobile phone, she was adept at tracking him down. She kept an ever growing list of numbers at which he might be reached. Paige also cultivated contacts with people where Sam was often to be found. This made it easier to get phone numbers to call him.

It was a little detective game she could enjoy from a distance, rather like Mycroft when one thought about it. The idea made her smile. This was how she had first encountered Bernie at the university and they had stayed in occasional touch. Sam had long since given up trying to work out how she did it. He recognised that her telepathic intuition and Mycroft Holmes deductive skills would usually result in her knowing where he was, probably what he was doing, and sometimes what he was thinking.

It was amazing how often they would be in parallel moods and just chatting would lift their spirits for a while. She knew him better than anyone, even their parents, and was his closest confidante. She was also a regular conduit of support and advice. They spent a few minutes exchanging their latest news and views. Paige was three years older than Sam and had her own family. She lived in Oxford and though they didn't meet that often nowadays, Paige at least made sure she phoned Sam regularly. She loved to wind him up, frequently using some Holmes trivia to drop casually into the conversation.

'How did you know where I was?' he would say.

'Elementary, my dear Watson.'

'Paige, I've told you a thousand times, Holmes never actually said that to anyone!'

'Oh yes he did, but you've not yet spotted it in the stories.'

'That's because it isn't there.'

'Ah, the same old Watson, you never learn that the gravest issues may depend on the smallest things.'

Hesitating for a moment, Sam then replied confidently.

'The Adventure of the Creeping Man.'

He grinned into the phone. The answering grin was at the other end of the line. He could see it clearly in Paige's grey eyes.

'Well done, Sherlock.'

She didn't mention Anna and her Jack the Ripper quest. Paige sensed he hadn't done any more to further things and she wasn't going to push. There would be another time and Sam had to come around to things his own way. If he arranged to see Anna again he would tell Paige when it suited him. Paige would know if he was in the right mood to spill the beans immediately he lifted the telephone.

Sam worked on for a while, absorbed in the documents and booklets he was sifting. The time passed quickly as it usually did here, and it was only when others were leaving that he realised it was time to go home. He liked going down to Southsea and always felt quite close to Sir Arthur Conan Doyle there. Some of the area hadn't changed too much and he could easily visualise Sir Arthur walking the streets. A fit and observant man, he would have much enjoyed his walks, perhaps putting together ideas for his writings.

Even today there were still many buildings dating from his time if you kept your eyes open and looked up occasionally. This was particularly true of shopping streets, where the ground floors were regularly gutted and the shopfronts were either mundanely modern or just downright trashy. Their brightly coloured logos might be designed to attract, but often did the opposite, repelling many people. In the older streets you only had to raise your eyes to see some original facades, often attractively and individually designed. Many of the names Doyle had used in his fiction writings also came from people and places he had encountered in Portsmouth and Southsea. Plus of course, the embryonic writer had conceived Sherlock Holmes here in his very first outing, *A Study in Scarlet*.

It was a lovely evening and walking right past his car Sam made for the sea, in no hurry to go home. He watched the Isle of Wight hovercraft disgorge its latest batch of travellers, then took a long walk enjoying the smell of seaweed in the light breeze. This was when it was great having no mobile phone; Sam was completely alone with his thoughts, in the fresh air and enjoying whatever nature had in store for him. The madness of the motorway could wait, he would let the commuters tear home in their frenzy while he walked the seafront alone. No doubt Doyle had done exactly the same thing before him, though Doyle could never have imagined the era of the motorway and the dreaded mobile phone.

Chapter 11
Baby Blue

Victoria Street, London – Present Day

Being seconded to the National Public Order Intelligence Unit was a pretty good number really. Darren Jones had enjoyed his time in Counter Terrorism Command, but the offer of something even more clandestine and exciting was a real lure. The elitism of only being responsible to your direct boss in CTC had slowly made him dismissive of more open and accountable ways of policing. He genuinely believed that to counter extremism in society it was occasionally necessary to step outside normal routes, and just deal with it. Darren liked secrecy and fighting fire with fire was sometimes the only way. Courts had proved to be ineffective in dealing with threats to the country, and human rights legislation was making a laughing stock of justice.

He had joined the police in Wales and craving excitement had transferred to the Metropolitan Police. Rising to Sergeant in the CID he had been invited to join Counter Terrorism Command after networking in London. Since 9/11 many things had started to change in the security services, priorities had moved on and CTC was expanded after the merger of the old Special Branch and the veteran Anti-Terrorist Branch. Darren had grabbed the opportunity. Proving himself a competent officer, he was soon trained in undercover techniques and showed an aptitude for intrusive surveillance.

Darren was intelligent and proved that he could use initiative and think on his feet. He slowly became aware that despite the need for warrants authorising surveillance, in practice the jobs were often simply rubber-stamped by a senior officer. Darren was one of those who didn't question things, and also realised that many of his colleagues held similar opinions. As is usual within institutions people gravitate together and are watched by their bosses. Darren became recognised as someone who was bright and would do what was required. The culture was changing of course, sexism and racism were disappearing and that was a good thing, though secrecy and the code of silence were never going to disappear so easily.

He was aware of the National Public Order Intelligence Unit and had no hesitation when his CTC boss Alan Macintosh suggested he was being headhunted for a job with them. Casually placed hints had made him aware that Alan was a great networker with contacts in the Security Service, formerly MI5, whose influence was considerable within CTC, both formally and informally. All these organisations worked closely together. Alan had told Darren that the NPOIU was a secondment and he would have to prove himself, but Alan would keep closely in touch with him and continue to act as his mentor.

Darren certainly didn't fancy undercover work. The idea of losing yourself for months or years didn't work for him. There had been a couple of cases recently where undercover work had gone badly wrong with negative and hostile press reports ensuing. He wanted to stay in touch with things and work out of central London so he could further his career by getting noticed. His logic was that out of sight meant out of mind, and undercover was badly out of sight as far as he was concerned.

After a few months with NPOIU he was called in and given a new assignment by his boss. The briefing was sparse. A girl called Anna Moretti was hunting documents or information concerned with the Metropolitan Police and Jack the Ripper. Nothing odd about that, but she could be on the verge of something that might be extremely negative for the establishment and the Metropolitan Police. His control handed him a ten by eight coloured photo of the girl. She lived in Kew, but spent most of her time in central London where she worked. She was to be watched and if she seemed to be opening up Victorian police scandals, her activities were to be disrupted and she would then be warned off. He was to keep his control fully informed of developments; he could disrupt on his own initiative, but not do any warning off without permission. Her phones were already being monitored and any relevant information would be fed to Darren immediately.

Darren didn't ask too many questions, he knew he wouldn't get answers. To ask where the case originated would have been naive. No problem, just do what was required. He was assigned three officers for the present, with the proviso that they would be called off at any time, if nothing much happened with the girl. Four officers weren't nearly enough for full round the clock surveillance but this case was probably going to be a part-time watching brief. They all had other work to do as well. He knew the three concerned. Angela with the curly hair would be his main driver, he decided. She was unflappable, and a bloody good driver, having done every course possible. She wasn't girly and could be one of the lads when she wanted to be. Darren had a lot of respect for her. John came next; he was a recent recruit, not very exciting but getting better daily at what he did. Then there was Rees, who was perhaps not the sharpest tool in the box but could always be relied upon.

Darren and Rees shared a Welsh background and the same sense of humour, but there the similarity ended. They got on well enough and enjoyed some institutional locker room banter. The good thing about his little team, he thought, was that they were all committed. There were no slackers amongst them.

He was really looking forward to this surveillance; it would make a change from the work he had been doing recently. The likelihood that Britain would embark on a programme of nuclear power station building in order to keep the lights on, was fast becoming a reality. The failure of renewable energy sources to supply enough for an expanding population meant the nuclear option was coming closer. Many people would be opposed to this and state monitoring of anti-nuclear activists was slowly ramping up. The database of people grew steadily with photos and personal information being added daily. That work would continue although the issue was still some way off at present.

Darren gathered his team and they all looked closely at the photo of the girl. It had been taken clandestinely from a vehicle, the wing mirror was apparent at the edge of the photo, and the image was good, though slightly blurred. It was a summer shot; she was walking along the street, apparently at quite a pace. Mentally he summarised: tall, attractive, good cheekbones, black hair and a bright blue halter-necked top, a real babe. She looked intelligent and focussed.

'Baby Blue,' he pronounced, 'that's who she'll be.'

The others nodded in understanding, knowing that this would be her code name when she was being discussed. Sexist it might be, but who was counting? Angela wasn't. Real names led to problems. They could listen in on people and that meant others might overhear them too. Darren gave them the same initial briefing he had received, and then sent the team off to research her, fixing another meeting in a few hours.

Very soon they had amassed a lot of information. Anna's home address, landline and two mobiles, plus parents' names and their mobile numbers. Anna's two email addresses and her mother's. No criminal record, nor her parents. Car owner, full licence, points for speeding recently. They downloaded the prospectus of a forensic science qualification that Anna was toying with as part-time home study. Her passport information was to follow shortly. Anna's employment details brought a surprise. She worked for a private investigation company based in Holborn in London. The name of the company was unknown to Darren, but according to the blurb, it carried out investigations of most types at home and abroad.

'Most of these agencies are run by ex-coppers, Angela. Find out who heads it up and we'll see if we have anyone there we can use in any way. Hmm, she's a proper little detective isn't she? Chasing Jack the Ripper, working for an investigation agency, and studying forensics. She'll be trying to join us next. Mind you, she'd probably be more use than you, Rees.' Darren sniggered at his own joke.

'What about social networking?' Darren suddenly asked John, who shook his head.

'Nothing yet, no Facebook, no Twitter, nor any of the others. She is on LinkedIn but she doesn't use it much, there's no recent traffic from her.' That was a shame; the easiest way to learn about anyone nowadays was online.

'Okay,' Darren nodded, detailing Angela and John to get to Baby Blue's workplace and follow her home or wherever else she went. Rees was to start digging into her emails and contacts list, and look for anything to do with Jack the Ripper.

Early the next morning they met again. Angela and John had little to report. Angela had got one of her favourite cars, a Toyota Land Cruiser in a light grey colour; it was fast, comfortable and merged in well. Being instantly forgettable it was very good for her purposes. Anna had returned home that evening via the Tube, and not gone out again. John had followed her on the train then met Angela near the house, which she had already reconnoitred. It was quite easy to monitor the place.

'A big place, two cars outside, hers and theirs,' Angela said. 'It's owned by her parents, she lives there with them, just the three of them. She seems to be living in one part of the house, maybe like an annexe, you know? Her lights were on very late but the parents' side of the house was dark. She has her own entrance at the side.'

Darren nodded. 'I don't expect the parents have anything to do with her activities but we'll keep tabs on their phones anyway for the moment. None of them made any calls last night.' Darren was well aware that the number of phone taps authorised by the Secretary of State was only a fraction of the taps actually applied in reality. However, he didn't care much, it wasn't his problem. Also, now that most people used mobiles they were much easier to tap remotely, so this formed a large part of their surveillance activities.

His mind moved on. 'Okay, what about her emails, Rees?'

'Nothing yet, but there's loads to look at, she's into these crime blogs about the Ripper and stuff. These people are all over the place, all round the world and it's going to take a long time to check them out, even if it's possible. She doesn't give much input, but she accesses lots of the posts. Something else as well, get this, loads of them are actual woodentops, and very senior too!'

Darren nodded again. 'So are you, Rees, so are you. A woodentop that is, but not senior.'

Rees grinned at the others, who were laughing at him. 'Some of them might be in this building,' he warned, shaking his finger at them. 'They all seem to be coppers, or ex-coppers anyway.'

'Not relevant,' Darren said to Rees. 'You need to spend a lot of time on those blogs and find out her lines of research. We want to know exactly what she is into at the moment, and what ideas she's pursuing.'

Darren pondered, remembering something that had been said at his briefing. He then addressed the three of them. 'It's probably true that some of these bloggers are police personnel, but many use pseudonyms and some infer they are serving officers when they aren't. We don't need to worry about that. Just treat it the same as the anti-nuclear people, a mishmash of enthusiasts, most of whom have their own agendas.'

Darren turned to look out of the window. He wondered idly if that was how this thing had come about. He knew he wouldn't be told anything, but was vaguely aware that the Whitechapel murders were still a very sensitive issue amongst a cadre at the top of the police hierarchy. If anyone was going to make a breakthrough in the case it was to be the police, not some amateur meddler who might expose age old incompetence, or even corruption in the service. At least if the police solved the crimes they could put their own spin on things.

Someone's worries had been triggered; perhaps it was one of these senior policemen who had become aware that an outsider might be getting close. Darren didn't know just how near his assessment actually was to the truth.

He dished out some duties to his trio and decided that today he would go and have a look at Baby Blue himself. He wanted to get out there in the field and be involved with the surveillance to get a personal perspective on her activities. Darren was also curious to see the girl in the flesh; she looked very attractive in her photo.

'What does she do lunchtime, I wonder? We'll see shall we? Angela, you're driving me today.'

Chapter 12

La Bella Italia

Kew, Richmond upon Thames – Present Day

Sitting in the bath with a glass of red wine in her hand, Anna Moretti pondered where she was with her Jack the Ripper quest. Anna was twenty-six years old; she worked as an administrator for a private investigation agency, lived in west London and had a degree in psychology and a post graduate criminology qualification. She had gained her interest in the subject of crime whilst at university, and her inquisitive mind led her inevitably to some of the great crimes in British and European history. She was morbidly fascinated and appalled by the violence and savagery meted out to the victims of many crimes, much of which seemed quite unnecessary if you just wanted to kill someone. Obviously the modus operandi employed by some killers was pure self-gratification and she wondered, not for the first time, what sparked that desire in some people.

Anna's ancestors on her father's side were Italian and her Mediterranean skin and prominent nose gave clues to her heritage. She was dark and attractive with no shortage of male admirers in her circle. Her father had indulged his little Anna Bella all her life, but this had been countered effectively by her mother who took a much more realistic view of her upbringing and had done her best to keep Anna level-headed. Her mother was an English rose but the only obvious traits she had bequeathed to Anna were her height and figure.

Anna's temperament was pure Latin, headstrong and passionate about whatever she got involved with. In that, she was just like her father, whose love for his English wife and his only daughter was the driving force in his life. What made Anna a little different from many of her contemporaries was the overriding interest that occupied much of her spare time, and not a little of her working time. Anna had become a fanatical Ripperologist.

The subject had started to consume her during her studies, and ever since, she had devoted most of her time and resources to the Whitechapel murders and the context in which they took place.

Anna shared a home with her mother and father. It was a big house with a self-contained annexe for Anna, giving them all space to avoid conflict. Even returning home after university hadn't been as difficult as it was for some people. She had moved into the granny flat as she called it, not seeing the point of getting a place of her own in London. It suited her controlling nature to be near them, but not with them. It also suited her doting father who was glad to have her nearby.

'I have everything I need here,' she told her friends. 'Why would I want to move out? It's easy to get into London and it's great to have Mum and Dad there when it suits me. They like having me around and we all have as much – or as little – privacy as we want.'

Anna's parents watched her irregular contacts with men with interest. Her two best friends were Sophie and Helen. She had known Helen since school, and they had both met Sophie at university, where the trio had become known as ASH. Anna was often out with a gang of friends, many of whom were men, but it seemed to her parents that she rarely dated anyone twice. They had learnt to curb their desire to see her settled and happy, but knew from bitter experience that the subject was to be avoided like poison. Casually they would ask how a date had gone and she would reply, 'Okay, thanks.'

Any further questions and her eyes would flash dangerously and the temperature would rise. The fact was that she was happy, doing what she did and enjoying her life, and saw no need of a regular boyfriend just for the sake of it. The idea of getting permanent with someone at the moment was an anathema to her.

Leaning back in the bath Anna thought over her last telephone conversation with Sam. She had detected his coolness towards the end of their talk and a woman's intuition told her he wasn't likely to contact her soon, if at all. She was aware he was piqued that she hadn't shared the numbers document with him, but felt possessive towards it and was finding it hard to give ground. Also of course he owed her nothing; it was her that wanted something from him, not the other way around. Anna swirled the wine gently in her glass, there was very little left so she reached for the bottle on the floor by her bathtub, relieved to see it was still half full.

She considered the matter again for a while. The truth was she needed his input. Anna was impatient to get to the bottom of the mystery and the tantalising possibility of solving the Whitechapel murders was almost tangible. She just needed to know more, a lot more, about Doyle and his life to build a profile and perhaps some evidence that he was the murderer. She also needed to find the meaning of the intriguing numbers document. Anna was certain it held the clue to the mystery of the Ripper.

To someone like her with a highly developed interest in crime and detection, the search for Jack the Ripper was the holy grail. Right or wrong she had to get on with it. In their meeting in London, Sam had demonstrated his scholarship of all things Conan Doyle, and for her to try to replicate that understanding would take years. If she turned to someone else the problem would be the same and Sam had seemed like a genuine guy. Somewhere in his brain was the proof she needed, though he wouldn't recognise it if he tripped over it. He was just too enamoured of Conan Doyle's reputation.

Savouring the wine as she emptied her glass, Anna made up her mind. She would make the first move now and contact Sam. It occurred to her that she needed to make a gesture and meet him half way, literally perhaps, she thought. I will go down to his part of the world, after all, why should he come to see me in London again? Also, she would use a little femininity to help influence him to spend time with her. Flirting? Definitely not, but her appearance could be subtly calculated to help her cause. Mentally she was already planning what she would wear when they next met.

Shivering, she realised her bath had grown cold. Placing her wine glass carefully on the windowsill she swiftly rose from the tepid water.

The next morning Anna emailed Sam before she left for work, telling him she would like to meet again to talk about Doyle. Remembering that a carrot might be needed she offered to come to Southampton, adding rather demurely the proviso, 'If you could find time to meet me?'

Sam powered up his computer and nursed the large mug of coffee in his hand, it was his favourite. It was a *Back to the Future* mug, bought for him in Florida by his sister on a family holiday there years before. In front of him now was Anna's email. Recalling Paige's words from their last conversation he smiled.

'It sounds really interesting; you should get involved and prove her wrong.'

Sam being Sam he had assumed Paige had meant with Anna's Jack the Ripper project, but of course Paige really meant more than that. Far too astute to say so, she had already divined from their discussions that this girl was someone who might distract him from his troubles with Indy.

He decided he would meet Anna again, but only so that he might prove to her that she was on a fool's errand. Sam tapped out a response. He was going to be away for a long weekend but could meet sometime after that if she wanted to come down. The reply came back quickly. She was looking forward to it and would be at Southampton Central station mid-morning on Tuesday, returning home later that day. He emailed her back saying that would be fine with him.

Sam's mind turned to the coming weekend. He had arranged to stay with friends in Battle, in Sussex, close to the site of the Battle of Hastings. Whilst down there he intended to renew his relationship with Windlesham, Sir Arthur Conan Doyle's home at Crowborough, which was also in Sussex. He hadn't been there for some years and thought he would like to take some photographs of the house this time. He would probably do this on Monday, and then travel home in time to meet Anna on Tuesday.

Chapter 13
A Writer in High Places?

East London – 1888

Victorian London wasn't the best of places to go walking at night. Whilst some parts were entirely fashionable and safe, others were unpleasant, oozing criminality and extreme danger. There were plenty of streets in the East End in particular where even the police feared to tread unless in considerable numbers.

The man's evening ramblings took him far and wide over London but today he was staying closer to home. He had received a note from his uncle and was going to meet him nearby. The only one he had any time for was this relative, a big man, a bluff professional who seemed to have some understanding of his thoughts and cared about him. Since the disappearance of his father when he was younger he had been brought up by his mother and her sister, who never mentioned the absent parent.

He had assumed that his father might be dead but nobody had ever confirmed it to him. From other relatives he heard whispers that he had gone to Australia. He heard nothing from him and begun to assume that he never would. This was why his uncle had come into his life and become the nearest thing to a father that he had. An educated man, his uncle spent much time nowadays writing, and had finally given up on orthodox religion. He had adopted spiritualism, and at the same time he harboured a hatred of Catholicism and all its ways.

The man would meet with his uncle from time to time and listen to stories about his life and work. They would have met more often but his uncle lived some distance away and was a busy man, moving in high places as his career had developed. The older man had become the nephew's source of information, knowing much about government, politics and other subjects. He had met and mingled with politicians, amongst them Home Secretary Henry Mathews, whom he had been shocked to discover was a Roman Catholic, the very first to be appointed to one of the highest offices in the land. Whatever next?

If a Catholic could be appointed to such a position, how long before a member of the Royal Family might espouse that faith? Earlier in his career Mathews had been accused of being a sympathiser to the Home Rule for Ireland movement before reinventing his politics later alongside his legal career as a barrister. His appointment to Lord Salisbury's government had surprised a lot of people.

The man's uncle had a real concern about Irish Catholics whom he saw as a serious threat to the stability of the Empire. The activities of the Fenians, the generic name that he used for those seeking Irish independence, were of concern to many in the establishment, and had been for years. Scotland Yard had spies amongst them and a special department had been created to monitor and disrupt their activities. His uncle had wondered if the Home Secretary might have hidden sympathies with the cause of Irish independence, this would be abhorrent, both to him and others. For that reason he felt Mathews was not really to be trusted.

Since the murders of Lord Cavendish and Thomas Burke in Phoenix Park, Dublin, anti-Irish sentiment had grown to greater heights. The English were horrified by this event and trust for anyone Irish was at an all-time low. Cavendish had been the brand new Chief Secretary for Ireland, and Thomas Burke was the senior Civil Servant. A group calling itself the Irish National Invincibles was blamed for the murders.

Their talk ranged over the situation and the man's uncle became slowly more animated, his voice rising slightly as he spoke. He went into a tirade against Catholics, and especially Catholic women who he saw as a threat to society. 'The Marys', as he referred to them, were the fount of all evil, they encouraged their men-folk to become seditious and they should be dealt with severely.

Home Rule for Ireland was unthinkable; it would lead to a clamour for full independence, both a challenge and an affront to the authority and government of the British Empire. In his mind, Home Rule was the thin end of the wedge, other countries would demand it and the Empire would be fragmented and lost, with Britain becoming small and insignificant.

His nephew nodded as he listened, he took it all in noting the vehemence with which his uncle spoke. He understood that the type of women his uncle despised were becoming a problem, their Catholic and Home Rule beliefs clearly at odds with the natural order of things. His uncle looked around him while he talked. Recently he had become concerned that he was under observation by people planning to assassinate him, and he confided in his nephew about this. The Marys, his uncle affirmed, were everywhere and especially in the East End. The 'stews of London' were full of them, and of many other types of undesirables. The big man told him that steps had to be taken to deal with the menace. His uncle asked to meet with him again soon, he would send a note to confirm the day and time.

When the older man had left, his nephew made his way slowly homeward. As he walked one dowdy street after another filthy alley, the blackened low quality brickwork of many of the buildings seemed to close in on him. Ill-fitting windows covered with filth looked down on him. There were buildings which had an almost impossible slant, looking as though they were kept upright only through the support and goodwill of their neighbours.

By a circuitous route he arrived home, he didn't remember the way and it hadn't been the most direct. However he had followed it unerringly like an animal in search of food, feeling his way by some instinct not by rational thought. He didn't greet his mother, just ate what she had prepared, then went directly to his room and did more reading. His current obsession still lay with medical knowledge and having received treatment recently that he hadn't agreed with, the man began to look deeper into the subject. Organs were the key to it, the answer to both his own illness and to others, he believed. His medical studies had no orthodox status; he simply obtained books and publications from wherever he could and read avidly. He was interested mainly in women, and in particular, their organs, both internal and external.

His latest drawings were simple but explicit allowing him to construct and to deconstruct them in his own way and for his own purposes. The women he drew came to represent the worst things about the female of the species. They were whores and Catholics, they were strident and ignorant, not unlike his mother and aunt. They influenced their menfolk in bad ways. *They were Marys.*

Chapter 14
Dark Annie

Whitechapel – 8 September 1888

Annie hadn't felt well that day, in fact for the last few months she had struggled hard to find her old vitality. Her night fevers and occasional chills had become worse of late, not helped by the fact that she had no home other than a lodging house in Crossingham Street, paid for by the night. This decline seemed to have started after the death of her husband John, although they had been estranged for a long time before that. Their marriage had simply been unable to bear the strains that were brought to it by family tragedy and a series of failed plans.

Annie Chapman had fond memories of her husband and despite their separation she knew that originally they had been good for each other. They had both liked to drink too much but that alone would not have divided them, it was simply the fall of the cards that had destroyed their partnership. She also realised that life was unlikely to improve in any real sense, now that her health was worsening. The thought of next winter on the grim streets scared her.

Only last week she had become involved in a fight with another woman at the lodging house, it was over nothing but a scrap of soap, which – precious as it was – should never have provoked such a fracas. Now she had a black eye and a bruise on her chest to show for it. Well at least the black eye had given her a conversation piece with friends, she thought. Dark Annie had become Dark Eyed Annie, one of them had joked.

The usual buzz of humanity in the Whitechapel streets had ebbed slowly away as the evening wore on. The weather had been cool, mostly dry and it had been a long night for Annie. Already the time was about one thirty a.m. and she called back to her lodging house to ensure she had a bed for the night, without avail. Not having the necessary cash and unable to call in any favours with the Supervisor, Annie knew she would have to go out again and earn some. She left, asking him to keep her bed free and telling him she would be back soon with the money.

Since then things hadn't gone well, the early hours had been frittered talking with acquaintances when she encountered them. She still didn't feel good and had little hope that things would change. The break up from her last partner had resulted in her suffering some depression, but for a while now the sickness had become physical rather than mental. All that Dark Annie really wanted was her bed and a good night's rest.

As time passed it made the prospect of her bed somewhat irrelevant unless she could get there soon. Finally, outside the Frying Pan public house in Brick Lane, she found a man, or perhaps he found her, and she agreed to go with him. At first glance he seemed to be a bit younger than her, and his worn clothing had obviously once been good. Age didn't seem to matter nowadays; it was young men who needed her favours, and old men. Come to that, she thought, it was any man seeking relief as a break from the daily grind of life. His demeanour was pleasant enough as they talked, though he had a nervous, tense manner and looked around them constantly, calling her Mary and observing everything as they strolled. She made no attempt to correct his use of her name, he didn't know her real name and why should he? Names weren't needed for their brief liaison, they might never meet again, and if they did he would either be buying or not, as the case might be.

It was now after five a.m. and they wandered down Brick Lane into Hanbury Street to find a quiet spot. It was the nearest vicinity she knew that would be suitable, its proximity to Brick Lane making it a short walk to do business. Annie was well aware that many of the houses had quiet yards in the back, used by her acquaintances, and often by herself. She stopped outside number 29 where they talked desultorily for a few moments, waiting until the street became quiet. A few people walked along the road including a woman who looked at them both as she passed closely by. The man turned his back to this woman and glanced frequently down the street. When she had disappeared and all seemed completely clear, Annie pushed open the swing door into a passage which led to the yard at the rear. The yard was surrounded by a fence about the same height as Annie herself. By now fingers of light from the approaching dawn were making their presence strongly felt.

Annie needed this client; she felt very tired and this was her last shot at getting her bed for the night, or at least this morning. She reminded herself this money must be saved. They paused by the fence and the man insistently requested his needs, repeatedly calling her Mary. Annie considered his new demands to be unnatural and was too tired to point out that she wasn't Mary, but things were going against her and she complied.

'Yes,' she said.

The man loosened his coat and moved in close facing her. As Annie looked up at him he gripped her firmly around the neck, she squirmed away, managing to gasp out the word 'no', though it came out as little more than a hoarse whisper. The man reacted quickly and violently, grabbing her throat again with no intention of letting her go. There were no more mistakes, this time he tightened his grip remorselessly around her neck, forcing her back against the fence behind her. The last thing she saw were two brilliant blue eyes gazing down at her with a fervour that defied normality. Her arms felt like lead and although she raised them to grip his wrists she had no strength to wrestle with him. Tighter and tighter he squeezed until she could breathe no more. Annie's consciousness faded and she slowly slumped to the ground, her head laying just inches from the step they had descended into the yard.

Swiftly, the man acted; taking a pace back he looked down the quiet passage. In it he saw nothing. Ignoring everything he went back to the body and stooped beside her. Extracting a long knife from his grubby frock coat he cut his victim's throat with unnecessary force then turned his attention to the lower regions of her body. Parting her legs he pulled her knees up into a position which suggested sexual intercourse, although that wasn't his focus now.

A watcher would have been horrified as the grisly work unfolded. Over the next few minutes he wielded the long knife, cutting into her belly wall and peeling it back over her shoulder, removing some organs in the process. He then made more cuts, removing her small intestine and placing it over her other shoulder. It was becoming easier to see as the dawn light crept into the yard, making his work less challenging. But still the blue eyes bored down on the task he had set himself.

He breathed heavily and fitfully, the act was causing him to experience an adrenalin surge, exciting him more and more. The excitement was heightened by the fact that he knew he was in a dangerous position, exposed by the dawn and with no easy exit. The only alternative way out of the yard would require clambering over high fences, although that didn't worry the man at all. He didn't have a name for it but knew that when he felt like this, sudden bursts of energy would easily enable him to make his escape.

Frequently he lifted his head to glance at the passage through the house towards the street, before being drawn back spellbound by the horrific savagery he had wrought. Finally the man wiped his blade on Annie's clothing and concealed it in his coat. Almost as an afterthought he emptied her pockets and seeing nothing he wanted, laid her few simple belongings near her feet. He then left the way he had arrived. Outside in Hanbury Street another man lingered some thirty yards away, a big man, well dressed with a moustache. The killer apparently didn't notice him; if he did so he made no acknowledgement and walked briskly away. After a few moments the other man followed slowly.

Chapter 15

Ruffs & Dimples

Sussex – Present Day

Leaving his friends in the town of Battle, Sam drove through to Crowborough; it was a damp and chilly Monday morning. He stopped just long enough to inspect and pay homage to the statue of Sir Arthur which had been erected in the town centre. The life-size bronze was a very good facial likeness and depicted Doyle with his hat and walking stick. It stood on a plain rectangular masonry plinth which carried the simple inscription:

Sir Arthur Conan Doyle
Resident of Crowborough
1907–1930

It was quite a while since Sam had been to the Crowborough area, and after viewing the statue he pulled up in the car park at the front of Windlesham Manor. Sam gazed up at the facade of what had once been a substantial family home with its two large and three small gables. Perhaps it was this very facade which had been the inspiration for the title of 'The Adventure of the Three Gables', which featured in *The Case-Book of Sherlock Holmes*. Doyle was renowned for pulling his ideas from anywhere or anything he encountered, often with disregard for accuracy and detail. He would simply see it or hear it, and then use it. Always keen to press on with his writing, extended research would only cause him to lose the momentum of his story.

Sam pictured his pen scratching as it raced over the surface of the paper. No word processors in those days, he thought, no going back later to edit or fiddle with the phrasing. If you wrote longhand you needed to be more decisive and precise just as Doyle had been. Perhaps he just hadn't seen the importance of checking details, after all, it was fiction so what did it matter?

Sam knew from his last visit some years earlier that the great man's house was now a care home for the elderly and was sure that Doyle would have approved of the use it was being put to. Sir Arthur had had many good times here with his second wife Jean and the children, after buying the house in 1907. He had been very happy in Crowborough and had delighted in taking walks and cycle rides locally.

The porch retained its rain canopy and the part-glazed wide wooden door reflected the tastefulness of its owners. Displayed beside the door was the simple green metal plaque noting Conan Doyle's residence here from 1907 onwards until his death in 1930. Though he had also spent time in the New Forest at Bignell Wood during the 1920s, this house had remained his main residence.

Entering the house, Sam was met by a nurse, he explained his historical interest and that he would appreciate being shown any areas associated with Sir Arthur. In the office on the right a young manager overheard the conversation and came out to speak to him. She was a twenty-something blonde in a dark business suit, the pencil skirt tailored expertly over her hips, terminating perfectly at the knee. A ruff necked white blouse kissed her throat as she moved, making a chaste change from the current rush for cleavage. Her hair was pinned up in a businesslike chignon showing her face to its best advantage. She asked if she could help him, offering a smile with cute dimples.

Sam explained why he was here, his background as a writer and his particular interest in the creator of Sherlock Holmes. The girl said she could show him some of the house, including the area which had been the main lounge or drawing room in Doyle's day. Other areas would be a little more difficult because of the residents. They walked through the house as she questioned Sam about Conan Doyle. She confessed that she hadn't read any Doyle books, but like everyone, she knew something of Sherlock Holmes and Doctor Watson, and had seen some of the recent TV programmes. She commented that it was a privilege to work in a place with such an illustrious former resident.

They stood by the original fireplace chatting as staff and cleaners passed through going about their tasks. Occasionally as she moved near, Sam would catch the fragrance of fresh soap while they talked. The manager remarked that she just hadn't realised how big a celebrity Doyle had been in his day. Realising she was interested, Sam expanded the background a little for her. He described Doyle as a Knight of the Realm, a war historian, sportsman, traveller and budding inventor who made suggestions about policy and tactics in more than one war zone to the War Office, though they had not all been welcome.

He had also been a surgeon in the Boer War and visited Egypt and Sudan, as well as later wangling a visit to the front during World War One. His concerns had been for the improvement, safety and training of British troops and with grim foresight of that war, he had started a rifle club whilst living at Hindhead.

Much of this was before he had purchased Windlesham. Sam told her that while living here Doyle had humorously christened it Swindlesham as a comment on the building costs he encountered whilst making alterations. The house he and Jean had fallen in love with had been a cottage originally but he had increased its size considerably. In its heyday it had seen large social groups, and the great long room in which people gathered was often used for dancing and music. Many society names had attended events here at Sir Arthur's invitation.

The blonde manager had absolutely no idea that both Conan Doyle and his wife had been buried in the grounds before subsequently being reinterred in Minstead churchyard, when the property had been sold. The estate had been more extensive in those days and Sir Arthur had added a wooden summerhouse in the grounds which he would use for writing during good weather.

They talked for twenty minutes or so before the manager said she would leave him to browse and that he should just come back to the office when he had finished. Making her way back she met the nurse, who smirked at her, raising her eyebrows in a questioning manner.

'What?' said the blonde, playing dumb and pretending she didn't get the unspoken message.

'Your visitor, he's very nice isn't he?' said the nurse.

'Well, since you mention it, isn't he just?'

'So I suppose in future you are going to show all visitors around the house for half an hour or so, and give them some very personal attention?' teased the nurse.

'Definitely not, only the good looking ones,' said the manager wrinkling her freckled nose with amusement. The dimples reappeared, and the nurse responded with hoots of laughter.

Meanwhile, Sam was deeply absorbed in the atmosphere of the past. He took a few photographs of the interior as it was today, and made a number of entries in the notebook he kept in his bag. There were some prints on the walls, both of Sir Arthur and of the house, allowing him to visualise the lounge as it had once been, without some modern dividing walls. A heavily carved Victorian bookcase held a stock of Doyle's novels for the residents to enjoy. Sam studied each of the framed prints, noting the changes that had been made and visualising the house in its peak years, with a grand piano and billiard table to welcome the family's dinner guests. He also reflected on some of the books that Doyle had written here, either in his study, or in his cabin in the grounds.

Eventually he made his way back to the office where the young manager was busy with a phone call. Patiently waiting, Sam thanked her. She rose from her desk and walked closer, planning to see him out. Holding his eye contact for much longer than necessary, she said it had been a pleasure, then volunteered to show him more of the house at some convenient time if he wanted.

'I'll give you my number and you can call me directly if you like,' she suggested.

'I'd like that,' said Sam automatically. He smiled and took the proffered card, oblivious both to the real invitation he was receiving, and to the fact she had carefully added pale lipstick whilst he had been browsing.

Bidding her farewell he left the building, the sun had now broken through the grim skies of the morning and Sam took a few shots of the house's facade. It was only when he sat in his car and started the engine that he reflected on the blonde's dimples, suddenly realising just how attractive she was.

Chapter 16

Ladies Who Shop

Southampton – Present Day

On the appointed day Sam was waiting outside the station as the dazzling smile breezed through the turnstile, her handbag snagging on the metal barrier as she did so. It was the largest bag he'd ever seen, what do women put in them? At their first meeting he hadn't really noticed so much about her, but Bernie's 'stunning' comment to the mystery club came back to him with a vengeance this morning.

Anna looked almost as tall as Sam today, her five feet eight or so increased by high heeled sandals with ankle straps. She wore black leggings, and a long, wide necked jumper. It was subtly arranged off one shoulder, allowing a black bra strap to play peek-a-boo. Toenails, fingernails and lipstick were all in a laid back mulberry shade. The whole effect was spectacular. Sam took it all in instantly and it left him thinking, *maybe under different circumstances...*

Dressed in his jeans and trainers with a shirt, his favourite shoulder bag and a keffiyeh around his neck he felt slightly underdressed.

Starting off on her best behaviour she shook his hand and thanked him for meeting her.

'It's my pleasure.' He grinned, amused at their mutual formality. 'Where would you like to go today?'

They didn't notice John as he hung back studying train times, following casually through the barrier a few yards behind her. Anna didn't know Southampton and told Sam she didn't mind where they went as long as she could get a large coffee. Sam had left his car at home, so he walked her to the WestQuay Shopping Centre, where they took the escalators inside, making for the food court high up over the city. Buying coffee in Cafe Giordano they got seated in the window area overlooking some of the port, drawing admiring glances from some 'ladies who shop' as they did so. As they settled down, John, dressed anonymously in a dark suit and open-necked shirt, entered the food court. He bought his own coffee and sat where he could monitor their exit.

Sam pointed out two enormous cruise ships docked for the day, dwarfing the terminal buildings around them, the outlook somewhat spoilt by the enormous blue and yellow box that housed IKEA. They chatted about the ships, Sam filling in some information for her. He remarked that around six thousand people would disembark and a similar number would embark today, as the two ships completed their turnaround within twelve hours. The city, he said, benefitted enormously from the cruise industry as the demand for goods and services was insatiable. The facilities and geography of Southampton had always made it the premier cruise port in the UK.

After this their meeting followed the pattern set by the last one. Once again there was some fencing around the issues and dealing with the niceties. Finally Sam asked her if she had brought the number sheet with her.

'Yes, I have it.' She delved in the massive handbag and produced her pad with a number of loose papers, from amongst which she extracted a photocopy. It was a sheet closely covered with figures set in four columns. At the bottom of the sheet the numbers faded out in a ragged edge. Along the top it bore the legend:

Bignell Wood

First and last lines contain a Ripping Yarn

Sam looked carefully at the sheet. 'What happened here?' he said pointing to the bottom where the numbers disappeared.

'I think it got scorched, the original had a brown edge as though it had been in a fire or something.'

'Where is the original?' asked Sam.

Anna hesitated and then said she wasn't sure, it had come into her possession via a roundabout route. Sam sensed again she was being evasive and once more felt irritation surge through him. He didn't pursue it, just shrugged it off.

'How do you know it's authentic? Without provenance it means nothing, there are only the words Bignell Wood that connect it to Conan Doyle.' Sam spelt it out. 'Anyone could create this and send people on some wild goose chase.'

'No, I saw it; it came as part of a bunch of domestic documents from Conan Doyle's estate. They were sold by Christies.' Anna protested.

'Yes, via a roundabout route wasn't it?' Sam returned sarcastically. She had again underestimated Sam's knowledge. He knew all about the Christies sale of papers that had so upset Richard Lancelyn Green and others. Precisely because of his specialism, Sam had a good overview of the various Doyle family factions and the dispersal of many bunches of documents over the years.

Anna went silent. She hadn't wanted to mention the episode in Seattle when she had obtained the document, but it was dawning on her again that this wasn't going to be one-way traffic. Sam just wasn't going to help her unless she levelled with him. He looked up from the document as the thoughts chased themselves through her mind.

'More coffee?'

Biting her lip she nodded and Sam disappeared towards the counter. Men! Why did they have to be so difficult? Anna thought. Sighing quietly Sam wondered yet again why he was here. Then his inherent good nature returned and with the two coffees he bought a couple of almond croissants. Anna watched as the blonde girl who served Sam smiled and joked with him. Little tramp, she thought, uncharitably.

For a moment the big smile came out when she saw the croissants, and after taking a huge bite from one, she told him something of the events in Seattle. She limited it to the fact she had been on a crime psychology conference, an acquaintance who was a Doyle fan had bought a small lot of papers and that was where she had seen the original of the number sheet.

Sam nodded. She was still defiant and made no apology for not telling him initially where the document had come from. For a moment he could visualise Anna as a little girl not getting her own way, the mental picture of her pouting and stamping her foot in anger brought a smirk to his lips. I bet she was just like that, he thought, and probably always would be.

He asked what she thought the numbers represented and she said she believed it was a code hidden in a book or story, the first and last lines of which might be significant. Then she came to the numbers in their four columns.

11	10	2	5
13	7	3	2
(Page)	(Line)	(Word)	(Letter)

'I think these might represent the page number, the line number, the word number and the letter number,' she said. 'It's a simple code but I'm sure that's what it means. Now I need the document or story it refers to, to find the message.' She paused. 'Sam, do you think it might be a code? Did Doyle use anything like that in his writings?'

'Yes he did,' said Sam. 'Off the top of my head he used a code in 'The Adventure of the Dancing Men', a short story where childlike figures were used to represent letters of the alphabet. More significantly for your theory, a character called Fred Porlock used a code from a commonly available book to communicate with Sherlock Holmes. It was in a novel called *The Valley of Fear*, and the code was indecipherable unless you knew the actual book that must be used to unravel it. Porlock was an informer that Holmes had an association with.'

Sam hesitated. 'So I have to admit that it is the sort of thing Doyle might have done if he had a secret to hide, not that it makes him a killer of course, that is plainly ridiculous!'

Anna's eyes shone at the news about codes, this was exactly what she had wanted from Sam, some corroboration of her theory that it was the sort of thing that Doyle might have done. She didn't bite back about his implied assertion that the rest of her theory was ridiculous, preferring to continue mining his knowledge while she was on a winning streak. She nodded, smiling as she continued.

'I also wanted to ask you if you'd had any more thoughts about the phrase at the top of the sheet.'

'Well, Bignell Wood was, and still is, a house in the New Forest not far from where I live. Doyle owned it and he and Jean conducted seances there quite often. It is situated in a quiet place well off the road, unlike Windlesham, his Sussex home.'

Then Sam moved on to the 'First and last lines contain a Ripping Yarn'. He told Anna that he had heard the phrase at a Sherlock Holmes convention that he had attended some years before. He explained that he hadn't seen much significance in it at the time, and hadn't thought about it since.

Anna asked about the convention and Sam obliged with some information remarking that it had been chaired by Richard Lancelyn Green. She drew a sharp breath.

'Richard!' she exclaimed. 'He was the last word on Conan Doyle and Sherlock Holmes wasn't he? Did you know him?'

'I met him.' Sam smiled. 'And he certainly was, he probably knew more than anyone else. His death was a tragedy for the whole Conan Doyle and Sherlock Holmes arena.'

Anna's eyes shone with interest, if Richard had still been alive she might have been talking with him now and not Sam, she thought. The partly eaten croissant forgotten, she gazed intently at Sam.

'Tell me about him, tell me about the conversation when the phrase was mentioned, what did it mean? How did the speaker come across it?' Her questions tumbled out, the researcher inside taking over as she probed for the missing bits of her jigsaw. Sam smiled to himself at her bubbling enthusiasm. He fixed his eyes on a tiny crumb of croissant that was stuck to the mulberry lipstick.

Patiently he outlined what he could remember from the session with Richard and a large group of others from several years before. The phrase had been in a short memo that probably referred to a story Doyle had written. The speaker concerned had been very keen to find any material associated with it, as it appeared to present a little mystery that he would dearly love to solve. Others present had supported this aim, though Sam hadn't seen it as anything very important. He went on to tell Anna that he couldn't offer any explanations at the time and had not got involved. The matter had simply gone off his radar since then.

'You must understand that there are loads and loads of little mysteries with Conan Doyle and Sherlock Holmes,' Sam explained. 'Enthusiasts are always delving into them. Some mean nothing but others may have some unknown significance. Doyle was a bit of an enigma at times.'

'Yes, my point exactly.' Anna leapt back into the fray. 'I think he had a lot to hide, I reckon he lived a double life, all his stories of secret rooms and stuff!'

Sam shook his head patiently. He tried to make the case that just because someone's life threw up inconsistencies that didn't make them a mass murderer.

Anna watched and listened intently, this time she didn't interrupt again until Sam had finished. She asked if Sam knew where the convention delegates had obtained the document bearing the phrase.

Sam shook his head again. 'I'm sorry; I don't remember anyone saying at the time.'

As he said it he knew he was still holding back slightly, why was he being secretive with her? He believed, though could not be sure, that Richard might have been behind the debate about the document. He may have had some reason of his own for this, but Sam had tuned out of the discussions eventually. He couldn't help but think that if the document was still out there, the Lancelyn Green bequest to the city of Portsmouth might just hold a clue to it. Come to think of it, if anyone had retained a copy of such a document it would be Richard. Sam could certainly look into that if he wished to.

He realised that by holding back he was responding to her in the same way that she was to him. He was playing tit for tat and it was silly. Sam felt disappointed with himself, but there was something else. Despite his ambivalence towards Anna he also didn't want to raise her hopes unnecessarily.

'It may be,' he relented a little, 'that there is some clue amongst Richard's collection.'

Anna's eyes shone again. 'Yes of course,' she said. 'Where is it? Can we go and see his stuff?'

'Ah, well, it's not quite that simple, the collection is vast, and is still being catalogued by Portsmouth Central Library. It's available to the public only by appointment, though some items are on display in the city museum.' Sam explained that the bequest had run to a number of large vans full of material including books, souvenirs and an incredible amount of documents and papers. The sheer volume of the collection overwhelmed people when they came to understand how much was in it.

'I have been helping them to categorise some of the stuff for a while now.'

Anna's eyes widened with incredulity. 'You've got access to it? You didn't tell me that,' she said accusingly.

'You didn't ask me,' said Sam swiftly. 'And you've only told me certain things so far, haven't you?'

She glared at him and the dark eyes flashed dangerously. Sam stared straight back, it was a standoff. Another fight had been inevitable from the start, he thought. Was it even worth trying to head it off?

'Look, Anna. See things from my point of view for a moment. You have this wild tale about Conan Doyle being the Ripper or knowing about the Ripper, you ask for my help in learning about him but you know I think it's all nonsense. I understand you want to keep things a secret but I can't help you if you don't share information fully.'

She tossed her head and the dark hair rearranged itself on her shoulders.

'I have told you everything.' She lied petulantly. It wasn't proving so easy to manipulate this guy as she had thought it might. Despite his feelings, Sam's good nature reasserted itself yet again, it was all so silly really, he thought. He grinned across the coffee cups to the croissant crumb on her lips.

'What are you laughing at?' Yet again, the dark eyes flashed dangerously.

His smile broadened. 'You look scary when you're angry, and...' he let the sentence hang.

'And what?'

'It amuses the other people in the cafe,' he said with a smile.

Anna took a cursory look around her for the first time, seeing a few eyes glancing curiously at them, no doubt assuming it was a disagreement between lovers.

As if! she thought angrily.

Had she been Sherlock Holmes she might have observed that John, who had followed them in, was the only person who never seemed to look in their direction. He gazed studiously across the food court as though deep in thought, occasionally looking back to the restaurant exit, and fiddling with his mobile phone. Observing this, Holmes might have deduced that his disinterest was feigned and that he was actually therefore monitoring Sam and Anna.

Anna tossed her head again, the long suffering hair returning to its customary position. Then suddenly the brilliant smile came out, enveloping Sam, and the atmosphere moved back from the brink.

'Phooey, okay, perhaps I'm a bit secretive,' she conceded. 'But so are you, fancy you not telling me about Richard's collection!' The way she said it made him sound guilty, like some naughty schoolboy!

Sam laughed at her. 'Well I've told you now, haven't I? Anyway, would you like to stretch your legs? I'll show you around town if you like.'

Sam took her on a walk around the old walls, starting at the Bargate, the original main gates to the medieval walled town. For a while she regretted wearing the killer heels but soon settled into it. Fortunately they were about as comfortable as heels can ever be and she had managed long days in them before. It was a bright, pleasant day, and completely oblivious to her shoe issues, Sam took her on a history trail. They saw the outsides of the Tudor House, the old Maritime Museum building and some good sections of the walls still in situ, erected by linking the outside walls of merchants' houses following the French raid of 1338. Anna took a few snaps on her phone, capturing Sam against the beige stone of the walls.

Some way behind them John was content. He was watching Anna's legs appreciatively as she perambulated gracefully along beside Sam. She was very good to follow; the job had some perks after all, he thought.

He wondered what they were doing but couldn't see anything significant. They just seemed to talk and argue from time to time. He sent regular texts to Darren, who already knew she wasn't staying over in Southampton, as she had a return ticket.

In addition to the older history, Sam showed Anna some of the remaining buildings from the golden age of cruising, an age that many felt was returning to the city as new cruise terminals were planned and constructed. Anna could hardly be described as a history buff with the exception of her Jack the Ripper obsession, but nevertheless she absorbed a lot of information from Sam and had the good grace to show interest.

Peeling off from the walk they lunched in a pub in Southampton's

Oxford Street, and preferring not to argue for the moment they confined themselves to less contentious subjects. As during their previous meeting, they needed a break, suspecting they would return to the arguing later, neither bending in their beliefs about Conan Doyle. When Sam went to the men's room, Anna fished her tablet out of the massive shoulder bag, quickly googling Richard Lancelyn Green and various Sherlock Holmes societies. Her eyes scanned the screen as she rapidly assimilated bits of peripheral information, including the location of the RLG collection in Portsmouth. Spotting Sam walking back she flashed the big smile, switching off the tablet.

'Just making a few notes before I forget.' She lied smoothly.

Comfortable in the pub they decided to stay for a while. Later they talked some more about their work. Sam told her that one day he would like to tackle a fresh biography of Conan Doyle. It was something that Richard Lancelyn Green had aspired to.

'As yet I don't feel I am anywhere near ready to do so. There have been many biographies about him, some better than others, but I'm going to bide my time. At the moment I'm too busy earning a living. It's a job for when I'm much older, and more material might become available.'

Sam added that he spent time slowly gathering information and background for the eventual biography, and made regular visits around the country taking photos and making notes. Anna told him more about her work and her fascination with criminology and the human mind. They talked long into the afternoon, both still studiously avoiding the difficult area between them. Eventually they worked their way back to the subject in hand. Anna had Richard Lancelyn Green on her mind and, not usually the most diplomatic person, remembered that when she had soaked in her bath planning this trip, some more concessions were in order. The smile was called into play and leaning slightly forward across the table she fixed Sam with her big eyes.

'I would appreciate it if you could help me trace where Richard found the phrase,' she said. 'It means a lot to me to try to get to the bottom of this mystery. If I could be the one to draw a final line under the Whitechapel murders, it would be the most amazing thing. It really is important to me, Sam. I just feel there's a nugget here somewhere.' The dark eyes widened suggestively, fixing Sam and drawing him in. Using his name and her eyes together was about as near as she would ever get to a plea.

'Okay I will try, but no promises about Richard's collection. It's vast, I can look when I go there next, but it really will be a needle in a haystack affair.'

Anna wanted to ask when he was due to go to Portsmouth, but sensed this wouldn't be a welcome question. She was realising Sam couldn't be pushed. She contented herself with meekly thanking him for the offer.

'Let's have another look at that document,' Sam said. Anna handed it over again and Sam started to examine it more closely this time. 'It's a shame it's not very clear,' he remarked. 'There might have been some other clues in it.'

'Yes, I had to duplicate it on an old fax machine and you know what they're like, it's not a great copy.' Sam looked at the top of the sheet.

'There's a mark here, it looks like the indent a paper clip might make.'

Anna peered at the mark.

'You're right it does, so perhaps the paper was clipped to another, or several. Yes, maybe even the one you heard about at your conference!' she said, eyes lighting up again.

'I'm not sure how it helps us,' said Sam. 'Was it a paper clip that made that mark? If it was, when was it attached? It might have been clipped to something much later. Did they even have paper clips as we know them at that time?' Sam mused on, posing questions that they couldn't answer. 'Well, Bignell Wood at least dates it to the 1920s, and Doyle died in 1930, 7 July to be precise,' Sam finished.

Anna's face fell, she hadn't thought of that, she was forced to concede that she knew little about paper clips and realised that Sam had put his finger on something that might be important. Now she had another task, this would have to be researched, and soon. Neither of them was particularly mathematical so they could find no obvious code in the numbers on the sheet, which appeared to be totally random. Sam looked carefully at the numbers and considered Anna's theory that the four columns represented the page number, the line number, the word number and the letter number from a book.

He concluded that they could fall into the ranges of those that would be generated by a fairly typical book. For example the first column which might represent the pages went to much higher numbers than the second column, and the third column didn't even seem to go above the number twelve. This might be the case as many books would not have more than a dozen words in one line. So, on this basis it looked feasible as a theory anyway. Sam had no better explanation than hers.

'If it's a genuine document and a code of some sort, then your theory looks good to me, we just have to find the right book I suppose.'

Anna was pleased and the big smile put in a fresh appearance, it seemed as though Sam might be coming around to her ideas. Also, she noted he had used the word *we*, implying that he would be helping her more in her hunt. She was starting to trust him a little as she learnt more about him. Sam smiled back at her.

'It isn't going to be easy; do you know how many books there are in this world?'

Finding nothing else in the sheet that meant anything, Sam turned the conversation back to Ripper suspects.

'Okay, without arguing about it, I still don't see why it has to be Conan Doyle,' he said. 'Surely there must be a hundred other suspects documented in one way or another.'

'Something over two hundred actually,' she corrected him. 'But many don't have any credibility at all; even some at the top of the list don't have any sort of evidence against them. In the last fifty years the 'Macnaghten Memoranda' has done much to put people on the wrong track, particularly perpetuating the myth that there were only five victims, the famous canonical five, and also trying to smear a suicide victim, Montague Druitt, against whom there is absolutely no evidence of guilt whatsoever.'

Sam knew nothing about Macnaghten so Anna obliged with some background. She had strong opinions on how the eventual publication of his memoranda had re-invigorated the hunt, then later split Ripper aficionados into factions.

'It's now thought that he wrote it for his bosses to refute some claims made by *The Sun* newspaper, who had suggested a man named Cutbush was the killer. Macnaghten tried to rubbish that claim,' she said.

'Sir Melville Leslie Macnaghten was first invited to join the force by his friend James Monro, who was an Assistant Commissioner. There was some politics around it, in that this was opposed by Sir Charles Warren, who distrusted Monro. His appointment was blocked and Macnaghten only joined the Metropolitan Police in 1889, after Sir Charles Warren's resignation, a resignation which came at the height of the Ripper crisis.'

Anna paused and collected her thoughts.

'Macnaghten later stated that he wished he had joined earlier, because he hadn't been involved during the hunt for the Ripper. The memo everyone gets excited about wasn't even written until 1894. It takes the form of a summary and contains a number factual errors, plus personal opinions and assumptions which can't be proven and would never be accepted in modern policing. In addition, it became apparent later that many senior people even closer to the investigation completely disagreed with his views. Perhaps the most interesting thing is that it was clearly written for people above him, it wasn't for public consumption but smacks more of a briefing document, or a response to a request for a report. Now there weren't that many people actually above him, other than the Commissioner, so you may suspect it was written to satisfy him or politicians, the Home Secretary perhaps?'

'I'd like to see a copy of this memo,' said Sam.

'I've got one at home, I'll bring it next time,' Anna responded quickly, too quickly, she suddenly realised. She had assumed there was to be a next time and she coloured slightly. Sam didn't appear to notice either the comment or her blush, just nodded and said thanks. Harking back to her earlier point Sam asked about the victims.

'Are you implying there were more than five victims?' he said.

'Oh yes, of course,' she replied emphatically, as though everyone should have known that.

'Macnaghten tried to draw a line under the murders for political reasons and to protect the Met from the damage to its reputation. More than five would have been a disaster for them; there were actually eleven murders on the Whitechapel file originally. It was a smokescreen, no more, no less. It was all about damage limitation. Unfortunately he succeeded in misleading many later scholars into thinking that he knew something when clearly he didn't.'

After a pause Anna continued.

'With regard to the number of victims, I would rather believe some of the eminent surgeons and policemen who were involved at first hand. Some of them became convinced that other murders were the work of the same killer. Remember, Macnaghten wasn't involved in the Ripper hunt and was only writing some time after the events. I fully accept though, that he had talked to all the senior detectives and was entitled to his own opinions. It was actually him who closed the file, in about 1892 I think.' She frowned, striving to remember.

Sam was fascinated and made a mental note to add some Ripper reading to the stack of books by his bed. He had a general grasp of the murders but Anna's comments made him realise how little he really knew. He wondered briefly if her statements were actually true or were her own opinions being relayed as facts, rather like her Conan Doyle theory. Although Sam had no way of knowing it, Anna was not a million miles from the truth in her assessment of Sir Melville Macnaghten's infamous memoranda. She had certainly sounded plausible, and rightly or wrongly he gave her credit for the work she had done regarding the matter.

'So how many do you think were murdered?' he questioned.

'A maximum of eight and a minimum six, I still don't want to be too precise about it at the moment. There are lots of disputed and unreliable sources of evidence, and occasionally new clues still come to light, even after all these years.'

In full swing now, Anna sailed through a list of some of the other suspects, a list that was familiar to anyone who had taken an interest in the case. She gave her considered opinion as to the merits of their candidacy, dismissing many of them with a short and pithy comment. She treated Sam to potted versions of the case against some of them, including Jacob Levy, Aaron Kosminski, Montague Druitt, Walter Sickert, Michael Ostrog, Joseph Barnett, Francis Tumblety and even Prince Albert Victor, Duke of Clarence. Sam smiled.

'Yes, I recall that he has been a suspect but he wasn't actually in London was he? Did I not read that he was in another part of the country when some of the murders were taking place?'

'Phooey, who said that?' said Anna.

'Well I read somewhere that it was documented... wasn't it?' said Sam.

'And you believe that?' Anna returned swiftly, she laughed, in full swing now.

'Well, I don't know, shouldn't I?'

'Listen, Sam, the Royals cover any tracks they want, they always have done, as soon as there's a whiff of scandal they close ranks and clam up tighter than a virgin's...' she tailed off, looking embarrassed.

It was Sam's turn to smile.

'A virgin's what?' he enquired innocently, grinning.

She tossed her hair impatiently as she recovered her composure.

'Anyway, you know what I mean, I'm not going to talk dirty just to please you, Sam.' Then she flashed him the ear to ear smile. 'The reality is the Royals have always had things to hide and they probably still have. It's all about image with them. You can be sure they pioneered the art of spin doctoring years and years ago. Governments are mere beginners compared to the palace mafia. I'm not saying the Duke of Clarence was guilty, of course. In fact it's painfully obvious he wasn't, but you can't just take things at face value with them.'

'I don't know much about them,' said Sam. 'I suppose I'm a passive republican really, I don't have any interest in them. It's okay if you are just a rich guy handing down the stately home and the money of course, but this dynasty notion... I disagree with the idea of bloodlines inheriting real power and authority. It's all a bit of an anachronism isn't it?'

Anna looked at him sharply for a moment, suddenly developing more respect for this mild mannered but principled man. There's some steel in there, but he's a deep thinker and quite a nice guy, she thought, even if he does view his friend Conan Doyle with ridiculously rose tinted glasses.

'Come on, Sam; let's get some tea and a cake, all this chat is making me thirsty.'

Finding a cafe on the way back to the station, they talked on for a while until Anna announced her intention to go home. She asked to meet Sam again soon and pursue the Richard Lancelyn Green connection to the phrase. Consulting her tablet once more she wrinkled her nose with disgust.

'I'm away with a girlfriend for a few days; would it be okay if we met after that? It would give you some time to have a look when you are next in Portsmouth.' She phrased it carefully, not wanting to push too hard. She realised from last time that wouldn't work.

Sam wasn't bothered. 'That's fine, where are you going anyway?'

'To Paris with Helen, one of my best friends, she loves it there, and we agreed to go for a long weekend a while ago.'

Sam gave his open smile.

'Mmm, Paris and Helen,' he mused, thinking of the 'Iliad'. 'Are you sure you're not going to Troy?'

Anna didn't get it for a moment, till he added more. 'Does she have the face to launch a thousand ships?'

Anna finally twigged, remembering he was a writer and a history buff. 'Oh yes, she does indeed,' she said firmly, thinking about Helen's complexion and voluptuous lips.

Sam nodded. 'Have a good time, I'm sure you will. We can speak next week.'

They wandered slowly through the city, once again avoiding any discussion of Conan Doyle as if by unspoken consent. Their day was coming to an end and it would be foolish to start arguing now.

Behind them as they wandered, the unseen John looked earnestly into the shop windows that he passed. The cafe had given him his chance; sidling close behind Baby Blue and the blonde guy he had heard something about a planned trip to Paris. Drifting away he sent another text to Darren, so he could check on her travel arrangements. All he had to do now was follow her back to London, and then one of the others would take over from Waterloo.

Chapter 17

Suspects & Suicides

London – February 1894

On another day, in another era and another place, things were getting difficult for Chief Constable Melville Macnaghten. He was in a tight corner, but it wasn't the first time and he was confident he would be able to square things with his political masters.

The pressure came quickly, out of the blue. Over the last couple of years he had boasted occasionally that he knew all the circumstances of the Whitechapel murders. He was also on record as saying that he wished he had been involved directly in the hunt, implying perhaps that he might have succeeded where others had spectacularly failed. Sometimes of course, things could come back to bite you in life and this was one of those things. Suddenly now this February there had come a new challenge to Macnaghten's perceived wisdom.

It came from an unlikely quarter, the popular press that he had little regard for, the press that had so unfairly attacked and ridiculed the Metropolitan Police throughout the reign of terror in Whitechapel. Now it was *The Sun* newspaper proclaiming that it had both sought and found the notorious Jack the Ripper. They had published their findings in a series of articles spread over five days, beginning on 13 February, in what seemed to be just a cynical and blatant attempt to sell their wares.

Though he read the articles with a growing anger and impotence, Macnaghten felt they should be completely disregarded. Indeed at first he had said nothing, leaving them to pontificate in their own misguided way. But unfortunately people were buying the paper, and raking up the whole ghastly business again, with all its comment about the ineffectiveness of the police in capturing the murderer. However, the real problem wasn't the public comment, but the fact that Members of Parliament were asking the Home Secretary if it was true. Had the newspaper really uncovered the killer, and if so, where were the Metropolitan Police positioned in all this?

The following week, the Commissioner had a word with Macnaghten, advising him that because of his 'apparent knowledge of the affair', the Home Secretary would be requesting his presence shortly.

On Thursday, as he had suspected it would, a note arrived from the Home Secretary asking him to attend at the Home Office, and Macnaghten duly did so. As a Member of Parliament Herbert Henry Asquith had been appointed directly by Gladstone to the Home Office two years before, bypassing junior ministerial positions as he did so.

'So, you have seen these reports?' said the Home Secretary. 'What are we to make of them?' he probed gently.

'It is all nonsense, the babble of ill-informed speculation, full of assumption and error,' Macnaghten replied firmly.

The Home Secretary stared for a moment. 'And yet they seem to write with a veneer of authority.' He continued quietly. 'And honourable members of the house would wish for answers, I am sure you will understand.'

Macnaghten nodded, saying nothing, wondering at this point what he could offer to the discussion.

There was a long pause again before Asquith stood and walked slowly towards his window. He was scrupulously dressed in a black three piece suit, with a crisp white wing collar and a jewelled tiepin. He folded his hands behind his back against the soft material of his jacket, staring outside at the cold grey weather.

'The Metropolitan Police, for whom you speak now, were criticised roundly, perhaps not without some reason,' he remarked, as though wondering aloud.

'I require from you a full written justification of events, and assurance that the proprietors of this newspaper are completely wrong in their discourse. You have the files; you have the resources and witnesses at your disposal to end this inconvenient blabbering.'

The Home Secretary turned and looked directly at Macnaghten. 'Not to put too fine a point upon it, Chief Constable, you will realise the need to protect your position before someone begins to wonder about your tenure with the police.'

Macnaghten grimaced inwardly, so this was the reality of politics, he thought. Now it was all to be his fault, and the drawbridge was steadily being raised before his eyes, to protect the Government. He was to be the scapegoat, if one should be required. This softly spoken politician had gently given him his instructions, and presumably the 'someone' was the Prime Minister himself, or at least that was the not so carefully veiled threat. The barrister in Herbert Asquith made him a canny politician, as Macnaghten had come to realise.

'By the end of the morrow, if that should be convenient to you. And now I must bid you good day.' The Home Secretary spoke silkily, bringing the conversation to an end.

Back in his office Macnaghten worked steadily through the files. Hundreds of civil service style Manila folders had been brought there at his bidding. In no way could they be properly assimilated in one afternoon, though he must do his best. He scribbled a few notes as he searched, picking up on various key points and interviews, adding these to everything he already knew from his years of discussions with senior detectives.

A well educated and clever man, Macnaghten saw immediately what had to be done. The individual, not actually named by *The Sun*, but identifiable to anyone who cared to investigate, must be discredited as a suspect. This person, a certain Thomas Cutbush, had a tenuous link to Scotland Yard. Because of this alone, he must be shown to have been eliminated from the enquiries by reliable officers. Of course it was of little use doing this unless the blame could be firmly laid at someone else's doorstep. Who could be better than a man who was already dead, conveniently meaning he could not defend his own honour?

Some other suspects could also be brought into play, allowing flexibility of view in case his chosen perpetrator should ever be proven innocent. That bit would be easy enough; the files were full of accounts of dangerous and deranged individuals, any one of whom might have laid claim to being the Whitechapel murderer. Foreign born suspects were the best type, a natural prejudice existed against them anyway and it was always easy to convince the public that foreigners were guilty of crimes. A Russian and a Polish Jew were carefully selected from the files for this purpose.

Some additional points had to be dealt with as well, the eleven murders still on the files must be whittled down to minimise the impact of this dreadful saga of events. Eleven unsolved murders, even though the number wasn't public knowledge, merely underlined the helplessness of the police force. That could be done simply enough, he reasoned. The George Yard murder of Martha Tabram could be passed off as a bayonet attack by two soldiers, and the appalling slaughter of Mary Kelly in Millers Court could be made to appear as the last one committed. The fury of the mutilations might finally have caused the murderer's brain to give way. The dates fitted well enough with the suicide of a young professional man, Montague Druitt.

That would certainly suit those in power at the time. The more recent cases of the two fallen women, Alice McKenzie and Frances Coles, bore enough differences to remove them from the fray altogether. Whether or not their assailant had actually been disturbed in his disgusting activities mattered little at this point. Also, there was enough disagreement amongst police surgeons and senior officers to rule them out without too much difficulty.

Lastly there was a need to discredit *The Sun's* work by finding some inconsistencies in their writings. To this end he read and re-read the dog-eared newspapers secreted in a drawer of his leather topped writing desk, adding to his scribbled notes from time to time. He sprinkled these notes with a few words like 'apparently', 'probably', and 'no doubt', carefully allowing his statements to be qualified at some future date if necessary.

Finally late in the day on Friday he settled down to write the first of what transpired to be seven pages of closely written script. That seven pages constituted what was eventually to become his ill-fated and much fought over memoranda, though all that was still many years away from the cold grey day in February 1894. His purpose had been to consign something to history, but he had no inkling that he was leaving a legacy that would reverberate down and on into the twenty-first century. Signing and dating the document he sat back in his chair, satisfied.

Chapter 18

A Ripping Yarn

London – 2003

For the umpteenth time Richard Lancelyn Green looked at the photocopy of a memo in his hand. He had found it amongst a considerable pile of papers Dame Jean Conan Doyle had kindly allowed him to copy some years before. The memo was filed loosely with a manuscript and some old household documents and bills, a small package of relatively unimportant Conan Doyle documents that Dame Jean had kept. It had intrigued him enough to make him copy it along with the other papers. At first it seemed innocuous but when you studied it many times, as Richard had, it threw up more questions than it answered.

It was definitely in Doyle's own hand, that much was certain. Richard knew that writing as well as his own. It referred to a Conan Doyle book or a short story, that much also seemed certain, but the manuscript that it had been filed with was much older than the memo. The memo was apparently written at Bignell Wood as this appeared at the top, but the manuscript was definitely from ACD's Portsmouth period, many years before. It had clearly been misfiled at some time during the past, and this was hardly surprising considering the vast amount of personal papers that Conan Doyle had left. These had later been divided amongst family, moved about and argued over legally, finally ending up in a variety of places around the world. Even to this day the locations of some documents were thought to be unknown.

Richard was probably the greatest living expert on Arthur Conan Doyle, as well as possessing the finest and most comprehensive collection of memorabilia and documentation concerning Sherlock Holmes and his creator. He was a scholar and also author of a number of works concerning Sir Arthur Conan Doyle including *The Uncollected Sherlock Holmes*. During his career he had been president of the Sherlock Holmes Society, and had travelled widely, lecturing and enjoying meeting other Sherlockians around the world. In the strange specialist world of the Doyle and Holmes fraternity, there were many rivals for his pre-eminent position, but Richard was secure amongst the people who would always respect him for the expert he was.

He had consulted a number of colleagues in passing about the memo in the last few months, speaking only to those who might throw some light on the cryptic message. In one day alone he had consulted a dozen people by telephone, and each time he had drawn a blank. The trouble was that few of them could actually match the depth of reading and research he himself had managed.

It had been easy enough to get a friend to raise the matter at a conference, so that he could gauge the reaction from those present, who had included the young Southampton writer and historian Sam Taylor. Sam for one had seemed disinterested and dismissive, seeing nothing mysterious in the memo. With a sigh, he put the paper down on his desk and gazed at the window. The conference exercise had yielded nothing of interest, and the sheet of paper appeared to smile at him mockingly.

Bignell Wood
First and last lines contain a Ripping Yarn

The message is for he who comes after.
Now I have done my duty.
Arthur Conan Doyle

Although he had seen it many times before, something about the paper suddenly became more significant. The document, as he well knew, was a second generation photocopy of the obviously old original and in the top left corner was the mark made by a paper clip. The document in Dame Jean's papers had nothing attached to it, but the outline of a clip could still be clearly discerned in the copy. At some time or other the original must have had an accompanying sheet or sheets of paper. Those attachments would surely hold the answer to the riddle!

It was true that small things were often vital. Some of Sherlock's own dialogue came to him as he thought it through. It had appeared in 'The Adventure of a Case of Identity'.

'It has long been an axiom of mine that the little things are infinitely the most important.'

The first time one read the note it appeared to be something that Doyle might have written to his publisher, commenting on a new book, but Richard was convinced this wasn't the case. Doyle had written many ripping yarns, as everyone knew. This note seemed too cryptic, although Conan Doyle had certainly always loved a mystery. If this had accompanied a manuscript, any manuscript, it appeared unnecessary. Richard was convinced that there was a hidden message somewhere and that Doyle was trying to tell something to someone who would come later, perhaps even after his own death. He was conscious that he only had part of the riddle in his hands, and it was meaningless on its own.

Could this have had something to do with Doyle's spiritual beliefs? In later life particularly he had been an uncompromising believer, and in true Doyle style, once he was convinced, nothing in this world would change his mind. It was one of his hallmarks, reflected Richard, once committed he would always see something through. Despite criticism by friends, family, strangers, or press, his bulldog approach took no regard of any of them.

No, this was about a crime he was sure. It mentioned a yarn, and invited someone to decide the truth for themselves. Most such yarns involved a crime, that was also apparent. But was it a fictional crime? If so it might have been a Sherlock Holmes story or another Doyle creation. Might it refer to a real crime? Somewhere there existed another piece or pieces of paper, unless they had been destroyed. That thought troubled him deeply. However, when one thought about it there was no reason to assume any attachments might have been destroyed. Haphazardly divided and hopelessly confused as Doyle's archive might now be, there was no evidence of any destruction of documents, with one clear exception that Richard knew about and deplored.

Letters and other written material by Louise Conan Doyle, his first wife, known as Touie, had not survived and were believed by many to have been disposed of by his second wife Jean. It was possible of course that any attached sheet might have been amongst those writings, but equally, there was no reason that it should have been. The memo apparently had nothing to do with Touie and was clearly written later in Doyle's life. That thought cheered Richard again.

His thoughts turned to where any document might be today. Doyle's rich archive was spread far and wide. Some items were in America, many in Canada, with still more in museums, some Richard even had himself. But a great part of the collection was still in the possession of members of the Doyle family. At the moment there was no real way to access many of them.

Richard went to fill the kettle. A hot beverage was clearly called for, and Holmes and Watson would undoubtedly have approved.

Chapter 19
Abandoned by a New Friend

The City of London – September 1888

At around 10 p.m. on 30 September, Police Constable Watkins made his first visit of the evening to Mitre Square. He approached from Mitre Street, circled the square in a perfunctory manner and returned to Mitre Street, picking up the route of his allotted beat for the night. He had walked this particular route many times and was familiar with the area. He knew how to time his beat in line with the instructions he had been given, and also where he could make up or lose time, shelter from any rain and rendezvous with constables on neighbouring beats. Like anyone who does a job regularly he knew all the wrinkles and made it as simple and pleasant as possible for himself. The Whitechapel murders had given patrol work a very keen edge recently and Watkins was on high alert, as were all policemen in the East End of London. Specifically, Watkins and his colleagues had been instructed to watch for couples together.

Catherine Eddowes slept soundly in a cell at Bishopsgate Street police station. Earlier that day she had been arrested following a drunken exhibition in front of onlookers. Her imitations of a fire appliance racing to a fire had caused great merriment before she had collapsed and slept upon the pavement. A nearby constable, alerted by the gathering, tried to arrest the woman as he was duty bound to do. It wasn't easy! As he raised her up, urging her to stand, she looked at him dreamily, smiled and sagged back to the ground asleep.

Eventually a colleague arrived and supported by the pair she was marched off to the police station, where the desk sergeant decreed that the offender be detained overnight. Later during the evening, as instructed, the constable responsible for the cells made frequent checks on her. Each time he looked she was fast asleep leading him to be confident that she would remain so. Occasionally she stirred but for the most part Catherine slept comfortably and well. Shaking his head at the folly of drunkenness he returned to the front desk.

Further to the south-east in Berners Street, a forty-four-year-old woman met her new man friend in a public house close to the International Club. This was a social club for working men, patronised largely by Jews and Russians. Her new friend was dressed as a gentleman, though perhaps as one who aspired to that status rather than actually inhabiting it. He was Jewish and Liz had encountered him through one of her cleaning jobs. She liked him, he seemed to care for her and though she knew little about him as yet, she had hopes for a secure relationship. Liz had no idea at this point that he was still married to another. Always one to take care of her appearance, tonight a single flower adorned her coat lapel; otherwise she was dressed entirely in black which suited her well.

Liz was a mild mannered and intelligent woman, except during her occasional drinking lapses. In the past she had been charged several times with being drunk and disorderly. Her friends called her Long Liz simply in recognition of the fact that she was taller by several inches than most of them. They were women of a similar type, though not Swedish born as she was. Liz resorted to street walking occasionally as she had through adult life, as a means to an end. She had been listed as a prostitute in her native Sweden before travelling to London to initially enter domestic service. It was something that Liz didn't seek, but she was realistic about it. Avoiding selling herself when possible she did whatever casual jobs came her way, including work as a seamstress and domestic cleaning. There had been a recent on–off relationship with a man but they had parted several times and at the moment it was off, at least as far as Liz was concerned.

On this particular evening she and her man had enjoyed drinks while waiting for the heavy rain showers to subside. Eventually they left the public house after some banter with several men sheltering in the doorway, and made their way along the street despite the fact it was still raining. They headed for another pub planning to wait for this shower to stop.

Apart from the rain it had been a nice evening so far for Liz, but all that was about to change. She hooked her arm through that of her new friend as they strolled slowly towards the International Club. Approaching them on the same side of the road was her ex-partner, and there was no way she could avoid an encounter. He glowered at her as he stopped right in front of them, pointing his chin truculently at the man with her. She addressed him calmly but it seemed he was spoiling for an argument and she knew from experience he could be roused to violence. Unhooking her arm from her friend, Liz motioned him away, asking him to leave her for a few moments while she spoke to the new arrival. Not liking the look of this man, her new man nodded acquiescence and stepped across the road, glad to be at a distance from them. There he waited, hoping they would soon part.

Liz spoke to the man for a moment or two, but when he suggested she go with him to a public house nearby, she demurred. She didn't have a good feeling about him and wanted to stay near the lights of the club where people were coming and going. The man disagreed, placing his hands on Liz's shoulders and pressing his thumbs into them in a controlling way. He glanced across at her new friend who still hovered on the opposite pavement. 'Lipski!' he shouted in an aggressive sneering manner. This had become a topical insult to Jews recently, following the arrest and conviction of a Jew by that name for the murder of a woman. The man grew angrier and demanded Liz come with him. Her refusal turned into an argument and the atmosphere became ugly. A third man walking by witnessed the incident and saw in the poor light two figures struggling. It ended with Liz being knocked to the ground, banging her head as she did so.

Concerned for his own safety and his reputation, Liz's new friend walked smartly away, closely following the third man who, assuming it to be a domestic matter, quickened his pace to avoid the incident.

Liz's ex-partner half-pushed, half-pulled the dazed woman a few feet into the adjacent Dutfield's Yard. It was a double gated but narrow entrance and extremely dark inside the yard. Her eyes were closed and clearly concussed she murmured something in her native Swedish. She slumped down beside the wall. The man, furious now, took a knife from his coat and bent down beside her, unable to control his actions. He made a deliberate slash, drawing the blade across her throat and partially cutting through the scarf she had arranged so neatly around her neck. A hundred yards away the sound of a horse's hooves approaching carried to him as he crouched beside her.

Meanwhile, Catherine Eddowes made her way smartly down Houndsditch towards Aldgate High Street. She was aiming to be back in her usual territory for what remained of the night, after leaving Bishopsgate Street police station. She felt reasonably well; her drinking was not habitual, but rather occasional like Long Liz. However, when she did succumb to a binge, it took her over completely for a day or so. As she had done earlier, she sung quietly to herself as she walked. She was a slim woman whose looks belied her forty-six years. Most people who knew her would have placed Catherine at around thirty-five.

The time was now about one a.m. and she had been released after a coherent conversation with the duty officer, thus confirming to him that she had slept it off sufficiently. Catherine had woken up singing softly and he had scolded her for being drunk but his bark was worse than his bite. Having watched her sleep and finding her chirpy and friendly when she awoke, he grudgingly softened and let her go. She told him she would probably get a good hiding when she got home, so in her mind she was already considering using a lodging house for the rest of the night, once she could raise the money. Giving her name to the policeman as Mary Ann Kelly, one of several false names she habitually used, Catherine left the station. She would never have used the name Mary had she had the slightest inkling that it might attract any unwelcome attention.

Catherine walked on, there were a few people about as usual, and the occasional police constable on night patrol. After a few minutes she slowed as a man walked towards her. Approaching cautiously she saw he was quite well dressed and presented a client possibility. Close to, she noticed his clothes were shabbier than she had thought. He nodded and smiled to her, gesturing back the way he had come and they walked together through a short alley. Emerging on Dukes Place they soon reached the entrance to Church Passage. Here Catherine paused to engage the man in her usual direct manner and he indicated his agreement to her terms for sex. They talked quietly for several moments, deciding where to go, and she rested her hand on his lapel as they conversed.

Three passers-by talked amongst themselves as they made their way home from an evening out. Only one of them slowed and glanced in their direction, the other two hurrying on past. Joseph Lawende, the man who glanced at the couple, had no idea that his two friends had resorted to fallen women themselves. They were both afraid they might be recognised by this woman, and their own sordid secrets painfully exposed. Catherine and her customer ignored the three of them. The client looked over her shoulder checking that nobody was close to them now. He nodded imperceptibly to himself, then took Catherine's elbow and walked her into the darkness of Mitre Square. Lawende was later to give a detailed description of the man he saw, but was subsequently protected from any further press questioning by the police.

Back at Dutfield's Yard at around one a.m. Louis Diemschutz attempted to turn his pony and trap into the entrance. He had done this many times before but this time the pony balked suddenly in the gateway. Unable to coax it into proceeding, Diemschutz cursed irritably and stepped down from the trap. He couldn't see much, the street was dark and the yard was even darker. Sensing more than seeing something in the way, he probed gently with the whip that he had in his hand. The whip encountered something soft and still and Diemschutz guessed it was a drunk blocking the way. This would explain the pony's reluctance. Unsure and fearing that it could be a dead body rather than a drunk, Diemschutz made for the door of the adjacent International Club.

Suddenly he became concerned for his wife who was working inside the building, and quickened his pace. Immediately he left the entrance of the yard a man emerged from the shadows and half ran, half walked away in a southerly direction. He turned right, then right again and walked more slowly back in the direction of Commercial Street. Enlisting the help of two men Diemschutz returned immediately to the yard, in which they discovered the body of a woman. The body was still warm and for a moment by the light of their lantern, it seemed she was sleeping. Her legs were drawn up towards the wall and it was then they saw she was quite dead, with her throat cut, blood trickling away from her neck.

Mitre Square was empty and very quiet. Reaching the wall in the darkest corner the couple paused. Glancing around in agitation, the man addressed her.

'Well, Mary.'

Catherine blurted out, 'I'm not Mary, how do you know… why call me that?'

'Because that's who you are, isn't it, Mary?' The man hissed suddenly, before grabbing her tightly around the neck and forcing her back against the wall with his body. He didn't look to be a particularly powerful man but seemed to find almost supernatural strength. The brilliant blue eyes shone and his right knee ground into her left leg as he pinned her firmly against the wall. He began to exert tremendous pressure around her throat. She struggled but it was hopeless. Catherine was in the grip of someone who had done this before. Her slight frame went limp but suspecting a trick he took no chances, keeping up the pressure on her neck for some seconds. Only then did he release her and as she dropped to the ground he stood back allowing her to fall.

Looking quickly in each direction he saw only the darkness, though he knew the constable would be around on his beat again within twenty minutes. The thought lifted him to new levels of excitement and his sensory awareness increased rapidly. Having been here on business he knew this area well, he was familiar with each exit from the square and wasn't daunted by the prospect of a chase if it came to one. He was an agile runner if he had to be.

'Swiftly, swiftly,' he whispered to himself. Drawing a long knife from his coat the man bent down beside his victim. Firstly he went for her throat cutting right across it dispassionately. He raised her skirts and opened her legs pushing the right one upwards. Her abdomen was exposed and now he worked furiously, never looking up. Within moments he had cut deep, locating and removing her left kidney and part of her womb. He then pulled her intestines out and arranged them over her right shoulder. There was surprisingly little blood and he was able to anticipate it, avoiding transferring much onto his clothes.

His mental clock started to tick louder and louder, forcing him to cease the butchery. Cutting away some of Catherine's apron he roughly wrapped his trophies, rose to his feet and walked regretfully away in the direction of Church Passage.

Less than ten minutes later PC Watkins entered Mitre Square again. This time by the light of his lantern he made out what seemed to be a body lying by the wall. Approaching, he felt the bile rise in his throat as his light showed details of the sickening scene before him. He turned suddenly, terrified there might be a knife-man behind him. Gasping and retching he stumbled towards the warehouse in the square where he knew the night watchman at Kearley and Tonge would be on duty.

Chapter 20

The Coffee Capital

London – Present Day

This time it was Anna's turn to reflect on the train heading homewards. She realised there was no real reason not to have told Sam the truth about her acquisition of the number sheet, and the thought took her back to the trip to Seattle and the circumstances of her discovery. Only ten feet behind her in the following carriage John sat reading his paper. Each time anyone came through the glass sliding door he could see enough of her reflection to check she was still there. He started to think about his dinner.

Anna had gone to Seattle to attend a criminology conference about a month ago. The conference was being held at the Hilton Hotel downtown on Sixth Avenue and was an international affair. Several delegates were from the British Society of Criminology, though none of them were directly known to Anna. Whilst there, she renewed an acquaintance with Jeremy Martinez, a Seattle based criminology student whom she had met briefly in Leicester, UK at a previous conference.

She relished her time in Seattle, arriving several days before the conference and exploring the downtown area in her free time. It felt safe and clean and she delighted both in the wonderful flower stalls and the sheer size of the salmon on sale at Pike Place Market. The flowers were so good she bought an enormous bunch to install in her hotel room for the duration of her stay. Anna took her coffee drug seriously, and after all, wasn't Seattle the coffee capital of the USA? Tully's and Starbucks started there and they weren't the only ones. She made the obligatory trip up the Space Needle and shopped for shoes at Macy's. She watched giant cruise ships sounding their sirens as they left to make their way up Puget Sound, through the Straits of Juan de Fuca and past the vastness of Vancouver Island en route to Alaska. Out and about in the city she revelled in the high temperatures, often reaching ninety degrees, when she went sightseeing.

Primed by her mother, Anna asked her hotel staff about the Jimi Hendrix statue, but they weren't sure where it was located. Somewhat surprised at the lack of knowledge about Seattle's famous son she asked a taxi driver who knew exactly where to go. He took her to the Capitol Hill/Broadway area where the bronze statue of Hendrix was adorned with gifts from fans. Anna took photographs to show her mother, who had met Jimi in his 1960s heyday in London.

The skies were blue and the Broadway area had a comfortable, if bohemian air about it. One or two crazies staggered around, shrieking occasionally at the world, so after her homage to the statue, Anna bought a couple of CDs and took another taxi back to the downtown area. She made a mental note to grill her mother again about those times in the sixties. Anna had always suspected a slightly racy past in her mother's youth, though when questioned she was always vague about it, albeit with a smile and a knowing look in her eye. Anna wanted to know a lot more, wondering about the iconic period in which her mother had come of age. There was an irony here, in that Anna was very secret about her own affairs so could hardly be surprised at her mother's reticence. Anna didn't see it that way of course.

Once the conference commenced she worked with groups of other criminologists, and in their free time Jeremy and a couple of others tagged along once or twice to show her more of the city. Anna had gone to the event at her own expense, using some of her annual holiday. She was happy to do this, extending her knowledge of the criminal mind, while indulging her love of travel.

It was while talking with Jeremy and others over drinks that the subject of Sherlock Holmes had come up. Delegates joked that it was a pity Sherlock didn't solve the Ripper case, and that maybe Conan Doyle should have done so. After all, he was writing at the time of the Whitechapel murders and could have got involved if he wished. It started Anna thinking. Jeremy told Anna his father was a Conan Doyle aficionado and collector who had purchased manuscripts, papers and souvenirs over many years. He offered to show Anna his father's collection at home in Madrona, near Lake Washington. He suggested they could get some dinner there at the same time. Anna agreed and the following evening Jeremy, who had been commuting in daily, drove them both from the Hilton.

A short drive took them to Jeremy's house which turned out to be a large mock Tudor style residence not far from Madrona Park. When they arrived at the house, to Anna's concern, his parents were not there, and Jeremy explained they were on vacation in Hawaii for a couple of weeks. He unlocked the front door and led the way inside. Anna hadn't expected this and immediately felt uncomfortable; despite the fact Jeremy lived here, a little warning sounded in her psyche. She had naturally assumed his parents would be present. Jeremy announced that pizza was on the menu, then before she could say anything he showed her into the study where his father's Doyle collection was situated.

It was a large, well laid out house with a lounge area adjoining the acres of marble worktops and dark cherry wood units in the open-plan kitchen. The study was full of memorabilia of one sort or another, a range of hardback books by Conan Doyle filled a bookshelf, and shelves on two walls held Sherlock Holmes collectibles.

Interested though Anna was, she felt uncomfortable again and turning to Jeremy she suggested that because his father wasn't there, perhaps he should take her back to the hotel. Jeremy wouldn't hear of it, insisting that his father loved to show his collection to people and would have wanted her to see it. She protested again but Jeremy shrugged off her concerns. He said he trusted her and obviously expected her to be careful what she touched in the study, as some of the older souvenirs would be worth a lot of money.

He demonstrated this trust by going off to attend to his pizza, leaving Anna alone in the study. Most of her concern, she admitted to herself, was to do with being alone in the house with Jeremy, whom she didn't really know well, in a part of Seattle that was new to her. She realised that she wasn't sure exactly where they were and also that her UK mobile phone didn't work properly in the States.

On the positive side, she thought, Jeremy really did seem a decent guy. He was a bone fide conference delegate and had given her no cause for alarm. Anna was used to men coming on to her, she was extremely vivacious and her zest for life communicated itself to men, many of whom found her an irresistible challenge. During her upbringing she had learnt how to handle them, generally managing to fob them off whilst still making them feel good about themselves. A neat trick if you could achieve it! Occasionally however, when someone pushed it too far her heritage would quickly assert itself, eyes flashing with anger she would deliver a put-down that was truly final. To get close to Anna a man had to be invited, to touch her or to sleep with her he had to be very special indeed.

Many men simply never grasped the nuances of getting to know women like her. Invitations might be extended but were not always verbal, they were in the casual touch of an arm, a coded comment or the glance offered over a drink. Things had to be at her pace and controlled by her. There must be at least the possibility of a romance and not just the age old excitement of the chase. Far from prudish, she loved taking her pleasure with the right man but her self-imposed standards meant they were few and far between. Anna wasn't in a hurry. Ruefully she reflected that she was a product not just of her ancestry, but of her parents who were still sharing the romantic relationship they had started in their twenties. She was quite sure now that Jeremy would make a play for her and started to hatch her response.

Drifting out of this reverie she got on with looking around the study and admired some of the Holmes souvenirs. Many seemed garish to the modern eye but reflected the enormous popularity of the character Doyle had skilfully created. The Holmes phenomena had taken off in America as powerfully as it had in the UK, making Doyle not only a celebrity, but a very rich man. She didn't know it but Doyle had made numerous visits to the USA, on promotional and lecture tours, during which he also found time to socialise with some of America's big names. Items on display in Jeremy's father's study included a Royal Doulton Holmes jug, two different deerstalkers, some small ceramics of Holmes and Watson, plus playing card sets and several calabash pipes which Anna noted had been recently smoked.

A brown leather folder on the bookshelf intrigued her and lifting it down gently she opened it to reveal a miscellaneous bundle of faded papers. They were related to Doyle and comprised an eclectic mix of household papers, scribbled notes to staff and one or two invoices from tradesmen. Only the latter were dated, making it hard to be sure from when the others originated. She flicked through them idly until she came to a sheet covered with columns of handwritten numbers. Along the top the sheet bore the legend:

Bignell Wood

First and last lines contain a Ripping Yarn

The bottom of the sheet faded out into a brown area which looked as though it had been burnt and plucked from a fire. Most of the sheet, with perhaps about three quarters of the numbers, was still readable but the bottom had been destroyed.

Anna frowned. What was this about? There seemed to be neither sense to the numbers nor any obvious sequence. Shrugging slightly she replaced the sheet in the folder as Jeremy entered the study.

'Found anything?' Jeremy breezed in with two opened Budweiser bottles. He handed one to Anna, they clinked them together and each took a pull.

'Yes, it's a really interesting collection,' Anna said. 'Your father is obviously a real fan.'

'He sure is, and he would have loved to show you himself. Anyway, pizza is ready,' said Jeremy, leading the way back to the lounge area.

They sat on the sofa eating pizza and drinking beer while the conversation ranged over their criminology interests, Sherlock Holmes and eventually Conan Doyle again. Taking their plates back to the kitchen Jeremy placed them on the worktop and slipped an arm around Anna.

Here it comes, thought Anna, who had known that he would make a move sooner or later. Smiling, she disentangled herself and moved just out of reach of his looming lips.

'Jeremy, I don't want you to do this. You're a nice guy but I'm not ready for anyone else at the moment.' Typically Anna, her lie was smooth and generous; she'd had time to think of something whilst in the study. A recent failed relationship would be a good excuse as well as implying that Jeremy wasn't the problem.

Allowing the message to do its work, she smiled again and embellished the story slightly to cover the awkward silence. She placed her hands on his upper arms and looked him square in the face.

'I got hurt more than I realised recently, I'm sorry but I'm finding it hard to get over. That's one reason I'm here in Seattle, to get away from things.'

Jeremy nodded quietly. He seemed to accept her explanation. Once again she sensed the need to cover the embarrassment and asked if he knew anything about the document she had seen in his father's study. He said he hadn't seen it so she took him to the shelf with the leather folder and showed him. Studying the sheet Jeremy professed ignorance as to what it meant. He was grateful for the diversion and felt he had been rather clumsy making a move on Anna. He had wanted her since the first time they met in Leicester and on seeing her again here in Seattle he had tried to cultivate the friendship. On one level he had certainly succeeded. She had made no previous reference to a recent affair, but after all why should she have done so? He pursed his lips as he considered the document.

'Well I really don't know, but one thing is sure, somebody fished it out of a fire at some point.'

'I think you're right. Listen, Jeremy, would you do me a favour? Could I take a copy of the sheet? I might find something out about it back in the UK.'

'Sure, why not? We can run it through the fax if you want.' He gestured to the machine on his father's desk. Anna smiled and went over to it before he could change his mind. She placed the resultant copy in her bag and put the original carefully back in the leather folder. She wasn't sure what it was about the paper that had intrigued her, the ripping yarn bit maybe? But something had, it was just one of those curious things.

They chatted some more, this time about the speakers for the next day, then Anna said she should get back to the hotel. She offered to take a cab but Jeremy wouldn't hear of it.

'I only had one beer,' he grinned. 'I'll take you back to the Hilton.'

The drive back in the darkness was quiet and short. Circuiting the block Jeremy pulled into a drop off area outside the hotel. Anna placed her arm on his and thanked him for the evening and for the pizza. As his car pulled away she slowly exhaled a long sigh of relief, and walked up the steps and into the hotel lobby.

The next day was to be the last day of the conference. Delegates assembled early, eager to hear the keynote speakers and to wrap up the proceedings. Keen to repair any damage, Anna made a beeline for Jeremy during the coffee recess and engaged him in conversation. She thanked him for his hospitality during her visit and for showing her his father's collection. He smiled ruefully saying his father's collection hadn't been the main thing on his mind, and he guessed he had made a fool of himself last night. Anna would have none of it.

'Not at all,' she said. 'I was flattered at the attention and so should any girl be. You're a great guy. It's just that I don't feel available at the moment. And by the way, thank your dad for letting me see the stuff.'

'That's no problem; he would love to have met you and showed you himself. He likes Brits, especially great lookers.' Jeremy grinned. Warmed by his attitude Anna gave him a hug and the big smile in return. She had to admit it, American guys really knew how to pay a girl a genuine compliment. They parted friends, agreeing to meet at any future conferences of interest, and promising to email. Later that evening Anna boarded a triple seven Boeing bound for London.

Chapter 21

Victorian Amateurs

London – 1890s

Early one summer during the 1890s a man living in the south of England corresponded with a friend in Scotland. He was asking for an opinion on the mystery that had gripped the nation for those desperate months during 1888 and occasionally since. They agreed to discuss the matter when they could next meet in London, and when they eventually did so, they laid some ground rules.

They would each study such evidence as was available to them, independently, then exchange their verdicts by post. Their frequent trips to London would allow them to make enquiries at first hand independently. The matter was to be kept strictly confidential for a number of reasons; for one thing the southerner's position in society meant that if he was proven to be mistaken, his reputation would be shattered. His career, to say nothing of his pride, would be ridiculed and he would be discredited.

His associate too, had similar concerns. His standing in his own profession was unparalleled and his almost legendary powers had ensured respect from anybody who knew him. By now, it had become known to many that he had inspired his friend and had been his mentor. Natural pride would never allow him to fail in such a matter. He was a top professional and didn't wish to be accused of meddling in something outside his area of expertise. They had both agreed there would be no going public, unless they had first proven their theories, agreed their findings and mutually decided to announce them.

For some months neither heard from the other. Then one or two short notes were exchanged, carefully and innocuously coded, and deliberately brief. Once read, the notes were destroyed by their recipients. They agreed that on a certain date each would post the other a name, with no other message, in an unmarked envelope. When the name had been noted, this message also was to be immediately destroyed. Only after this would they meet again and discuss their findings. It was a novel approach but not so unusual in the circumstances. The matter demanded attention and these two keen brains were determined to have their way in solving the mystery.

Both eagerly awaited the delivery of the all important note. On the appointed day the southern dweller opened his first and on seeing the name written, his heart took a lurch as he groped for the seat behind his desk and sat down heavily.

The name was the same as he had sent to his associate.

The enormity of the moment overcame him for a second, then suddenly he felt the strength flow through his veins. He was right, he had to be right, his associate had agreed. He was analytical, astute and a person to be listened to.

The reaction of the man's Scottish associate was not dissimilar, but he beamed as he read the name in front of him. Their instincts, he felt, had been proved correct. His pupil, as he liked to think of the other man, had deduced the same result through processes that he himself had pioneered. Where they went from here of course, was quite another matter. More cryptic notes followed and a fresh meeting was arranged in London some weeks hence. On the appointed day the wiry Scotsman was waiting, sitting quietly inside the foyer of his hotel. He rose as the big man entered, shook his hand warmly, and weighed him up.

'My dear fellow, grand to see you again, prosperity suits you, and your tailor is a good fellow. Still playing cricket I see?'

The big man was also born in Scotland, though his origins lay in yet another country and his Scottish accent was softer and less pronounced than the older man's.

'Nothing changes then,' said the big man, smiling. 'It took you but seconds to sum me up on this occasion. I really dare not enquire as to the matter of the cricket.'

The elder man was in fine fettle, he glowed with the praise. Ever the showman he delighted in impressing his audience, whoever they might be. His lean ascetic face creased with mirth.

'I could not resist the comment,' he said. 'But of course it was a jest. I knew from reports about you that you still indulge your love of the English game.'

The big man guffawed aloud.

'Excellent,' he said. 'I knew I would enjoy our meeting today, let me arrange a hansom and we will talk over old times as we go.'

In the bright light of day the two men appeared unconcerned as they strolled through the Whitechapel streets. They stopped and peered into alleys, yards, public houses and lodgings alike, the big man occasionally making notes in a leather-bound notebook, as something took his attention. Frequently the Scot's sharp eyes observed something on which he would comment to the other. Both men were conservatively dressed as gentlemen, yet with no hint of richness or decadence in their attire.

Two days later the big man's eyes gleamed as he slipped the revolver into his overcoat pocket. He had owned it for some years and though he never used it, nowadays it felt like an old friend. The coldness of the hard metal gave him confidence in what promised to be a most unusual encounter. He had explained his intentions to the older man after their dinner and to his absolute delight the Scot had agreed to accompany him, enthusiastically, though not without some trepidation. Leaving the Reform Club he walked slowly and purposefully towards the hotel where his friend was staying.

Once again the older man was waiting, bright eyed and ready, but his nervousness was hard to conceal, even to a man well versed in self control. This time he was on the other side of the consulting table as it were, and was tensely facing the unexpected. The other night after a good dinner, an even better claret and excellent company it had seemed like a remarkable and exciting adventure. Now he had had time to reflect. Although he had no doubts about his initial diagnosis, the propriety of this particular expedition seemed rather less of a good idea. However, this was one he would see through to the end. Partly for the big man, who he regarded as his protégé, partly for the love of the chase, and partly to see if his conclusion about the identity of their subject was correct.

The big man also was nervous but hid it as well as he could. Ever the man of action, the bluff sportsman with the secret life was now slightly overawed by his mission. He wondered briefly if he had bitten off more than he could chew. He thrust the thought aside in his usual way, convinced of the righteousness of his actions and reflecting that this had to be seen through to the end. It was simply too important to allow weakness to surface, there was too much at stake and the mission owed a great responsibility to people. That alone was enough to steel him as he neared the hotel.

It was cool but dull in the late afternoon. After a long steady handshake with the Scot, the big man could not resist saying, 'Come, Watson, the game is afoot!' They both smiled at his allusion to Sherlock Holmes, the detective of popular fiction, whose exploits had become so widely sought after by an eager public.

The cab driver dropped them at the end of Burnley Road. The southern dweller had spent a long time planning this, wrestling endlessly with both the problem and its resolution. Eventually he had decided to involve the Scot, not only in the chain of activities which had led to this moment, but now in what might be the final act. The two walked the short distance to the house that was their destination. With a final glance at each other they approached the door. Before the big man could raise his hand to the brass knocker there came an almighty shouting and wailing from deep within the house. As they hesitated, the sound of a muffled shot came from within, followed by a grim silence.

The man of action took over. Grasping the door knocker the big man used it furiously. There was no response but the door seemed a paltry affair unable to resist a determined assault. Without hesitation he shouldered charged it and almost ran inside, the jerky steps of the Scot hard at his heels. Instinctively they went down the passage to the kitchen from where it seemed the sounds had emanated. From behind the door came the sound of a desperate, almost primeval whimpering, and opening it they were confronted by a tragic scene.

A young woman was on her knees near to the prone body of a man, shot through the head, with a revolver still in his hand. Blood spattered both the floor and the chair which stood beside the body. No-one else was present. The woman cried uncontrollably. The big man, suddenly moved by her grief, approached her and bending down, placed reassuring hands around her shoulders. The Scot scanned the scene taking everything in, his agile mind subconsciously assessing exactly what had transpired. He dropped to his knees beside the body and a rapid examination told him what his eyes had already suspected. There was no hope in this world for the victim. The big man spoke softly to the woman.

'We are both doctors, what has happened here? Who are you?'

The woman turned slowly to look up at him, her eyes wide, uncomprehending and wet with tears. 'I am his daughter. He has not been well for many years, but just this last few days he had a face like thunder and would barely speak at all to me.'

'Did he say why he was driven to this shocking end?'

'No, I asked him what was troubling him this evening,' said the woman. 'But all he said just now was, "They know, they have found me out… It shall be over," and then he suddenly…'

Her voice faded and she looked again at the body in front of her. Then she spoke again.

'I expect he meant the Catholics, he has been worried about them for a long time now. His doctor came to him this morning but it didn't help.'

The Scot's sharp eyes met the big man's over her head, and he raised his eyebrows quizzically. Just then a slight sound and a muted hello came from the passage. The big man took charge and went to meet the new arrivals, an elderly couple.

'We are neighbours,' said the man. 'We heard a noise.'

'I am a doctor,' said the big man briskly. 'There has been a tragic accident, would you send immediately for a constable, and perhaps your good lady would attend this young woman in the parlour.'

'Yes, yes,' said the man turning for the front door. Behind the big man, the Scot shepherded the young woman along the hallway to the front room. Bemused, the elderly woman accompanied her into the room and sat beside her, holding her hand.

A small crowd had gathered on the pavement by now, most trying to peer into the dark passageway of the house. The Scot went to the front door and spoke authoritatively,

'There is nothing to see here, please be about your business.' Whereupon he partly closed the door. It would not latch properly since the big man's assault upon it, but remained just slightly ajar concealing the interior from view.

The two went back to the kitchen. 'Well,' said the Scot, 'a pretty turn of events, what do you think now?'

'He knew the game was up once I made the appointment to see him. My pretext of talking about his experiences did not fool him for long. Perhaps he thought we were Catholics. However, this was, I must confess, not at all expected.'

Hearing more voices in the street, the two looked at each other again. 'I think we should leave now, and meet with the police at another time,' said the big man.

'I concur entirely,' replied the Scot, he had already observed the garden and found no rear access to a lane or anything similar.

'I fancy we shall have to leave the way we came.' Closing the door behind them, the two strode down the front steps and away down the road without a backward glance.

Later, ensconced in the bar at the Scot's hotel with a much needed brandy, they discussed the unexpected turn of events and the twist that it had given to their quest.

'I am entirely of the opinion that we were correct in our identification of the culprit,' said the big man. 'Also, his pre-emptive suicide, to my mind, is conclusive proof of his culpability.'

'Yes,' said the Scot. 'The range of possibilities really allows no other safe conclusion in this horrific matter. It was significant that he felt compelled to commit the act in front of someone of his own kin. One might expect it to have been a solitary end in the usual way of things.'

The big man nodded. 'I believe we must now contact the police, but suggest that we do so at a senior level and first decide precisely what we should tell them.'

'It would suffice to say that we were enquiring about his career and we unfortunately arrived at a bad moment. Senior colleagues of his will have been fully aware that he had been ill for some years and may not be too surprised at this outcome,' the Scot suggested. Then he added, 'If we are to be truthful with anyone it had better be at an even higher level than the police.'

'Agreed,' said the big man. 'Then I suggest we make an appointment to see the Commissioner as soon as we are able. In the meantime, my bed awaits me at the Reform Club.'

Chapter 22
A Lesson Learned

Present Day

The Ripper quest had started again at university. Anna, as ever, was vivacious and sociable. It assured her a constant group of friends and acquaintances, many of whom were men. She was in her element and enjoyed life. There was a lot of drinking, some drug usage and many casual relationships, most of which, being picky, she carefully avoided. Her interest in the history of serial killers, and particularly the Whitechapel murders, was developing and she was always ready to discuss the subject.

Anna would talk with anyone who was well read on the murders or had an angle to push. There were more than a few students with a passing interest and the never ending list of suspects was always being thrashed over. She gathered books on the subject and spent time online, reading and filtering some of the mass of information there. Also, Anna perused blogs and often laughed at their ideas but was sparing with her own contributions, realising she had little to say yet.

It was then that she had met Nick.

Initially he was just a conversational friend on the fringe of her group. He was a part-time Ripper enthusiast and they naturally gravitated together sometimes. Nick had views about the Whitechapel murders that Anna didn't always agree with; however he was certainly knowledgeable about most of the players in the tragedies. He claimed to have a relative high up in the Metropolitan Police who was privy to inside information about the police investigation. Nick planned to write a book with him in due course which would, he boasted, finally name the killer.

The analyst in her seriously doubted this, though she was curious. The more she thought about it the more unlikely it seemed. Why would such information not already be public? Ripper data and files had been pored over for years and new clues were avidly sought by enthusiasts. If Nick and his relative really had anything to say why hadn't they done it already? What were they waiting for?

Anna quizzed him repeatedly but he wouldn't disclose the name of his relative or any details of their findings. He would talk only in generalities about the case and not say anything to identify any particular suspect. It didn't make sense to Anna, and she eventually gave up pushing the matter, after all, why would he invent something like that, unless it was just to impress people like her?

She thought more about Nick during her summer away from university and unconsciously begun to idealise him into something more than he was. In his absence she started to imagine he could be the type of man she wanted. Maybe it was just the time in her life; she was kidding herself she was ready to find a man she could spend time with.

Anna didn't see Nick again until they returned to university in September. She teamed up again with her best friends Sophie and Helen. As before, once ASH were reunited the three became as inseparable as ever.

ASH were very different individuals but each complemented the other two perfectly. Sophie had auburn hair and pursued a slightly hippy lifestyle. This was reflected in her passion for boho which she refused to abandon whatever the latest trends. Her dreamy air and wide eyes concealed an intellect as sharp as the scissors she wielded on her friends' hair. The hobby of hairdressing had come early to Sophie; she had grown up cutting her family's tresses and was never far from a box of hair colour and her styling equipment. She would materialise with pink or blue streaks in her hair, and often a diamond nose stud. Sophie had made herself responsible for ASH's styles and cuts, though had never yet managed to persuade Anna to try any other colour than her natural raven locks.

Helen was the only one of the three who knew exactly what she wanted to do. She was going to be a journalist and couldn't imagine life any other way. She would write and write, observing and commenting on everything, only stopping when Sophie and Anna dragged her to the pub. Once there of course, she loved it, but had to be convinced each time that she should leave her work behind. Helen was a blonde, straightened hair in tune with the times and a jeans and jumpers girl at heart. She was blessed with a lean figure and a wide gash of a mouth à la Cameron Diaz. Helen's most endearing quality was her modesty and she genuinely had little idea how or why she attracted people. On the occasions when ASH got dressed for a special evening and Sophie applied the make-up, Helen would bloom like the English rose she truly was. Out on the town ASH was a force to be reckoned with, their striking and varied looks drawing glances from as many girls as guys, the sisters envious while the guys lusted.

Old groupings reformed and the Ripper chats continued, as did the drinking sessions and the rest of the social whirl. Alongside it all some studies managed to work their way into the equation. Nick had brought his motorbike from home and Anna delighted in riding pillion around the district. During one particular evening of drinking and fun he had started to pursue Anna seriously. She ignored much of it, going along with him because he was good company and she had to admit, good looking with it. She was a sucker for dark Latin types and his contemporary three-day stubble attracted her. Nick definitely had an air of risk about him and like many others before her, Anna was drawn to him.

She was aware Nick had been out with lots of girls but that was hardly unusual for a good looking guy. Now he seemed to have set his sights on Anna. Despite herself she became flattered and although taking his remarks about her beauty and intelligence with a pinch of salt, she started to spend time with him. She wanted to see him as the man she had idealised that summer, so persistently ignored his flaws and a warning from Sophie about his affairs. So it went on for a while, and he made a beeline for her each time they met, teasing her with things that he and his relative knew about the Whitechapel murders.

One evening it happened. Sometimes there isn't a right time. This was one of those situations. They had a few drinks and went to her flat, laughing about things that had occurred that evening. This wasn't unusual but matters normally ended with some heavy kissing at the door. Tonight she invited him in for coffee, though of course that never materialised. The high spirits continued, everything seemed much funnier when they had been drinking. They sat on the sofa, kissed passionately and Anna didn't resist. He was good kisser at least, if nothing else. His right hand slid under her tee shirt in the classic manoeuvre, caressing her left breast. Anna felt weak but it had been a long day and she had been drinking, part of her also knew that she had wanted this and had led Nick on. Before long the point of no return was reached, some clothes were discarded and the sex was soon over.

Afterwards, Anna didn't remember much, Nick left and she slumped into bed to sleep it off. Next day she felt cheap and had broken one of her own rules, as no precautions had been used. Having drunk alcohol but no water, she was also dehydrated and had a violent headache. Anna didn't really have regrets, only perhaps that it just hadn't been the right time. Also, the earth hadn't moved on this occasion, so all in all it wasn't a great experience. The process of obtaining the morning after pill made her feel like a slut and was something she vowed not to repeat.

ASH's network confirmed that Nick hadn't stopped his habit of seeing other girls. Sophie warned her, not for the first time, after seeing him in town. It occurred to Anna that she had glossed over her suspicions about him and had gone against her own subconscious doubts. She made an appointment to get checked for STDs and despite herself, started to worry a little.

Having decided she wouldn't sleep with him again, the typically forthright Anna told him so over coffee in Caffè Nero. She wasn't rude, in fact she was quite tactful but he didn't like it. Nick's demeanour confirmed that what she already knew about his activities was true. Studying his body language she realised it was unlikely that he would ever stay with one woman for long.

Although she enjoyed his company, particularly when part of a group, she knew now this wasn't a man she wanted. Anna would have been happy to remain friends with Nick so they could continue their mutual interest in criminology. She made a point of telling him so, but with some people that just couldn't happen once a sexual bridge had been crossed. Nick even proposed repeating their experience that evening but that was never going to happen.

'Haven't you heard what I just said?' she responded slightly incredulously.

Nick had always been used to getting what he wanted with women; his looks and charm were in demand. Rejection, however sensitively delivered, was not something he could easily handle. He left the cafe alone, an ugly twist on his lips as he did so. Watching him leave, Anna raised her eyebrows, wondering just what it was about men and their egos. Now she could see the faults in Nick that she had so conveniently ignored.

Over the next few days, things became worse for her. ASH's intelligence discovered that Nick had bragged to male friends about sleeping with Anna, bigging up his own prowess and implying that she had been smitten and couldn't get enough of him. Anna was angry; naively she had thought they might both be discreet about their one night stand.

A few evenings later Anna was in town with Sophie and they saw Nick on his bike parked near a pub. Sitting on the gas tank facing him with her legs astride him was a blonde in a denim miniskirt which left little to the imagination. Their faces were inches apart as they drank from the pub's plastic glasses. Though fully dressed, their pose was provocatively intimate and unmistakeable. Anna didn't hesitate. Leaving Sophie in her wake she marched over to him.

'It didn't take you long to move on did it?' The girl looked at her defiantly and Nick said nothing. 'Enjoy him while you can,' Anna addressed the blonde. 'He'll be with some other slapper tomorrow.'

Executing a smart about-turn, Anna walked back towards Sophie. As she did so Nick's voice came floating after her, taunting her.

'Have you found Jack the Ripper yet? I'll bet you never name him, but I will. Don't forget I've got the inside track.'

Sophie grabbed her arm tightly and walked her away. Anna was angry, but this time it was with herself.

'Why did I do that, Sophie? What's the matter with me, was I over the top?'

Sophie squeezed her arm. 'You were just a little,' she said gently.

'Why do I do these things?' said Anna bitterly.

'Well... you wouldn't be our Anna if you didn't totally overreact sometimes. Don't blame yourself, it's part of who you are, that lovely Latin streak of yours. Anyway, take my advice and ignore the guy from now on, he's just not worth it.'

Anna resolved to take Sophie's wise words onboard. She briefly wondered if part of the reason she had been with Nick was to find out what he knew about the Whitechapel murders.

My god, she thought, am I a tart sleeping with someone to get information? No, it wasn't that, and she knew it. But even so, a lesson had been learned and she would never sleep with anyone for personal gain. Anna realised that by her outburst she had allowed Nick to easily provoke her in the way he had.

'Have you found Jack the Ripper yet?' The words rang in her ears.

To Anna's wounded pride this was a clear challenge. She would ignore Nick but one decision had become lodged in her mind. She would find and name Jack the Ripper, whatever it took. Now it had become personal.

A few days later her results from the doctor's surgery had turned up. All was well and on the very same day her period arrived, smack on time as usual. The relief was palpable as she hugged Helen and Sophie when they met for a large glass of wine. They joyfully toasted the trinity of ASH and resolved that the threshold for their amorous flings would have to rise. They would seek out only the very best of men from now on, make them wait ages for sex and always carry condoms.

'In fact there is no time to waste, we should start right now,' said Sophie, whose big eyes were roaming restlessly around the bar. Helen and Anna laughed till the tears fell. It had been a cathartic moment for Anna; she was truly over Nick, who was consigned to the recycling bin.

However, the flame of her Ripper ambitions had never burned so brightly.

Chapter 23
Irish Eyes

Spitalfields – November 1888

November was producing some difficult days for Mary Jane Kelly, it had turned colder and she didn't relish the coming winter. Her room was cold unless she could afford to light the fire; she was well behind with the rent and knew she must pay up soon. It wasn't the first time but the arrears had accrued quickly, to much more than was usual. Money had been earned during her evenings of late, but had been squandered on her drinking habit. Mary had been warned by her landlord John McCarthy, that failure to pay up would mean eviction sooner rather than later. She knew that McCarthy's man would call tomorrow for the rent. Mary had to do something and determined that tonight she would work hard and drink less, thereby at least being able to pay off a proportion of her arrears.

Mary was a pretty girl, with striking Irish eyes and a curvaceous figure. Very attractive to men, she seldom had difficulty in drawing them to her when she wished. The main thing that let her down was her habit of arguing with people, particularly when under the influence of drink. At times like this she would go too far and become abusive, even to her friends. For this she had earned a sometimes undeserved reputation.

She had lived in Millers Court for a few months, at first with her latest consort Joseph Barnett, who was in and out of work regularly. When he was not earning anything she resorted to prostitution and had recently invited a girlfriend, Maria, to share the room with her on an occasional basis. This sent a clear message to Barnett who had moved out, then fallen into the habit of calling round from time to time. The presence of another girl in her life had given her some comfort and they often enjoyed a drink together before separating to earn their nightly keep.

By nine p.m. Mary was working, and working well. She was determined to keep going and sung to herself between clients. She sung often, in the street and in her room, the songs she had learned as a child taking her back to those carefree days. Sometimes she would become maudlin and combative when flushed with drink, but not tonight. During her frequent visits to and from her lodgings she saw other prostitutes she knew, waving and occasionally singing to them as she went. Unfortunately a fair proportion of the money she was earning was disappearing over the bars of the public houses she used, but Mary was optimistic, tonight was going well and there was plenty of time left for her.

In the early hours Mary visited the Ten Bells public house, not for the first time that night, it was one of her nearest and she was a frequent visitor. Resisting the temptation to go inside and drink she stood on the corner waiting. Often people collected outside and before too long she saw a tall, well dressed man with a distinctive moustache approaching. With the perception of a woman twice her age she knew immediately what he was there for. Guessing that he would only be in the area to meet someone like her, she caught the big man's eye, then he spoke quietly.

'Hello, Mary.' They struck up a conversation and eventually walked slowly off towards her lodgings. She felt safe with him because she actually recognised the man and knew his profession. If she wasn't safe with him then who would she be safe with? They had not done business before but she was aware he had been with other girls of her calling. The street was busy near the public house and Mary had no reason to notice a younger man who lounged against a wall in the shadows of Fournier Street. A few minutes later, with her new client beside her, she arrived at her room.

The man chatted easily enough with Mary. Entering her room he looked around and then, requesting some extra time, he offered to pay accordingly. Mary agreed and having lit a candle she took off her clothing with the exception of her shift and sat on the edge of the bed.

Suddenly the door opened quietly behind them and a younger man walked into the room, the first man looking towards him as if in recognition. Neither man spoke. Mary looked at them both, startled.

'Oh no,' she said firmly. 'Oh no.' She suspected they both wanted her at the same time. That wasn't acceptable to her and she rose from the bed, looking toward the first man for help. He gave no reaction at all, just stared expressionlessly at her.

It was then that the second man struck; suddenly moving swiftly towards the bed he pushed her back down. With both speed and ferocity he grasped her around the neck, holding her down with one knee as he did so. Mary looked again at the first man, beseeching him with her big Irish eyes, but he just stood quietly watching.

'Murder,' she managed to shriek weakly but was quickly stifled by the man. Still struggling violently, Mary slowly lost consciousness and then lay still. The big man with the moustache stared for a moment and then walked to the door. Closing it firmly behind him, he was gone.

The younger man turned the key in the door lock. It was only then that the grisly orgy started to unfold in earnest. Alone with his victim the man could indulge his horrific fantasies to the fullest extent. Unlike the streets outside he was in a secluded environment, no constable was due to patrol, no nosy bystander would happen along, no interruptions were likely. It was just him and the Mary; he had been given a bonus tonight in his work. A shudder of delight shook his body, a primeval light shone in the blue eyes as he leaned over her body.

On the very same day Sir Charles Warren put down his pen having signed his letter of resignation. By a bitter coincidence he had finally concluded he could not manage the police effectively while policy differences existed with the Home Secretary. Warren had discussed the matter with his wife and they agreed that his hands were being tied behind his back, and he should not continue. The honourable thing was to resign. After some two and a half years of sparring, and much criticism, he had had enough.

Would the discovery of Mary's terribly mutilated body have changed his mind? He was to ask himself this question again and again in the coming weeks and months, but the answer was no. He couldn't have prevented it despite the best efforts of his force. They were no nearer than they had been after the frenzied stabbing of Martha Tabram back on the August bank holiday. It would now be for someone else to take on the mantle of the unwieldy and difficult organisation that Warren had led.

Chapter 24
Anna Gets What Anna Wants

Victoria Street, London – Present Day

John and Angela were arguing about who should go to Paris to watch Baby Blue, both wanting the task. Angela spoke some French and had been there before; she thought that gave her first claim. John felt he deserved the job, he had put in some long hours lately and Darren owed him. Rees wasn't interested in going; Paris was full of foreign people, wasn't it? And they drove on the wrong side and ate snails; they were totally out of order.

Walking into the office Darren soon put the matter to rest.

'No-one's going, we would need two of us and there's no budget, the job doesn't warrant it. This girlfriend she's booked the tickets with checks out okay, so I think it's just a jolly. What we will do though is keep an eye on Blondie while she's away.'

John grimaced and Angela shrugged. Oh well, she thought, she would have to wait for the trip she had been promising herself.

Anna's weekend in Paris went really well for her. Initially she was annoyed with the timing because of the trail she was on. She was picking up a lot from Sam and was keen to keep going, convinced she would find that special something about Doyle that would clinch things. Waiting for their flight she explained to her friend Helen that she was on the trail of something and needed Sam's input to help her.

'Oh yes,' said Helen, sensing a juicy story. 'He must be pretty hot if you would rather stay at home than go to Paris.'

'No, it's not like that at all.' Anna laughed. 'This is still to do with my thing, Jack the Ripper, and this guy is helping me.'

Helen raised her eyebrows in mock surprise. '*Helping you?*' She emphasised the words slowly. 'I'll bet he is. I've heard it called some things but not exactly that before. Now what does he look like? I want to know *everything*.'

Anna described Sam briefly, admitting that he was quite attractive, then remembered she had some pictures on her phone that she had taken around Southampton's old city walls. She leafed through them, found one of Sam and handed the phone to Helen.

Helen gasped. 'My god, he's beautiful, no wonder you've been keeping him all to yourself. You dirty little tart, just wait till I tell Sophie!'

Anna convulsed with laughter as the banter went on. She grabbed the phone back and stared at Sam's image herself, seeing a broad shouldered guy in his late twenties, very unruly blonde hair, and his eyes crinkled against the sunlight. He wore stone washed jeans, a blue shirt and a faded keffiyeh. Anna studied the picture carefully, Helen was right, he was beautiful. He wasn't really the type Anna went for, perhaps that was why he just hadn't registered in that way. Dark, Latin style men with stubble were her usual stereotype, and anyway with this guy it was just business.

After more protestations she finally gave up trying to persuade Helen that there was nothing more to it than Jack the Ripper.

'Oh well, it's a shame for this guy, whoever he is,' Helen said. 'Anyway, remember what we used to say about you at school? Anna gets what Anna wants.'

Anna shook her head. 'It isn't always true you know, I don't always get my own way, and certainly not with this guy.'

Helen laughed. 'Not always, just most of the time I think. Roll on Paris, you can get whatever Anna might want there, I'm sure.'

Anna's eyes glinted. 'We'll see shall we? Let's make sure we have a great time eh? It's a pity Sophie isn't here, ASH would be back together and she'd soon find some guys for us.' Helen looked at Anna's profile and smiled to herself. They didn't need Sophie.

'We don't have to find them, they'll find us!' Helen said confidently.

Anna laughed. 'You're right,' she said, linking her arm with Helen's as they sat back waiting for the gate to open.

Arriving in Paris they abandoned themselves to the city and thoroughly enjoyed it. They spent their days walking and sightseeing, lunching in cafes and soaking up the atmosphere. Anna wore flatter shoes this time, saving the killer heels for the evenings.

Once, in the Louvre, Anna saw a man who looked like Sam from the back, he appeared to be absorbed by some sculpture, oblivious to the hordes of tourists and school parties around him. She thought for a fleeting moment that Sam would love it here, and then wondered if he had ever been. Anna felt she should have asked him, realised how little she knew about him, and decided she must find out more.

Anna and Helen drank a lot of wine and were chatted up by French men – whom they flirted with and then evaded. They visited the Notre Dame and the Musee D'orsay, then shopped and shopped again at Galeries Lafayette. Finally the pair came home exhausted, their flight delayed and landing ninety minutes late at Heathrow.

Anna said a quick hello to her parents that night and announced her intention to lie in for a while in the morning. She was grateful she had one more day off before work. In the event she awoke early after a dream about the Ripper in Paris left her shaken and uneasy. Knowing she wouldn't sleep again she made coffee and toast, taking it, her mobile and her tablet back to bed. At least she would be able to catch up on her messages.

There was an email from Sam hoping she had a good time in Paris. Smiling to herself she responded. She was keen to meet again and see if Sam had any news from the Richard Lancelyn Green collection. Despite how annoying Sam could be, she also quite wanted to see him. They exchanged a few messages that morning. Sam was due to come to London soon to visit the British Library, but wasn't sure when it would be. Fearing that it wouldn't be for a while, Anna volunteered to go to Southampton again next Saturday.

Once again they met at the station. This time Anna wore jeans and black ankle boots with chunky heels, in case she was inveigled into another history walk with Sam. As usual the massive shoulder bag accompanied her, and as before, her tablet jostled inside it as she walked.

Sam reflected that their meetings had a routine. Usually there was a warm up session, then some fencing and arguing about her theories, and later a period when they shied away from controversy. Perhaps this was because they didn't want to part enemies. That way they left the door open for another meet. He was looking forward to today and knowing her need to get caffeinated, he led her to a coffee shop before suggesting a visit to Southampton City Art Gallery, a short stroll away.

Unwittingly they made it hard for Angela who was detailed to shadow Anna today. Initially she followed them into the gallery building, checking it out and using the ladies while Sam and Anna went upstairs to the exhibitions. Then she wandered around the adjacent library, finally posting herself just outside when she realised they were certain to exit the building via the main entrance. She couldn't join them in the gallery, it simply wasn't busy enough. They would remember her being there if they should notice her later on. Texting Darren she consoled herself that the weather was good today, and if the previous pattern was followed, Anna would get a train home later. Angela had no car available so she would have to play it by ear and use whatever means might present themselves to stay near her subject.

They moved on to a pub next where they could eat when they felt like it. Getting some beers in, Anna wanted to know more about Richard Lancelyn Green and was full of questions. She had encountered his name on the Internet during her initial Doyle research, before coming into contact with Sam. More had been added after her last trip to Southampton but nothing that helped her quest.

'Anyway, tell me more about Richard. How did you know him?' Sam started to talk and as usual with Anna, the questions tumbled out. Once again he marvelled at her enthusiasm and her inability to listen for long without interrupting. He was able to tell her that he didn't know Richard well, but had been in awe of his knowledge and lifelong collecting passion. His knowledge of Richard's death came only from press reports.

'I've seen some stuff on the net, what about this thing – you know, the 'Curse of Conan Doyle'. Also, the suggestion that his death might have been like the plot of a Holmes story. Which story is it? What is it all about?' She was referring to some of the more outlandish theories that had surfaced on the Internet. Sam grimaced sadly at this, the look on his face saying it all. Then he laughed at her questioning technique.

'Which do you want first then, the Doyle curse or the Sherlock Holmes story?'

Oblivious to his amusement she replied decisively, 'Please start with the curse, then the story.'

'Okay, and I think I'll have the soup and then the pasta.' Sam grinned at her.

'Ha,' she returned, icily deadpan, before relenting and allowing him a small flash of the dazzling smile.

'Alright, the curse then,' Sam said. 'I don't think anyone really believes in that, I claim to know a fair bit about Sir Arthur Conan Doyle and I can assure you there is no evidence of a curse of any sort. It's like the curse of Tutankhamen. It's actually just some nonsense that can't ever be proved. If you string together a number of people associated with anyone famous, you will come up with events that just occur naturally. They get sick, they have car crashes, and sometimes they die. It's life, or death, I'm afraid and things happen to people. There's a side to our nature that makes us unable to accept this and want to find supernatural causes for things.'

'Well, how did the curse thing start then?' Anna prompted.

Sam shrugged. 'ACD's first son Kingsley died in 1917 during the First World War. Kingsley was in the army and was wounded, but actually died of flu I believe. There was a terrible epidemic at that time. None of his three children from his second marriage to Jean had children, and both of the boys died when they were relatively young, in middle age. His younger brother Innes also died during the First World War but none of these things can be put down to a curse. It's just not a tenable suggestion I'm afraid. His daughter from his first marriage, Mary, and his daughter from his second marriage, Jean, both lived, but didn't have children.'

She nodded at that, a bit disappointed there was no juicy curse theory. 'Okay, what about the Sherlock Holmes plot then?'

'Well the reason for the theory was that this story told the tale of a person who commits suicide in order to get someone else hung for their murder. It's an ingenious way to set someone up, though rather final for the person who kills themselves! The story is called 'The Problem of Thor Bridge', and it appears in *The Case-Book of Sherlock Holmes* which comprises the final set of Holmes short stories. It concerns a beautiful governess called Grace Dunbar who is arrested for the murder of her employer's wife. Her employer, Neil Gibson, a rich American, is in love with her but unable to advance the relationship because he is still married. The assumption is that Grace Dunbar murders Gibson's wife in order to take her place.

'His wife is found dead at Thor Bridge, a stone structure over the narrow join of two small lakes called Thor Mere. She has been shot once, no sign of a struggle, and a revolver is later found on the floor of Miss Dunbar's wardrobe. The governess admits that she had been at the bridge, and had even written the note arranging the meeting, which was found in the dead woman's hand.' Sam relayed more of the story and then described the conclusion.

'It turned out that the wife shot herself but planned the whole thing to blame Miss Dunbar, of whom she was passionately jealous. The method she used was to tie the revolver, one of a pair, to a piece of string with a large stone attached to the other end, suspended over the parapet of the bridge. She had already concealed the matching gun in the governess's wardrobe, with one round fired. When she shot herself, the revolver sprang away from her and into the lake, badly chipping the parapet as it did so, and disappearing into the water. The fresh chip was observed by Holmes leading him to eventually deduce what had happened. He replicated the event with Watson's gun, thereby proving exactly how it was done. It was a classic Holmes story, maybe not the best, but extremely inventive and compelling.'

Anna had for once listened quietly.

Across the road on the green space opposite the pub Angela walked casually past again, confirming that Baby Blue was still with Blondie.

Sam continued. 'The idea of such a suicide, planned so as to blame someone else for murder, was advanced as a theory about how Richard died.'

The grimace came back to Sam's face. 'Obviously many people are keen to spot or invent secret conspiracies to fit their own theories. Whether they have any validity of course, is quite another question.' Anna caught his disdain, which she assumed was a dig aimed at her own Conan Doyle theory, but uncharacteristically for her, said nothing. Another thought was already foremost in her mind.

'How many Sherlock Holmes stories are there?'

Sam raised an eyebrow. 'There are four novels and fifty-six short stories.'

'And do you know all the plots and characters as well as you do this Thor Bridge one?'

Sam grinned, somewhat sheepishly, wondering where this was going.

'Yes I guess I do. I've been reading and re-reading them since I was a child. I also used them in my university studies.'

'It's amazing that you can do that, keep re-reading stories, then just pick one and know all about it. I have to say, you really do know your stuff!'

As Sam nodded his thanks, a crafty gleam came into Anna's eye.

'Of course that could be the only story you actually know out of them all mightn't it? Perhaps I need to test you on another one,' she said sweetly.

Sam grinned again. 'Try me.'

'Mmm, I might just do that.' She rolled her eyes at the ceiling, pretending to ponder a list of Holmes stories, and then produced the only one she could actually remember hearing of.

'Now let me think... Okay, *The Hound of the Baskervilles*, tell me about the principal characters and the plot.'

Sam relaxed back in his chair, enjoying the challenge. This was an easy one; other more obscure stories might have caught him out a little.

'Well, as you know, this one is a novel, not a short story, so perhaps I'll just give you a summary. Holmes is introduced to the case by Dr Mortimer, a local physician who lives near Baskerville Hall on Dartmoor, after the sudden death of the current Baronet. Mortimer relates the tale of the curse of the Baskervilles which goes back to around the 1700s when Sir Hugo Baskerville was killed by an enormous hound.

'When exactly in the 1700s?' challenged Anna with a smile ghosting around her lips. 'I thought you knew all this stuff.'

'I may be a nerd, but I'm not quite that bad. Anyway, I don't know which year it was, alright?'

'Okay,' conceded Anna with a grin. Sam continued his narrative.

'Following the death of Sir Charles Baskerville, in the presence of some footprints of a giant hound, the baronetcy is inherited by Sir Henry Baskerville, an American. His butler and housekeeper are a Mr and Mrs Barrymore. In addition, other principal players are the eventual villain Stapleton and his sister Beryl, who Sir Henry finds very attractive, though she eventually turns out to be Stapleton's wife, masquerading as his sister.

'In addition there is also Selden, a convicted murderer on the run from Princetown jail, and of course the star of the show is the spectral dog, who actually turns out to be Huckleberry Hound!'

Sam couldn't resist throwing in a joke to get his own back. Anna's face was a sight to behold as she digested this last bit of information.

Sam collapsed laughing. 'It's all true I promise, except the Huckleberry Hound bit of course,' he said. 'Watson is sent to accompany Sir Henry for his safety and report back to Holmes in London. However, Watson is unaware that Holmes has also gone to Devon and is secretly hanging out in a prehistoric hut circle on the moor. It transpires that Stapleton is a distant relative of Sir Charles Baskerville, and has a claim on the estate. Of course, in the end he pays the price for his dark doings, by drowning in the Great Grimpen Mire. The dog, which is an overgrown mastiff, also meets a violent end at the hands of Holmes and Watson.'

In truth, Anna had been impressed by Sam's knowledge, and there had been no need for such a challenge, but she was clearly enjoying the verbal sparring with Sam. She couldn't admit she had never read any Holmes stories but privately decided that she had better do so when time allowed.

'Okay, Sam, you know your stuff and I'm impressed. Perhaps we won't run through the other fifty-eight stories now, maybe another time, eh?' With her mind still on what she saw as Doyle's double life, Anna asked about his first wife Louise and her early death. Sam filled in some gaps for her.

'Well, he met and married her in Portsmouth as you know, then when he started to become successful and was writing full time they lived in Norwood, south London. I know what you're getting at, Anna, and it's true that he was often in central London by train from Portsmouth and later from Norwood. Yes, that was the Ripper period, but Doyle was only one of thousands using the trains during those years.

When Louise was diagnosed with tuberculosis they spent time in Switzerland for the clean air. Then Doyle decided to build a house from scratch in Surrey. He called it Undershaw and the building is still there. The air in Hindhead was thought to be exceptionally clear on the hills around the Devil's Punchbowl.'

'What's that? The Punchbowl?' Anna queried.

Sam grinned at her. 'It's a natural valley in Surrey, a beauty spot. It's a great place for a walk, there's a lot of nice countryside in Surrey. I might go down there next weekend; would you like to come with me?'

The words came out suddenly and Sam scarcely recognised his own voice. He hadn't even thought about it, but there it was. Anna cocked her head, a slightly surprised look on her face, which she quickly removed from view.

Sam continued, rapidly giving both of them an exit strategy.

'Well perhaps it'll be a bit boring actually; Hindhead isn't exactly Whitechapel, not many knife murderers about, at least not that I know of.' He smiled.

'Yeah I'll come down, why not?' She smiled back. 'I'd like to see his old house. Maybe I'll learn something useful.'

'Well, if you're sure, don't feel obliged,' Sam said.

'Not at all, I'm up for it, what time are you going anyway?' Once her mind was made up, as usual there was no stopping Anna.

They took another walk around the city avoiding the Saturday shoppers before getting some tea. This time Sam knew just the place. In the Marlands Shopping Centre was a shop which served fresh loose leaf tea, in a proper pot.

'It's probably the best cup of tea in Southampton,' said Sam, and after imbibing, Anna was forced to agree. Looking around furtively, she dug deep in the big shoulder bag, discreetly producing a packet of chocolate biscuits. Seeing Sam's quizzical look, she explained.

'You just can't get chocolate biscuits in a cafe these days. If they had them I'd buy them. I don't want their big sticky cakes, but I'm addicted to these. Some are broken but they taste better that way,' she chattered on, sneaking a biscuit across the table to Sam.

Angela made a circuit of the local shops, checking regularly on them. She had picked up a little conversation here and there and relayed it to Darren; there was nothing in it that meant much to either of them. She made a point of watching their body language whenever possible, trying to psyche out their relationship.

Between biscuits, Sam asked about Anna's Paris trip and she spent a few minutes recounting the highlights to him. This time she remembered to ask if he had been there, finding that he had been to the Louvre and rather weirdly, was a fan of classical sculpture.

Anna told Sam about the sculpture she had seen there, and without mentioning the guy who had reminded her of Sam, asked him what the attraction was. She had been just about to discuss paper clips and their indentations with him, but asking about sculpture got her more than she had bargained for.

Sam started slowly. He mentioned his interest in the development of Greek sculpture from early, more symbolic pieces, through to the stunning and idealistic portrayals of beautiful young athletes and gods. He moved on to the adoption of Greek culture by educated Romans and their subsequent penchant for realism, making observations about some well known pieces. In full flow now, he started to talk about the eventual resurgence of such sculpture during the renaissance. Sam then became quite lyrical about Bernini and Michelangelo, both of whom he credited with leaving so many treasures for us today.

Anna was intrigued, once again she was seeing a new side to Sam, and although the subject didn't grab her, she had no heart to dampen his enthusiasm.

'For me great sculpture captures a split second in the life of the subject, at a moment of great passion, pain or drama. Often these are life changing incidents for the subject. Of course, painting can do this as well but it's the three dimensional aspect of sculpture that is the attraction. I believe Michelangelo felt like that, he was a sculptor first and a painter second. His knowledge and depictions of the male physique have never been bettered, and probably never will. Of course in those days there was no real distinction between the disciplines, these guys were architects as well as creators of works of art.'

He paused, then mentioned the 'Ecstasy of St Teresa of Avila', one of Bernini's greatest pieces. Sam kept away from the controversial debate about the Spanish nun's visions, the similarity to an orgasmic experience, and the subsequent criticism of Bernini's carving as a sexually explicit image. It was a great conversation to have, but maybe not today with Anna, he decided.

Sam talked some more, getting as far as Rome's Galleria Borghese, before suddenly realising he was becoming boring. He tailed off quickly.

Anna grinned at him, seizing her chance. 'Now I'm going to tell you all about another gripping subject, paper clips!' she announced with a flourish.

'You remember the mark we were looking at? Well it certainly looks like a clip and they were definitely used in the 1920s. They were even around in the 1890s and there was at least one patent in the US before that. The Vaaler clip, a triangular invention, was around in 1900, and the type of mark we have, similar to modern day clips, is called a Gem.' Anna whizzed on, saying that there was every possibility that the original document had been secured to another one early on with a Gem type clip.

Sam smiled. 'Well done, you have such an interesting life, researching paper clips, I really envy you,' he mocked gently.

'Well, yes I do actually; it's very exciting, a bit like you and your sculpture.'

Sam held up both hands, embarrassed. 'Touché.'

Anna opted to get an earlier train home explaining that she had to go out somewhere that evening. Sam saw her to the station and agreed once more to keep in touch if he found anything in Portsmouth.

In the carriage behind Anna, Angela sat quietly, thinking. She now wore a different tee shirt and was sporting glasses with plain glass in them.

Once settled on her train, Anna considered her day with Sam. I'll use next Saturday to learn more about Doyle, and about Sam, she mused.

Thoughts cantered swiftly through her butterfly mind. Why is he inviting me down to Hindhead with him? Is this a pickup or something? If so, he's out of luck. I just want to know more about Doyle and solve this puzzle. Was he the Ripper or not? If not, did he know who it was? Those were the questions. Sam is easy enough to work with, just a little blinkered, that's all. I don't want his body; his mind will do. I don't think he'll try it on, but if he does I'll have to deal with it like Jeremy, and like a few others, she thought, slightly ruefully. She recalled Helen's words about his looks, yes he was good looking, but a distraction wasn't on the cards. Then the end of their conversation came back to her.

'I can pick you up on Saturday if you want,' Sam had said. She had started to object but he went on quickly. 'Look, it's no trouble, I'd be happy to. We'll make a day of it and I'll drop you back that evening.'

Anna had smiled with good grace. 'Okay, thanks. I'll be waiting; so whatever you've heard about women getting ready to go out doesn't apply to me.'

'That's fine.' He had smiled and visibly relaxed.

They had then chatted inconsequentially for a while and parted on their usual cordial basis. Interesting, she thought now, looking back it was pretty clear he wasn't setting up a date. Anna's mind fluttered on, considering this, considering that.

She made another mental note, if this Devil's Punchbowl place was a walking area she needed to take flatter shoes than usual. I'll have to be an outdoor girl for the day, that's probably what he likes anyway, thought Anna, picturing some mousy girl with a cagoule, awful trousers and no make-up. She had divined somehow that Sam was between girlfriends or getting over one, though he hadn't discussed anything with her. Anyway, her Converse trainers would do, she'd wear designer jeans but with an outdoor coat in case of bad weather... So, she thought, in actual fact it might turn out to be a fun day!

Before she knew it, and to Angela's great relief, the train arrived back in London.

Chapter 25
Stir-Fries and Butterflies

Southampton – Present Day

Sam wandered back home feeling slightly deflated. It had been an enjoyable time with Anna today and he had no plans for this evening, though it certainly sounded as though she had. Why had he asked her to visit Hindhead with him? Sam didn't really know. Usually, he was happiest poking around in a place like Undershaw on his own. During his last visit, a while ago, he had imagined Arthur and Louise entertaining guests whilst the children played happily in the grounds. Still, Sam reflected, maybe Anna's company was a plus, perhaps it was meant to be.

His flat was quiet, much too quiet. He wandered around aimlessly, and the very first time Indy had stayed there overnight came to haunt him, her presence was still here. He sank down on the sofa and cast his mind back, was it just a few months ago?

She had been to Sam's a number of times but never stayed longer than the evening, they would usually have a meal, make love, then disliking television they would play a few games of cards with their coffee. Afterwards he would walk her to her car to go home. Indy was good at card games; she was competitive and kept an ongoing tally in her handbag, gleefully reminding Sam that she was dozens of games ahead of him.

When she had agreed to stay over one Saturday, Sam was pleased. She would be able to have more than one glass of wine before leaving and they could relax for the weekend. Before she was due he had tidied the place. He blitzed the bedroom, changed all the bedclothes and thoroughly cleaned the bathroom. Then Sam went shopping for dinner, deciding on a stir-fry and red wine, keeping things simple in his usual way. Sam had left his study well alone, preferring that just the way it was, dusty, untidy, with a smell of old books, but comfortable and reassuring.

She had arrived on time, no sari that night but a black pencil skirt, black tights and modest heels, topped by a striking magenta jacket over a Grecian necked cream silk blouse. No costume jewellery this time either, just a plain gold chain around her neck. In a small overnight bag she had just the essentials, some jeans for Sunday and an extra bottle of wine. Before dinner, Indy had suggested a bath and they had taken their wine with them, soaping each other carefully, and of course, for much longer than was necessary.

Afterwards, stir-fry man had prepared dinner in his tee shirt and jeans while Indy applied scented moisturiser to her body. She put on fresh satin underwear, turquoise with cream lace edging, and a matching housecoat she had brought with her. Finally she had redone her make-up and let down her shoulder-length hair, pushing her fingers through it and shrugging it into place while she studied herself in the mirror. She cocked her head at her own reflection, musing that it changed her face so much when her hair was down. Decision made, she left it down. Then she had poured more wine for them at the table, dimming the room lights as she did so.

Dinner had been a masterclass in eroticism, little had been said but there had been an abundance of eye contact. Indy ate with one hand, economic in her intake and her movements, occasionally feeding Sam something from her fork. The intimacy of the gesture had not been lost on him. She had twinkled at him over the twin candles he had placed on the table, her eyes full of the promise of what was to come. Sam had wholeheartedly embraced her waiting games, now understanding the value of eking out mental foreplay even over several days. On the one hand he was bursting to hold her, but on the other he was relishing this extended teasing. They had lingered over dessert, milking the sexual tension before rising to take the dishes to the kitchen.

Indy reached up and hung her arms around his neck.

'I suppose you want a game of cards now?' she teased.

'Not exactly,' smiled Sam, suddenly scooping her up, one hand under her legs and the other under her back. She squealed with laughter, her housecoat falling open, showing toned legs and a small delta of the satin knickers. Indy smiled, watching his face and waiting while Sam savoured the view, then she planted a kiss on his nose, suddenly serious.

'Take me to bed please, Sam.'

They had made love twice in Sam's king-size bed, the first time inevitably short and urgent, as the waiting had done its work. The second time much longer... measured and more intense. Afterwards they were weary, and spurning the washing-up they settled down to sleep.

Sam had dreamt peacefully, he lay in a summer meadow with his eyes closed and the warmth of the sun on his body. All around him were wildflowers, their sweet scent hanging in the air, calming him, relaxing him. Then a large coloured butterfly alighted on his face, its wings gently tickling as they brushed over him. It was a beautiful dream and he smiled softly in his sleep. The feathery touch fluttered over his cheeks, his forehead, his eyebrows.

Murmuring, he had awoken to find Indy kissing his face lightly. It was still pitch dark and he heard her whisper.

'Kiss me again, Sam.'

Suddenly mischievous he whispered back, 'Where?'

She gave her usual little giggle. 'Well you can start with my mouth,' she said. 'Then I'll leave it up to you.'

The next hour, the darkest of the night, had slipped slowly by. A beautifully choreographed ballet of movement unfolded. With the duvet discarded they had sought each other by touch alone. Restlessly they had pursued their ritual of foreplay and seduction, rising and falling, repeatedly deferring, then finally seeking the inevitable conclusion.

The butterfly's wings grew stronger, more demanding. The butterfly pushed Sam's shoulders flat to the bed and pinning him there, rode him, first at a walk, then a trot and a canter, and finally the unstoppable gallop to the edge. With a single cry she swept over, taking him with her. Then they were both falling, falling... down into the depths.

Sam's heart was pounding, and Indy knelt over him, first soothing his temples with the balls of her thumbs then kissing his heart and speaking softly to it, shushing it to slow down and normalise. She knew she had pushed him, wanting more, but he had responded magnificently and her own pleasure had been incalculable.

Afterwards, Sam retrieved the duvet and Indy her satin knickers, then like two friendly commas they had snuggled together, her back pressed against him. She felt the soft hair on his chest touch her shoulder blades and wriggled back further into him. His arm flopped over her and he gently cupped one breast. Then they had slept again, exhausted.

On the Sunday morning they had driven into the New Forest to get coffee and a long lazy walk. It had been a weekend to remember, and that was exactly the trouble now.

Sam groaned. Then finally snapping out of it, he jumped up from the sofa. Suddenly strong and determined he phoned Dave to see if the love god was available tonight. Dave was and they agreed on a city centre pub. Sam grabbed his jacket and wallet to head out for a couple of hours. Dave was in excellent form and soon spied a couple of Polish girls to chat to.

'I'm in there, Sam, I can tell they both want me,' he said. 'I've been getting the look, you know, that look that women give me. We have to go and say '*dzień dobry*' or something to them.'

Laughing out loud Sam looked at his watch. 'Mmm, well I think that means 'good morning', Dave, and it's now the evening. Perhaps we should just say 'Hi' instead.' He then surprised Dave by walking over to the girls with a smile and a hello. Catching Dave completely on the hop, he took control of the introductions.

Sam felt much better after a few beers, some uncomplicated male company and his chat with the Polish girls. Agnieszka, the blue-eyed blonde had captivated Dave without any trouble although Sam thought the round-faced Justyna had lovely eyes. Eventually the girls went their own way and Sam had walked home to catch up on his phone calls. He preferred it that way, feeding his aversion to mobile phones he would call several people from his landline, all in one go. He spoke to James from the Mystery Club, agreeing a drinks date, he called his parents, getting all the news from his mother, and finally he rang his sister for a chat.

Chapter 26

A Woman's Intuition

Victoria Street, London – Present Day

John confirmed to Darren that Baby Blue was safely in work again today and her phone was still being monitored. The four of them sat around the office to review progress.

Darren was holding court. The other three reported everything they knew and the team sifted it thoroughly. John had made no further progress on the Internet, Anna's use of social sites was virtually non-existent and though she still went out some evenings, it appeared to be purely for drinks with friends. Her emails produced very little and nothing to do with Jack the Ripper. She contacted two friends regularly, Sophie and Helen, but the messages were chit-chat. Her route to and from work was usually the same. Sometimes she would dine with her parents, and at other times the lights would be on all evening in her part of the house.

Rees had spent hours and hours on Ripper blogs looking for traces of her input but there wasn't much to show for it. She accessed many sites but left virtually nothing in contributions. It seemed that she was just reading stuff. Anna also accessed genealogy sites and census records, presumably to do with her Ripper enquiries but again, it revealed little about her findings. Angela reported in detail about her trip to Southampton, and the subject turned towards Blondie.

Darren took up the thread.

'Okay, so she went to Paris, not with Blondie, that was just a holiday, her emails to this friend Helen pretty much confirm that. She's met this guy three times now, they've had to travel to meet and everyone else she's been with has been simply social. What is his significance? Why is she seeing him?' Things went quiet in the room.

'He's helping her with research,' Angela said softly. 'She thinks he's got something she needs.'

Rees and John sniggered.

'She could get it from me alright if she wanted,' Rees suggested crudely.

Darren looked at him pityingly.

'She's not blind you know, she'd want a real man.'

'That rules you out then,' Rees had bantered.

Angela raised her eyes to the ceiling.

Darren grinned at her. 'Calm down, boys, how do you know this, Angie?'

'Women's intuition, since my day in Southampton with them I've done a lot of thinking about their body language. They're definitely not at it, it's not a love thing even though they argue a lot,' she said cynically. 'It's not a platonic friendship either, that would be very rare between two attractive people of their age. We know he is a writer and she is a Ripper person, I thought maybe she wanted him to write a book. But it seems that she is asking him for information, and if it was a book it would be the other way around.' Angela summed up her theory for them.

'So, she wants information, he's got it, or she thinks he knows something that will lead her to the Ripper.' Angela finished her speech, and Darren nodded slowly.

'It works for me; I think you're right, well done, Angie.' He turned to John. 'So now John needs to find out much more about Blondie, what is it he knows that Baby Blue is after?'

By the next day John had found out a lot about Sam, most of it of absolutely no use to the team. Darren told him to keep on it, to make Blondie his main focus for the present.

Chapter 27
The Cloak of National Security

London – Present Day

Since leaving university Nick had tried a couple of career avenues without managing to find anything that was both satisfying and lucrative. His interest currently was in hunting down, buying and selling classic cars, definitely satisfying but not yet very lucrative, and not very time consuming either. At least that gave him time for Jack the Ripper. His interest hadn't waned, if anything it had increased, but his main motivator in this had now become to beat Anna. Since her verbal assault on him he had determined that no woman would better him, especially not a frigid bitch like her.

Nick kept in regular touch with his uncle who was now a Commander in the Metropolitan Police. His uncle was still interested in publishing a book in Nick's name, but seemed to be cautious in his willingness to push things at this time. Both of them were still seeking the Ripper, using pseudonyms online in their blog interactions with others. So far, the Commander had been unsuccessful in unearthing the legendary hoard of missing case files that people believed still existed. However, he certainly wasn't giving up on that particular project.

The rumour, of course, was that sensitive files had been spirited away by senior people intent upon protecting the Metropolitan Police's reputation. It was certainly true that there were people who thought the Ripper investigations had been botched and obvious clues not linked or followed up properly. The publication of this hoard of files would lampoon and damage the force as much today as it would have done at the time. There was also no doubt that many, many police files concerning the murders had disappeared over the years, and the dearth of documents at the National Archives in Kew supported that theory strongly. For this reason Nick's uncle was carefully and slowly exploring his contacts within the cabal for information. As yet he had nothing to feed to Nick, but was always hopeful. It wasn't something you could push with people, it was important to remain cautious and discreet with his contacts.

Nick wasn't in touch with Anna of course, but a mutual friend had told him she was working at an enquiry agency in London and was still researching the murders. This fired Nick to discuss her with his relative and warn him that she was capable of breaking the case and stealing their thunder. Over a quick lunch with his uncle he wondered aloud how she could be stopped.

His uncle listened silently. What he wasn't telling Nick was that he could do something to slow down her enquiries, both through his position and his informal membership of the cabal. Eventually he nodded, telling Nick he would consider the situation and see if anything could be done. He knew it could, but discretion had to be absolute and Nick's position as an outsider was a security risk.

Nick was aware that his uncle was active in the National Public Order Intelligence Unit but didn't understand the organisation or its allegiance to the Association of Chief Police Officers, who were actually a private limited company. This device meant that they didn't have to respond to enquiries under the Freedom of Information Act. The flexible chain of command within the organisation meant that if it chose to, much could be done with very little accountability. The cloak invoked by the words 'National Security' could easily be drawn over any activities that were best not made public. That same minimal accountability extended across its relationships with those of a like mind within the Security Service and Counter Terrorism Command.

When Nick had gone his uncle returned to his office, fetching out his third, and rarely used, mobile phone and sent a short text to arrange a meeting with a friend. Like most people in his position he had a police mobile, a personal mobile and a third mobile obtained clandestinely so it could never be identified to him.

Meanwhile, Nick continued his researches. He really didn't know who the Ripper was but it had been a useful boast at university and had got him into the beds of a few students, the main trophy amongst whom had been Anna Morretti. The satisfaction of that episode had soured badly though, after their last encounter.

Nick wasn't entirely in the dark about the Ripper however, his knowledge was considerable and he was trying to rule people out. His theory was that if he eliminated suspects one by one, eventually he would be left with someone who was really credible as the elusive Ripper.

This wasn't a new idea of course, but Nick thought he was the man to do it. To give him his credit he was being single-minded and pragmatic in his research. He was currently working on eliminating the theory that Joseph Barnett, sometime lover of Mary Kelly, was the culprit. Again, it wasn't a new theory, though somewhat involved, and Nick was trying to prove that it wasn't credible in order to eliminate Barnett once and for all. He was documenting this ruling out process so it would form the bulk of his eventual book, the jewel in the crown of which would be his naming of Jack the Ripper. By disproving a number of other individuals Nick would add strength to the candidacy of his named suspect. He believed he just needed the hoard of documents in order to nail the case.

As he worked he studied the account of Mary's last movements from the statement of a certain George Hutchinson. This individual had given an extremely detailed a description of a man he saw with Mary. The more the statement was examined the more it seemed impossible. How could Hutchinson observe so much about someone who was only in sight for a short time?

Nick leaned back in his chair and folded his hands behind his head. In the early hours and with poor lighting, would this labourer, an untrained observer, really notice and be able to describe someone's eye lashes or specific details of their tie pin? Why would this Hutchinson also have waited outside Millers Court for forty-five minutes or so whilst Mary was inside with her client? He said he had waited there till about three a.m. Why? Had he been a lover of hers? Was he concerned about her? Jealous?

Hutchinson had admitted that Mary had asked him for sixpence, which he didn't have, so he had obviously known her fairly well, and probably been a previous client. What was his agenda? He only came forward after the inquest had finished, why was that? Worried perhaps that he might become a serious suspect himself? What if Hutchinson was honest and truthful? The timing of his sighting was good. If this was the case he may have supplied the only truly detailed description of Jack the Ripper we would ever have.

Nick sighed. Hutchinson was tantalising, we just didn't have enough information about him and his involvement. There were questions begging to be asked but it was all too late unless more information could be found. Damn that hoard of missing files! He moved on to study what was known about Maria Harvey, Mary's friend who had moved into Millers Court with her, causing Mary's rift with Joseph Barnett over her presence. He opened a new Word file on his laptop and headed it up 'Maria Harvey', then he started to browse again.

Anna had also heard the story of the missing police case files, but she wasn't sure what to make of it. In fact she and Nick had talked about it briefly in happier times, now of course he must be cursing the fact that he had discussed anything with her. She gave a sour smile; the memories of her own angry outburst still just the tiniest bit raw. Could there really be a stash somewhere which might contain the final vital clues? It seemed a little fanciful, the idea that some senior police or home office official might be part of a conspiracy to conceal the truth, in order to protect the reputations of institutions. She thought again about Nick's supposed relative high up in the Metropolitan Police, surely if he knew the whereabouts of the documents, their planned book would already be on the shelves.

The other possibility was that documents had been taken home by officers retiring from the force, for their own reasons, maybe to write their memoirs. This was known to have happened in the past when all files were paper based, and was actually quite a feasible possibility. If it happened the documents had probably been destroyed, a grievous crime against future researchers. The other idea was that they had been filched by collectors. That also was known to have happened sometimes and was a likely scenario. Perhaps the only hope was that someone would discover a box of documents in some dusty attic somewhere and go public with it. In the meantime however, she might as well forget it; there was little she could do about the hoard unless it turned up.

Chapter 28
The Ruined House

Hindhead, Surrey – Present Day

On the appointed day Sam pulled up outside Anna's home. He was early, but not nearly enough to catch Anna out. She had already warned her parents.

'He's not a boyfriend, it's just business. No peering out of the windows or curtain twitching, if you do I'm leaving home!' It was only half in jest, and they both knew it. Her mother smiled at her, secretly planning to run upstairs in a moment and watch from there.

'Of course, darling, we understand.'

She swept down the path in jeans, trainers and baggy top, the big handbag swinging off one shoulder and the wide grin encompassing her visitor. Her glossy pale pink lipstick was caught beautifully by the weak morning sunshine.

As they pulled away down the road the grey Toyota slipped into position behind them, Angela was at the wheel and Darren sat yawning beside her. In front of them, Sam had the radio on for traffic news, turned down low so he and Anna could chat over it. Once on the A3 they made some headway and were soon in the vicinity of Hindhead. It was much quieter now than Sam remembered it last time, due entirely to the construction of the dual tunnels of the bypass. Pulling into the National Trust car park at the Devil's Punchbowl Sam reached behind his seat for a flask. Knowing her habits he had come prepared.

'Want coffee?' he asked and the big smile came out in response.

'You know the way to a girl's heart, don't you?' she said, then instantly regretted it. It sounded too intimate, as though they were on a date. It was her that had been suspicious of him and now here she was acting girly. For Christ's sake, Annabelle, get a grip, she thought.

'So what was happening in Doyle's life when he was here?' she asked studiously.

Sam poured the coffees, stretched out in the car seat and sipped at his.

'Quite a lot, he was here for a few years. I'll try and recall as much as I can for you. He wrote some of his best known stuff here including *The Hound of the Baskervilles*. He also wrote *The Return of Sherlock Holmes*. Doyle had Undershaw built on a plot of land near Portsmouth Road which cuts through the middle of Hindhead over there.' Sam nodded in the direction of the main road.

'Of course there wasn't much traffic then, most of it was horse-drawn. Doyle got his first car when he lived here, he had a chauffeur who had been sent away to learn about the car, but Doyle drove himself as well. It was a novelty for rich people back in those days, and motoring was a real adventure. Undershaw was a state of the art property when he built it, though it probably wouldn't excite people today. It's pretty large, eleven bedrooms originally, with fantastic views out from the front of the house.'

After a sip of coffee, Sam went on. 'I'm looking forward to seeing the old place again before they finally redevelop it. It was a great example of a well-to-do gentleman's house in its day. It's pretty much in ruins now, vandals have been in and it's all a bit sad. Originally the grounds were around three acres and Doyle installed a miniature railway plus other modern conveniences. One novelty was an electricity generator for the house. Remember, it was gas lamps and candles for many people in those days.'

Anna's eyes widened as she tried to imagine it all, picturing this as a once sleepy village. She was happy to take it all in, and enjoy her coffee. Sensing that Sam had more to say she cocked her head towards him as he continued.

'I'd also like to pop into Grayshott and pay a visit to St Luke's church while we're here; it's very close by and there are several Doyle relatives buried there. His first wife Louise is there, and also both their children, though many, many years apart. Kingsley died at the end of the First World War and Mary died much later in the 1970s. Also of course his mother Mary, 'The Mam' is buried there, so it's quite an important site for Conan Doyle fans.'

Anna nodded, sipping more caffeine; it had been thoughtful of him to bring it, knowing she was addicted. Once again Sam's knowledge was proving extensive and informative. She was constantly finding out what an important figure Conan Doyle had been in his time, and that he still had such a following even now. The man had been a giant. The idea that the future of one of his houses should cause controversy and arouse such public interest more than a hundred years later was a complete surprise to her.

An hour later they were still in the car park. About a hundred yards away Angela was parked at the extremity of the car park, screened by a few wispy bushes, having first driven past, then turned back and gingerly followed Sam in. Darren was watching out, making periodic visual checks on Sam's car.

'What the hell are they doing in there? If it was dark, I'd know what they were doing, but it's mid-morning for god's sake!' Angela smiled at his impatience.

'I'll go and try to get some coffee shall I?'

Darren nodded. 'Good thinking, Angie, I need one.'

Angela wandered off to the National Trust cafe, not glancing in the direction of Sam's car. She was dressed deliberately in nondescript clothes and her manner was instantly forgettable. She was an expert at the art of blending in, and the waiting didn't worry her at all. She had more than her share of patience and probably more than Darren, John and Rees put together. Surveillance was often boring but she liked it. As long as she could get to a ladies or a coffee shop from time to time she was quite happy in her job, and as she often said, it beats working any day. The irregular hours also suited her, a few days working very long hours then a few days off was a good way to work, she thought. Surveillance was okay; it allowed you to be nosy and gave you a lot of time to think when things were quiet. It was the opportunity to think that had made her realise the true nature of the relationship between Baby Blue and Blondie.

Waiting for her coffees she thought about Baby Blue again. What was she all about? Angela didn't have much interest in the Jack the Ripper story, wasn't it just some historical pervert slashing women on the streets? And it had all happened so long ago. Why was it important now? Unless, of course, the girl was actually about to name the culprit. She shrugged to herself. Angela found herself envying Baby Blue, with her stylish clothes and striking looks. The way she carried herself shouted confidence and self-esteem, and to Angela she looked like a supermodel on her day off. Everything I'm not, she thought bleakly for a moment.

Angela was a petrol head. *Top Gear* was her favourite TV programme and she loved cars and motor bikes. Being behind the wheel, any wheel was good for her soul. She watched the Grand Prix season on TV, loving the men who drove the cars, scrupulously recording any races that were on when she was working. Angela liked leather seats and lowered suspension. She liked a workshop environment where the bonnets were up and the overalls were king. She liked the men who hung around cars and bikes. Angela didn't have a partner at the moment but she wasn't too bothered. The job always got in the way and she hadn't had a really good relationship since her college days.

She paid for the coffees and headed back to Darren. Just as she did so Blondie and Baby Blue got out of the car and walked towards the main road. Darren passed her, swiftly grabbing his coffee on the way.

'I'll stick with them, stay near the car and I'll call you in a mo. I don't think they'll be going far,' he said.

Sam and Anna crossed the road at the main crossroads, dodging the traffic and making their way left into Hindhead Road. Just a few yards along on the right-hand side Sam ducked through a gap in the rails and walked down the bank. It caught Anna by surprise, but then she saw he was descending some old steps that were almost completely covered by leaves. He turned and grinned up at her, offering his hand to steady her as she came down.

'Come on then, we're here,' he said. 'That's Undershaw right there.' He pointed into the undergrowth. Carefully ignoring his hand she descended the steps to stand beside him. It was heavily overgrown on both sides and Anna peered through the trees, just making out the outline of a big red brick building a few yards ahead of them. She had hardly expected the building to be so close to a main road.

Sam led the way to the back of the building. It looked shattered and desolate and there were signs of demolition where some sort of extension had been taken down. They made their way round towards the front of the building, ducking under the overgrown foliage.

'Watch out for nasties on the ground,' said Sam.

'What do you mean?'

'Broken drink bottles, syringes maybe. Just be careful.' Anna looked down and shrugged. She had worn her Converse trainers today, good move.

Emerging at the front of the house Sam ran down a slope to a flat grassed area where he turned and looked back up at the building. He pulled a camera from his shoulder bag and took a few shots of it.

'It's probably the last time it will look like this, boarded and broken. One way or the other, the building will change soon. It's a moment in time,' Sam said sombrely.

Making her way down to join Sam, Anna looked up and took stock of the long brick structure, the upper facade of which was hung with red Victorian tiles. The windows of the ground floor were solidly boarded and many of the upstairs ones exhibited broken panes. It had a desperate and melancholy air about it. In front of the canopied main door a few stone steps led down the little bank to the garden, which fell away enhancing the incredible views from the house.

Darren had been taken by surprise as they had ducked into the grounds, where they rapidly disappeared into the undergrowth. He hung back a little way and phoned Angela.

'They've gone through a hedge. What is this place? There doesn't seem to be anything here. Get onto the ranch and give them the co-ordinates. Find out what's here.' He rang off and followed them cautiously. Angela phoned London.

Sam was walking Anna around the ruins of what had been a substantial house. After Doyle had sold it, Undershaw was used as an hotel for many years until finally closing around 2004.

Now it was just sitting there, once proud, but now sorry for itself and awaiting a new and uncertain future. Sam pointed out features of the property such as the large bay windows that Doyle had insisted on to give fresh air and sunlight for Louise. The multiple gables gave it the look of a Swiss chalet.

Tucked out of sight behind the house, Darren's phone yapped quietly, it was a silly ringtone but rather discreet, like a little pet niggling at its owner. Angela relayed what she had found.

'It's a derelict building, there's some planning going on about redevelopment. But the significant thing about it is that it once belonged to Sir Arthur Conan Doyle, the author.' Darren thought about it.

'What has he got to do with it? She's a Ripperologist not a Sherlock Holmes fan isn't she? Or is she? Okay Angie, thanks.'

Back on the flat grassed area in front of the house Anna looked back up at it again. She didn't really like the look of the building.

'It looks a bit odd,' she commented. Sam nodded.

'I know what you mean, it has been extended. Originally it had three gables, the large one on the left and the next two. You can see the extension jutting out on the right side, just past where the third small gable was added. It has given it an unbalanced look.' Sam thought, and then added. 'I've got an old black and white photo of the original house back at my place. It looked much more of a home then, I'll show you sometime if you like.'

Sam moved away to take some photos, while Anna looked around the remains of what must have once been a lovely garden. Her eye was caught by some barely visible steps shielded by the heavy growth. She stepped up them, pushing away branches, and peering through saw a green gazebo which was completely hidden from view. Moving in closer she got a real surprise. The gazebo had been adorned with Sherlock Holmes carvings. Her eye took in a silhouette of Holmes wearing a deerstalker against a painted landscape and sky, and around a central table were seatbacks carved with what she assumed were the titles of Holmes stories, 'The Resident Patient', 'The Naval Treaty', etc.

Excitedly, Anna turned back only to find Sam had disappeared. Frowning, she looked around and saw a man peering around the side of the house. Thinking it was Sam she was about to shout, then realised it wasn't him. She stayed quiet, easing herself carefully back into the undergrowth. Her first thought was that they were trespassing and that this might be the owner. She wasn't worried about it, after all they weren't doing any harm, but she didn't want to spoil things for Sam. 'Where the hell is he?' Anna wondered aloud.

Peeping out again, she suddenly saw Sam come into view, some way further down the garden. He was wandering around, taking the odd photograph back up towards her. She looked back at the house and saw the man, whoever he had been, was gone. Not wanting to call out she gestured violently at Sam, finally attracting his attention. He made his way back up the garden to where she stood.

'Come and see this,' she said as he neared her, pointing into the bushes. She glanced quickly back to the house again, but the other man was nowhere to be seen. With a theatrical flourish she held open the branches and motioned Sam to go inside.

Sam looked into the gazebo and whistled softly with amazement. 'Wow, that's incredible, I had no idea this was here. It must have been put in by the hotel for their guests.' He went inside and sat down, examining the story titles, looking around in rapture.

'Imagine having afternoon tea in here, how good would that be!' he exclaimed.

Anna was absurdly happy with her discovery. To find something to do with Sherlock Holmes that Sam didn't know about really pleased her and she was delighted with his reaction.

'When I brought you here, I thought I'd save this gazebo till last,' she joked. Sam grinned back at her.

'I'm glad you did, this is great,' he said, extracting his camera again to take a few shots of the structure, which was now showing signs of rotting in places. A fox had ended up inside some time ago, his remains still in the corner where he had come to die.

'At least it was a peaceful place to go,' reflected Sam.

Darren was still prowling around the grounds beside the house, keeping well away from them. He watched as Sam and Anna wandered around the garden chatting. Finally they made their way up the main drive of the house and out onto the busy Portsmouth Road. He rang Angela again.

'I think they're on the way back, be ready to move, and pick me up.'

As they walked back up the road Anna stopped again. She had spotted one of the original pedestrian entrances to the house, also half-hidden behind leaves. The old wrought iron sign proclaimed, Undershaw Hotel. She pointed it out to Sam who took another photograph. For the second time that day, she had made a little discovery for Sam and it made her feel good, pleasing the control freak inside her.

They moved on to Grayshott and went to the Fox and Pelican for lunch, which Anna insisted on buying. During their adventure this morning the atmosphere between them was the best it had been, but unfortunately that wasn't to last.

Sitting in a snug with a bookshelf divider behind them the subject that bedevilled them came back with a vengeance. Anna insisted there was no reason why Doyle couldn't be the Ripper. Of course when it was put like that it was difficult to dispute.

'There's no reason it couldn't be a hundred thousand other men either,' Sam said for the umpteenth time. His obstinate streak was usually well buried, but Anna and her fixation on Doyle's guilt was guaranteed to dig deep enough to find it.

At this point Angela came into the pub to use the ladies and check on their whereabouts; once again they were arguing and didn't even see her as she passed by. She shook her head in disbelief, what were they rowing about now? She heard the word 'Doyle', and it had been his house just up the road, but so what?

Needled by what she saw as Sam's obstinacy Anna produced one of her little gems.

'*When a doctor does go wrong he is the first of criminals. He has nerve and he has knowledge*,' she said triumphantly. 'Doyle got his man Sherlock to actually say that in a story he wrote, I found it in some quotes online.'

'Yes I know,' said Sam wearily. 'It comes from 'The Adventure of the Speckled Band', I've read them all, remember?'

'Well it is highly suggestive don't you think? He had obviously thought about himself going wrong, it was in his mind.'

Sam shook his head. 'It doesn't have to mean that at all, it just means he was a good writer who was finding realistic things to say.'

Anna repeated some of the other things she had said at their last meeting, embroidering them skilfully into a patchwork of possibilities mixed with facts and psychology. Sam wasn't having it and things got a bit heated over their meal until a few people glancing their way made them quieten down. Anna picked moodily at her tuna salad and things went silent.

Not saying much they moved on to St Luke's churchyard to find the Doyle family graves. Meanwhile, Darren and Angela were parked in the main road a hundred yards away making do with a sandwich from the local Co-op. The graves were easily found, Sam had been to the churchyard before. Louise had died first, in 1906, then Kingsley, her second child had died some twelve years later. His grave was next to his mother's. Louise's first child Mary had finally died in 1976 and her memorial had been added to Kingsley's, 'Reunited'. On the other side of Louise the Celtic cross of Conan Doyle's mother's grave stood, reaching a little higher than the others. 'The Mam', her daughter-in-law and two of her grandchildren commemorated. Sam took a photo of the three headstones.

Darren was bored. Angela was quite happy. It wasn't a bad day out in the country, she mused, dry and fairly warm, and the sandwiches for lunch had been quite decent.

Eventually after touring St Luke's Sam and Anna made their way back to the Fox and Pelican's car park to retrieve his car. Sam suggested a walk at the Devil's Punchbowl, and afterwards they had a welcome pot of tea at the cafe. He was in a better mood now, and after inspecting the fare on offer at the counter, Anna sneaked a chocolate biscuit to him, realising perhaps, that a peace offering was needed. She didn't want to lose Sam entirely, just through a single argument. The broken biscuit did the trick, amusing Sam with her need to snack regularly. They talked more about their work over tea and Anna suddenly remembered the man she had seen at Undershaw. She told Sam about it and asked if he had any idea who it might have been, but he didn't.

'The site isn't fenced and there are no signs warning people to keep out,' he said. 'Of course someone owns it, but we were doing no harm and it is a historic place, so it is reasonable to go and have a look at it.'

Anna agreed. 'If it had been the owner he would have told us to get out, but he almost seemed to be hiding,' she said. Suddenly another thought came to her. 'Hang on, let's see your camera, you might just have got him on there. You were taking shots as he looked around the edge of the building.'

Sam handed it over. Expertly, Anna scanned through the photos he had taken, zooming in on the building to look closely at each one.

She gave a triumphant cry, 'There he is, look, just at the left side of the building.' Sam moved his head nearer to peer at the screen on his camera, suddenly aware of her proximity and the raven hair that tickled his cheek. Anna made no attempt to move away, she quickly zoomed the camera to the max, so Darren's pale face appeared at the left side of the image. At that level of magnification it was blurred and they couldn't make out any distinguishing features. The face meant nothing to them and it only appeared in the one shot. In the next frame the head had disappeared entirely.

'Oh well,' Sam said, moving away somewhat reluctantly. 'It was probably just someone looking around the site like us, unless it was the ghost of Undershaw,' he joked.

Having had their obligatory row over Doyle earlier, they once again avoided the subject as they set out on the way home.

John phoned Darren with more info about Sam. He relayed new findings about his job and contacts. They already knew about 'Samuel Taylor the writer', knowledgeable about the Victorian era. But crucially, his personal interest was in the fictional detective Sherlock Holmes and his creator, Sir Arthur Conan Doyle.

Darren did more thinking as Angela tailed Sam back to Anna's home. That was the connection with this big ruined house explained, but what the hell did it have to do with the Ripperologist? Perhaps it was just a fun day out after all. But something niggled at Darren, he fell silent. Angela joked that at least he had visited Undershaw now and learned a bit about it.

'Yes,' Darren said with heavy irony. 'I'm so excited about it I can't contain myself.'

Chapter 29

A Sequence of Events

Present Day

Many Doyle and Holmes aficionados and researchers never did figure out why Sir Arthur Conan Doyle had wanted to change the order of the stories within *The Case-Book of Sherlock Holmes*. It was the final series of short stories, published some three years or so before Doyle's death. The running order had been changed in some later versions so that 'The Adventure of the Retired Colourman' had become the last story, displacing 'The Adventure of Shoscombe Old Place' from its original position at the end of the volume.

At the same time, 'The Adventure of the Illustrious Client' replaced 'The Adventure of the Mazarin Stone' as the opening story. These changes had caused some misunderstandings, with later Holmes aficionados not realising that technically the last published Holmes story was in fact 'The Adventure of Shoscombe Old Place'. Of course, it had to be said that most normal people just didn't care, but to an enthusiast things like that were crucially important!

Through the years there had been debates over the change to the order and most people had assumed that it was a publishing decision to improve the sequence of the stories. That was however, until Richard Lancelyn Green had unearthed a memo by Sir Arthur to his publisher. This requested that the order be changed and 'The Adventure of the Retired Colourman' should be the last story, as he had always intended it to be. In the briefly, almost curtly worded request, he also specified that 'The Adventure of the Illustrious Client' should always be utilised as the opening story of *The Case-Book*. The request made it clear there was no room for negotiation and left no doubt about the seriousness of his wishes.

The strange thing was that no reason was given in the document, nor could one be found in any of the rest of his prolific writings. The favourite theory was to do with readability; one story might set the scene for another or be able to flow better into the next, although an analysis of this always divided people and could be easily argued either way. The changes seemed to show little real advantage.

Another idea was about the chronological dates of Holmes cases, but this had never been an issue before, Watson had been happily picking them at random from his archives for years, this was an established principle, and had never been a problem. Everyone knew that *The Case-Book of Sherlock Holmes* was the last collection of stories, and the dates varied.

It was another one of those little quirks that Conan Doyle had left behind him, Richard had reflected. It probably wasn't important but why had he wished the sequence to be so? Did it have any real significance or was there just some mundane view of the running order that he wanted for his own reasons? A copy of the memo document was filed in Richard's collection.

Sam Taylor had also wondered about the memo in passing, and had discussed it with various interested friends. No light had been shed on the subject, and as usual with these things, some people dismissed it as irrelevant, and others were intrigued by the puzzle. It was an interesting one though, and would be fun to delve into, Sam thought. He consigned it to the list of Doyle quirks that he would investigate again one day, if he ever had time. For the moment he himself had plenty of writing to do and investigating Sir Arthur's little mysteries could wait. Heaven knows there were a lot of them and history was an easy thing to get bogged down in.

Right at the moment he had Anna's quest occupying some of his time and that was quite enough to deal with. His mind wandered back over their meetings and her haughty, imperious ways. She had a soft centre though, just now and then it would appear and quickly disappear. He smiled at the thought.

It was another day for Sam to catch up on his phone calls, there were three messages on his answer phone, one was business and two were from Dave the love god. Dave's first message wondered when Sam would come to his senses and go out on the beer again; his second one was to remind Sam that there were young women in the city who needed urgent attention. Sam chuckled, their last evening out had been good for him, and Dave was absolutely right, there was no reason why he should be living like a monk. He picked up the phone and dialled the love god's mobile.

Chapter 30
Finding the Nugget

Southampton – Present Day

Sam awoke early on Monday and decided he would visit Portsmouth today. He had been mulling over the subject of Anna and her mysterious phrase the evening before and now felt he had to see it through.

'First and last lines contain a Ripping Yarn'

Then, during the night his brain had remembered that one of the delegates at the Sherlockian conference had used exactly the same words to describe the phrase as Anna had back on their second meeting.

'There's a nugget here somewhere.'

It was strange how the brain worked, he reflected. It seemed that if you went to bed with a question hanging, often the brain would work on it whilst you were asleep. This was rather like a computer working in background as you processed something else on it. It really was a marvellous attribute, he thought, how blithely we take the complex functions of our bodies for granted. The brain was a miracle of the evolutionary process but could become clogged with unnecessary material. He recalled Sherlock Holmes' famous saying that his brain was like an attic, if you filled it with too much junk, there was no room for the important stuff.

Of course it had been the conference that had drawn his attention to the phrase a few years before, and some of the debate came back quite clearly. He could see Richard now, wittily summing up proceedings after the event. During his intermittent contacts on the fringes of the Sherlockian fraternity, Sam had frequently learnt something of interest or pursued a new angle on Conan Doyle from a chance remark.

At the time Sam had other researches on his mind and it hadn't struck him as important. Perhaps it still wasn't. Having no explanation for it, he had shelved it quickly in favour of other tasks. Now that he was in the perfect position of having unlimited access to Richard's bequest, he resolved to try to find it. Sam was partly involved in cataloguing the collection, so had as good an understanding of the bequest as anyone. He knew where he would begin as soon as he arrived in Portsmouth.

His expedition started well, he parked again in a road on the edge of Southsea Common and walked from there. Sam hated parking in tiny little slots in car parks and avoided it when possible, he enjoyed walking and the air today was fresh and breezy. Once in the office he met his contact Jean and they updated on progress to date. Sam went into the large room where many of Richard's papers were kept. Other memorabilia from the collection was stored in various places wherever it could be accommodated. Eager to start sifting through much of the loose stuff, Sam was soon left alone to play. The hours drifted by as he pored over Richard's papers, frequently becoming sidetracked in areas that were of special interest to him. It was a remarkable collection but many of the papers and thousands of pamphlets had yet to be sorted, so he really was facing a daunting task.

After a couple of hours he slipped out for a coffee, but even whilst drinking it he was eager to be back in searching mode. Re-entering the big storeroom Sam focused on his project.

'I must look for that document,' he reminded himself, it was too easy to just enjoy reading everything he came across.

Working through yet another box he came across a bundle of papers fastened together with a rubber band. Knowing he was probably looking for a single sheet of paper he flicked part way through them. Some were going brown with age. Most were old domestic papers, invoices and lists, but they were clearly from the Doyle household, one was a copy of a note from Doyle to his publisher in the 1920s about the sequence of the stories in *The Case-Book*.

'Oh yes I know that one, I was thinking about it only recently, now where did this bundle come from?' Sam muttered idly. Placing them face down on the table he finished rifling through the box and straightened up. As he did so the paper that was now on the top caught his eye, it was a modern photocopy with some printing on the other side. Picking it up, the elusive phrase jumped out from the sheet. He read it quickly; the memorandum was short and sharp.

Bignell Wood
First and last lines contain a Ripping Yarn
The message is for he who comes after.
Now I have done my duty.
Arthur Conan Doyle

'Got it!' Sam hissed to himself, smiling suddenly at the thought that he now held a document that the secretive Anna dearly wanted. She would be ecstatic when she saw the paper and he looked forward to the moment. Looking closely at the sheet, Sam's mind started to consider what it might mean. He realised he was now going through the same process that other Sherlockians had some years prior and the sheet just didn't make any real sense to him.

Just then Jean showed her head around the door. 'Sorry Sam, we're all going now, it's late,' she said walking away again.

'Okay, Jean,' Sam called after her. 'I'll be right there.' Knowing he had to hang on to the paper, Sam suddenly folded it in half and placed it in his shoulder bag. This was something he would never normally do, but Anna's quest was intriguing him and somehow he sensed that time was against them. Resolving that he would replace the paper on his next visit, he left and walked back towards his car. As he drew near he groaned with despair. The driver's side window had been smashed and the door was slightly ajar. Peculiarly shaped fragments of glass littered his seat and the floor. The glove pocket gaped open and the back seat had been pulled down to gain access to the boot from inside.

Exhaling slowly he looked around the car, there hadn't been anything of value in it and nothing seemed to be missing with the exception of a few articles he had written for the *Southampton Echo*. They were old copies and the loss didn't concern him in any way. Curiously enough, a small bag of loose change that he kept for parking machines was still in the door pocket. It was quite visible and held a few pounds in various denominations of coin. Frowning, he put the purse in his shoulder bag and headed for a nearby hotel to call the police.

About two hundred yards away across Southsea Common two men sat in a green Renault. Angela was on a couple of days off. The passenger, Darren, had binoculars trained on Sam. John was in the driving seat, casually checking his mirrors and watching the traffic as people made their way home from work.

An hour or so later Sam got on his way, he was tired now and irritated at the mindless damage to his vehicle. More things to sort out, he grimaced to himself in the mirror.

The wind buffeted him through the broken window as he drove slowly home along the M27. He thought again about Anna. Her initial reluctance to fully involve him had nettled him, as had her refusal to name the source of the number sheet on their second meeting. He understood she wanted to protect her sources of information, but it was absurdly cloak and dagger. She was taking it much too seriously. Still, he thought charitably, during their later meetings she had become much more amenable. It had reached the point that they almost seemed to enjoy being together, except perhaps for their furious row in the pub near Undershaw. She still thought Doyle was the killer, she was a control freak and impossibly argumentative, but she could be good company as well.

Sam was really pleased he had found the sheet containing the little memorandum; he would tease her with that before disclosing the message. The thought brought a smile to his lips, he was actually looking forward to seeing Anna again. Their verbal sparring brought out her passion for her subject and although Sam didn't show his own emotions in such a demonstrative way, he was passionate about his own interests. This helped him to at least partly understand what drove her. Now, he thought, he had something concrete to bring to the table. He guiltily decided he would photocopy the memo and keep the original safe in his apartment until he could get it back to Portsmouth. Sam was aware he had committed a cardinal sin in removing the document.

Arriving home late, he parked the damaged car in the car park of his building, wondering if more damage would be sustained overnight. Once he had emptied the car he copied the memo and hid the original safely in his library. Then, too tired to cook, he walked down to his local for a beer and something to eat. The green Renault was parked nearby,

John followed him into the pub and bought a beer. Having ascertained that Sam wasn't meeting anyone, he sent a text to Darren who had stayed with the car.

Looking again at the memo, and refreshed by a beer, Sam started to wonder which story or book it referred to. He forked some chicken curry into his mouth and thought carefully about it. As Sam and other Doyle experts were aware, Doyle was notorious for not dating documents and letters, though he would sometimes put his location on the top, as he had done this time. So, Sam thought, we don't have a date but we did have a place right there in the heading. Bignell Wood was clearly where he had written it.

Bignell Wood was a very secluded property in the New Forest not too far from Minstead, which Sam knew so well. A little stream ran close by and the house was surrounded by woodland. Doyle had purchased the property for his second wife Jean as a holiday home, and because of its seclusion it became an ideal site for their spiritualist meetings. This at least enabled Sam to date the memo approximately, helping to narrow down the book or story that it must refer to. He hadn't been to Bignell Wood lately but he could visualise it well enough.

Suddenly another thought came to him; there had been a house fire at Bignell Wood in Doyle's time.

Sam flattened his new copy of the memo onto the pub table to examine it more closely. Across the bottom of the sheet ran a faint ragged line looking similar to the copy of the number sheet Anna had. It was clear the two originals had been clipped together at some point and suffered the same fate of scorching or burning. It was a very long shot, but it was a fact that there had been a fire at Bignell Wood and this lent a little credence to the authenticity of the documents.

He smiled as he recalled the humorous comments Doyle had made at the time about the locals who helped remove furniture and effects from the house. He had remarked that some had moved his possessions much further away than was necessary, a witty reference to some pilfering attempts.

Well, well, the sheet even carried Anna's Gem paper clip mark; she had been right about that. Sam felt sheepish as he recalled teasing her about paper clips and her subsequent riposte about his sculpture interest. He realised he had banged on about it and the thought made him cringe.

Leaning back in the pub Sam tried to mentally work through a list of Doyle's writings in the later part of his life. There were an awful lot of them! He looked again at the memo:

Bignell Wood

First and last lines contain a Ripping Yarn

The message is for he who comes after.

Now I have done my duty.

Arthur Conan Doyle

What sort of Doyle story would it be? A famous one, perhaps? After all, why associate such a message with any book that wasn't widely read. Doyle, despite disappointment at not being recognised for what he considered his best work, had always been famous for Sherlock Holmes. He had reluctantly come to accept this and made his fortune from Holmes. Doyle had been more than happy to exploit the detective from time to time as a cash cow, as long as he could maintain the quality of the stories. Sam's reasoning continued. So... could it be a Holmes story?

Why not? The very last batch of Holmes stories were written in the 1920s, with the exception of one, and were published as *The Case-Book of Sherlock Holmes* in 1927. It was at least a likely lead. Draining his second pint Sam walked home; unaware that someone was casually following him. Darren, in jeans and a leather bomber jacket, kept his distance and observed Sam as he let himself into his apartment building. When the door closed behind him, Darren turned and walked the short distance back to the car. Once in the passenger seat he spoke briefly on his mobile to the telephone monitoring office in London.

Back home, Sam locked up and went straight to his bookshelves. Unerringly he put out his hand and pulled a copy of *The Case-Book* from the shelf. It was an old copy from his youth and exactly where he knew it to be. Despite the apparent clutter it was strange how a book lover could always lay their hands on the one volume they wanted. Sam was already anticipating the pleasure of disclosing his find of the memo to Anna. Of course, if he could solve the mystery of the 'first and last lines' as well as having found the memo, it would be the icing on the cake. Opening it at 'The Adventure of the Illustrious Client', the very first words sprung out at him.

'It can't hurt now, was Mr Sherlock Holmes' comment when...' Sam turned eagerly to the end of the story. He had read them all countless times, but couldn't recall the exact wording of the beginnings and ends. 'My friend has not yet stood in the dock.'

Might that have been some oblique reference to Jack the Ripper? No, it was Watson clearly referring to Holmes himself and it didn't mean anything to Sam. The opening words had been promising but the closing ones didn't strike any chords. Disappointed, he flicked to the back of the volume, suddenly wondering about the last story. It was 'The Adventure of the Retired Colourman', and scanning the final page he saw it.

'You can file it in our archives, Watson. Some day the true story may be told.'

Surely, Sam thought, this could be the right book; if so it was the whole *Case-Book*, not just one story. He put it together.

First line – *'It can't hurt now.'*

Last line – *'You can file it in our archives, Watson. Some day the true story may be told.'*

Well, this looked encouraging. What were the odds on finding phrases like that in the first and last lines? It certainly intimated that there was a secret there somewhere and if the papers were genuine, Doyle was either having a practical joke or had a serious message to impart. Drawing his pad toward him, he wrote down the words exactly as they appeared. He then folded the paper together with the copy of Doyle's memo and put both safely in his bag to show Anna when they next met.

It was very late and he could do nothing more tonight.

Sam sat back and closed his eyes. Inexplicably, Indy's face appeared in his mind, her soft eyes seeming so sad.

Chapter 31

Mycroft Calling

Southampton – Present Day

Finding Anna's nugget in Portsmouth, having his car broken into, and lastly his lengthy research in the pub had added up to a long day for Sam. The following morning he was slumped on the sofa nursing his second mug of tea when the phone jarred him.

'Go away,' he muttered, reaching for the offending instrument and tucking it firmly into his shoulder. It was his sister. She was chirpy today. Paige listened and commiserated about his car problem, before telling him it was a banger and about time he got a better one anyway.

'Don't you start,' said Sam. 'That's what my pal at the garage said.'

'Mmm, well you know he's right don't you?' she replied.

'Maybe he is,' Sam conceded.

Paige wanted to talk about their mother's birthday which was looming large in her diary. They discussed it for a while and agreed they would make a surprise visit to their parents, to take her out to a restaurant. Paige would set it all up with their father. Of course their mother would probably know anyway; growing up they had struggled to keep anything from her. In their young lives her psychic abilities had become a legend.

The conversation moved inevitably to Anna's quest for Jack the Ripper. Sam updated Paige about his latest disagreements with Anna, and said he had found something that might help her in her quest, when he saw her next.

'She's one of those impossible women who is always right and never listens to anybody else. You know, a bit like you, Paige,' he added slyly.

Paige smiled to herself as he described his argument on the day out to

Undershaw. She noted that despite their squabbles he was still trying to help Anna and was going to see her again. She then asked more questions, playing her Mycroft to Sam's Sherlock, and adroitly zeroing in on the question of Conan Doyle's known movements during the Ripper era.

Sam told her that whilst a few dates might be identifiable, the convenience of the railways meant anyone could travel around quite freely and easily. Conan Doyle had been living in Portsmouth at the time, and had certainly visited London regularly. Sam said he felt it would be impossible to prove either for or against his involvement.

There was a grin at the other end of the line from Oxford.

'Impossible eh? Well,' said Paige, 'it is an old maxim of mine that when you have excluded the impossible, whatever remains, however improbable, must be the truth.'

The line went silent as Sam struggled with the quote. Eventually he responded.

'Ha! 'The Adventure of the Beryl Coronet' – Holmes to a certain Mr Holder.'

'Bravo, Watson, but why did it take you so long?'

'Well, I had to think about it, although it's one of the best known Sherlock quotes, it also one of the most misquoted, and there are different versions in several stories.'

'And?'

'It's too early in the bloody morning!'

Delighted, Paige beamed down the line.

'Wait till you have children, then you'll have to be up early, brother.'

'Paige, it isn't going to happen!'

'We'll see,' she said. 'Weirder things have been known, though I pity the kids!'

Sam told her he planned to go to the British Library and do some research sometime in the next few days. He would be trying to see Anna again whilst he was there. It was his turn to phone Paige next and he promised he would do so in a couple of days' time. Well satisfied she rang off, realising that Anna was certainly taking his mind away from his lost love.

Chapter 32
The Mysterious Case of the Boxed Papers

London – 2004

The curious memo and its missing attachments were hardly the main thing on Richard Lancelyn Green's mind right now. It was earlier that year that a bombshell announcement had been made, a substantial tranche of Doyle papers were to be sold by public auction at Christies. Since then he had ceaselessly worked to halt or postpone the sale. It was firmly his belief that these papers originated from a collection that Doyle's daughter Dame Jean had wished to be lodged at the British Library.

Some other interested buyers also wondered about provenance and sought assurance that all aspects of the sale were legal. They did receive that assurance and most remained interested and keen for the sale to go ahead.

Richard, however, thought very differently despite the fact that his work to stop the auction had so far been unsuccessful. His latest attempt, writing to Christies, had received no positive response. It seemed that people either didn't understand or didn't care about the importance of the papers to Britain and its literary heritage. He knew the American market would dominate the sale and the likely fate of much of the material would be to end up in the hands of affluent private collectors. Richard had many friends in America and respected their right to purchase such material. However, this instance was a bit different and for him, Britain was the only place for the papers to reside. The British Library would have been the best custodians, where students and researchers could access the material.

It seemed the problem had arisen because of divisions in the ranks of Doyle's family; this had led to a particular collection of memorabilia being boxed and then forgotten in a London solicitor's office for many years. It was just like a Sherlock Holmes mystery, despite the fact that three thousand or so letters and many personal effects of Doyle's were known to exist; it seemed incredible that they had been lost to the world for so long. How could anybody have predicted that the treasure trove would be rediscovered? But it was, and suddenly the hoard had come back to public prominence after many years.

Apart from the personal correspondence to and from family members, there were letters from other famous people, including Winston Churchill, Oscar Wilde and George Bernard Shaw. Also in the hoard was the much written about and rarely seen brass plate from the fledgling doctor's practice in Southsea, Hampshire. Other gems included an original manuscript of *A Study in Scarlet*, still showing its first working title as 'A Tangled Skein' neatly crossed through. The hoard was to be auctioned in lots, divided into different types of correspondence and other artefacts.

Richard picked up the telephone and dialled another of his acquaintances, Samuel Taylor, the Southampton Victoriana expert and quietly rising star of Holmes and Doyle miscellanea. Sam had a good brain and could be relied upon for a balanced opinion. But before the phone rang at the other end Richard hung up abruptly. Sam wasn't a lawyer and it was starting to look as though the fate of the papers was going to be decided solely by legalities.

He felt despondent and had wanted to talk the latest position over, but now he was starting to doubt people. In recent times he had discussed the matter with many fellow Sherlockians, colleagues and friends, they had generally all agreed with his concerns but were unable to help. He wondered suddenly if those conversations had been wise. What if someone was secretly supporting the sale and working against him? Perhaps he had confided in too many people. He hadn't yet discussed the matter with Sam, who he hadn't heard from recently, and now he felt perhaps he couldn't.

Taking a leaf out of Doyle's book, someone had wittily christened the whole matter, 'The Mysterious Case of the Boxed Papers'. Under other circumstances Richard would have been highly amused but this matter was too important for frivolity.

Sam had also wondered about the sale, but he took his usual philosophical stance. If some of the material became unavailable after being sold that was a shame. If it was a legal sale then that was just the way things went. The papers hadn't been available for many years anyway, and few people even knew they still existed. There was always the hope that at least some material would be available in future to scholars, maybe the British Library or other institutions would obtain something from the sale if funds could be found.

In the event the auction went ahead as planned on 19 May 2004, and almost one million pounds sterling was raised by the sale. From the one hundred and thirty-seven lots auctioned, one hundred and four were sold, with the remaining thirty-three failing to reach their reserve price.

As it turned out, the British Library successfully obtained quite a few lots, as did some other libraries, institutions, dealers and private buyers in the UK, Canada and the USA.

The doctor's famous brass plate from his Southsea practice fetched more than £20,000 with its distinctive black lettering.

Dr. Conan Doyle
Physician & Surgeon.

The tragic side of the whole affair was the sad and unexpected death of Richard Lancelyn Green prior to the sale. His friends and associates in the world of Holmes and Doyle were shocked and dismayed, with many believing that he would never have taken his own life, others not so sure, and a few convinced of foul play. Ultimately the Coroner recorded an open verdict, indicating that there was doubt about how the death had come about.

So, while 'The Mysterious Case of the Boxed Papers' didn't reach its much hoped for totals, a substantial amount of material was sold for considerable amounts. One particular lot of miscellaneous material was shipped to America, split into smaller lots and resold during the next few years. As a result of this a small bunch of papers ended up in the study of a collector's house in Seattle. Anna's curiosity and her nose for a mystery had resulted in a copy of the number sheet travelling back with her to the UK, where she had started to follow her quest in earnest.

Chapter 33
Silent Laughter

Southampton – Present Day

The next day, some forty-eight hours after he had found the memo, Sam received an email from Anna. It politely thanked him for meeting her again, told him she had really enjoyed the day at Undershaw and then, almost casually, asked if he had any progress from Portsmouth. Her timing was good. Yesterday he got his car back, the window fixed and shining. Then he had spent time at the university, finally getting home later in the afternoon.

He now felt that he wanted to solve this mystery, if there was one, and for the first time he was really keen to get on the trail. If only, he mused once again, to prove to the difficult Anna that it was a dead end and she was wrong. Not bothering to reply to her email, he rang her mobile number straight away.

Anna was surprised but pleased when 'Sam Home' appeared on her mobile screen.

'Hi Sam, I'm at work. You talk and I'll listen.' She spoke the last bit quietly, letting him know she was in an open office.

Sam shook with silent laughter. That'll make a change, he thought, but resisted saying it aloud.

'I've got good news for you, I found the document and it has the paper clip mark.' He heard the intake of breath and sensed her excitement down the phone line.

'That's fantastic,' Anna said. 'When can I see it?'

'Call me when you can speak freely and we'll talk,' said Sam.

'Okay,' she said obediently. 'I'll be out of here in an hour or so, will you be at home?'

'Yes I will, I've got loads to do,' Sam replied.

Hanging up the phone Sam tried to concentrate on his work again.

Forty minutes later the phone rang, it was Anna, bursting to know all about it. Sam couldn't resist teasing her, asking her repeatedly what memo she meant before finally giving in to the barrage of insults and telling her he had definitely found the missing sheet. Suddenly cautious about security Anna said, 'Don't tell me what's on it exactly, just tell me if it carries the phrase we spoke about.'

Sam felt she was being melodramatic but respected her view, confirming that the headings were exactly the same as that he had seen on her number sheet.

'It certainly looks like a match to me,' he said. 'The writing is the same as well.' He glanced down at the sheet on his desk.

Bignell Wood

First and last lines contain a Ripping Yarn

The message is for he who comes after.

Now I have done my duty.

Arthur Conan Doyle

'So the heading is exactly the same, put it with my information and it has to be important, just as I thought,' Anna said excitedly.

He reminded her that it also had the telltale paper clip mark; at the other end of the phone she listened carefully, then insisted Sam describe exactly the position of the mark to her. It appeared to correspond with the mark on her number sheet, showing that the originals of these two documents probably had been clipped together in the past. Sam approved of her questioning; it was just what Holmes would have done in this situation.

The importance of paper clips, thought Sam. It had a nice ring to it, a good Conan Doyle title for a short story. Perhaps he could use it in one of his own writings. The humble clip had played its part in this mystery.

Sam didn't say anything about his possible identification of *The Case-Book of Sherlock Holmes*, preferring to keep that and tell her face to face.

If she was so worried about people overhearing her it would be better to wait anyway. Anna was delighted and impressed with Sam's discovery of the memo, and was good enough to say so. His modest response was understated as usual.

'It really wasn't much,' he said. 'I had a bit of good luck in Portsmouth, at least until somebody broke into my car.'

Anna sympathised about the vehicle and Sam told her he would get a train to London, possibly even tomorrow, and meet her if she could get time off work.

'Of course I can, they owe me time all over the place! Just tell me where and when!' Sam promised to contact her first thing in the morning and rang off. In an office in Victoria Street not far from Anna, John took off his headset and reached for a glass of water.

Sam had planned to spend a couple of days in the British Library in London soon anyway, so he booked a hotel in Bloomsbury for three nights. It was a place he had used before when researching. Dashing off an email, Sam told Anna about his plans and invited her to meet him at the hotel if she could. He re-read the message, pondering whether it sounded suggestive, then shrugged, thinking she wouldn't have to stay over if she didn't want to. He clicked on send.

John picked up one his mobiles and rang Darren straight away. 'Blondie just rang her. He's found a document with a paper clip mark on it, and some special phrase or other. She got all excited about it and they're going to meet again, possibly tomorrow, he's going to let her know. He'll be coming up here by train, so it'll be Waterloo again.'

'A paper clip? What's all this about? How can she get excited about a bloody paper clip? Did he say anything else, John?

'Yes, he told her his car had been broken into.' Darren could hear the humour in John's voice.

'Oh, that's a shame isn't it, thanks anyway, John, I'll call you back.'

Darren thought about it. Baby Blue's excitement meant she was on a hot trail. Angela had been right, Blondie was helping her to research something, and he had found it. The girl was going to meet him again. They needed to stick close to her now and be ready to intervene if necessary. After a couple of minutes he rang John back.

'I want to know when and where they're meeting; it could get a bit busy now. Stay right on this one, John, and check their emails tonight.' Then he dialled Rees and Angela telling them to be on standby for an early start tomorrow.

Chapter 34
Quite A Three Pipe Problem

Bloomsbury, London – Present Day

When they met the following afternoon at Sam's hotel, Anna was bursting to know all about the memo. Savouring the moment, Sam continued the teasing he had started on the phone. Innocently he enquired about her health, mentioned the rainy weather they were having and started to ask what she was doing at work recently. Her face grew more and more stormy and her mouth set in an unforgiving line. Anna bit her lip, her controlling nature hating the fact that he held the upper hand, she played along for another minute or so then leaned forward in her chair.

'Sam,' she hissed sweetly, 'if you don't show me that memo I'm going to kill you, and don't think I don't mean it!' The dark eyes bored relentlessly into his and a hint of red tinged her high cheekbones.

Sam smirked back. 'Oh, that memo? Yes of course. Now let me see... did I bring it with me?' He patted his pockets absentmindedly, finally opening his bag and extracting the paper. 'Ah yes, I must have done, here it is.'

'You've had your fun, now show me will you?' Anna snatched the proffered copy and carefully examined it. 'This isn't the original is it?'

'No I've got that safe, but even this copy of a copy bears the paper clip mark.'

Anna compared the two papers in her hand.

'Yes I can see that, it's in exactly the right place to correspond with my number sheet.'

Anna relaxed, looking up now. 'Thanks, Sam, it's really good of you to search for it like that, I do appreciate it. So now the question is, what does the 'first and last lines' bit refer to?'

Sam lapsed into Holmes speak. 'Well, it is quite a three pipe problem and I beg that you won't speak to me for fifty minutes.'

The look on Anna's face was priceless as she seriously considered if this guy was bonkers. Sam laughed aloud.

'It's okay, Anna, just something Holmes said to Watson when he wanted to think about a problem he was trying to solve. It's a quote from 'The Red-Headed League', one of his short stories.'

'Oh, of course it is,' said Anna blankly, still wondering what the hell he was talking about. 'So going back to my question, what does the 'first and last lines' bit refer to?'

'Well, I may even be able to help there,' said Sam casually. 'I spent a bit of time researching stuff Doyle wrote during the 1920s, the period that he owned Bignell Wood, and came up with one possibility from *The Case-Book of Sherlock Holmes*.

Once again the look on Anna's face was worth it. Nonplussed, she looked as though she didn't know whether to hit him or kiss him. Exasperation at his teasing was being chased across her face by admiration and thanks. She didn't know what to say.

'Tell me, please tell me about it!' she said in the end.

'I'll do better than that, I'll show you.' Sam dived into his shoulder bag again and pulled out a battered paperback copy of *The Case-Book of Sherlock Holmes*. He showed her the first statement from 'The Adventure of the Illustrious Client', which carried the words, 'It can't hurt now'. He riffled through to the end of 'The Retired Colourman' and pointed out the final text. 'You can file it in our archives, Watson. Some day the true story may be told'.

Sam showed her the other piece of paper from his bag, on which he had scribbled the whole of the text:

'It can't hurt now.'

'You can file it in our archives, Watson. Some day the true story may be told.'

'This may be nothing but a red herring, but I thought you'd want to consider it as a possibility,' he said.

'Of course, thanks very much, you've saved me an awful lot of research, Sam, and I really do appreciate it.' The big smile came out, bathing him unconditionally in its rays for a few moments, making Sam respond similarly. Then rapidly it was back to business for Anna.

'If this really is the 'first and last lines' bit then all we have to do is decode the message from the number sheet,' she said excitedly. 'You remember I told you in Southampton I think the numbers represent the page number, the line number, the word number and the letter number. I'm sure it's a simple code but I just have to crack it. If this is the book I can do it now!'

Sam gave her the paperback and extracting a biro and pad from her handbag, she started to check out the first page number.

Sam looked at his watch, it was past five o'clock and he was ready for a drink. Asking her if she wanted one she opted for a Coke.

'I've got to go soon, I'm out tonight,' she said.

He hadn't asked if she was staying over and apparently she wasn't. Slightly disappointed Sam went to the bar to order. He looked back towards where Anna sat, her forehead was furrowed and her lips were turned down in disgust. She pulled irritably on one of her hooped silver earrings. He realised she wasn't breaking the code and he shared her frustration.

Suddenly it came to him. Leaving the barman to pull his pint he walked swiftly back to Anna's sofa.

'Anna, it isn't going to work!' She looked up, still frowning as Sam continued.

'This is a modern paperback, only printed in recent years. If Doyle put a code in, it would be a completely different print. The pages, lines, etc. would all be different from this edition. We're talking about a book printed ninety years ago or so.'

Anna realised the logic instantly. She was angry with herself.

'Oh phooey, of course, I'm wasting my time aren't I? How stupid of me. Damn it, how can I prove if this works or not?'

Sam was already considering this question. He wandered back to the bar, returning with their drinks.

'If he really did create a code, it must have been when the book was first available, that means you will need a first edition of *The Case-Book*. They are quite rare, and very expensive. I think it was published by John Murray.' Anna looked up at him saying nothing.

Sam continued, once again offering his help. 'Look, I'm in the British Library again tomorrow, I bet they have one, but you normally have to order things in advance. I could try and get one for the following day if you are free?'

The big smile came out again. 'Would you really do that? Thanks, Sam. I'll come over tomorrow after work and check in here if they've got a room. I'll ask them now before I leave.' Anna looked at her watch. 'I really must go now.'

Anna managed to book a room at the hotel for the following two nights without trouble, then ran outside to get a cab. As her taxi left the hotel, Angela's Land Cruiser pulled out and followed.

Chapter 35

The Clay Pipe

Whitechapel – July 1889

John McCormack arrived rather the worse for drink at the lodging house in Gun Street where he shared a bed with his common-law wife Alice. He had worked the morning shift in his job as a porter and stopped at a public house on his way home for a drink. One drink became several as he engaged in animated discussions with acquaintances at the bar. Alice was waiting impatiently as she had expected to be able to go out and obtain some essentials before now. John didn't wish to argue, the drink and his early start had tired him and all he wanted now was to sleep it off.

Dipping into his waistcoat pocket he extracted some coins, passing one shilling and eight pence to Alice. Grumbling, she took the money and made to leave.

'Mind you pay for tonight before you go out,' he asserted before throwing himself fully clothed on the bed. Alice, still angry that he was late and had been drinking without her, didn't reply.

'Pay for tonight indeed,' she muttered to herself as she left the building. 'I'll pay when I'm ready and not before.' Alice had not been able to indulge in a smoke since yesterday when she had used the last of her tobacco. The clay pipe she favoured was in her pocket and as she strode down the street her first intention was to get some tobacco, and her second was a drink.

Later, Alice returned briefly to their lodgings, by now she was the one swaying a little and had smoked several pipes, though her mood had not improved much since the afternoon. John still lay on the bed and she answered sharply when he asked again if she had paid for the night. Following a couple of further exchanges she left the building again, vowing not to return until much later. This time her anger was mainly directed at herself, guilty because she had spent the bed money on tobacco and alcohol. She knew she could raise the cash again by resorting to selling herself. It was something she did when the pitiful income from her work as a washerwoman fell short. Putting her chin in the air Alice McKenzie made for the nearest public house.

Sergeant Edward Badham was on his rounds in Whitechapel. His mission was simple; to check on a number of constables who patrolled the streets, making sure they stayed on their beats and were where they should be. He tried the doors of a few businesses as he went, ensuring that they were locked securely. Woe betide a constable who had missed anything while the Sergeant was out and about. Badham had been promoted to Sergeant about eighteen months before and was transferred to Whitechapel early in 1888. He rapidly became familiar with the area and had been involved in the aftermath of two victims of the Whitechapel murderer.

It was Badham who had been responsible for wheeling Annie Chapman's mutilated body to the Whitechapel mortuary. Barely two months later fate involved him again as he had become one of the first officers to attend the site of Mary Kelly's murder in Millers Court. The appalling sight that greeted him would stay with him forever, as it did the rest of the band of professionals who were obliged to attend the scene.

Approaching the pub and seeing several loiterers outside, Alice asked who would buy her a drink. Her request was directed generally and was a ploy that she had often used to pick up a client. It was useful for the men too because it offered an easy way to fall in with her if any of them were interested. On this occasion there were no takers and she set out resolutely for the next public house in the street. Outside a pie shop, a little further on, a man stood on his own, jingling a couple of coins in his pocket. Noting the sound of money Alice slowed up and asked him to buy her a drink.

The man she fell into conversation with had an air of wild authority about him, a man perhaps who would not take no for an answer. He seemed civil enough though his reticence to enter the public house struck her as curious. He assured her he had no wish for a drink at the present time, though Alice had other ideas. She insisted that he buy her a drink, following her usual practice of obtaining alcohol in addition to the money for her services. The man reluctantly followed her into the pub and complied but soon made it clear he was ready for business. Alice persuaded him to stand one more round, after which he firmly clasped her elbow and steered her out and away from the lights of the pub. By now it was late and was as dark as it would get that night.

In the distance a policeman walked towards them on patrol, the outline of his rain cape clearly silhouetted in the yellow light of a street lamp behind him. Seeing the policeman, the man holding her elbow steered her across the road past another pub which was now closed and into Castle Alley. As they made their way down towards a darker area she could see that no-one else was around and all was quiet. It didn't occur to Alice that this man seemed to know where to go. Most men she met relied upon her to lead the way to a secluded place. She knew the alley well and would probably have made for here anyway. It was one of a number of places she used when her occasional business needs demanded.

Around half-way down the alley they paused, each looking back and forward to establish their privacy. All was clear and they moved to the side just beyond two carts which obscured the view from one direction and also blocked out most of the light from the nearest lamp. The ground was damp now and the faintest of drizzle settled on their heads, their shoulders and their clothes. There was no discussion; they both knew they would remain standing for this transaction. Facing him now, Alice stooped quickly to grasp her skirts. But as she straightened back up he was ready. Grasping her neck firmly he used his whole body to force her back against the grimy brick wall behind her.

From that moment Alice was lost, her consciousness fading rapidly as he half supported her, half pushed her to the ground. She lay partly on one side, mercifully unaware as he pulled a knife from his jacket and cut twice across her neck. The blood ran immediately, trickling into a small puddle near her head. Quickly the man knelt on one knee beside her, oblivious to the damp that seeped into his trouser leg. Raising her skirts he surveyed the scene in front of him. Then he made light movements with the knife, cutting, but not particularly deeply as he considered exactly where to begin. Finally he made a downward cut some inches long at an angle across her belly.

Suddenly his survival mechanism sensed something and standing up quickly he looked either way into the gloom. Somebody was near, approaching from the northern end of the alley. Making a rapid decision he wiped his blade and walked hurriedly south towards Whitechapel High Street. Within seconds he was anonymous again and mingling with the human traffic of the night.

The narrow confines of Castle Alley were made difficult to negotiate by tradesmen's carts strewn along its length between Old Castle Street and Whitechapel High Street. It would be one a.m. in about ten minutes and for Constable Walter Andrews 272 of H Division, it wasn't the first time he had walked this alley, either tonight or on previous nights. The last time he had completed his beat through here was thirty minutes earlier at twelve twenty a.m. or so. It was drizzling slightly more now and had been doing so for a short while. The alley had three lamps spaced throughout its length but despite this nobody would have credited it with being well lit. Conscientiously, and as instructed, Andrews again tried each door that he came to. A scant few minutes before he had met Badham on his rounds and the Sergeant had gruffly questioned him as usual.

'Alright?' the Sergeant had said.

'Alright, Sergeant,' said Andrews in a similar tone. That was the extent of their exchange.

His first glimpse of the woman came as he walked past a cart, one of two together near the alley's central lamp. Above her badly scuffed and buttoned up boots, the two different coloured stockings she wore contrasted strongly with the pallor of her upper legs, which shone luminously in the poor light. His eyes were drawn to where her brown skirts were pulled up, cruelly exposing her genitals and abdomen. The pale flesh, damp now in the drizzle, added to the ghostliness and horror of the scene before him. Andrews gasped involuntarily and looked first behind him and then down the alley, there was no-one in sight in either direction. Despite this he sensed that someone was, or had been, close by.

Shining his lantern he looked back down at the woman and saw now that her throat had been slashed and a number of cuts were apparent on her belly. His mind racing, he registered the fact that this had just happened. Blood still flowed from her neck even as he stooped beside her, rich red on the damp ground. Hesitantly he reached out to her body which was warm to his touch. As he did so, footsteps echoed down the alley from the direction he had come.

Rising from the body, Andrews ran the short distance back up the alley, blowing loudly on his whistle as he did so. A certain Isaac Jacob, whose footsteps had been heard by Andrews, found himself roughly questioned and marched back towards the victim by the constable. Within moments Sergeant Badham, who had been less than two hundred yards away checking on another constable, was back on the scene and issuing instructions.

By this time Alice's assailant was some hundreds of yards away, walking confidently but somewhat aimlessly. He would like to have carried out more surgery on this Mary but his keen antennae had sensed the approach of a constable before he had decided where his incisions would take him. The man was more confused now about his mission than during last year, but his awareness of the risk of discovery and capture was as keen as ever. Things were more difficult now, he conceded; despite the fact he had not dealt with a Mary for many months, Whitechapel still seemed alert and suspicious. There was nothing to mark him out as unusual; he was just a man with a wet mark on his trousers at the knee.

The man was well aware that until recently police plain clothes patrols had remained intensive. This was the reason he had postponed his activities for a while. He did not know, but might have assumed that with the murder of this Mary, such patrols would be heavily increased again. In the event this was precisely what was to occur as London fell in thrall once more to the Whitechapel murderer.

After the surgeon had finished his initial examination, three constables were detailed to lift Alice onto their hand cart. They handled her reverently, moved at her plight, smoothing her clothing and covering her with a blanket. As they lifted the body her pipe was exposed on the cobbles along with a solitary farthing, still dry where they had been covered by her skirts.

The clay pipe had been smoked for the last time.

Chapter 36

The Women of Whitechapel

Bloomsbury, London – Present Day

Anna was actually sorry she had to leave the hotel. She was due to be out that evening, but it was a family gathering and she wouldn't have missed it for anything. Despite this her mind was constantly on the riddle of Conan Doyle, making her sometimes distant to the people present.

The following evening they met again at Sam's hotel. Anna had taken a taxi from work, checked in, dropped her bag in her room and made her way back to the bar. Making themselves comfortable on the same sofa as the previous evening, they contemplated something to eat and drink. Looking around the bar, Sam thought this is getting to be a habit, a nice habit.

'Well, I could do with a glass of wine and just a one course dinner or something,' said Anna.

'That sounds good to me,' replied Sam, rising to go to the bar. He had already booked a table in the restaurant. 'Red or white?'

The big smile came out to play. 'Red please, Mr Taylor... and it's my turn next,' she added firmly. No-one was going to get away with buying her drinks unless she returned the favour.

She was still restraining herself. Whilst dying to know if Sam had managed to trace an original copy of *The Case-Book*, she had learned that he couldn't be rushed. His laid-back, steady approach to things was something of an anathema to her. Her approach to life had always been impulsive and full on; she thrived on going all out and was never one to worry too much about the details. In Anna's mind they could always be sorted out later.

Standing at the bar it occurred to Sam that she was desperate to know about the book. Delivering two oversized glasses of red wine he sat down, tossing Anna a bag of crisps that he guessed she would want. Her snacking habit had become part of their relationship. He announced as he did so that the library had a first edition copy of *The Case-Book* and that he had managed to reserve it for the following morning.

The big smile became as wide as he had ever seen it. Anna thanked him for the good news, and the crisps. She busied herself opening them, while Sam took a look at the menu card. He realised he was looking forward to the evening very much.

Dinner in the hotel turned out to be average. During the meal they agreed the bar was much better than the restaurant, and they would go back there shortly, the ambience was pleasant and Anna thought the barman was cute. As they ate, she had another gentle go at trying to convince Sam about Doyle.

Sam looked at her closely. She was becoming animated again, chattering away, her dark hair bobbing as she emphasised some point or other. Slowly he tuned out of her conversation, wondering what Holmes would have made of her story had she visited him in his Baker Street rooms. He was imagining how things might have been in those times, with Mrs Hudson showing the lady in. Holmes would have seated her by the fire and introduced Doctor Watson.

'You have our undivided attention, Miss Moretti, please take your time,' Holmes would have said.

There was no doubt Watson, ever the ladies man, would have been quite taken with Anna. Mentally, Sam slipped back into the dialogue.

'She seems an excellent and eloquent witness, Holmes. And a remarkably handsome young woman as well I may say.'

Sam looked down so she couldn't see his eyes had glazed over. He tried to hide his smile. His fictional reverie had Holmes giving a response to Watson. It was one of his better known quotations.

'But it is a capital mistake to theorise before one has data. Insensibly one begins to twist facts to suit theories, instead of theories to suit facts.'

Sam was still convinced that this was what Anna was doing. It was something we all did occasionally when anxious to solve a problem.

Despite her expertise as a criminologist, she was allowing herself to fall into one of the oldest traps, a trap that was still catching policemen and investigators on a daily basis.

'Am I keeping you awake?'

Sam jerked his head up suddenly.

The big eyes regarded him dispassionately like a specimen in a jar. He couldn't read anything in them.

'I'm sorry, Anna, I was just thinking about something else.'

'Yes, well I'm sorry I'm boring you,' she returned levelly.

It was Sam's turn to give her a big smile.

Leaning forward across the table he looked straight into her eyes. 'You're not. Whatever you are, Anna, you're not boring.'

Mollified, she smiled back, the frostiness melting instantly.

Back in the bar, they relaxed again. The adopted sofa was rapidly becoming their personal space, Anna thought. It felt good and was adding a frisson to the occasion. This was the first meeting they'd had when one of them was not going home and it was a good feeling to have no time limits. Believing that she owed Sam after his detective work on the document, she took the opportunity to tell him about her acquisition during her Seattle trip. She explained about Jeremy and his father, the Holmes and Doyle fan, leaving out Jeremy's attempt at seduction.

Sam wondered why she hadn't told him in the first place, but said nothing. It was her concern, and at least she was telling him now.

About this time Darren arrived at the hotel and found John hanging around. John updated him, confirming that Baby Blue and Blondie were now in the bar having a drink. He hadn't yet got near enough to overhear them because there weren't too many people in there. Darren nodded.

'Are they checked in?'

'Yes, he did yesterday of course and she did tonight when she came from work. She has been to her room and dropped her stuff, but that bloody big shoulder bag of hers is still with her. Neither of them have a car here so it's only going to be the Tube or taxis.' Darren nodded again, wondering how he could get closer to them; he might just wander into the bar and play at being invisible.

'I'll take it from here, you go and check her room, see if there's anything in her stuff. Make like the assistant manager if you get disturbed. My phone is on silent, text me if you find anything. And don't get caught,' he added.

Sam and Anna moved on to talk about Jack the Ripper and what sort of profile he might have had. 'It is a complicated business and not always well understood,' admitted Anna, nursing her second large glass of Shiraz.

'Profiling is often discredited, sometimes by people who know little about it. It's been around for some years but many people still distrust it. Of course the strength of probabilities is also the main weakness, just because something is probable you can never say it will apply in every case. However, it is increasing in usage all the time. It wasn't so long ago that many police forces rejected it along with the use of mediums, but nowadays most forces use various types of profiling to assist them.'

Anna continued her explanations. 'There are different types of profiling. There's psychological, or offender profiling, plus crime scene profiling, which you often see on TV cop shows. Geographical profiling is really interesting and comes into its own where you have serial offence sites; it can be possible to target almost exact areas where the offender will strike next, or actually lives. If they'd had it in the 1880s things might have been different.'

Sam sat back in the comfortable sofa, enjoying Anna's own profile, the Roman nose giving character to her face. Tonight the raven hair was gathered tightly back and tied at the nape of her neck, some little tendrils escaped from each side, curling softly down by the same hooped silver earrings she had worn yesterday.

Anna warmed to her theme and explained her admiration for Doctor Thomas Bond, who without being aware of it was an early profiler of Jack the Ripper. Bond was asked for his opinions by Sir Robert Anderson of the Met and he carefully studied the medical evidence given at the inquests of four of the murders, those of Polly Nichols, Elizabeth Stride, Annie Chapman and Catherine Eddowes. He also performed his own autopsy on the body of Mary Kelly, and he then set down his thoughts. He did this in his capacity as Surgeon to 'A' Division of the Metropolitan Police.

In summary, Bond's opinions concluded that the Ripper:

Was physically strong, daring and cool

Had no real medical knowledge

Had periodic attacks of homicidal and erotic mania

Made sudden attacks with no warning

Was not necessarily covered in blood after the crimes

Made the attacks from the right side or front of the women

Was inoffensive looking, probably middle aged

Would be respectably dressed, with a cloak or overcoat

Was solitary and eccentric in his habits

Would be of no regular occupation, but with a possible pension or income

Was likely to live amongst respectable people, who may have had some suspicions about his mental state

Anna couldn't resist pointing out that some of this would have fitted Doyle at that time.

Sam shook his head. 'Some of it might, but some of it definitely doesn't. It would fit thousands of men. Anyway, carry on.'

Anna then went on to talk about the FBI's Ripper profile, created in 1988. 'Don't quote me, I'm only giving you what I can recall,' she warned him before listing some of the key points.

A white male, 28–36 years of age

Easily able to blend in with his surroundings

A quiet loner, withdrawn and asocial

Living or working locally

In a menial job, employed Monday to Friday

The product of a broken home, and raised by a dominant female figure

Drinking in local pubs prior to the murders

Likely to have been seen walking through Whitechapel during the early hours

Probably interviewed by police at some point

Probably not involved in writing the 'Jack the Ripper' letters

Not likely to commit suicide after the murders stopped

Once again Anna couldn't resist insisting that some of this profile matched Doyle.

'He was, in effect, the product of a broken home, and raised by a dominant woman,' she said.

Sam disagreed. 'A quiet loner? Withdrawn? It doesn't fit him well at all. He was a sportsman and a doctor, a very sociable guy.'

Anna shrugged her shoulders defensively.

'You can't expect everything in a profile to fit someone, and anyway, there are some things we can't tell about Doyle and his secret life. Who can say? But this was the FBI, and I think it's a good profile, like the one by Thomas Bond.'

Sam went to replenish their glasses, and returned to the sofa. There were about four or five people in the room and it was still fairly quiet. Darren stood at the other end of the bar; he had turned away from Sam and was contemplating the old fashioned wallpaper. He had picked up smatterings of their conversation including the references to profiling and the FBI. Darren pondered carefully. Was this girl actually profiling the Ripper? Had she found anything of importance?

'So that's Surgeon Bond's views and the FBI's version a hundred years later,' Sam said. 'What about Anna Moretti's professional opinion?'

She glanced sharply at him from her sideways position on the sofa, sensing sarcasm in his query, but there was none. Sam gazed openly back with a questioning look on his face. She relaxed again, realising that he was genuinely interested.

'My own analysis shares common threads with Bond and the FBI. Much of their work, though separated by a hundred years, has real resonance for me. My profile is conservative and includes only the bits I think are likely to be factual, I'm fairly happy with it. I'll admit there's one problem that I can't square, not yet anyway.'

Intrigued, Sam asked what it was.

'Well, it's to do with the age of the murderer,' said Anna. 'I support the analysis that says he would be mid-twenties to mid-thirties because I believe that is the age when his problems and compulsions will have matured to boiling point. However, I can also see reasons why he would be a middle-aged man and I know exactly where Thomas Bond was coming from. This is a real problem for me and I've looked at the ages of the credible suspects many times. So far though I'm sitting on the fence, it's the only bit of my profile that has a question mark.'

'Mmm,' murmured Sam. 'I can't help with that I'm afraid, it's just not my area. We always talk about the Ripper as him, what about the idea that it was a woman?'

Anna shook her head firmly, her dark hair glistening in the subdued lighting of the hotel bar. 'No, it's not likely, to my knowledge there has never been a solo female serial killer with sexual connotations of any sort,' she said. 'Admittedly these were not sex attacks in the usual sense because there seemed to be no direct sexual activity by the assailant, but there were terrible mutilations to the abdomens and sex organs of the victims. These areas were definitely targeted by the killer.'

Though she spoke as a scholar or academic about the terrible injuries to the victims of the Ripper, Sam sensed a new tenderness in the way she described the women and their plight. The passage of time had turned the murders into a historical puzzle that many wanted to solve. It was easy to forget that these were real women, horribly murdered then mutilated ferociously, denying them their chance to fulfil their lives. Just like people everywhere they made their way through the daily struggle, sometimes angry, sometimes sad, sometimes drunk and sometimes hungry. Even so, their natural optimism would often shine through, despite desperate poverty and the need to resort to the world's oldest profession from time to time.

'On the whole they were cheerful souls,' Anna said. 'It comes through time and time again when you read reports from people who actually knew them. They were women of their times with all the same problems that being poor brings today. Most of them strove to find work in order to avoid going on the streets. We have no decent photographs of most of them; all we see are grim pictures of dead bodies in black and white when no-one is going to look very nice. But despite that some of them were fairly good looking women. Elizabeth Stride was a tall and quite attractive lady of Swedish birth. She spoke languages, drew glances in the street, and always dressed as well as she could, perhaps by adding a flower to her lapel, or wearing a nice scarf. When she wasn't drunk she was known as someone who would do a good turn for anyone.' Anna paused. 'I don't suppose you want to hear about all of them,' she said.

'I do,' said Sam firmly. 'You make it sound so interesting.'

'Well, Kate Eddowes was a cheerful chirpy lady. She was slim with hazel eyes and popular with people who knew her, though her downfall was her drinking habit. It got her into trouble, sometimes spectacularly. This happened when she made an exhibition of herself and got arrested the day before she died. She was very intelligent according to her friends, and before her split from her family she had three children. She looked much younger than her years, people believed her to be in her thirties, not the forty-six she actually was when she died.

Martha Tabram, who divides serious researchers even today, was certainly a Ripper victim in my opinion; in fact she was very probably the first. The similarities are too common to be ignored. If we had seen Martha murdered after Polly Nichols, people would have had no doubt that she was also his victim. Because she was murdered first, people didn't realise that this was a serial killer beginning his work. Martha had two sons and her marriage only broke up after she became a heavy drinker. I'm afraid drink was the downfall of most of these women.

'Polly Nichols, though an alcoholic, was forty-three when she died but according to friends she also looked between thirty and thirty-five years old. She was a short lady, fine featured with high cheekbones. When sober she cared a lot about her appearance, was known as a woman who kept herself clean and was very well liked. On the night she died she was proud of her new bonnet and felt it would attract clients easily. Most women wore bonnets then, often made of straw, dyed black. Polly's had a green velvet trim.'

Anna took another sip from her glass and swirled the wine around. She held it up so the light shone through the ruby liquid. For a long moment she contemplated the lees running slowly down the glass before continuing.

'We don't know enough about Alice McKenzie who was another disputed victim. She may be disputed but there is no disagreement about the fact she was brutally murdered. Some senior policemen and politicians were desperate to convince the public that she wasn't a Ripper victim. She was murdered only about nine months after Mary Kelly. She didn't have such severe injuries but that could be explained if the killer was disturbed, which he may well have been.

'Another point is that Surgeon Bond was clear that he saw the same modus operandi in her case, and this is a man I have great respect for. Alice was said to be a hard worker, when she could get employment as a washerwoman. She had a freckled face and was partial to smoking a clay pipe.'

Sam nodded. 'A bit like you then,' he teased.

'I'll ignore that for the sake of our friendship,' Anna replied haughtily.

Sam grinned. He was enjoying his regular teasing of Anna, and now it appeared that she saw him as a friend. That was progress after some of their earlier clashes, he thought.

Anna continued her narrative.

'Young Mary Kelly was undoubtedly a real looker, by her own account she had been the mistress of a well-to-do man who took her to live in France. Although she soon returned from choice, she would never have got that far if she hadn't been beautiful. She was born in Ireland and reported by friends to be quite intelligent and artistic. She was about five foot five, tall for a woman then, and had those classic Irish good looks, with the eyes to match. It seems she had a buxom hourglass figure. Inspector Walter Dew, one of the policemen involved in the hunt for the Ripper, described her as attractive. Many of the officers in the Ripper hunt knew her and would often see her around Whitechapel. Again, when she wasn't drinking she was quiet and well-liked by people.'

Anna flashed the big smile at Sam, adding that Mary Kelly also loved to sing, which often got on her neighbours' nerves, particularly in the early hours.

'Frances Coles, not universally reckoned to be a Ripper victim, was also a looker. She was thought to be the prettiest of them all and only turned to prostitution for some unknown reason after a fairly good start in life. There are one or two contemporary illustrations of her which are quite striking. If she was a Ripper victim, she was certainly the last. She was also the only one found still alive, by a new policeman on his beat. It's absolutely certain her killer was disturbed and if he was the Ripper, he had no chance to continue his mutilation of her. The policeman even heard footsteps walking away fast. Walking, mind,' said Anna, 'not running, so if that was the killer he was a cool one.'

Anna continued with her descriptions.

'Annie Chapman was not quite so blessed with health or looks, she was quite stout by the time she died and was known to be suffering from a serious illness, probably tuberculosis. But when she was younger there is a photo of her with her husband John Chapman which shows how little and cute she had been, about five feet tall, with a tiny, tiny waist.'

Anna paused, and momentarily Sam could see a tear in her eye.

'You know, Sam, even a prostitute can keep her dignity but the terrible thing was that theirs was taken away, and of course now that we only have those awful photos of them they can never get it back.'

Sam listened intently as Anna made her speech. This was a new Anna, someone he hadn't seen before. She showed real compassion and it made him reassess his opinions of her. He felt moved at her emotion about the women she described so articulately. Sam now understood that part of her desire to trace the Ripper was her anger at the injustice shown to the victims. Like most people he had never really dwelt on the human tragedies of the killings before, probably because of the time that had elapsed.

Gazing at Anna in the warmth and intimacy of the hotel bar, Sam was suddenly afflicted by her beauty – internal and external. He realised that she was an exceptional woman, despite her controlling tendencies and the conflict in their relationship. The wetness in those dark eyes got to him. Like men since time began he was being drawn to a woman showing naked emotion. Sam knew he wouldn't forget this moment. Their constant sparring had masked her beauty as a person until now. He remained silent as Anna turned to look at him again.

'It was a man's world back then,' she said ruefully. 'It wasn't really the men's fault of course, these were "fallen women, unfortunates" as they were called. But you know all about those times anyway don't you?'

Sam nodded, not trusting himself to speak. His knowledge of the Victorian period was considerable and he had a good grasp of the conditions people lived in, both in the West and East End of London as well as the provinces.

Sam cleared his throat. 'You're right,' he said. 'I hadn't really given much thought to the human side of it. They were real people struggling with their lives like poor people anywhere. Overpopulation and lack of job opportunity was a major problem. Women didn't have the vote of course, and men filled all the professions. I see exactly what you mean. It was a human tragedy of the worst possible kind.'

They fell silent as Anna nodded, sinking the last of her drink. 'I'm bushed,' she smiled. 'I'm going to bed.'

'I'm going soon too,' said Sam. 'I'll just get some water first, see you for breakfast?'

She nodded again and left the bar. Sam went to get his drink. There were only about four or five people still drinking. As he picked up his glass a man in a brown leather jacket finished his pint and left. Outside, John grimaced at Darren.

'Nothing at all in her room, there's no tablet or other device, no papers, nothing.'

Darren nodded. 'I hope you didn't leave any traces. We don't want her knowing anything, not just yet anyway.'

John looked offended. 'What do you think I am? I was very careful. She won't know.'

But Anna did know. Returning to her room later she had a feeling something wasn't as it had been. There had been a presence there. Someone other than the housekeeper she had met earlier, a cheerful soul. But housekeepers don't move your stuff about. She looked over her few things. A couple of tops, black jeans and spare underwear, and in the bathroom sat her roomy washbag full of paraphernalia. She couldn't be sure but the feeling persisted.

Sam didn't need the glass of water but had figured that if they went up to their rooms together she might think he would make a pass. He was starting to think he actually wanted to, but preferring to avoid embarrassment he waited in the bar for a decent interval. All of a sudden he remembered he hadn't contacted his sister as promised. Paige was scrupulous at keeping in touch and Sam was determined that he would always make the effort to do the same. Looking at his watch he frowned.

It was too late now. Paige would have the children in bed and would either be asleep or relaxing with her husband. He felt a little guilty. He had been totally absorbed this evening with Anna. It had been the best evening he'd had for some time. They were going to the British Library in the morning, he would phone Paige tomorrow.

Chapter 37
Library Games

Euston Road, London – Present Day

The showers persisted as Anna and Sam walked swiftly from Bloomsbury to the British Library. A keen wind blew raindrops into their faces making it a miserable experience. Small groups of smokers huddled in doorways clutching cigarettes. Shaking off their coats in the library entrance they decided to split. Anna headed down to the locker room with their bags, while Sam bounded up the first fifteen steps towards the rare books and music room. Showing his Reader Pass he walked quickly into the large L-shaped room and made for the desk to pick up his reserved copy of *The Case-Book*.

Whilst Sam was collecting it, Anna arrived with her notebook and pencils, seating herself in one of the central rows. When he sat down she leaned across him to switch on the reading lamp, Sam catching the aroma of her perfume as she did so.

Several other people had arrived by now and were settling into their reading. In the time honoured way of most people they headed for different areas, staying as far from each other as possible. A student picked up a volume from the desk and seated himself and his dreadlocks on the row of tables nearest the entrance. Further along the same row an elderly white haired gentleman perused his volume with a slight smile on his face. Behind Sam and Anna another couple whispered together, working quietly a couple of rows back.

Handling *The Case-Book* carefully, Sam opened it and laid it in front of Anna. He unfolded the code sheet, smoothing it out on the desk before him. Then he quietly gave her the first page, line, word and letter number.

'Eleven, ten, two, five,' he whispered. She turned to page eleven, slid her finger both down and along the page and wrote C in her notebook on the desk beside her. Sam whispered the next four numbers, 'Thirteen, seven, three, two,' and she wrote down the letter O. After a few moments of this a word started to appear:

CONFESSED

'That's it, the code is working,' she breathed excitedly. 'I knew it, Conan Doyle is making a confession.'

'Maybe,' demurred Sam. 'We'll see, shall we?'

Privately he was excited. It could be no coincidence that a real word had materialised from the book on their first attempt. They worked on quickly and the next bit started to appear:

CONFESSED AS GUIL

Suddenly there was an interruption as two people strode into the room and headed straight for Sam and Anna. It was one of the attendants, a pleasant Asiatic girl, and accompanying her was a young man in jeans and a leather jacket.

'I'm sorry,' began the young girl, 'we've been told to withdraw all rare volumes from readers at once.'

The young man reached out towards *The Case-Book* in front of Anna, who instinctively grasped it and said, 'What do you mean? What's the problem?'

'It's a major security alert,' said the girl. 'I apologise, but we have just been informed about it.'

'Yes,' said the young man reaching out again for the volume. 'Sorry about that,' in a tone that suggested he wasn't sorry at all.

'Hang on a mo,' said Sam. 'We've nearly finished our task, just give us a minute or so.'

'No exceptions,' said the man bluntly. 'All rare volumes are to be returned at once.'

'This is ridiculous.' Anna was blazing by now, as the other occupants of the room looked intently at the fracas that was developing. The elderly man had stood up and the student near the door was agape.

'We're both long-term readers here, and we've got urgent work to do, how the hell can you come in and start mucking us about like this?'

The young man made another reach for the book saying, 'I'll take that.' Anna, on her feet by now, automatically stepped back with it clutched to her chest.

The girl looked distressed. 'Please, Madam, don't damage the book,' she said.

Seeing out of the corner of her eye Sam giving the slightest of head shakes, Anna reluctantly surrendered the volume to the man, who promptly turned and walked out of the room with it.

'What the hell was all that about?' Anna rounded viciously on the young girl who looked close to tears by now. 'Who was that bloody idiot?'

'I'm sorry,' said the girl. 'Nothing like this has happened since I've been here, the police arrived a few minutes ago and spoke with my boss, it's a security alert apparently.'

'Okay, I suppose it happens sometimes,' said Sam, pinching Anna's elbow sharply as he spoke.

Anna recovered rapidly and gave the girl a weak smile. 'I'm sorry,' she said. 'I didn't mean to cause a fuss.' She picked up her notebook and pencils and they headed towards the door. As they went through she angrily turned to ask Sam why he wasn't backing her up. Sam cut her off, murmuring in her ear.

'Say nothing, let's get outside,' he said.

They retrieved their bags, then via the front courtyard, Sam led the way swiftly down the road to St Pancras station. Every time Anna spoke he shook his head. Making their way into Costa Coffee he bought two Americanos, and steered her to a table at the back. From here he could see out into the station through the glass. John had followed them from the library; glancing casually into the coffee shop he confirmed their presence without even breaking his stride. He walked on to the end of the concourse before phoning Darren on his mobile. Darren had already been through *The Case-Book* with no result. The stories were boring, old school, from another age. He didn't know what he was looking for and he couldn't find any marks or signs of anything unusual.

By now Anna was smouldering again but under control. 'What's going on?' she said calmly. 'Why the silence?'

'This is serious,' Sam replied. 'I don't know what's going on but we are being followed. That guy in the library was in the hotel bar last night; he stayed for a while when we were talking. He had a drink and glanced around as though he was looking for someone. It was us he was looking for. I wouldn't have known him again, but I recognised his leather jacket when he turned in the reading room. It's got a distinctive stitching pattern on the back, and last night I saw it when he left the bar.'

'If they're police why would they be following us? I don't get it. Are they trying to find the same thing as we are?'

Sam shook his head. He was still watching through the glass all the time. People were coming and going via the escalator up to the Eurostar platforms above. 'I'm not sure, but let's consider what we do know before we rush off anywhere else.'

They ran over the series of events that had led up to their visit to the British Library, debating what had happened in the last few days. Anna remarked that looking back, it was clear she and Sam were the objective of the policeman's interruption.

'Otherwise,' she said, 'they would have started at the nearest people in the reading room instead of making straight for us. Also, he must have been a real policeman, because surely the British Library would have verified he was genuine.'

Sam agreed. 'They must have had contact at a senior level, and it all happened so fast. Somebody had some real clout. I wonder now about my car break-in at Southsea, nothing was taken, not even my parking cash.'

Anna considered this, then went silent for a moment. 'Well, it sounds silly but I thought someone had been in my room last night when we were having a drink. I can't be sure but it was just a feeling I had. You know how you leave your stuff sometimes, don't you?'

Sam nodded as Anna continued.

'I've got a friend who knows a lot about surveillance of the public by police; he has encountered it on a protest march and has written about it for the civil liberties movement. I could contact him and see if he can tell us anything.'

'Okay, why not?' Said Sam. 'Now let's sum it up, someone is after the same thing as us, or is trying to prevent us from working it out. It looks like it's the police, but we're not going to be put off by that, whoever they are. I think we should first change our hotel, lose these guys, and make plans to find another copy of *The Case-Book*. I'll get my pal Bernadette onto that one, you remember you met her at the library, that's what started all this!'

'Of course,' grinned Anna mischievously. 'It was her that told me about your Doyle obsession.'

Sam smiled, not rising to the bait. 'You contact your friend about the surveillance angle and we'll see what happens. I also think we should act as though we are not aware anyone is following us, at least for the moment.'

Pleased that he kept saying 'we' Anna warmed to him. At least he wasn't backing out of her quest.

'Sam, are we in danger?' she said suddenly.

'I don't know really, but I can't see that a couple of Doyle and Ripper enthusiasts are a threat to anyone.' He smiled at her, looking away from the window for the first time since they had arrived.

She gave him the full megawatt smile in return. 'It's really quite exciting, isn't it?'

Sam laughed. 'You didn't think so in the reading room. I can see the look on that old gentleman's face now, when you started up. I bet he'd never heard language like yours in the British Library before.'

'Anyway,' Anna chimed in, ignoring his remark, 'the last word we got was GUIL – that has to be GUILTY, so far we have got: CONFESSED AS GUIL, so I'm sure it is a real confession by Doyle.'

'We don't have any evidence of that yet,' said Sam. 'Agreed it is a message, but I'm not convinced about Doyle confessing.'

'Oh phooey,' she said, getting up from the table. 'I bet I'm right anyway.'

Leaving St Pancras they made their way back to the hotel, resolving not to look behind them or give any indication they knew they might be being followed. The rain had stopped but the clouds still sped across the sky whipped along by strong south-westerly winds. They agreed they would check out and move to another hotel, one that Anna knew at Blackfriars. Safely back in Bloomsbury, they went to their rooms to get their stuff, arranging to meet down in the lobby.

Sam was down first and phoned Anna's hotel to reserve two rooms. After checking out he asked the concierge if he could get them a taxi to the rear entrance. Handing over twenty pounds Sam asked him if he would keep their departure secret if he was asked.

'Our friends might want to catch up with us,' he smiled. Anna had just arrived behind Sam, and the concierge happily agreed to Sam's request, his knowing look at Anna insinuating they were lovers having an illicit affair. The thought never occurred to Sam who missed the moment entirely. Seeing the concierge's thought patterns, Anna gave him a suggestive wink, a smirk curling the corner of her lip.

About an hour after they left the hotel, Paige called and got the front desk. She had consulted her long list of numbers for Sam and remembered he used this hotel occasionally. It was a long shot and didn't find its target. They told her they were unable to confirm whether a Sam Taylor and any companion were resident or not. Paige put the phone down and thought. She wasn't worried, but Sam had said he would ring and so far he hadn't. She smiled to herself, if that was because he was staying in a hotel with a beautiful woman, then why would he remember to phone his sister? Paige was content with that.

Chapter 38

Patriotic Wellingtons

Bloomsbury, London – Present Day

Meanwhile, Rees was in a coffee shop close to the hotel. He could see the front door easily and was sure that if the subjects came out he would know. He watched a young woman walk past in Union Jack wellingtons, extremely indecent blue shorts and a white lace camisole. Yes... all girls should dress like that, he thought, pondering whether another coffee was a good idea or not. The trouble with coffee was that it was a diuretic and when you were watching people it wasn't always easy to find toilets. Earlier, he had followed the two of them back from St Pancras where he had taken over from John. The sun had appeared now and it was quite warm, though the winds were still strong and gusty. Angela was due here soon, bringing Darren who had finished his fruitless search of *The Case-Book* in the library.

Angela was actually only a few yards away, Darren lounging in the passenger seat, his restless eyes everywhere. Several taxis emerged from a side street one after the other, pausing as they joined the main road. Idly he watched them, suddenly seeing a profile he knew well in the rear of one of the cabs.

'Baby Blue!' he shouted, making Angela jump. 'Blondie's there too, make a turn and get after them.' He scanned the road, not seeing Rees anywhere.

Angela did as she was bid; braking hard then completing a fast U-turn at the expense of a red bus that was closing rapidly. She open-handed the driver as she shot in front of him, seeing rather than hearing the language he was using about her manoeuvre. She was two cars back from the target taxi now and was comfortable that she could stay on his tail. Darren took out his phone to contact Rees who was completely oblivious to the incident, and still considering the possibilities that wellington boots might present.

They pursued the taxi all the way through Kingsway to Aldwych, then left into the Strand and Fleet Street. Finally it turned right into some narrow streets after the Temple, ending up at the drop off area to another hotel. Angela followed cautiously, then stopped short on the corner as they watched their subjects walk through the revolving door with their bags.

Darren wondered aloud, 'Are they on to us yet?' He knew they would be completely thrown by his intervention in the library, but did they actually know they were being followed? If they were changing hotels it would seem that they did. He made a decision. 'I'll watch the car, go and stick this on their luggage if you can,' he said, handing Angela a tiny GPS tracking device. 'They nearly lost us that time; this will help if they try it again.'

As it happened it was absurdly simple. There were several people milling around in the reception area and the staff were busy. Baby Blue had left her wheelie bag parked behind her while she talked to Blondie, so Angela just sauntered past, stooping momentarily to drop the device in an unopened zip pocket on the bag. The whole thing had taken just a few seconds. She wandered on up the stairs, out of the front revolving door, then back round the block to where Darren waited.

'Easy peasy,' she said getting back into the driver's seat. 'It looks like they're waiting to check in.'

Chapter 39
What Happens in the Vaults

Blackfriars, London – Present Day

When their taxi dropped them at the Crowne Plaza in Blackfriars, Anna explained to Sam that the hotel had entrances on two levels. One was to New Bridge Street for pedestrians and another at the back, where taxis would drop guests in Kingscote Street close to the front desk. This was where they were now, it would make it difficult for anyone to hang about observing them. Any watchers would probably have to wait outside where the winds and showers made it unpleasant. That idea gave them both a happy thought as they waited to register.

'We are quite near Whitechapel; I could give you a Ripper walk if you like,' said Anna, staring at the wall with quite uncharacteristic shyness. 'My own I mean, not the advertised walks,' she added quickly.

'That would be nice,' said Sam, and he meant it. After her descriptions of the case last night, he was fast becoming a Ripper enthusiast. As he spoke a woman with curly brown hair walked past their bags behind them, barely slowing as she headed towards the stairs.

'Okay,' Anna said briskly, 'my turn to get dinner as well on the way.'

The front desk receptionist gave them rooms 221 and 321. 'That's good,' chuckled Sam. 'I've got the Sherlock Holmes room, 221.' He added the '221b Baker Street' for her benefit, but she didn't really get it. Anna took the other key card, noting she was on floor three.

'Well I'll be higher up than you, girls on top,' she retorted.

Inside 321 Anna paused at the mirror to add a final touch of her favourite perfume. An hour or so had passed since they had checked in. Both of them found time for reflection as they had showered and changed. She planned a drink with Sam in the hotel's bar 'Voltaire' before they ventured out to Whitechapel. Anna knew the place well; the bar had vaults which came complete with their own cell doors and real privacy.

They met downstairs and Anna made straight for the long bar, telling Sam that she knew somewhere where they couldn't be overheard. The barman greeted them and bustled off to fetch a bottle of Shiraz and some snacks for Anna. Sam looked at the slogan on the table, reading it aloud:

'What happens in the vaults stays in the vaults.'

Anna looked around, the vault was actually very intimate and she suddenly felt a little embarrassed, it looked as though she had set up something romantic. Nothing could be further from the truth, she told herself, she had just been seeking privacy. Rather defensively, she quickly made the point that they just needed somewhere to talk quietly.

Sensing her discomfort, Sam agreed, saying that he was glad she had suggested it. With that out of the way, the arrival of their bottle and the dim contemporary lighting created a relaxing environment. They settled back in their chairs, enjoying the ambience. There was no-one else around and having served them, the barman disappeared about his business. Sipping their drinks slowly they discussed their extraordinary experience at the British Library, and then they laid their next plans.

Using Anna's mobile, Sam emailed Bernie explaining he was in London and urgently needed a first edition of *The Case-Book of Sherlock Holmes*. Anna then emailed her friend Steve asking him if they could meet soon. His reply came in straight away; it was a one liner, just saying to meet him at the old place when she could. Anna told Sam that Steve meant the pub he used; he was there most days at some time or other. Because of Steve's experiences he would never discuss anything important on the phone or by email.

It didn't take them long to finish the bottle, Anna looked at it regretfully then suggested that they should go.

'Well,' she said brightly, getting up from her seat, 'at least the weather's dried up, let's go to Ripper land, I could do with a bite on the way, I'm starving.'

Anna led the way as they walked out through the City, both of them remembering not to stare behind them. They stopped only once, to look at the Bank of England and whilst they paused, Sam risked a slow glance back the way they had come. He saw nothing to alarm him. They made their way on through Cornhill and Leadenhall Street to Aldgate.

As if by mutual agreement they both avoided the contentious subject of Conan Doyle's involvement in the Whitechapel murders. There was no need to spoil their evening with arguments, and somehow things had changed. They were much more united now that a common danger was stalking them. Sam was determined to learn more about Whitechapel from Anna and she was equally keen to give him an interesting evening. True to her word she paid for a meal and drinks at the White Hart on the corner of Gunthorpe Street.

'This area is the heart of it, where it all started,' asserted Anna as she pointed out the depiction of Martha Tabram on the wall at the rear of the bar. 'Right next to George Yard, as it used to be known, and that's Martha Turner or Tabram if you prefer, up there.'

While they ate, it had grown dark and chilly outside, appropriate for the experience they were about to have. Clutching their coats about them they set off. Over the next three hours Anna was to take Sam on a physical and spiritual walk through Whitechapel and Spitalfields. Her discussions ranged across the murders and the lives of Victorian people as Whitechapel rapidly absorbed thousands of new arrivals. Many of them were migrants from different countries and cultures.

She was a good speaker – if excitable and jumpy – but Sam was fascinated by her description of those times. His respect for her had taken a quantum leap since her touching portrayal of the victims last night. Was it only last night? Sam's own knowledge of the period was considerable, but he had rarely heard things described so well and so passionately by anyone else.

'You have to imagine,' she said, 'what it was actually like in the evenings at the height of the Ripper crisis. Prostitutes only daring to go out in threes and fours, vigilantes patrolling, police numbers doubled and people being stopped and challenged at every corner. It truly was an unreal situation. During the day groups of well-to-do gentlemen were out seeking clues to the Ripper. Street urchins were offering to show tourists the murder sites for a fee, plus as many gory details as they could take, not all of them factual of course!'

Anna guided him around all the main murder sites plus a few others of interest. She started in George Yard outside the White Hart after their dinner. Although it had been renamed Gunthorpe Street and the building that Martha Tabram died in had been demolished, it still retained much of the grim atmosphere it had in the 1880s. They walked through, pausing at the site of George Yard buildings while Anna described the discovery of Martha's body on the stairwell in the poorly lit building.

Then she marched him the half mile or so east towards Durward Street, to the site where Polly Nichols lost her life in the road then known as Bucks Row. Pausing in the shadows, Anna pointed out the vast bulk of the Board School which had loomed over Polly and her attacker, and was still looming over Sam and Anna now. It was eerily possible to imagine the fear of Polly's last moments on the unforgiving slabs of the pavement at the entrance to a stable yard.

There were many tour groups that didn't make it down Durward Street as there was little to see. Also it was slightly off the beaten track, being the most easterly of the murder sites. Returning to the central area they saw tour groups being conducted on their nightly circuits of Whitechapel. This caused Sam some astonishment at the size of the Ripper industry. There was a compelling interest that drew thousands of people from all over the world, even after 120 years or more. They smiled at one group which numbered well over one hundred people, straggling along after their cheery guide. Sometimes they would turn a corner into a quiet dark street where the atmosphere was quite gripping. Sam could clearly imagine just how things were in the 1880s, whilst underlying it all was the futility, the poverty and the tragedy that pervaded the story.

From here Sam was taken to Henriques Street – known at the time as Berners Street – and the scene of Elizabeth Stride's murder in the entrance to Dutfields Yard. The area was now the site of a school and a brick wall ran across the entrance to the yard. This was the first in what became known as the double event, two brutal killings on the same evening within a short distance of each other. Anna was non-committal about the Dutfields Yard murder.

'The popular belief is that Elizabeth's attacker was interrupted before he was able to mutilate her body. She was the only one who had no abdominal injury so this adds weight to the case for interruption. The theory is that her frustrated attacker tried again, succeeding with Catherine Eddowes a short time later, when some horrible mutilation was inflicted. Of course, as always, there are other possibilities. Some people believe the double event to be a coincidence, with Catherine being a genuine Ripper victim and Elizabeth the subject of a domestic assault.'

'What's your verdict?' asked Sam curiously.

Anna shrugged, turning back to smile at him. 'You tell me. Of course you'll have to do your research first, and then you can argue for what you believe.'

During all this time, Angela's car wasn't far away. Using a technique of dropping and picking up her two passengers, she, Rees and John kept discreet tabs on the two. Darren was back home now resting, he had rightly predicted this as a Ripper walk and didn't feel it would reveal too much. He was working on his plan for tomorrow morning concerning *The Case-Book*. His team would have to be up and about early, with the exception of Rees who would be taking his turn to sleep in late.

Arriving at the busy and colourful Brick Lane, Anna pointed up to the top of the building facade of what was now a balti restaurant. The terracotta tiled logo which still survived bore the legend 'Ye Frying Pan' and showed two crossed frying pans which had given the former public house its name. The Frying Pan pub had lain in the heart of the Ripper's territory and there was no doubt that some of his victims, and probably he himself, had drunk there.

By now Sam was totally lost. He had kept a good sense of direction for a while but Anna's winding route and the dark, sometimes sinister streets had confused him. She told him they were back only yards from where they had started in Gunthorpe Street, before she sailed on up Brick Lane with its enticing restaurant smells, and into Hanbury Street.

Here they were to find the site of the murder of Annie Chapman. Number 29, in the backyard of which the murder took place, was long gone. Nowadays on this side of the road stood a dismal brick building covered with tired graffiti and tattered posters. Interestingly, Anna told him, Annie Chapman's murder featured the strange matter of her few possessions being arranged adjacent to her body. It was also notable for the fact that a female witness believed she had seen her talking with a man outside the house. Was that man Jack the Ripper? Was it actually

Annie Chapman she had seen? If so, this happened minutes before the murder took place in the rear yard, and may have been one of the only sightings of the Ripper. Another witness, a man in the yard next door, said he had heard voices through the fence. All he could swear to was the word 'no' and a little later the sound of something, or someone, falling against the fence. Were these Annie's last moments?

Though the site was impossible to relate to, immediately opposite there still remained some houses of the 1880s. Refurbished of course, some clearly showed the style of the street at that time, allowing Sam to visualise the scene. He imagined it in grainy black and white pictures of that period. It was difficult to visualise the Victorian world in colour.

Anna expounded her theories, telling Sam of her plan to produce a new account of the whole affair.

'There are loads of books about Jack the Ripper already,' she conceded, 'and a few that can be considered really definitive. But, there is always new evidence coming to light, and I really feel I could approach it from some new angles. Of course, if I can nail the murderer, that would be the icing on the cake. Then I'd really have the motivation to write it.'

Sam was honest in his response. He told her that she should do it; he was impressed both with her knowledge of the subject and her graphic descriptions of events.

After leaving Hanbury Street, Anna steered them to the Ten Bells pub on the corner of Fournier Street, another venue where prostitutes and their clients of the time drank and socialised. Even tonight, many people stood outside the pub, just as they would have all those years ago. Some things never really changed, Sam reflected. Just feet away was Christ Church, Spitalfields, built, like many other London churches, to try to counter the ungodliness that Christians felt was endemic in the area. The spire stood like a beacon above them, its outline unchanging through decades. Derelict for many years it was now lovingly restored and a wonderful haven from the busy streets around it.

They paused outside the Ten Bells while Anna described the locality of the most gruesome of the murders, that of Mary Kelly in her own room at Millers Court, Dorset Street.

'There's not much to see there so I'll tell you what I know first,' she said. Though often thought to be the final murder, when the killer had reached a peak of savagery, Anna was sceptical. They walked the few yards to visit what was left of the site. Once again the building was gone but Anna pointed out the tell-tale kerbstones that defined the old entrance to Millers Court. Mary had lived in a ground floor room at number thirteen, the number certainly proving unlucky for her.

Next they walked down and through Goulston Street the site of the infamous graffiti:

'The Juwes are the men that will not be blamed for nothing.'

This was where a piece of Catherine Eddowes bloodstained apron had been found, and that was what linked the message to her murder. The graffiti had been removed immediately on the orders of Sir Charles Warren, who had been concerned about the potential for civil unrest if it had been left in place.

Moving on they walked to Old Castle Street, where in Castle Alley, Alice McKenzie had met her terrible end. She was another of the disputed victims, though as Anna pointed out, the police who found her, and many people at the time, were convinced she was murdered by Jack the Ripper.

Continuing now in a southerly direction they crossed Whitechapel High Street and headed for the site where Frances Coles met her end. Hers was to be the last of the Whitechapel murders on file and in many people's opinion, she was not a Ripper victim at all. Anna said she had an open mind on this case, but told Sam that the killer was undoubtedly disturbed during the act and fled the scene. Frances was found by a policeman and was still just alive when he arrived. Following strict orders he remained with her even though he could hear the sound of a man walking away. The immediate site wasn't accessible, being a closed railway arch accommodating a private business, but the area still gave much of the atmosphere it would have had at the time.

The final stop on Anna's tour was Mitre Square, nowadays informally known as Catherine Eddowes Square, as witnessed by the stencil markings on the wall. It made an enduring tribute to Catherine. At night, and it was getting very late now, the square was still and silent. Somehow it really conveyed the atmosphere of fear and danger that it must have had so many years ago.

The stories Sam heard from Anna touched him, and now it all felt so real and tangible. Standing here in Mitre Square, just the two of them, he could hear the chirpy voice of Catherine Eddowes as she left the custody officer at the police station. Anna shivered involuntarily, it was late and cold.

Back on the main road they hailed a cab to the hotel, tired and without thoughts of being followed. They had seen nothing and felt that their escape via the back entrance of the hotel in Bloomsbury had lost their pursuers, at least for now. Unfortunately they were quite wrong. As their cab pulled into the hotel's drop off area, Angela's grey Toyota drove slowly past the end of the road, stopping just yards further on. The passenger door opened and Rees walked quickly back to the corner. He was just in time to observe the pair entering through the revolving glass doors.

Deciding against a nightcap they both made for their rooms, where, tired from their long day they were soon asleep. As Sam drifted off he remembered he still hadn't called Paige.

Damn it. What a weird day it had been, but a great evening!

Chapter 40

The Big Man in London

Whitechapel – 1889

The big man's routine had been changed recently and he had things to attend to, though some days he found it difficult to reconcile the interests of a double life. This was one of those days. It was an afternoon in late July and his occupation allowed him the freedom for his mission. Today he would meet his nephew again for an early dinner.

After some essential work was completed and lunch over, he decided to walk. He was a lover of sport and had been used to physical exertion, so the prospect pleased him. His route followed the Strand past the Royal Courts of Justice, opened a few years before, then through Fleet Street and Ludgate Hill, heading east. The man looked with interest at everything he passed. Observation was important in his profession and he had found that it paid dividends. Perhaps it was as well, he thought, that others were not as observant as he was. His walk continued out through the City to Aldgate. In the past the big man had few concerns about being attacked, but lately he had realised that people like himself could be perceived as a threat to Catholics. However, he wasn't a public figure so continued to walk unhindered by fear, relying on his anonymity.

As he left the bounds of the City, the environment changed suddenly and noticeably. Just yards away to his left lay Mitre Square and Houndsditch. Just beyond that the angular tower of St Botolph's church cast a long shadow in the afternoon sun. The public here appeared shabbier; when they did possess good clothing it had seen better days. He strode along confidently, seeing people about their business, a number of them wearing worried looks since the recent murder of Alice McKenzie. The event had brought a fresh crop of sightseers, keen to draw their own conclusions about the latest Whitechapel atrocity.

The previous and most shocking murder, that of Mary Kelly, had taken place in November last year. The months since then had convinced the public and police that the danger had finally passed. In the case of the police however, this had been based more on hope than judgement. Little could they imagine that another murder in the heart of Whitechapel would bear a similar signature to those of Jack the Ripper. Much effort was put into assuring the public that Alice's murder was unconnected. But many senior policemen and the eminent surgeon Thomas Bond were clear that the modus operandi was identical. The same sudden assault, the throat skilfully cut from left to right, and the lacerations to the abdomen. Albeit these were lighter ones, which could be accounted for by the attacker being disturbed. Commissioner James Monro, in temporary command of the police, had agreed it was the Ripper and immediately increased the numbers on patrol in Whitechapel yet again.

The big man had a very good mental map of the area, he had relatives who lived a little further out, and resolved to visit them soon. In addition he had pored over his street guide many times and had walked the ground. During his walk he sidestepped piles of rubbish, rotting vegetables and patches of slime, the origins of which were unknown and unspeakable.

His mind turned back to the Whitechapel murders and a slight smile twisted his features. The police had been predictable and his specialist knowledge told him that they would never catch the Ripper unless he decided to be caught. Many things had been recommended and tried already by Scotland Yard, from doubling patrols to drafting in hundreds of plain clothes police. Last year it had also been suggested that policemen should be dressed as women to act as decoys.

The proposal was that smaller and more effeminate constables would be chosen, provided they were capable types who could defend themselves and apprehend the killer. It hadn't been tried... yet. Perhaps now after the murder of Alice McKenzie it might. Suggestions had also been made that the killer was a woman but that idea had little currency amongst senior detectives. The details of walking beats were changed often but the killer seemed one jump ahead, one might almost think he was aware of police strategy. Once again, it was going to be a long night for those patrolling the district.

He paused to observe many of the alleyways he passed, thinking about these meandering rivers of filth and detritus. How they had gradually become the uncared for thoroughfares of the flotsam and jetsam of society, people who had nothing, aspired to nothing and would inevitably amount to nothing.

Since the disappearance of his brother the man had assumed a little responsibility for his nephew, left fatherless. Having spent time with the boy now that he was grown, he felt some affinity with him. He had clearly listened and understood the problems facing both his uncle and the country. Undoubtedly, he was still on the path he had been assigned during last year.

Eventually he arrived at their meeting place, they took dinner in a simple eating house and talked quietly while the big man looked around, ensuring there were no eavesdroppers. Despite a recent pause, his nephew was competent in his mission and had natural aptitude for the work. He possessed the family skills in secrecy and seemed comfortable with the ambiguity of a double life. The big man was satisfied that he had put the younger man on the right road to success, success that would have only one outcome.

By the middle of the evening the big man was sure he had done all that he could. Wishing the younger man well and handing him some money, he made his way back towards the West End. As dusk fell, he left behind the menacing streets of Whitechapel.

Chapter 41

The French Connection

Blackfriars, London – Present Day

The next thing Sam knew was someone banging loudly outside. Wondering for a moment just where the hell he was he grabbed the hotel dressing gown and opened his door. It was Anna. Bouncing in fully dressed, she brandished her mobile phone.

'Your friend Bernie got back to us, there's a copy in a shop in Cecil Court, they open at nine, oh and they want a lot of money for it, but I thought we might beat them down or something,' she finished lamely. She hadn't really thought about paying for it yet.

'That sounds good, give me a mo and I'll get myself together,' said Sam running a hand through his hair. Anna regarded the white towelling gown and his tousled blonde locks as if seeing him for the first time. Suddenly she remembered her friend Helen's comment about him being beautiful.

Mmm, actually he was.

'Okay fine, I'll see you downstairs,' she said, backing quickly out of the room.

Alighting from the Tube at Leicester Square they walked the few yards to Cecil Court. Most of the shops were still closed but a few others had their green metal shutters and gates open ready for business. Sam had been here before, finding the collection of bookshops much to his liking. Even when Charing Cross Road was busy, this quiet little haven with its green shop fronts made a pleasant place to browse in the centre of London.

It was nine twenty-five as they entered the shop. A middle-aged man with steel-rimmed glasses wished them a well spoken good morning. Sam asked him about the first edition *Case-Book* and a strange look came over the man's face.

'I'm sorry, I don't have it,' he said.

Anna's face fell. 'But my friend did an online check last night; you showed one as definitely available.'

'Yes of course, I'm sure, but I'm afraid it's gone, we have just sold it.'

'What? You mean today?' said Sam.

'Yes,' replied the man. 'I'm sorry if you've had a wasted journey, it's a real coincidence.'

'Isn't it just!' burst in Anna, swiftly interrupted by Sam who, smiling at the man, asked casually.

'Could you tell me who bought it?'

'It was a young man; well actually there were two of them. They were already waiting when I arrived to open up this morning.'

Sam turned to Anna and winked, hoping she would play along.

'I bet it was James, he always does this to me when we are both after a book.' Sam turned back to the man and asked what he looked like.

The shopkeeper did his best to describe them, stating they were under thirty, both in jeans, one with fair hair and a black fleece and one with dark hair and a brown leather jacket. Sam felt Anna's eyes boring into him as the man mentioned the jacket.

'Well thanks,' said Sam. 'It sounds as though it was James after all, I suppose he paid in cash, he usually does.'

'As a matter of fact,' said the man, 'he did.'

Leaving the shop they walked back towards Charing Cross Road. Anna was seething and could barely contain herself. 'The bastards, what's going on, Sam?'

Sam stopped. Shrugging, he looked carefully back along Cecil Court towards the St Martin's Lane end of the street.

'I just don't know, but there are clearly two things we need right now. Firstly a powwow about what we do next…'

'And?'

'Some breakfast, I'm starving.' He grinned.

The big smile made its first appearance that morning. 'Me too,' she acknowledged.

Seated over breakfast in the corner of a cafe just off Leicester Square they discussed the latest development. Anna was demolishing a second bacon sandwich with her coffee. Where did she put it all? Sam wondered. The chilling realisation dawned on them that Anna's email was being monitored. The only contact regarding their need for another first edition of *The Case-Book* had been with Bernie by email yesterday. They were quite sure any conversations in the hotel vaults last night were not overheard. There had been no-one around in there at the time.

'These guys are professionals, we can't really hope to keep ahead of them,' declared Sam. 'This is getting serious, they have resources and know how to play these games and we don't. They are probably watching us now. We can only use your mobile for things that don't matter from now on. I always thought mobiles were a problem, now I know they are!'

'Worse than that,' said Anna, 'we can't use it at all, they can track where it is.'

'Of course, I was a bit slow there,' agreed Sam.

Things went silent for moment; they glanced carefully around the cafe. 'I think we need to meet Steve, my college friend. I used to think he was paranoid but now I see what bothers him about surveillance. If anyone can help us, he can,' said Anna.

'That's fine, but they know about him, he emailed you back didn't he?'

'True,' she returned, 'but he didn't say anything, only to meet at the old place when we could, it's actually a pub in Hammersmith we used as students, but they don't know that. He is probably there most lunchtimes, if we could shake them off first.'

'Okay, but how do we lose them?' Sam looked out through the glass cafe door, seeing no-one suspicious, though he didn't really expect to.

Anna had the bit between her teeth now.

'I'll tell you where we can meet Steve, then we split up so it's harder to follow both of us. We make our own way there, stopping and waiting from time to time to see if we are being chased. If one of us thinks we are, then don't arrive at the venue until we are sure we have shaken them off.' Anna looked past Sam, comprehension dawning in her eyes. 'This cafe has two exits; we can go different ways from here,' she chirped triumphantly.

Sam looked around, they had left Cecil Court and entered Bear Street from Charing Cross Road, but there was another door into Cranbourn Street which led back towards the Tube station.

Sam cautiously nodded his agreement. He wasn't entirely happy about separating from Anna, but knew she would absolutely hate the idea of him being protective. 'You're right, so how will I know Steve if I'm there first?'

The brown eyes bored into him again. 'Five feet ten, round face, short dark hair, drinking real ale. But I'll probably be there before you anyway.' She smiled sweetly.

Looking around again Anna moved closer and quietly gave the name and address of the pub to Sam. For a moment he became acutely aware of her perfume and felt her warm breath on his ear. She leaned away, then suddenly moved in close again, the perfume was back and this time her breast brushed his arm.

'It's about eight or nine stops on the Tube,' she whispered. 'You try that way and I'll get a taxi or something.'

They stood up to go, Sam looked at Anna. 'Take care,' he said briefly.

'You too.' The wide smile returned. 'Last one there is a numpty.'

Sam walked fast, making straight for the Tube station as though he had no idea he was watched. A few yards away in Leicester Square, John, in his black fleece, was galvanised into action. Without taking his eyes from Sam's back he rang Darren. 'They've separated, where are you?'

Darren's voice came back immediately. 'I'll be there in five.'

Starting to follow Sam, John mouthed into his mobile. 'I'd better stick with Blondie; can you try and find Baby Blue?' As he walked past the cafe he glanced inside. There was no sign of Anna. 'Sod it,' he said.

Sam sped quickly down the stairs, a plan already forming in his mind. As he reached the Piccadilly Line platform a train pulled in, he got straight on, then looked out behind him as others boarded. Several people got on including Black Fleece who was one carriage back. The train pulled out immediately. Within seconds it seemed they were slowing at

Piccadilly Circus, where Sam left the train and walked towards the exit. Black Fleece followed slowly, keeping his distance. Sam walked away as though going towards the street exit, then casually swung around and returned to the same platform. He looked unconcerned but fought his instincts to look back; he was sure now the guy in the fleece would be close behind him. John realised that Blondie was trying to lose him and things were going to get more difficult.

Déjà vu, thought Sam as he leisurely boarded the next train, turning casually as he did so and seeing Black Fleece out of the corner of his eye further down the platform. This time Sam waited till the train reached Hyde Park Corner, then when the doors opened he leapt off and sprinted towards the exit. Knowing rather than seeing the man behind him, Sam suddenly appeared to change his mind, turned and walked back the way he had come. Black Fleece had nowhere to go, so he walked on past Sam who then literally ran back, squeezing through the doors of the same train just before they shut behind him.

The satisfying hiss of the Tube doors closing sounded just like the 'Yeess' Sam silently expelled as John realised he had been beaten. Sam could hardly believe he had tricked a professional but was under no illusion that he had won the game. He felt like the guy in *The French Connection* film who had pulled a similar trick all those years ago. Beginner's luck, he thought soberly, suddenly wondering what had become of Anna.

Anna's journey had been surprisingly simple. Leaving through the other door of the cafe she walked back down Charing Cross Road to St Martin-in-the-Fields where she got in the first taxi she came across. As they pulled away she looked behind them, scanning for anyone who looked as though they might have been following. She saw nothing. Once they got away from the Trafalgar Square area she asked the cabbie if they were being followed.

'Who are you then, luv, MI5?' The cabbie smiled, then, 'Do you want me to find out for you?'

'Yes please,' said Anna. Immediately the cab took a left turn into a side street, the cabbie watching carefully in his rear view mirror. He then made a right turn, then a left, then another right and slowed down in a long quiet road, still watching behind them. Nothing appeared in his mirror and he made another left, then a right followed by a final right before joining the road they had originally been on.

'Absolutely nothing, luv,' the cabbie smiled in his mirror at Anna. 'You're safe to meet James Bond as planned.'

'Thanks, I really appreciate it.' Anna dished out his reward, the big grin lighting up his rear view mirror, and settled back with a sigh of relief.

In the meantime Angela had dropped Darren on Charing Cross Road and he walked swiftly through into Leicester Square.

'Stay close, I'll call soon,' he said. They tried to keep a car nearby for surveillance, though in London it was often public transport and cabs that made getting around easier. Angela planned to circuit the vicinity and wait nearby until contacted, her ID allowing her to park pretty much anywhere she wanted. She pulled the Toyota into a loading bay outside an arcade of tacky little shops. This would do for the moment, she was only a block away from Darren. If he stayed in the Charing Cross Road area she would probably be facing the right way to pick him up. She looked down at the passenger seat where Darren had left his newly acquired copy of *The Case-Book*. Yawning, Angela switched the radio on low, propping her mobile upright in the centre console.

Darren realised he should have anticipated a split, although as the two targets had been together for some forty-eight hours now they seemed to be inseparable.

Fuck it, this pair are getting tricky now, he thought. They had nearly lost them at Bloomsbury yesterday, only picking them up again through sheer luck. Mind you, the girl would use her phone soon, he was certain. They always did. 'Girls and their phones,' he muttered with derision. The tracking device was still in a pocket of Anna's overnight bag at the Crowne Plaza. They would go back to the hotel later at some point, even if only for their bags, he was certain.

Pulling out his phone he called Rees who was off duty, still asleep, his phone on silent.

'We've lost Baby Blue,' he announced to the message service. 'John is on Blondie's case; call me when you are up.'

Darren quartered the area thoroughly, all of Leicester Square as far as Piccadilly and then a section of Charing Cross Road. Finally he called Angela then wandered down toward St Martin-in-the-Fields for a coffee.

Chapter 42
A Friend in Need

Hammersmith, London – Present Day

As Sam entered the bar Anna half rose to greet him, for a split second a look of concern had filled her eyes, but almost immediately the big smile appeared like sunshine.

'Sam, this is Steve,' she said. 'I'll get you a drink while you say hello.' Sam knew better than to argue with her. Eying up the beers available he made his choice and turned to Steve. By the time she returned they were talking generally about the Internet.

Anna picked up the conversation on a practical note. 'Steve, if they are watching us what can we do?'

Steve held his finger up to his lips. 'We need to make sure you're clean,' he said. 'Your handbags may have been bugged which means they know where you are now.'

Sam eyed Anna's massive handbag playfully. 'There could be any number of bugs in there and we'd never know about it.'

Anna looked frostily at him for a second then hooted with laughter, tossing her hair in his direction. 'Steve, can you see what I have to put up with?'

Steve volunteered to help them search, tipping Sam's man bag out onto the table. Anna was suddenly reticent, remembering what might be in hers that she wouldn't want these guys to see.

'Hmm, I'll do my own if you don't mind,' she said turning to the next table and shielding the contents with her body. It took quite a while to work her way through the stuff, as Steve and Sam exchanged a humorous knowing glance. Having checked carefully she shovelled everything back into her bag and zipped it with relief. Steve pronounced Sam's bag as clean, then sent them both to the toilets to check their clothing.

Returning to the table they felt free to talk openly. Anna gave Steve a potted version of what had happened to them so far, ending up by saying that with any luck they had lost their followers for now.

'Yes, there is just one problem with that,' said Steve. 'You used one of my email addresses to contact me, they could easily find my home, it's a piece of cake for these guys. Though fortunately there's no reason to link us with this place.'

Anna looked around the pub nervously, but no-one had entered since Sam and it was a quiet at the moment.

'From now on you must assume that everything you do is being watched, obviously phones and computers are out. Of course, they will pick you up again. People don't stay lost for long. Also you need to leave your mobiles switched off, and take out the batteries and SIM cards.'

Anna cooed, laughing, 'Sam doesn't have one.' Steve turned to Sam with an old fashioned look on his face, was there anyone who didn't have a mobile? There might be somewhere perhaps; Steve was picturing some old lady who lived in a care home in Brighton.

Sam grinned back at him. 'Long story, I'll tell you one day,' he said. Meanwhile, Anna got busy taking her phone apart and dropping the components in her bag.

Steve started to relay facts and information. He had a slow calm manner, the sort of guy who wouldn't be ruffled by much. Before speaking he would pause, carefully weighing up what he was going to say. His comments had little embellishment, and immediately Sam felt that he was hearing the truth from him. Anna had known him and his wife for some years at university and had kept in touch, though not understanding his commitment to civil liberties.

On the Tube journey Sam had imagined Steve might be a Rainbow Warrior, idealistic, heart in the right place, dreadlocks, and a career in protesting about pretty much anything. The reality could not have been more different. Steve was a married man with young children, conventionally dressed, a software designer, and a deep thinker, concerned about the society he lived in and selective about the causes he supported.

His study of civil liberties went back to his student days. Steve's main activity nowadays was online, contributing to networks supporting free speech and the exposure of establishment cover-ups. He acted for several such websites as technical engineer on a no fee basis. All in all Steve was quite a traditionalist who valued his way of life and wished it to continue. Sam liked him immediately.

'There is an inner establishment in Britain, but of course it's not a formalised thing. It's based on a set of beliefs and interests that want to preserve certain doctrines. The things they want to protect include their version of democracy, both houses of parliament, the monarchy, the secret services and the police forces, which supply the executive arm of the establishment. Particularly the police's special departments! It's simply a gentle infiltration of services at a senior level, rather like a set of terrorist cells. Everything is done informally; casual remarks are made to test people's affiliations and the 'right sort' of people are cultivated. There is no actual membership of course, nor is anything in writing.

'These people aren't all bad of course. Think about it from the other side, Sam. When we see governments collapse abroad, and military coups or radical revolutions, they seem to come out of the blue. Even natural events can trigger a breakdown in culture. Look at the New Orleans flood disaster, a small step from normality to near anarchy. It indicates that the notion of a civilised society is just a veneer, and frightening changes can happen almost without warning. A moment of madness through people power could change the community, and might install some disastrous or repressive regime. That could happen here quite easily, though most of us find it impossible to imagine.'

Steve went on slowly. 'Perhaps these people feel that keenly and are simply acting to head off any likely problems. Many see threats in everything around them and their paranoia is easily spread to others. The root fear is an overthrow of the government by some unnamed and fearsome alternative. The foot soldiers following you are just that, foot soldiers. They don't have a personal agenda but have been told to keep tabs on you by their boss and perhaps, frustrate your attempts to do whatever it is you are doing. As far as the guardians are concerned, the end justifies the means. Their objective is always to keep things as they are, change worries them.'

'Give me an example,' Sam said.

Steve nodded and paused carefully. 'I went along to a climate change protest in London a while ago and watched some coach parties arriving. Amongst them were retired pensioners, even a vicar. The police tactics were to try and intimidate them as they got off their coaches. Many of the police were dressed in full riot gear which depersonalises them, they look like Robocop and they take on the character. Again of course they are just foot soldiers following instructions, but you feel you are dealing with a machine, not a human being.

Some officers filmed everyone, using their cameras blatantly, almost into people's faces. Those officers will have been from one of the secret units, busy adding to their database. Because they have facial recognition software they can film people in crowds, then confirm their attendance at different events. It was like a movie of some Third World dictatorship in action. Most of the folk arriving were quite shocked. They weren't touched physically of course, but implicit in the encounter, was an unspoken threat. You are not welcome here; you are now known to us and at risk of arrest etc., etc.'

Steve paused again. 'Remember, these people hadn't done anything wrong. They were arriving to join a demo which was entirely lawful. It's the insecurity of the guardians which makes them view any sort of protester as a threat to the status quo.'

'Why do they do this then?'

Steve considered again before speaking. 'Because they can is the simple answer, and they have the ability to do so. Most security forces are organised in such a way that accountability can be shuffled off in various directions if it needs to be. Some appalling events have taken place in recent years. Penning in of protesters without allowing them to disperse or find a toilet, assaults on members of the public in demonstrations, with sometimes fatal consequences. Also the deliberate covering up of police number badges, I could go on and on. But we must keep it in perspective of course, this is nothing compared to most countries in the world today.'

'What organisations are allowed to do surveillance?' said Anna.

'You should know that doing your job shouldn't you?' said Steve.

She wrinkled her face. 'I've never thought about it; of course my company does surveillance all the time, legally I hope!'

Steve pondered her original question before replying. He told them that there were several organisations capable of doing this, the secret intelligence service MI6, the security service MI5, Counter Terrorism Command, and the National Public Order Intelligence Unit. There were close links between all of these, formal and, more significantly, informal.

'However, there is little doubt that the people conducting surveillance on you are either from CTC or more probably the NPOIU. They are a highly secretive unit which used to answer only to the Association of Chief Police Officers, but now report to the Metropolitan Police. They work out of a base at New Scotland Yard. In addition to surveillance and intimidation, they have sent officers underground to infiltrate different groups. Sometimes they stay for long periods in order to establish trust.'

Steve went on slowly.

'This is their style. These are the people who are responsible for gathering intelligence on, and acting against, political parties, trade union activists, as well as animal rights, and anti-globalisation groups both here and in Europe.'

Anna, who had been patiently waiting, chimed in indignantly. 'Aren't these operations only supposed to be carried out against extremists?' she said.

Steve looked up from his drink, nodding.

'Yes, that's exactly what their guidelines say. Of course one man's extremism is another man's normality and freedom, or woman's of course,' added Steve, smiling at Anna. 'How can anyone measure it?'

'So how could a Ripperologist come to be so dangerously subversive?' asked Sam, smiling a little as he observed Anna's reaction to this description of her.

'Well, Ripperologists who demonstrated they were getting to the bottom of the mystery might be monitored, at least on a loose basis, when nothing more important is happening,' Steve pronounced. 'Look, I'm no Ripperologist, it's too exciting for me,' he joked. 'But I can view it as an outsider and see what security risks might arise in the guardian's minds.' He paused again.

'There are two clear prongs to this that come to mind initially. Firstly, any association with royalty or a senior political figure would spook them. Any proof of involvement by such a person would be destroyed, and the people with the proof would be publicly discredited by any means available. This would be in order to protect the establishment from scandal, of course.'

He looked at Anna apologetically. 'They could do that quite easily, I'm afraid. There are many people who would see it as a clear threat to the establishment and would fear the rise of republicanism. Obviously to the guardians that would be unthinkable.

Secondly, the Metropolitan Police came in for tremendous criticism over their impotence at catching the criminal – and ever since. They are very prickly about their reputation. We only have to think about a few high profile failures in recent years. Now that the National Public Order Intelligence Unit reports to the Met, that would fit quite nicely. Anyway, you guys know much more about Ripper politics than I do I'm sure.'

'Yes,' Anna took up the conversation eagerly. 'I see what you mean on both counts, Steve. In addition to being a suspect the Duke of Clarence was rumoured to have been caught in a raid at a brothel with other establishment figures. The Met was supposed to have hushed that up on orders from the Home Secretary. In fact the Duke certainly wasn't the Ripper, even if there may have been other unsavoury aspects to his life. But the Met certainly did get a bashing over the Whitechapel murders with senior officers falling over themselves to defend their own reputations and that of the police in general. Some wondered privately if the killer had inside information from Scotland Yard, their greatest fear being that the Ripper would turn out to be a policeman. An unwritten rule of the service imposed a code of silence. It meant that one never criticised the organisation for being incompetent, even after leaving. The unwritten rule is well documented by senior people like Robert Anderson in their memoirs, most of which are self-congratulatory, even though they didn't catch the Ripper!'

Anna stopped in mid flow, looking puzzled. 'Actually, there's one thing I don't get, Steve. Lots of Ripperologists are definitely serving or ex-policemen. It's hardly criminal stuff is it?'

'No of course not, but they're not political. They're just guys like you, they're detectives who want to solve the mystery and love a puzzle. Naturally if any of them made waves or came up with any inconvenient proof, they might also get the treatment you're experiencing.'

Sam wanted to know more about the code of silence in the Met that Anna had mentioned.

Steve nodded again. 'It's still very much there today,' he observed. 'The Met don't talk out of school even if they are aware of unethical acts by colleagues. It's a somewhat perverted code of honour, but unfortunately it doesn't help justice. Of course, now and again they will hang someone out to dry because they have no choice, or the press have fingered someone. This actually makes them look as though they are extracting rotten apples, and then the problem is over. The world soon moves on.'

After a long swallow, finishing his beer, Steve continued. 'It's not just Ripperologists naturally, they're probably small fry.' He grinned at Anna. 'But people who promote civil liberties, high profile celebrities who are "outspoken lefties", trade union officials and, even humble website nerds like me can be monitored. I don't flatter myself that my Internet traffic is being monitored all the time; it's only when something big is brewing, some national demonstration or something.'

Steve smiled, modestly down-playing his own role.

'These people see potential republicans overthrowing the monarchy, and even the Government. Sometimes they may be right to worry. Occasionally perhaps we come close without knowing it. Think about the opposition to the war in Iraq, and before that the death of Diana, Princess of Wales. Also, in the past, petrol price demo organisers have certainly been intimidated and monitored closely.'

Sam chimed in. 'Surely the police and others need to get warrants to tap phones and computers, don't they?'

Steve picked up his empty glass and studied it regretfully.

'That's what we read in the papers, yes. But think about it. Even newspapers can easily arrange intrusive surveillance when they want to, unofficially of course. We now know that don't we? It's not just a rogue reporter, though that's what they wanted us to think originally. They have been shown to have accessed phones incredibly easily, especially mobiles. Think what can happen in the security services where they have sophisticated equipment to hand, and are in a unit that is virtually unaccountable. When your boss says use it, you use it, it happens all the time. It's often simply a matter of routine, particularly at sensitive times.

'The rules say that in serious cases authority must be sought from the Secretary of State, but in many other cases decisions are taken internally, decided by a senior officer. The rules say a level of security appropriate to the degree of intrusiveness, whatever that might mean.'

Steve continued. 'A number of past Home Secretaries have stated that they don't know what really goes on within the security services, and perhaps more worrying, they don't want to. In other words, they suspect dirty doings but politically can't afford to know about them. The security services can do pretty much what they want, and conceal it if they have to. That's the nature of secrecy, the end justifies the means.'

Feeling tired, Anna silently went to get more beers.

As soon as she had gone Steve leaned forward and motioned Sam closer. He spoke urgently, but still slowly and deliberately. 'Sam, I've only just met you, but you must understand this could become a bit dangerous. I don't want to alarm Anna too much but you should be careful. Because I don't know the full implications of your enquiries I can't say if any direct action is likely. Unfortunately, accidents can be made to happen. Anna is a great friend of Jenna's and mine and I don't want to see her in any danger.'

'Direct action? What's that?'

'Well it's very unlikely that they'll use violence, but anything could happen if someone is really on your case. Probably you may just experience intense intimidation. You see, the watchers often want you to know they're there. Intimidation has a purpose, to scare you off. Ordinary people are soon cowed if they are being stalked and menaced by someone.'

Sam pondered everything he had heard. It sounded very sinister, a world away from the society he thought he lived in.

Steve leaned back. 'Ah, more beer, just what we needed,' he said as Anna arrived.

'You can get the next round, I feel like a waitress,' she shot back at them.

Steve offered to take them to his place to stay, but felt that after Anna's email to him, they would probably be located quite easily if they did so.

The three of them debated what Sam and Anna should do. It seemed they had given the slip to their pursuers at the moment, but couldn't stay hidden for long. Also, Anna desperately wanted to get a copy of *The Case-Book* to decode the message. Obviously they couldn't communicate with Bernie again about bookshops, so needed a completely fresh avenue.

'It's getting late,' Steve said. 'This pub has rooms and you've lost the watchers at the moment, so why not stay here for the night? I can meet you in the morning and we can work out what you do from here on.'

'Good idea.' Anna nodded. She and Sam went to the bar to ask if they had any rooms free. The woman said there was only one available tonight, a double. Sam glanced sidelong at Anna, who stared straight ahead.

'Can we see it please?' she said decisively.

'Of course,' the woman said. She picked a key from a row of hooks behind the bar. 'Through that door, upstairs and it's on the right, room three.'

Anna led the way. It was a spacious room with a bathroom, a large window overlooking the street and something she had hoped for, a sofa under the window. She looked in the bathroom and glanced around the room.

'Could you manage on there?' She gestured to the sofa.

'Yes, but we don't have to. You can take this room and I'll find somewhere else,' Sam replied.

'There's no need. It's getting late. You don't know the area and there really isn't much around here. We'll be fine... if you don't mind sharing that is.' She looked directly at him for the first time since their conversation with Steve.

'Of course not.'

They returned to the bar, paid for the room and rejoined Steve, who announced that he was going home. He said he would do some thinking and bring his laptop in the morning to show them more stuff they needed to know. Warning them both to be careful, he left them alone in the pub to confer.

Sam and Anna swapped notes on their respective journeys to the pub, Sam playing down his new found skills in dodging the guy on the Tube.

At this moment at least they felt they had definitely eluded their pursuers. Anna glanced at her watch.

'There's a few shops down the road, as we don't have any stuff I'll just go and get some bits. Anything you want?' she said.

'A razor would be good,' said Sam, fingering his stubble, 'but watch out.'

She nodded. 'I will, why don't you have a look at the menu? Plus of course work out where we go from here.'

Chapter 43

Room at the Inn

Hammersmith, London – Present Day

Anna had no concerns about sharing the room with Sam. She knew what he was, a decent guy who wouldn't try to take advantage of a situation. Nearby she found a M&S open late. She picked toothpaste and brushes, a green and a black one. None of that one pink, one blue nonsense, she thought. She bought Sam a razor, shaving gel and deodorant, a big tee shirt she could use as a nightie and some black underwear for herself. Then she went to find some for him.

Scanning the racks, some dark blue silky trunks caught her eye. There was a hunk on the packet. Unsmiling, he brooded, stubbly and dark with an impossible six pack. He oozed that bad boy attitude that women love. She fingered the stretchy Lycra material absentmindedly; then chose medium sized and tossed them in her basket. Perhaps it was the hunk who sold it to her. It was the first time she had ever bought underwear for a man, and she found that she was quite enjoying the idea.

'I could make a habit of this,' she muttered, turning away.

Meanwhile, Sam was deep in thought. It was while Anna was shopping that he realised that James from the Mystery Club might be able to help them. They needed a vintage *Case-Book*; James was a dealer and had his fingers on the rare book pulse. When it came to obtaining books either James or Clive at The Final Chapter were the men. James and his wife Beth were close to Sam and lived in Minstead where Sam had been brought up.

I should have thought to ask his advice first, Sam thought. It's not likely he is being monitored in any way. I'll give him a call from here; he'll know where I can get a first edition.

Sam used the pay phone in the pub and Beth picked up straight away. She passed the phone to James who listened intently as Sam gave him a sanitised version of events, telling him that Anna and he were in London and needed to locate a first edition copy of *The Case-Book of Sherlock Holmes* most urgently. He emphasised it had to be a first edition, nothing else would do.

A smile spread over James's face as he listened. 'You came to the right man didn't you?' he said, not quite able to conceal the pride in his voice.

'You don't mean... You've actually got one?' Sam stuttered.

'Of course,' said James delightedly, then unable to resist, 'I'll let you have it for a very reasonable price. As you know, I am a poor man!'

'You bastard,' Sam laughed, then quickly added, 'It was Holmes speaking to the Duke of Holdernesse.'

'Sam, what are you banging on about?' James had absolutely no idea what Sam meant; unaware that he was paraphrasing Sherlock Holmes' words from 'The Adventure of the Priory School'. Had it been Paige of course, the quote would have been carefully chosen to drop into the conversation.

'No, no, no, forget it, just forget it, James. Look, we have to see the book urgently; can we come down later tomorrow?'

'Why not? We'd love to meet the mysterious Anna.'

'Thanks, friend, just keep the book safe will you?'

Hanging up, Sam went smiling back to his seat and picked up the pub menu.

Returning from her shopping, Anna looked tired and pale but when Sam told her about their stroke of luck she visibly lit up with excitement, firing more questions, this time wanting to know all about James and Beth, his books and where he lived. She slipped a carrier bag with Sam's shopping onto the seat beside him.

The pair had dinner in the pub and talked till late, delaying going to their room. They split the bed covers between the sofa and the bed, and then Anna used the bathroom while Sam sat on the sofa, peering out at the street below. Nobody was about, a street lamp shone almost opposite and nothing much moved. He could hear the shower hissing gently behind the closed door. She came out wearing her new underwear and tee shirt, sat on the far side of the bed and swung her legs under the covers in one smooth movement. Sam didn't see any of it; he was still watching the street.

He took a shower himself, enjoying the hot water on his body; it was soft water and felt silky, unlike the hard water area he lived in. It wasn't the sort of hotel that had dressing gowns, so he ripped the blue trunks from the brooding hunk's packaging and slipped them on. Then he tried to settle on the sofa. Their murmured goodnights sounded subdued.

Neither of them slept easily at first. There was an awful lot on their minds.

Anna thought about the bizarre situation they were in, trying to stay one jump ahead of some secret police force. Then there was the mystery of the Doyle code that she hadn't yet cracked. It seemed so near and yet so far, did it lead to Jack the Ripper? Or was it something totally unconnected? The things that Steve had said this afternoon, did they really happen in Britain today?

Overlaying all of that, they were two young people sharing a room overnight. They had all shared rooms as students regardless of gender, though usually there were more than just two of them. Anna knew Sam wouldn't make a move, and she wasn't sure if she wanted him to or not. Definitely no, actually, it wasn't the time or place. He was good looking but that wasn't enough. She needed to be romanced, and not in some London pub. They were being chased and she wanted to be free of secret police watching her. But nevertheless she was glad he was in the room with her.

The light filtered dimly through the old flower patterned curtains from the street lamp outside. Sighing softly she turned gently over for the umpteenth time, eventually falling asleep.

Sam also ran over events in his mind. The questions couldn't be answered; they would have to see this through until it was resolved one way or another. Anna was asleep, he heard heavy breathing from the double bed and grinned inwardly, that could be exaggerated into a snore to tease her about one day... if he dared!

His mind turned to the present moment and he gave a wry smile, it reminded him of the films we had all watched, where the scene was played out. It was a cliché of course, the male and female leads, on the run, sharing a room. The guy would be on the sofa, which was never comfortable. There was always sexual tension, and the camera showed us they were both lying awake. There were numerous versions in the movies. Sometimes they ended up making love, often they didn't, perhaps they just cuddled. Maybe they woke in the morning and just smiled at each other. It depended how corny the movie was, but it was always a great scene to include.

Sam felt the same as he had in the Bloomsbury hotel. He wasn't going to try his luck with Anna. Beautiful though she was, her prickly temperament didn't encourage one to try. Who needs the inevitable put down? Anyway, these certainly weren't the circumstances for either love or lust. Eventually exhaustion triumphed and he too slept deeply for what remained of the night.

When Steve turned up they all enjoyed a pub breakfast. Steve unsheathed his laptop and showed them a few articles from websites and national newspapers. He gave them a rundown on some of the latest comments, reading from his screen.

'About the National Public Order Intelligence Unit that I mentioned yesterday. They keep secret files on individuals and refuse to say how many there are, or who they are. We know the database runs to thousands. Undoubtedly some innocent people do get tagged as "of interest to NPOIU" they may have no criminal record but have merely attended a protest meeting of some sort.'

'These characters of interest, just what sort of people are we talking about?' said Sam.

'How long have you got?' Steve grinned. 'As I said yesterday, it largely began with trade union strikers like the miners, and animal rights activism, but those areas have receded a little so lots of other people are now of interest. They could be anti-hunting, possibly from the Green movement, petrol price activists, or anyone who organises protests of pretty much any sort. Radical students, climate change demonstrators, Heathrow runway protestors, left or right wing celebrities who tweet any serious political comment. Anti-anything people, the list goes on.

'The guardians, as I like to call them, also instigated a change in the terminology used by the police to describe the actions of protesters, lawful or otherwise. They are now involved in monitoring "domestic extremism", a deliberately unquantifiable description, which doesn't have any status in a legal sense. This terminology has been adopted during the last few years. Of course it gives licence to carry out covert surveillance on pretty much anyone that the guardians wish to. The nationwide network of automatic number plate recognition cameras (ANPR) are used to log sightings of any registrations that are flagged as "of interest" to the NPOIU. These are then added to their database, so they know where people travel to.'

Steve brought it back to Anna and Sam's situation.

'As we said yesterday, this is where Ripper researchers might come in for two reasons. One, the Royal connection rears its ugly head now and again, the poor old Duke of Clarence won't go away! Two, that the Met might have covered up their own Ripper findings. Either scenario being proven would probably finish one of them for good, even today. Unthinkable isn't it?'

Sam felt better after breakfast and his mischievousness had returned. 'I'm glad I'm not a Ripperologist, it's safer to be a boring writer who likes sculpture,' he said, needling Anna, who tossed her curls and snorted, not deigning to reply.

Steve smiled at the banter between them, then showed them more stuff on his laptop.

'It's not very interesting but here's a definition of "covert surveillance". Its status is governed by the Regulation of Investigatory Powers Act and it's broken down by the Home Office into three main types.' Steve grinned at them.

'I'll put it in layman's terms... *Intrusive Surveillance* – may take place in people's homes or vehicles, bugging, filming, etc. *Directed Surveillance* – watching people in public places to gather private information about them by following, filming, etc. The sort of thing councils do to trap benefit cheats. Lastly, *Covert Human Intelligence Sources* – just gobbledegook for going undercover to gain information. It could be either an officer or a paid informer. Each year there are four to five thousand cases of surveillance of one sort or another. Takes some believing doesn't it?'

Steve continued. 'Of course most of the press aren't particularly interested; the only bit they like is whether the undercover officer has sex to get information. The salacious details are of much more interest than anything else, and it sells more papers.'

Steve reckoned Sam and Anna were being subjected to both directed and intrusive surveillance, and warned them accordingly. He spent much of the morning with them, matching Anna's caffeine intake cup for cup. By midday they were ready to go. In the event they decided to forget their overnight bags, they could contact the hotel later and ask them to hold their stuff.

Anna was taking another look at the number sheet and the partially completed note from the British Library, she studied them with a frown on her face.

CONFESSED AS GUIL

She was desperate now to get back on to her quest. Steve stood up to go. Anna hugged him warmly and promised to keep him informed about what happened next. Sam shook his hand, thanking him for the way he had opened up a whole new world for them. Anna folded the number sheet and the notebook page and slid them into her front jeans pocket. Picking up the massive handbag, her body language was saying it all. Let's go. Their next move would be to get back to Waterloo and take a train down to Southampton, where Sam would take her to see James and *The Case-Book*. It was to be a fateful decision.

Chapter 44

Bagged on a Train

London – Present Day

Darren sat outside Pret a Manger scowling at the coffee in front of him, waiting for John to return. Receiving John's phone call earlier he had gone straight to the Leicester Square cafe, arriving moments after John had left tailing Sam, only to find that Anna had disappeared. After his abortive search of the area Darren decided that coffee was necessary. Later, John phoned again, reporting that Blondie had evaded him. Darren knew John had had little choice when the couple split. The orders were to follow and watch, intervening only to try and prevent Blondie and Baby Blue from receiving materials or other information they tried to access. He phoned Angela and told her to stand down but to stay near the car and be ready for a call. Next he reported the latest development to his control, who told Darren to stay on it and to call in later.

It seemed that Blondie and Baby Blue now knew they were being tailed, and that was a shame. It was going to happen sooner or later and it meant the gloves were off, he could now try a little warning or two. He might have lost them for a while but that didn't trouble him too much. They couldn't stay off his radar for very long. Darren had a lot of thinking to do, and this was his opportunity. He looked skywards as he first considered what had happened since he had been assigned to this task. He mentally reviewed the surveillance yet again, starting with London. The couple had met, seemingly for the first time and had just spent hours talking. Then there had been John and Angela's separate day trips to Southampton. John had seen them discussing documents in the shopping centre cafe, then they had talked a lot more and walked around the town as well.

He was absolutely sure that Angela was right; the girl was after information. The break-in to Blondie's car at Southsea had revealed nothing. They knew who he was and what he did for a living. He was a writer who lectured sometimes and knew a lot about Victorian and Edwardian times. Christ, how exciting, thought Darren cynically. It was obvious now that the guy had just been working in Southsea that day.

The incident at the British Library came next, what was it they were trying to do? When they left he had examined *The Case-Book of Sherlock Holmes*. He had scanned each story quickly, drawing a blank, there was nothing relevant about Jack the Ripper or the Metropolitan Police. The book contained no handwritten messages, or marks of any sort. Reluctantly it had been given back into the care of the library. There was something in that book though... he now had another copy, it was in the car but he saw little point in wading through those old stories again. Darren recalled that Baby Blue had some papers she used in Southampton and in the library. He needed to see those papers. Perhaps a little theft or intimidation might now be helpful.

Finally, he turned his thoughts to how they would regain contact with them, reasoning that they would probably go to the hotel where their bags were, or use the train network to get wherever they were going next. There was also the likelihood that the girl might use her phone again at any time. Blondie never seemed to use one. That was a bit weird, Darren thought. What was the guy up to? He looked up and spoke as John approached his table looking apologetic.

'Forget it, mate. Get a coffee and go over to the Crowne Plaza again. Their bags are still there, and I want to know when they turn up or check out. Find out from the desk staff.'

'Okay, what about you?' John said.

'I'll be at Waterloo, keep in touch.'

Sam and Anna took the Tube back to central London, changing to the Northern Line for the last few stops before Waterloo. When they arrived at the station Anna declared her intention to freshen up while Sam bought coffees to go. Returning with fresh lipstick, she spotted a sandwich kiosk and rushed off to get one.

'You must be starved, you poor dear, I'll get you a baguette to keep you going.' She delivered it back, but not before consuming almost half of it first.

'Whose baguette?' grinned Sam.

'Yours of course, I'm just testing it for you,' she laughed at him.

Darren watched from the gallery vantage point, his lip curling up as his reasoning about their movements proved to be correct. He phoned Angela then came down to join Rees who was waiting on the concourse below. They both boarded the 16.05 train for Weymouth, a couple of coaches behind Sam and Anna.

This was a fairly quiet train, perhaps the last one of the afternoon before swarms of commuters would take over. Sam and Anna had a choice of places and found corner seats with a table. Sam sat by the window and Anna gratefully parked the big handbag on the floor at her feet, sinking back beside him and sipping her coffee. Already it seemed to have been another long day.

Darren was immediately back on the phone, first telling John to get off duty and get some rest then Angela to parallel the train down to Basingstoke, then Southampton and wait at the station. He then reported in again to his control, giving better news this time, in monosyllables in case of nosy passengers.

'They're still on it, whatever it is,' remarked Darren to Rees, staring out of the window. 'We might have stopped them getting the book they wanted but they're still on it. I want her handbag, that big one.'

Rees raised his eyebrows mockingly and hammed up his Welsh accent, as he often did with Darren. 'There's lovely, but is it really your colour?'

Darren smirked back. 'Alright you plonker, she's got information in it. Women have everything in their bags don't they? You'll have to get it; they'll recognise me from the library. This is how it works...'

The train slowed down to stop at Basingstoke, and Anna and Sam were both looking out of the window as Rees made his move. He swept past making a grab for Anna's bag. As he did so, the train was nearly at a standstill and his plan was to hop straight off and out of the station precinct in seconds. Rees grabbed the bag, which was much heavier than he expected, but Anna's speedy reaction surprised him. Hanging on grimly to one of the handles she stood up to struggle with him. Sam was right behind her but as he rose to grapple with Rees, Anna blocked his way, tugging at her bag. Hemmed in by the table, Sam just couldn't reach around her.

Two women sat opposite, not understanding what was happening, frozen in their seats. Anna was shouting now and Rees was starting to panic at the thought of failure. In seconds it came to a head. Rees lashed out violently at Anna, punching her hard in the face and splitting her lip. Sam lunged desperately past her, managing to connect solidly with Rees's shoulder, then landing a second blow on his ear. Rees staggered back under Sam's onslaught, but Anna lost her grip on the bag and Rees was away. He had timed it well and as the door slid open at the end of the carriage, he sprinted along the platform towards the exit. Anna had fallen heavily back against Sam, winding him and cracking her head on the back of the seat as she did so.

Peeping from behind the glass door at the other end of the carriage Darren noted Rees's coup with satisfaction.

Angela was waiting, she picked up Rees outside Basingstoke station and tore off down towards the M3 for Southampton, one eye on the GPS and one eye on her speedometer. She didn't want some motorway patrol officer stopping her to complicate things. Rees rummaged in Anna's bag, then phoning Darren, he reported there was no paperwork only what looked like an essay on criminal psychology. He re-assembled Anna's mobile and Darren told him to phone the office and pass on her contacts list.

Anna was spitting blood, literally and figuratively, cursing all bag snatchers and their ancestry with choice Anglo-Saxon words. As Sam got his breath back she was rubbing the bump on her head and accepting commiserations from the two women who were sat opposite. Rubbing his sore knuckles Sam felt grim, this was getting bad, things were escalating and he still didn't know who was pursuing them or why. He wished they still had Anna's mobile but realised immediately they couldn't use it anyway. It was of little use reporting this to the police, these guys probably were the police and by the time they did anything it would be too late anyway. Things were moving fast, way too fast.

By now they were nearing Southampton and Sam was angry that their movements were being anticipated so easily by their pursuers. He had a long fuse but it was burning down quickly. In his anger he realised it wasn't about Jack the Ripper any more, it was about their safety. This was becoming dangerous and personal.

'Luckily they didn't get my tablet or my notes; they're all still at home. He got my phone though, the bastard,' Anna said bitterly.

Sam wondered silently if her stuff actually was safe at her home, but said nothing.

He had planned to get a taxi out to James's house at Minstead but suddenly decided against it. Their pursuers would expect him to alight at Southampton; he used the station often and had met Anna there twice, the last time only a few days ago. So much seemed to have happened so quickly. Now Sam desperately wanted to break the cycle of predictability which made them so easy to monitor. He decided they would travel on to Brockenhurst where his parents lived and commandeer his father's car. Sam wanted to be in control of their movements and public transport didn't give that flexibility. It occurred to him that they might still not be alone on the train, even though the one guy had got off with Anna's bag.

He told Anna of his plans and she nodded silently, a tissue pressed to her lip. Her anger had given way to the realisation that this wasn't a game, her bag had gone, her phone and what else? Sam borrowed a mobile from one of the women sitting opposite and phoned his parents' home. His father picked up straight away, adjusting immediately to the urgency in Sam's voice as he heard Sam's request to borrow his car. He didn't question him, but agreed to pick them up straight away at the station.

With a sigh of relief Anna slid her hand into her jeans pocket touching the papers pressed against the front of her hip bone.

'Well that's one good thing,' she said to Sam, breaking into his thought patterns about getting to James's house. He turned to see her face, still pale, but with a return of the defiance and obstinacy he had come to recognise as her trademarks.

'What?'

'I've still got the number sheet and our bit of the translation; those slimy bastards aren't going to get it that easily.'

Sam grinned for the first time in a while. The feisty Anna was back, and he was glad. They were now on track for James and Beth's house to search *The Case-Book*. He squeezed her arm in response.

At Southampton, Darren was completely wrong-footed. Knowing

exactly where Sam lived and convinced they would alight there he had told Angela to wait out of sight with Rees. Peering through the glass door at the end of the carriage he saw the couple rise, then head for the other end, as though they were about to get off. Making for the nearest door he stepped onto the platform to find there was no sign of them. Darren bobbed his head this way and that, trying to see past people. For a few moments he was nonplussed then he clicked. Blondie had tricked John earlier, might he be doing it again now?

Darren got back on the train and looked where they had been sitting; there was no sign of them. He walked cautiously through as the train pulled out, carefully inspecting each carriage. There they were, sitting half-way down in the last compartment as the train picked up speed. Darren sighed, why couldn't these two behave like most people did? He raised his phone to his ear, telling Angela he was still on the train; she was to find out where the next stops were and follow the train – fast.

'It's a Weymouth train, wherever the fuck that is,' he said. Rees scampered into the station to find out while Angela kept the motor running, moving into the taxi area to collect Rees as he emerged.

'Brockenhurst next,' Rees said tersely as he got into the car again, a timetable pamphlet in his hand.

'Where's that?' Angela said.

'Search me, somewhere west of here, get going and I'll check.' Rees pulled the GPS from its suction pad and ran his fingers over the screen, finding Brockenhurst station as fast as the satellites would allow. Angela was already on the main road, following signs to the west as Rees navigated.

'A35 to Lyndhurst, then south to Brockenhurst. It's only a piddling village, we should find it alright,' he said, yawning. 'After that it goes to Bournemouth and some other places.' Rees rubbed his shoulder where Blondie had punched him, it was really painful and he knew a bruise was on its way; his ear was red and felt hot from the other blow. Angela was silently wondering how far they might have to go tonight and whether they could catch up with the train anyway.

'Okay, let's go,' said Sam as they got off the train at Brockenhurst, grabbing Anna's hand he ran her up the stairs and over the footbridge to make for the car park beside the station. Anna stayed close as he made straight for where he had asked his father to meet them; an area which he knew would be in shadows at this time of day. It was almost dusk now which pleased Darren who followed them slowly, hanging back to avoid being seen. Sam stopped near the car park entrance, checked back behind them, then stood scanning the road.

Seconds later his father arrived, his home was only minutes away on the edge of the village and he had left immediately after Sam's call. As he turned his four-by-four into the car park Sam's father smiled. In the headlights he saw his son waiting, a slim pale girl with glossy dark hair and enormous eyes pressed close against his arm.

'Nice one, Sam,' he murmured to himself.

'Thanks, Dad. I really appreciate this, I'll explain all later. We have to get to James's house. And this is Anna by the way,' he finished, by way of an introduction. Anna shook his father's hand and thanked him for picking them up.

His father got out of the car and Sam took the wheel, heading back to his parents' house. Darren was unable to get the number and watched frustrated as their tail lights disappeared into the town. Fidgeting, he waited for the others to arrive. Striving to get control of the pursuit again and disrupt the couple, he had already phoned his office. They quickly found a retired historian by the name of Taylor living in the village, and gave the address. Darren phoned it through to Rees who got busy with the GPS again.

'At least we're not going to Weymouth then,' said Rees, and with his mobile tucked into his shoulder he gave Darren a running commentary on their progress. Within minutes they were there. The pickup was seamless, Angela barely stopping as she swung into the station car park while Darren jumped into the back seat.

'It's an old pale red Jeep Cherokee, couldn't get the number, heading that way,' Darren gesticulated back into the town, the way she and Rees had just come. Angela reversed fiercely, making a commuter jump, then pushed the gear stick into first before accelerating back onto the main road with a squeal of tyres.

'The GPS won't speak to me fast enough, give me the turns,' she said. Glued to the little screen Rees did as he was told, as they headed towards the address listed for Taylor.

Sam dropped his father back at his house, engine running and promising to return the car tomorrow. His father asked Sam to unclip his front door key from the bunch in the ignition, and smiled his goodbyes to Anna. He didn't comment on Sam's haste, knowing him as well as he did, simply reminding him, as always, to watch out for the wildlife on the Forest roads.

Swinging the old Cherokee around, Sam worked his way back to the main road for Lyndhurst, raced up it and headed towards the junction for Emery Down.

Angela arrived at the Taylor address just after Sam had gone, and hesitated. There was no Jeep there. Darren, who had been studying a road atlas in the back seat, decided they were going north to Lyndhurst.

'There's nowhere else, they have to be going that way,' he pronounced.

Sam was explaining to Anna that although some main roads were fenced, most forest roads weren't and there were many collisions with wildlife caused by people driving too fast, particularly at night. She had never been to the New Forest and had no idea that ponies wandered freely through the villages, woods and open heathland.

'It's not just ponies,' Sam told her that there were cattle let loose to graze as well as plenty of wild deer and even pigs in the autumn. He had been pushing it on the narrow and bumpy roads, and suddenly had to brake hard.

Bracing herself against the dashboard, Anna was intrigued and thrilled as a pony wandered across the road, stopping in front of them. It was followed by another, with a third one on the grass verge that she simply hadn't seen in the fading light. Only one of the three bore a reflective collar. Sam told her that some owners put collars on their animals but many didn't, for a variety of reasons.

'My god, this could be really dangerous, those poor ponies!' she exclaimed. Sam made no reply, squeezing swiftly around the animals and away.

Some way behind them the lights of a car appeared, glinting in the dusk. It was closing on them quite fast now.

Back in Brockenhurst, Sam's father updated his wife on Sam's brief visit. Surprised that he hadn't come in to see her, she asked what was going on, and where the car was.

'He's in a tearing hurry; he has to get to James's house, but don't ask me why. He said he'll explain soon, so give him a chance. You know what he and Paige are like when they're not ready to tell you anything.'

Sam's mother nodded.

'There's some good news anyway,' said his father.

'What's that?'

'He's got a new girlfriend, and she's an absolute stunner.'

'How do you know it's his girlfriend?'

'If she isn't, he's stupid, and Sam's never been stupid.'

'Well, well.' His wife smiled at him, the grey eyes looking into the middle distance. 'Perhaps he's getting over Indira at last. It's a shame really, such a lovely woman and she made him so happy. I bet Paige knows all about this girl, I'll ask her. She'll be phoning soon.'

'How do you know that?'

The grey eyes twinkled at him. 'You'll see.'

Chapter 45

Three Ponies, One Collar

The New Forest – Present Day

Seeing what she hoped might be Sam's rear lights in the far distance ahead, Angela took control of the chase. Darren, seated in the back, was testy since nearly losing Blondie and Baby Blue at Southampton, and she knew he wanted – no – he needed, to get back on top of the game.

'Seatbelts,' she snapped at both passengers, viciously tightening her own. The lower belt cut across her belly and the upper strap pressed tightly on her sternum. Bumping over the uneven tarmac, she gunned the motor of the powerful Toyota through Brockenhurst, stretching her arms out full length to the wheel, the classic ten to two position.

They followed the route to Lyndhurst, catching the car in front and finding it was a black hatchback with a young woman driving. Overtaking rapidly they pushed on. When the first decision came, Angela was fatalistic and breathed her usual mantra.

'If in doubt go left,' so she took the left fork. A few moments later she had the same decision, another fork, so she went left again. They were now on the A35 cutting west across the New Forest towards Christchurch and at the same moment she and Rees caught sight of a vehicle making a right turn opposite a pub. Could it be an old Cherokee? They couldn't be sure, having it in sight for less than a second before it disappeared.

Darren made the decision for her.

'Go with it, let's do it,' the words emanated from the back seat. She made the turn to a place called Emery Down. Angela's adrenaline was up; this was what she was trained for. Thatched cottages, the road narrowing, bumpy and winding, cars parked haphazardly outside houses and gateways. She saw everything, dealt with everything, anticipated everything. Except for one thing.

Immediately after leaving the main road, and without thinking about it Angela rumbled the Land Cruiser over the cattle grid in the road. She had seen it, logged it, and accelerated over it, but what didn't compute was its meaning. Like Anna a few minutes ahead of her, this was her first time in the New Forest. So far her route had been fully fenced, but the implication of the grid was that animals were loose on the road, anywhere and at any time. The four by four in front of her had been travelling fast but Angela knew that if this was her man, the driver wouldn't have her expertise and would find it difficult to lose her. She didn't know what would happen when she caught them, that was up to Darren, who would be thinking about it now.

Telepathically Darren chimed in. 'Just keep on his tail; if it's them the important thing is not to lose them, they're obviously not staying at the Brockenhurst address so they could be going anywhere now.'

While they drove Sam was giving Anna a little more information about James and his book business. He described the niche James had carved for himself in the import and export of books. His business had changed a lot since the early days when it was simply buying and selling volumes, the advent of digital media and the price of paperbacks dropping through the floor had changed many things. But James had worked with it, selling on the Internet, embracing new ideas and conducting a lucrative trade with America as well as the domestic market. He had a reputation for supplying goods promptly and exactly to the advertised specification, he also understood the importance of cash flow and setting modest prices so that stock turned over. He used a light industrial unit in Southampton for his business, though like most booky people, his home was loaded, pressed into service with the constant overflow of material.

Rounding a bend at speed Angela suddenly ran into serious trouble. Just feet ahead of her bonnet the reflective collar of a pony shone in the centre of the road. She stamped on the brakes, knowing in a split second that she mustn't hit the animal. Not out of some squeamishness, but for her and her passengers' safety as much as anything, a pony coming through her windscreen was just not a good idea. Flashes of some terrible crashes she had witnessed in her job came into her mind, the tragedy of broken bodies scattered on cruel tarmac.

The brakes were good, and had been serviced recently but like most brakes they were just slightly unbalanced, one side pulling a little more than the other. Anticipating this, Angela gripped the wheel tightly and put the vehicle into a controlled skid, whizzing past the animal with inches to spare, then straight off the road. They bumped suddenly down into a shallow ditch and up again onto the open heath beside the tarmac. Rees shrieked out as the ditch bounced them severely up and down, his head colliding with the roof lining. Earth and gravel sprayed out from both nearside tyres. The offside front of the car came to rest against a section of rotting log, the bumper panel collapsing and falling off with a nasty sound. It lay forlornly in the grass.

Darren had braced himself as best he could against the back of Rees's seat in front of him. Fortunately the seat had remained locked in place. Rees had slipped partially through his seatbelt and seemed to be crouched in the footwell. Angela remained firmly seated secured by both her belt and the steering wheel. As they came to a stop she looked around at both of them.

'Fuuuck,' said Darren slowly. Angela put the Toyota into neutral and pulled the handbrake automatically. They all released their belts and stepped gingerly out of the vehicle. The pony with the reflective collar meandered off the road and slowly disappeared into the darkness. Two others stood silently by, staring at the car's occupants with curiosity, wondering perhaps at the strange things humans did. Their breath was steaming slightly in the cool air as their compatriot with the collar led the way. One, then the other, started to silently follow.

Darren took charge again.

'Are you both okay?' he demanded, getting firm nods in return. 'That's good. Well done, Angie, you saved our arses there.' He patted her on the arm. Angela smiled tightly, praise indeed, she thought, starting to walk around the car to look for damage.

Rees chimed in. 'What the fuck are these doing here?' He was gesturing toward the ponies indignantly. 'I banged my head on the roof, what's the matter with people around here, letting these things out on the road. Christ, they must be loonies, aren't they?'

Despite losing his quarry Darren was good humoured now, relieved at their narrow escape.

'Yes well, they're country folk, bumpkins like you I expect. Now, I may have to charge you with damaging police property, since you nutted the roof of my car.'

His mind was already back on Blondie and the missing four-by-four vehicle. Not one car had passed since they had left the road so spectacularly.

'We've lost a headlight and the front panel but everything else looks alright,' Angela reported. She put the Land Cruiser into reverse then drove it cautiously back onto the road, bumping slowly over the ditch and checking her dashboard for warning lights as she did so. Rees threw the front panel into the boot, then he and Darren got back in and fastened their seatbelts, much more tightly this time. Darren looked back at the ground torn up by their tyres.

'Okay, let's go before the local plod turns up.' He continued thinking aloud. 'I don't think they're going far, he's borrowed a car, where might they be? Rees, zoom the GPS screen out and look at the map, what's around here? Where are the nearest towns?' Darren groped on the floor of the car for his road atlas again.

Angela slowed as a junction in the road loomed up; Rees told them it was Minstead to the right down a single track road, Cadnam was a bit further on or they could head for the A31 which led to the motorway. Darren interjected.

'No, he's not going to the motorway; he wouldn't have come this way. Try this Minstead place first, we'll cruise these villages and look for their car.' Angela swung the wheel obediently, the road was heavily rutted and narrow, puddles everywhere from some recent rain. Moments later there was another junction.

'If in doubt, go left,' she muttered.

Soon an isolated house appeared on one side of the road, then another, then several more as they approached the village. Angela slowed down checking in every gateway and opening they passed. Close to the centre of the village she spotted a Jeep Cherokee, its roof bars standing higher than the two saloons parked near it. Approaching slowly she could see there was no-one inside it, her window hissed down softly as she stopped alongside. In the quiet night air all three of them could hear the ticking of hot metal as Sam's father's car cooled down. A few yards away, James's house was the only one ablaze with lights.

'Nice one.' Darren grinned in the back seat. 'Back it up, Angela, and park a little way down the street.'

Chapter 46

The Prettiest of Them All?

Whitechapel – 1891

The 12 February had crept slowly into the 13th, and the time was around two fifteen a.m. A few minutes behind the unseen couple ahead of him, Ernie Thompson patrolled steadily, it was his first ever night alone on the beat. As a new police constable he had been through his training and pronounced competent. Like the couple before him he also entered Chamber Street from the direction of Leman Street, proud of his new independence and watchful of everything around him. He had already walked this beat many times since ten p.m. and was determined to stick to the instructions he had been given.

In the darkest part of the archway Frances and the man halted. Suddenly and without any warning he threw her brutally to the ground, cracking her head on the floor. Inebriated and dazed she was unable to cry out as he grasped her chin with his left hand. He knelt beside her, still covering her mouth forcibly, fumbling to draw a knife from his right-hand pocket. Pushing her chin back violently and exposing her throat, he quickly, almost frantically, slashed at her neck. He realised as he did so that he was muddling through things, somehow he had lost his fluency. It had been a while since he had felt moved to attempt an attack like this, but the problem of the Marys still remained. Suddenly the man's keen hearing picked up the sound of faint footsteps. His heightened senses and almost telepathic instincts made him rise and back away from the body, his work not completed, not even started. As he retreated a low moan came from his victim.

Quickly, he walked through the rest of the arch and waited just out of sight, hoping to resume when the passer-by had gone. That hope was dashed as Constable Thompson shone his lamp on the body, and after a moment began furiously blowing his whistle. Frustrated and angry with both himself and the Mary, the man strode away, mindlessly humming an unmusical tune to himself. Constable Thompson couldn't see anyone but he did hear the sound of a person walking firmly away from the scene.

As her assailant backed away the last thing he saw was Frances' new bonnet lying beside her, and her older one still attached to the skirts she wore. He didn't believe the constable would follow as he knew they were trained to stay with any person they found needing assistance. True to his instructions, Thompson remained with Frances, something he was later to question in his mind again and again.

The 12 February had been a fairly routine day for Frances. Her family knew nothing of the details of her present life, though she now believed that her sister had perhaps an inkling of her circumstances. Thankfully her father knew nothing and she wanted it that way. He was a proud man and at his age would be badly affected if he knew how things were with her. Frances had a lot of time for her father and visited him as often as she felt she could. Less than a fortnight ago she had accompanied him to church, something she did regularly.

Several years before, she had sunk into depression after giving up her regular job for health reasons. She liked a drink and a good time but the drink gained an insidious hold, as it did with so many others. Without stable income she had drifted steadily into prostitution as a way of supporting her habit, moving from one address to another. It hadn't been too difficult for she liked men in general, though there was little satisfaction in her couplings with most of them. All the time she had kept up the pretence with her family, even now they believed she was living in a respectable street, when in fact she spent her nights in a series of lodging houses.

She realised that in her last meeting with her sister she must have looked disreputable, her soiled clothes betraying her real way of life. It was difficult but she resolved to maintain distance from now on between herself and other members of her family. Frances believed she could work her way out of the life she had espoused, though she didn't know how this could be done. Whatever happened she would still see her father, in that she was adamant, also it would be easier to keep the truth from him.

Frances had regular clients; she was both popular and attractive, though it never led to any financial security for her. Most of her acquaintances and clients came and went, sometimes reappearing after weeks or months when they had money for drink and entertainment. So it was with James Sadler. On Wednesday, 11 February he was discharged from his ship and met Frances in a public house. They had shared a liaison once before and this time was no different, he had money and they agreed to spend the night together.

The night turned into next day and in one public house after another the two of them steadily drank their way through much of the money James had left. During the afternoon Frances called into a shop where she had put down a deposit upon a new bonnet. James gave her the money and by the time she collected it she was barely able to stand upright. Leaving the shop they went to another pub to celebrate. She wore the new bonnet immediately, after pinning her old one, with some difficulty, under her outer skirt for safety.

During the evening they parted after a row. Eventually Frances started to sober up, and later on, in the early hours she was back in Whitechapel. Whilst talking to an acquaintance, Ellen, who was also a prostitute, she saw a shabbily dressed man approaching. The two immediately sized him up as a client. After some harsh words and a scuffle between Ellen and the man, during which he slapped Ellen, the man propositioned Frances. Despite being warned off by Ellen, Frances decided to ignore her and struck up a conversation with him, culminating in them walking off together.

It was difficult making small talk with the man. He seemed tense and a little distant sometimes, often cocking his head as though listening, then loud and erratic the next. He would look around wildly, his blue eyes staring into the distance. Ellen's words of caution came back to Frances briefly and for a moment fear touched her. There hadn't been any grisly deaths amongst the ladies of the street for some time now; Jack, the so-called Ripper was long gone. Some said he was drowned in the river, some said he was locked away, still others thought he had taken ship to another country, from whence he had arrived in the first place.

Shrugging off the feeling, still woolly from her heavy drinking, she strolled with him down Leman Street towards Chamber Street, where she knew the three railway arches that linked the adjacent streets would be dark. She had used the arches before as had many others. There were plenty of dark places in the area and they wandered into the somewhat poorly named Swallow Gardens.

Though Frances didn't know it, Constable Ernie Thompson was already fairly close behind them. Close, but tragically not close enough to either save her, or to apprehend the man who was to cruelly end her young life.

Chapter 47

A Study in Scarlet

The New Forest – Present Day

Seeing no lights behind him, Sam drove as fast as safely possible through the unfenced roads, adrenalin flowing as he strained to see animals in the half light. He pointed out a small deer grazing watchfully just outside the tree line.

'Wow!' Anna exclaimed. 'Just look at that.' Sam leaned forward in the seat peering into the rapidly darkening road ahead.

'It's a muntjac,' he said. 'There's a few more of them about at the moment, their numbers have increased, but they're shy and you don't usually see many.' Before long and with some relief he entered the village of Minstead and parked his father's car.

James and Beth welcomed them warmly into the house. Sam quickly impressed the urgency on them and explained they had been followed earlier, and weren't sure if they had lost their pursuers or not. As with his father, he promised to explain all shortly. Without further ado James led them to the long bookcase on one wall of his lounge. Anna stood back, expecting him to take a volume from the shelves, but instead he reached behind some books and moved a lever. Silently a section of the bookcase swung open revealing a dark oak door behind. James unlocked it, and with a flourish motioned Anna and Sam to go in.

'Welcome to the "study in scarlet",' he said proudly.

Sam had been here many times before, but Anna looked around in amazement.

'This is fantastic, a secret room. Are you another one of these Sherlock Holmes... people?' She had been about to say nutters, aiming at Sam, but suddenly realised James might be the same, and she was a guest in his house. Most of the walls were covered in bookshelves and much of the floor space was taken up by boxes awaiting despatch somewhere. The room was piled with books both ancient and modern but any pieces of visible wall were clad with faded red wallpaper.

'No, not at all,' said James. 'That's just Sam, it's not really a Sherlock Holmes thing, but Beth liked the red wallpaper and christened it the study in scarlet. If it was actually a Sherlock Holmes room I'd never get Sam out of here, would I?'

James stepped over to a shelf from where he plucked a copy of *The Case-Book*. He removed it from the extra dust sheet which covered it and handed it to Sam.

'There we are, Sam, published by John Murray, Albemarle Street, 1927.'

'Thanks James... you're a legend.'

'Do we need gloves for this?' said Anna.

'No, no,' said James. 'It's a book to read, it will stand handling as long as you are careful.'

Back in the front room Anna pulled the papers from her hip pocket and laid them on the table, the number sheet and the partially written message she had started in the British Library. Focussing on her task, she set rapidly to work, counting softly as she ran her fingers down and then across the pages. As she pored over the book her expression relaxed and a slight smile lifted her lips. The message, so rudely interrupted last time at the British Library, was finally continuing to emerge. She added scribbled letters to her sheet.

CONFESSED AS GUILTY...

Sam realised she would work faster on her own, he stood back letting the light fall on the book to aid her visibility. Impatient though he was, he could see it was a one woman task, and he had come to respect her speed and agility of mind.

A few minutes later Anna looked up and wordlessly handed the paper to Sam, her face inscrutable. As he glanced at the name she looked out of the window and motioned him away from the slightly open blinds. Another car was now quietly parked several houses away with at least one dark figure in it. There was nothing special in that, but it had no lights on, and by now darkness had fallen completely.

Sam weighed things up quickly. Switching off the front room light he spoke rapidly, 'James, call the police will you? It's those guys again, we have to go. Don't tell them we were here.'

'Okay,' said James. 'Out of the back, quickly, over the fence you can make it through the gardens.'

James ran back to the study, locking the door and closing the bookcase in front of it. Anna grabbed the number sheet and the precious message paper, folding the two tightly together and slipping them once more into the pocket of her jeans. She then followed Sam through the kitchen to the back door. Clambering over James's fence into someone else's garden they made their way cautiously back towards the main road. Rees stood silently a little way down, but they didn't notice him. The pub was already busy tonight and loud chatter emanated from the doors and windows.

Backing away from the lights of the pub, they stayed in the shadows around the rear of the war memorial and slipped up a dark lane towards a church, Sam leading the way.

'We can hide in the church, I know a place they will never find us,' he whispered. They entered the churchyard through the lychgate, passing the central bier, and Sam made his way swiftly to the gravestone of Thomas White. Knowing every inch of the unusual church, he was confident they could evade anyone there, Sam groped in the little niche cut in the gravestone for the key that used to be kept there years before.

Rees, who thought he had spotted the couple, signalled up the road to Darren who was still near James's house then walked on quietly up towards the church.

'Damn,' Sam hissed, realising the church would surely be locked nowadays, finding the key had been a long shot. 'No key, follow me.' Looking behind him, in the faint light from the village he thought he could just make out the figure of a man walking slowly up the lane, or was he imagining it? Leaving the church he led the way between the gravestones of generations of local people. The fence on their right seemed impenetrable so Sam headed around towards the grave of Sir Arthur Conan Doyle and his wife, Jean.

'We have to hide the message quickly,' said Anna. Reaching the grave Sam fumbled on the plinth.

'There's a pipe here,' he said quietly. 'Stuff it in the bowl.'

'What?' Anna whispered incredulously.

'Just do it,' he said. 'No time left, if they're police they could take it off you.' Wordlessly, Anna obeyed.

Glancing back towards the church Sam wondered again if he could discern a darker area which might have been a man following. With sudden inspiration he turned to the bench seat under the tree, just yards from the grave.

'Emma-Kathleen,' he whispered, 'keep us safe.' Standing on the bench he motioned Anna to join him. 'Up in the tree, quick!'

Putting one foot on the back of the bench she disappeared up into the old oak tree, wondering what the hell he was rambling about and modestly thankful for the fact she was wearing jeans. Sam grabbed the ivy, swinging himself up. He pushed her bottom, urging her much higher in the tree and with some difficulty followed her himself. She climbed on up, then they crouched silently, high in the branches, much too high for Sam. He froze, Sam absolutely hated heights and they were at least thirty feet up now, probably more.

'What did you mean?' she whispered.

'Shh,' came the fierce reply, as Sam gripped tightly onto the enormous branch next to him. Peering down they saw a man approach the grave, as their eyes acclimatised themselves to the darkness. Sam was thankful for the leaves on the tree, pretty sure that no-one would be able to see them from the ground. Rees halted and stood completely still, listening keenly for any sound that would betray his quarry. It was probably only a minute or two but felt like an interminable wait, then Darren approached quietly, having skirted round the other side of the church. The few leaves underfoot gave the slightest of rustles as he walked. His hand hung down beside him with something metallic glinting in it. A torch? A gun? Anna suddenly gripped Sam's arm with fear and despite his concern about their precarious situation he noticed the aroma of her perfume.

'Nothing,' Rees said quietly.

'Nor me,' said Darren. 'They must have gone over the fields, but just hang on a mo.'

The two stood silently for another long minute or so, tuning in to the darkness for any clue that would help them. Darren looked casually at the tree, and then moved slowly towards the bench underneath it. Suddenly there came a distant commotion from the direction of the pub. Raised voices came from the lane, and seconds later people were in the churchyard. A group came around each side of the church, joining up as twenty or more figures headed noisily toward the Doyle gravesite.

The two men slipped silently away towards the perimeter fence of the churchyard. Sam and Anna had no idea what this meant. They stayed put, barely moving in case something gave them away. Breathing out slowly in relief, Sam smiled to himself in the dark as he felt Anna still gripping his arm, her perfume filling his senses. Shivering slightly she pushed even closer against him, her hair in his face. He forgot his phobia about heights; she was calming him though she didn't know it. His nose touched her scalp and she smelt good, Sam's eyes closed and his mouth formed a silent kiss. Then realising what he was doing, he stopped. But he felt in no hurry to move.

The newcomers were right underneath the tree, noisy, lighting matches as they looked around.

'Nobody here,' said one of them. 'Arthur and Jean are okay.' Following this the figures slowly drifted away in the direction from which they had come, some going each side of the church, arguing, their voices growing fainter as they went.

After a few minutes Sam and Anna climbed back down the tree and cautiously moved towards the grave. Retrieving her precious message from the pipe Anna tucked it safely in her pocket as they walked back through the churchyard. When they reached the gate, it became clear that the hunters were now potentially the hunted. The rotating blue light of a patrol car could just be seen reflecting along towards the pub, and a large number of customers, mostly men, were still milling around in the lane and on the green, chatting in groups. It was obviously them who had arrived in the churchyard, saving Sam and Anna from discovery by their pursuers.

James was on the green with Beth looking around anxiously. His face lit up as he walked swiftly towards them. 'Thank God you're alright,' he said. 'Luckily there was a gathering of Sherlockians in the pub so I told them that those guys were Conan Doyle grave vandals.'

Sam grasped his hand and shook it. 'Thanks, James, that's two I owe you.' He looked around and smiled at the nearest group of Sherlockians.

'There's no-one up there now,' he announced, gesturing up towards the churchyard. His words triggered a murmuring of relief from some and disappointment from others.

Sam turned back to James, who wanted to know what had happened.

Sam put his arm around James's shoulders, as Anna patted her jeans pocket where the message now resided again. 'Buy us a drink, James, and we'll tell you all about it.' He grinned with genuine relief.

On a corner table in The Trusty Servant, with fresh drinks in their hands, they updated each other. James said Beth had actually been on the telephone to the police when a woman knocked on his door saying she was a plain clothes police officer. She had asked if he was James the book dealer and said she was warning about a rare book thief in the area. She gave a loose description of Sam. The woman had flashed an identification card then asked James if he had a copy of *The Case-Book of Sherlock Holmes*, because she had information that the thief might burgle James's house seeking it. She suggested that James could lodge the book with the police for safety.

James riposted by saying he had never seen anyone of that description, didn't have such a book and his wife was speaking to the police right now because he didn't like the look of some men he had just seen outside. Whereupon the woman had given him an old fashioned look and backed off.

The local police had arrived shortly afterwards, and didn't really seem interested, though they made a show of looking around the area. James and Beth had then locked up and gone to the pub telling the Sherlockians there were grave vandals about, whereupon a number of them headed towards the churchyard. The pursuers' car had since disappeared from near James's house, but the local police still lingered, no doubt joking over the eccentricities of village characters.

'I don't think we'll be troubled by them again tonight,' said Sam who then tried to update James and Beth on their adventures. He told them he had initially planned to hide inside All Saints church where he knew of several places. If he had got the key they could have locked themselves in. Unfortunately the key to the church hadn't been where he expected it to be, in the slot cut in the gravestone of a certain Thomas White who had died in 1842.

He explained for Anna's benefit that the wording had originally referred to a 'faithful husband' but the story went that his wife had the word 'faithful' removed from the gravestone when she later found evidence of infidelity. This had left a slot in the stonework where the mason had cut deep to expunge the offending word, in the process creating a useful aperture that was ideal for keeping a key. Unfortunately for Sam, the key was not kept there any more.

There were more interruptions from Anna who demanded to know who Emma-Kathleen was. Sam patiently explained that the bench he had sat on so many times under the tree was dedicated to Emma-Kathleen Robinson and he had in fact climbed the oak tree himself many times when he was younger, though not as high as they had tonight. The tree, he informed her, had been struck by lightning more than once since Sir Arthur Conan Doyle and his wife Jean had been re-buried there. Some people still believed that this was a sign of God's displeasure because Doyle had renounced Christianity in favour of spiritualism.

'What a load of old tosh,' she said dismissively, 'about the lightning I mean, not you and your Emma-Kathleen! Mind you, I'm glad there wasn't a thunderstorm tonight.' Secretly she was pleased with Sam's local knowledge and the insight into his childhood in what looked to be a lovely village.

Anna produced the crumpled message and rolled it open on the table. 'Well, at last we have it,' she said.

CONFESSED AS GUILTY OF THE

WHITECHAPEL MURDERS

T CUTBUSH

Sam read the message. 'So who is he? And what do we know about him?'

'Quite a bit actually,' said Anna. 'Though not as much as we would like to know, he's been a suspect for a while, but has never really been high on the list, Charles Macnaghten certainly tried to scupper any idea that he was the Ripper. But now it looks as though Conan Doyle was sure he had got a real confirmation. You might remember, Sam, I mentioned Macnaghten when we were in Southampton that time. A couple of writers have already fingered this guy for the crimes, but he hasn't really caught on.'

Sam nodded; he leaned back in his chair and took a drink from his pint. A smile played gently on his lips and he faked an air of puzzlement.

'So, let me get it straight in my mind, Anna, are we are now saying that Arthur Conan Doyle *wasn't* Jack the Ripper?'

The dark eyes skewered him fiercely for a moment and then she feigned disinterest. 'Oh phooey, I was wrong about that little bit of the puzzle, but some people are never satisfied are they?'

She turned to James and Beth and gave them the enormous smile. 'How do you put up with him? Has he always been picky like this?'

Sam laughed aloud, spluttering on his beer at the way she seemed able to gloss over anything to justify her own position. The woman was totally impossible.

Anna's mind went back to the oak tree, neither of them had mentioned it but being crushed up against him had been nice. Feeling his face in her hair, for a moment she had imagined that he might kiss her, but he hadn't. If he had, she thought, I would have responded, but maybe there was time yet, who knew?

Chapter 48

Sisterly Love

The New Forest – Present Day

Sam's mother sat quietly by the phone, a crossword on her lap. As soon as it rang she picked it up.

'Paige, how are you all?' She smiled across at her husband who shook his head with laughter.

Paige wanted to know if they had heard from Sam. He was some days overdue with her call and she knew he wouldn't have forgotten. By now she was actually a little worried and had a bad feeling about things. Her mother was immediately able to reassure her.

'Sam was here tonight, briefly, I didn't see him, but your father says he's gone to James's house on urgent business. He's okay, but in a fearful rush so I expect that's why he hasn't rung you. He's borrowed his father's car for a while.'

Paige commented that Sam's own car had been broken into and that it was about time he got a new one anyway.

Her mother continued, 'Perhaps he'll get a mobile phone one of these days, and then we'll all know how he is. Anyway, don't worry, everything's alright. Also, he's got company, a real beauty, according to your dad, who still thinks he's an expert in these things!'

Paige smiled with relief, on two counts. One, that Sam was safe and well, and two, that the mysterious Anna was with him. They were obviously still on her Jack the Ripper quest, and that pleased her.

'Good,' she said, 'I'm glad he's okay. I've been giving him phone hugs now and again while he's been down; I hope he'll call me back soon.'

'He will,' said their mother, 'very soon, probably tomorrow morning,' she added decisively.

Paige shook her head, smiling.

Chapter 49

Make-up & Biscuits

Minstead, the New Forest – Present Day

When Darren and Rees split up to try and find Blondie and Baby Blue, Angela did some quick thinking. She didn't like the way things were going and the guy who answered the door had been truculent and primed, Blondie and Baby Blue must have briefed him in their short time there. As soon as she got back to the car and told Darren, he had left to search the area. Rees had already wandered down the road to the village green and the pub. Angela backed the car away and seeing a house with a 'for sale' board she rightly divined it was unoccupied. It was funny how you just had to look at a house sometimes and you knew there was no-one at home. Reversing the Toyota into the drive, gravel crunching under its tyres, she switched off her remaining headlight and waited, phone at the ready. A tall beech hedge screened the car, the gentlest of breezes moving its leaves. Angela lowered the front windows to hear any sound of Darren or Rees approaching.

Glancing down she saw Baby Blue's handbag in the front footwell where Rees had left it, and decided to have a snoop. As she unzipped the top the familiar smell of a woman's bag wafted out, a mixture of old make-up and cinnamon biscuits. Rummaging through she picked out several lipsticks in different shades, the inevitable tube of moisturiser and another of No7 make-up, five biros with different hotel logos, one of them broken, three tampons, the mobile phone that Rees had already examined, a packet of tissues, a small tube of antiseptic hand wash, an umbrella, a notebook with nothing in it, a pair of black knickers and some loose change.

Angela smiled. Christ, this girl was worse than most! The list went on,

Anna's purse with credit cards and a photo of her parents, seventy euros in an envelope, hair grips, one silver earring, half a packet of dark chocolate digestive biscuits, some popsocks, chewing gum, and a condom in a battered packet, looking past its sell-by date. Last but not least there was a make-up mirror with Disney cartoons on the back, clearly of sentimental value.

Despite herself, Angela felt a sudden pang of sympathy for Baby Blue. It was horrible for a woman to lose her handbag, and she remembered Darren telling her that Rees had punched the girl in the face on the train. Angela had been envious of the girl's looks but it wasn't Baby Blue's fault that she was attractive. She suddenly decided to get the bag back to the girl, sod what Darren might think. They didn't need it now and Baby Blue wasn't Angela's enemy.

She phoned John who was at base, updating him cryptically and checking that he had the contents of Baby Blue's phone that Rees had passed to him.

'Yep, I've got all that,' John said. 'We got very little from it that we didn't already know.'

Ringing off and stepping out on the road she looked down the street. The lights of the pub were just visible with some commotion going on outside, where the slowly rotating blue light of a police car reflected back to her. The house she had called at was now in total darkness. Angela took another torch from her glove compartment intending to guide Darren and Rees to the car when they appeared. With Anna's bag in the other hand she strolled down to James's house and hung it on his gate. A few moments later Darren emerged from someone's drive, closely followed by Rees who was quietly cursing about some barbed wire he had encountered leaving the churchyard.

Putting two fingers in her mouth Angela whistled at them softly, flashing the torch light once, and sprinting back to the car. She sensed now they would be making a rapid exit.

'Go, go, go, the game's over, for tonight anyway,' said Darren, panting heavily as they got into the car. With a little wheel spin firing a shower of gravel at the empty house behind them they were gone, Angela driving more cautiously this time after her brush with the ponies. She was now focussed on getting them back to London and hoping the loss of her headlight and front panel didn't attract any attention on the way. Glancing at the GPS she headed towards Cadnam. Getting his breath back in the back seat, Darren was already on the phone to his boss.

Rees yawned; it had been a long, long day. His head still hurt and the barbed wire had scratched his legs. 'Where's the handbag?' he said looking down into the footwell.

'I tossed it,' said Angela, shortly.

Chapter 50

Bathwater on the Stairs

Minstead, the New Forest – Present Day

Finishing their drinks, the four of them left the pub, Beth insisting that they stay overnight and make use of her guest rooms. James was now anxious to forsake The Trusty Servant for his precious books and manuscripts, and was glad to have overnight company. As they approached the house Anna gave a little cry of pleasure seeing her bag hanging on the gate. She grabbed it, clutching it to her.

'Where did that come from?' she said. 'I thought it had gone forever.' Sam was more suspicious.

'Hold on, it might have been bugged now, this could be a Trojan Horse,' he said quietly, lifting a finger to his lips. 'We'd better check it,' he added, whispering now.

'I'll do it,' Anna whispered back hastily, remembering her discomfort at the pub with Steve. Bloody hell, déjà vu, I must clear this bag out sometime, she thought. As Beth unlocked the front door Anna made for the kitchen with the suspect bag. For the second time she found nothing.

Soon they were all comfortable in the front room, tiredness was setting in now, and Anna went off for a soak in the bath while Beth went to make up some beds.

Sam took a mouthful of the scotch and water in front of him. James fussed around the bolts on his doors and checked the alarm settings. Sam stared at the crumpled scrawl of the message and the photocopy of the scorched number sheet. It seemed to be something of an anticlimax; Doyle had certainly named the man he had identified and confirmed as the Ripper. He must have been certain otherwise he would never have named the man, Sam was sure about that. All the same something niggled at him. Upstairs he could hear the water running and felt glad they were both safe and well.

His eyes turned again to the papers, picking up the number sheet he looked at it properly for the first time since they had received it. It was an A4 photocopy of a slightly smaller, older sheet of paper. The numbers were handwritten in that neat compact way that typified Conan Doyle. Anna had quickly decoded the simple sequence that gave the message.

Obviously it was designed to be innocuous as a sheet of numbers but was also meant to be simple to crack. Once the finder had realised there was a message, the sequence was one of the simplest you could devise. Doyle had meant it to be found by anyone who was really interested in his archives; his object had not been to make it indecipherable. Sam pulled the scrawled message Anna had written down across the table.

CONFESSED AS GUILTY OF THE

WHITECHAPEL MURDERS

T CUTBUSH

Idly, Sam compared the numbers to the words on the paper; he could see the slight gaps between the sets of numbers to indicate a fresh word was starting. Nine sets for the first word, two for the second word and six for the third word, etc. Further down the sheet he could see the single line of figures that represented the T before Cutbush.

Suddenly he stiffened and sat upright in his chair. Before the numbers faded into the irregularly burnt area at the bottom of the sheet, there were more numbers. They had only got part of the message. He thought back to earlier that evening, Anna had obviously recognised the name of Thomas Cutbush as a longstanding Ripper suspect. At the precise moment she had passed him the name on her sheet, their three pursuers had arrived at James's house. She either hadn't noticed or hadn't had time to see the extra few numbers on the sheet. They had immediately left on the run with no time to even consider the message.

James was nodding in his chair as Sam sprang up. 'James, James, get *The Case-Book* out again,' he demanded urgently.

James woke up abruptly. 'What? Now?' he said.

'There's a bit more to the message,' said Sam. 'Quick, let's do it.'

Without a word James moved swiftly to the other end of his lounge and opened the secret door in the bookcase. In moments he had returned with the volume he had so recently replaced there. For the second time that night he took off the extra dust cover and laid it on the table. Sam pored over it immediately.

'I won't be able to do this as fast as Anna but I'm damned if I'm going to get her out of the bath.'

'No, best not,' said James dryly, 'bathwater on the stairs and all that...'

Sam laughed and returned to his number sheet. He turned the pages rapidly, trying not to damage the rare volume. As he decoded each letter after counting out the lines and words, he noted it on the creased sheet Anna had used earlier.

The next bit of the message slowly emerged. Now he had:

CONFESSED AS GUILTY OF THE
WHITECHAPEL MURDERS
T CUTBUSH AND C CU

And there the message abruptly ended. The numbers ran out at the burned edge of the sheet. There was absolutely nothing else to be got from it.

'Damn.' He looked at the message. He had a little more but what was it saying?

AND C CU

James looked over Sam's shoulder silently taking in the message, then stared at Sam, his eyes widening. 'Two Rippers?' was all he said.

Message in hand, Sam took the stairs two at a time!

In a borrowed dressing gown and with a towel twisted round her wet hair, Anna looked pretty good. He hadn't seen her without any make-up before, but her olive skin needed none. Sam silently approved, thinking maybe it wasn't the best moment to joke that she scrubbed up well. She was still very conscious of the facial bruise Rees had given her, a yellow and black area plus the remnants of a split lip, though none of that detracted from her natural beauty.

She sat with the message in her hand thinking carefully. She examined the number sheet again, checking Sam's findings now that they had wrung every possible letter available from the message.

Two Rippers? This was a turn up. What did it mean? Who or what the hell was C CU? During her researches Anna had come up against every Ripper permutation. These included the idea that it was a woman, 'Jill the Ripper', advocated by Conan Doyle himself at one time. Also the deranged Doctor theory, strengthened later by the 'Macnaghten Memoranda', but effectively crushed by the first-hand knowledge of Doctor Gordon Brown and others. And of course, the idea that there had been two killers, but she had never yet felt there was any real evidence or even pointers that this might be the case.

As she well knew, Thomas Hayne Cutbush had long been a suspect, fairly high up the rankings of the two hundred or so argued about by Ripperologists to this day. Periodically, like others, he would be in or out of fashion according to the latest information and your point of view. His candidacy had risen again in recent times with the release of his medical records from Broadmoor Hospital, though tantalisingly, they revealed little new information except to confirm his violent tendencies.

Suddenly something came to mind and the irresistible smile spread over her face. Sam felt his temperature rise and it wasn't just because she had come up with something. Anna looked up.

'I think I've got it,' she said. 'It's weird but then the truth always is isn't it?'

Sam and James waited patiently.

'As I said before, there have been a couple of books floating the idea that Thomas Cutbush was the killer. David Bullock cites him as the murderer. Another is by AP Wolf and he not only talked about Thomas, he raised the scenario that his uncle Charles may have been an important factor in solving the mystery. Both of these books are extremely well researched.'

She paused. 'Charles Cutbush was Thomas's uncle and a very senior policeman. He was a superintendent in fact, one of only three in the Metropolitan Police at that time. He may have been very close to his nephew. So what Conan Doyle is telling us is that both of them were involved in the murders.'

She pencilled a few extra letters on the message and handed it to Sam. Now it read:

CONFESSED AS GUILTY OF THE
WHITECHAPEL MURDERS
T CUTBUSH AND C CUTBUSH

'At the time of the Melville Macnaghten memo, *The Sun* newspaper was busy implying that the force would be severely embarrassed if they named Thomas Cutbush. Macnaghten's memo was written – for his superiors – to deflect heat from the police and from Superintendent Charles Cutbush. You remember, Sam, I gave you my views about Macnaghten and his memo before?'

Sam nodded, that was coming back to him now. He still hadn't had a chance to read the memo or any other Ripper material.

She paused in the middle of her speech looking blank. Then a strange light came into her eyes. Sam and James said nothing; they could see she was back on the trail in Whitechapel all those years ago.

'Of course,' she said. 'Of course.'

Sam's patience was exhausted. 'What? What?' he demanded.

'I'm sorry, Sam, but I've just remembered the rest of it. Initially Superintendent Charles Cutbush was personally directly involved in the early Ripper enquiries, but was then put in charge of pay and supplies. As a desk warrior he doesn't feature too much in the later police hunt, perhaps because he was sidelined, but...' she paused for dramatic effect.

'Thomas Cutbush was found to be a lunatic and Charles Cutbush also definitely had some mental illness, in fact he was becoming a serious embarrassment in a senior role and it is thought he was quietly pensioned off to get him out of the way.'

She paused again, switching to her own modern parlance to summarise things.

'The police knew he was going round the bend, and to prove it, he did commit suicide while in retirement afterwards. He was mad and he shot himself. It ran in the family, they were both nutters.' She finished abruptly with a flourish.

It was silent as her words sank in. Suddenly it all seemed to make sense.

Anna added a few more points as she pieced the bits together. 'I think the whole thing was covered up, there was too much at stake. Lots of senior policemen said they knew who the Ripper was, but most of them just wanted to be self-important. Perhaps one or two people *really did* guess the identity and had to do something. They couldn't name Cutbush; one Cutbush would lead to the other! Can you imagine the fallout if the public got wind of it?'

Sam nodded seriously as he replied, 'It wouldn't just bring down the Metropolitan Police, it might have brought down the Government. There would have been riots, anarchy, if it was thought that the police had a murderer in their ranks. Or even worse still, if they knew who he was and covered it up. You remember what Steve said about their code of silence and what he thought about it.'

She nodded her agreement.

'Do you really think that's what would have happened?' James asked Sam.

'Yes I do, it would be unthinkable, and it would shake the Empire to its roots. Cover-ups have happened throughout British history, there was, still are, politicians who think ordinary people shouldn't know everything. Although things seemed fine in the Empire, there was still plenty that could go wrong. The Bloody Sunday riots in 1887 involved both Sir Charles Warren and the Home Secretary Henry Mathews who was widely disliked. That sort of event can easily lead to much more serious trouble if it's badly managed.'

Sam paused, he was very tired now, suddenly the events of the last few days were catching up. He finished off his thoughts.

'It only needed an event like the Ripper to be mishandled, then things would really blow.'

Sam looked across the table at the bruised face opposite him. 'Good old Conan Doyle, he sussed it out, and do you know what? I'm really not surprised. Anyway, James, I'm going to bed, I'm done in,' said Sam.

'What are we going to do with this message now?' said Anna.

'I don't know, put it under your pillow and we'll see tomorrow,' smiled Sam. 'Goodnight, James.'

Chapter 51
The Great Escape

East London – 1891

In March, shortly after the murder of Frances Coles, Thomas Cutbush was taken into custody. He lounged on the simple bed which formed the sole furnishing of the grim holding cell in which he was locked. All his clothes had been taken from him with the exception of the grubby stained white shirt that he wore. Left alone he looked around him, slowly becoming aware that he was imprisoned. A moment of lucidity washed over him, at this point in his life he still had much to do. The walls closed in, suffocating and confining him. Then the rage surfaced momentarily and he fought to control it, slowly his anger subsided, replaced by the cunning he had so often employed in the past.

His arrest had taken place after one of his frequent rows with relatives; with the exception of his uncle these people seemed to be sent to try him. Berated about his behaviour once again, this time by another aunt, he had finally grasped the woman around her neck, and had pulled his pocket knife as if to slash her throat. It was only then that he had been manacled and taken away, suspected of being a violent lunatic. He now felt betrayed, and by his own family indeed. In his view they were all clearly insane.

It was usual in these circumstances for the authorities to get the offender off the streets, so he had been taken to the infirmary in Lambeth for an initial assessment of his condition. Their early attempts to question him had been fruitless, and more than one of the police and warders involved were convinced he might have been responsible for the Whitechapel murders. Certainly, his sudden violence and latent strength made him a very dangerous and unpredictable individual. Now he was to be removed to the asylum's inner building where he would be registered, bathed and given a medical examination. Four orderlies were designated for this task. They arrived at his cell with a gown to dress him in, and peering through the observation slot they could see that he appeared calm and resigned.

The four entered the cell and one orderly approached, telling him to come along with them. Suddenly and with unbelievable speed Thomas arose violently, knocking over the first man, then punching another viciously in the face. The remaining two were caught by surprise, one received a knee in the groin and doubled up swearing and gasping with pain. The last man, vainly to block the doorway, was grabbed by his neck and had his head smashed hard against the brick wall. Not one of them was able to deploy his truncheon in any sort of meaningful retaliation. In a flash the prisoner was through the open door, his shirt tails flying up as he did so. The lack of clothing seemed not to hinder him as he ran from the building, then leapt at the eight foot wall in the courtyard. Grasping the top with both hands he kicked his leg up to one side and swung himself on to the top. Oblivious of the cuts and scratches he was receiving he paused for a second to survey the crowded street on the other side of the wall before dropping swiftly down onto it. A shout from inside followed him, suddenly muted by the wall which now divided them.

By this time whistles were blowing and the alarm had been well and truly raised. Fifty yards along the wall was a large double gate, from which one of the orderlies emerged, shouting for people to stop the man. Some way further down the street a constable responded to the whistles and gave chase. There was no time to lose and Thomas ran straight into the door of the first house he encountered. As so often in the area, it was unlocked, allowing him to run straight through and out of the back door. He left a woman who was the occupant shrieking in shock behind him.

Over several garden fences he leapt still oblivious to the fact he was unshod and had nothing on save his shirt. He tried another door further along the same road, and finding it also unlocked, he paused inside. The silence told him it was unoccupied so casting about he found just what was needed, some men's clothing which he swiftly put on. His luck continued, by the back door stood a pair of working boots and they fitted him without difficulty. Pausing to take a hat from the hat rack he pushed it hard onto his head to complete his new ensemble. Thomas then opened the front door and calmly and casually strolled away. Glancing back over his shoulder he could see a crowd of people outside the door of the first property he had entered.

Thomas was well and truly on the run now. Later, still engaged on his nocturnal ramblings and unable to return home he stopped a man and his companion in the street to talk to them. He asked the man for help explaining that the police were seeking him, and then alarmed them both by talking and gesticulating wildly. Each time a cab passed he told the couple that it contained the officers who were hunting him. He said a reward of £500 had been offered for his arrest as Jack the Ripper but he was not guilty, he wasn't the man they wanted. His entreaties struck the man and his companion as desperate, and this, coupled with his ill-fitting clothes and the blue staring eyes, made them feel vulnerable to assault or worse.

After making his excuses the man and his lady companion hurried away, but it wasn't long before they had reported the matter to a police station. There they were able to give a very detailed description of the man they had met.

Thomas was apprehended again within a few days, given away by his outlandish behaviour and garbled conversations with anyone he encountered. On 14 April 1891 he was due to be charged in the name of Thomas Hayne Cutbush with the stabbing of two women, but was found to be a violent lunatic. After being taken down he was transferred to Broadmoor on the following day. There were to be no further escapes for Cutbush junior.

Chapter 52

The Morning After

Minstead, the New Forest – Present Day

The next morning the four of them sat over breakfast in Beth's kitchen. Anna and Sam apologised again for their invasion of their hosts' house and the danger they had brought with them. They discussed the adventures of the night before and Sam, concerned for the safety of Anna and his friends, came up with a plan to get the watchers off their backs. It was a plan that involved some emails and a phone call. A phone call that they hoped would be overheard...

Anna borrowed Beth's computer and, prompted by Sam, swiftly created a document detailing her discovery of the Doyle Memorandum, along with its eventual conclusion about the two murderers. She didn't name them, preferring to keep that information closer to home for the moment. She also listed the encounters and harassment they had experienced from their pursuers, including the train journey and the assault and robbery she had suffered. Tellingly, she stated that they must have been police in order to have had the clout they showed in the British Library. Finally, Anna and Sam collaborated to come up with descriptions of any of the individual police officers they had become aware of. Anna emailed a copy to Steve, assuming it would be intercepted, and then using her own mobile, she rang him directly.

Her purpose, at Sam's insistence, was to ensure that any listener realised that the cat was out of the bag. She told Steve that she had some important information and would phone him back in one hour. This would ensure that anyone monitoring would be ready to listen in. On her second call she told Steve that she was sending the document to many others including a friend in the national press. She chattered away as though the thought of anyone eavesdropping was the last thing on her mind.

Steve quickly realised what she was up to and a broad smile crossed his face. He made a few comments along the lines that there was no point in anyone bothering her now, as the game was clearly over. He had her document and he and many others would follow it with interest. It was a good performance. Darren knew it was finished, and so did Sam. Darren pursed his lips and shrugged at John who sat opposite his desk. Finally he picked up the phone to speak to his boss. It looked as though his team would be back working on their list of anti-nuclear power activists shortly.

Soon, Anna got back to the subject of the Ripper. Borrowing Beth's computer again she blitzed sources of information, confirming and checking out her findings. Her fingers flew over the keyboard and her face set with determination as she wrote up her piece on the two Cutbushes. Anna paused only when James made coffee for them all, gratefully clasping her mug with both hands she discussed the case in more detail.

'There was definitely a suspicion that the Met covered up their knowledge of the killer because he was the nephew of Superintendent Cutbush. Yes, the weakness of the case against Thomas Hayne Cutbush has always been that the murders supposedly ended in November 1888 with the mutilation of Mary Kelly. If Cutbush was the killer why would he stop in that November, when he was still at large? The old idea was that the killer's own savagery finally made him flip and commit suicide, but that's unlikely. As we understand nowadays, it isn't unknown for serial killers to take a break and even begin killing again in different ways. If, as many people believe, the killings resumed later, then he comes back into his own as a suspect. It depends upon who you believe were the Ripper's prey. If you accept that Alice McKenzie and Frances Coles were his victims, then Thomas Cutbush fits, and fits very well. He was finally incarcerated in April 1891, soon after death of Frances Coles. At that point the murders definitely ceased.'

Sam was intrigued. 'What else ties this guy into the killings? What is the rest of the case against him?'

Anna racked her brains.

'I'll have to check on this stuff again, but what I do remember is that his court appearance decided he was insane for hereditary reasons and through over-study. He was said to have furiously researched medical books, and roamed the streets at night, returning covered with mud, and some people said, blood. His aunt Clara was on record as saying he was violent, and in fact we know he definitely was. He made one violent escape, threatened asylum staff later and even attacked his own mother when she came to visit him. Some three years after he was put away, *The Sun* newspaper published their series of articles which outed Cutbush, saying that he was in an asylum. They even sent staff to see him in Broadmoor. They didn't name him directly, saying that he had relatives in high places, and that of course made some people very inquisitive.'

'*The Sun* also made the statement, which many subsequently agreed with, that when the killer was committed to an asylum, the murders finally stopped. It was a very significant point. They also printed statements from witnesses who encountered him and their experiences.

'I did once read their articles, they display evidence that they were well researched and written in good faith. The paper spent a lot of time and energy following it up. There is no question that the people who did the interviews and wrote the articles believed without doubt that they had identified Jack the Ripper. *The Sun* cites lots of evidence that points directly to him, and lists nine murders that they say he was responsible for.'

'Well, it sounds as though you've cracked it, Anna, well done,' said Sam.

Anna didn't actually purr, but she looked like the cat that had got the cream.

Standing up, Sam turned to James. 'Excuse me a moment, can I borrow the phone in your study, James?'

'Who are you phoning?' said Anna, as bossy as ever.

Sam grinned. 'My sister, she's going to kill me. And then my parents, and Bernie as well, I owe them all some thanks.'

Chapter 53
For He Who Comes After

Whitechapel – April 1905

The April day was damp and overcast as six well-dressed gentleman walked slowly along Commercial Street towards Spitalfields Market. The constant threat of showers had caused several to carry umbrellas. The weather was well suited to their mission; a sunny day might have softened the experience, made things less serious and grim than they had been some seventeen years prior.

Accompanying them were a couple of senior Scotland Yard detectives. From time to time one or another would gesture with his stick, indicating a point of interest to the others. These were influential men and the detectives had been assigned to accompany and guide them. Earlier that morning the group had met at Bishopsgate police station for the onset of their tour.

Now and then they would pause and cluster around, discussing some detail of the gruesome Whitechapel murders in which they were interested. The gentlemen were all members of a London dining society, The Crimes Club. By this time they referred to themselves as Our Society, but were known to others as The Murder Club. From time to time its small but elite membership listed some of the most eminent men in the country. Drawn from various professions they all had an interest in serious crimes. Amongst their numbers were surgeons, civil servants, authors, lawyers and academics. Occasionally in their visits to crime scenes they were accompanied by senior police officers, a few of whom were also members.

On this occasion one of the six was Dr Frederick Gordon Brown, a police surgeon who had been involved in some Whitechapel murder post mortems, and had given evidence to some of the inquests. Another was a coroner who also had been professionally involved.

During the day the group visited nine sites where serious murders had occurred, and several other places of interest including a lodging house or doss house. But two of them had a secret they could not share with the group. It was not the first time that they had visited the sites and they were privy to the identity of the men who had committed the Whitechapel murders.

Conan Doyle, by now Sir Arthur Conan Doyle, was a well-built man sporting his trademark moustache. He was aged around forty-five, and his companion Professor Joseph Bell was a wiry Scot just over twenty years older, with bright eyes and a jerky stiffening gait.

Bell had been Doyle's mentor during his medical training and had made a lifelong impression upon the young student. What had really stuck in Doyle's mind had been the incredible powers of logic, observation and deduction which Bell would regularly demonstrate to his students. These skills were, as Bell had insisted, absolutely vital to a doctor and would be of limitless use to him when making a diagnosis. What Doyle had achieved later was to transplant those skills to another discipline, that of the private detective. When he had done so, hey presto, Sherlock Holmes lived and breathed. The rest was history. Later on, Doyle had credited Bell with his inspiration in those famous words he had written to him.

'It is most certainly to you that I owe Sherlock Holmes.'

Nearing the end of their tour, these two hung back a little from the rest for a private word.

'Well, it's more than ten years since we were last here in the area, and I have to say it feels like a lifetime away,' Bell remarked.

'Indeed it does,' said Doyle slowly. He also still had his soft Scottish accent, though less pronounced. 'Such a pity in a way that it turned out how it did, and people still none the wiser.'

'Sometimes it is best that people don't know everything eh?' said Bell. Suddenly he looked up at the bigger man shrewdly. 'You're not thinking that maybe they should be told just now, are you?'

After a moment Doyle shook his head. 'No, the secret is safe enough, though I feel it must come out one day.'

'Aye, but still we live in troubled times and it would mean an unprecedented upset for the police and Parliament. They might not be able to prevail.' Bell smiled. 'Maybe when we are gone eh? None of us are going to live forever,' he chuckled mirthlessly.

'Perhaps I'll leave a few clues before I go,' smiled Doyle. 'It would be an unnatural shame for the future if there was no answer to the conundrum.'

Bell's eyes shone with pleasure. 'That's a capital idea, and you are the best man to do it. You'll probably have twenty years more than me and the public love a mystery, as you know only too well. And what a rare ripping yarn it has been!'

That evening the two talked long and earnestly over dinner at their hotel. They talked about the old days when they had first met and Doyle had qualified as a doctor in Edinburgh. Also they recalled their individual and shared clandestine visits to Whitechapel years previously, reliving a mutual fascination with the Whitechapel murders. The eager desire to solve the mystery without committing themselves in public had been central to their activities. For these two successful and well known men it would have been disastrous to have announced a name which might subsequently have been proven wrong.

They reminisced about their initial decision to swap letters bearing the name of the suspect and how they had both come independently to the same conclusion about Thomas Hayne Cutbush. What a shock it had been to both of them that they had named the same man! In turn, that had led to the discovery that his paternal uncle was Superintendent Charles Cutbush, a sick man, but one of the highest ranking police officers in the Metropolitan Police.

They remembered their great relief when they ascertained that Thomas had finally been adjudged a lunatic and was incarcerated in Broadmoor, from where he was unlikely to escape. They went on to talk more about that tragic and distressing night when they had gone to confront his uncle. Charles Cutbush had been forced into retirement by the police, who suspected his involvement, through him leaking information to his nephew.

After that had come their timely but discreet exit from the sad and violent circumstances of his death. There was little doubt in their minds that Superintendent Charles Cutbush had influenced his weak minded nephew to both join him, then supersede him, in the eradication of fallen women. These were the hated Marys of Whitechapel. Their keen incisive minds had put the trail of clues together in true Holmes style. The Superintendent's loathing of Catholics was well known as they had discovered from his colleagues, and they had no doubt that the elder Cutbush was just as guilty as the younger. It had been his certainty that the game was up that had caused him to blow his own brains out when their visit was imminent.

Following on, there had been clandestine discussions with the Home Secretary. It had been tacitly agreed that the less that was said about the policeman's illness and death the better. Now that the Whitechapel menace had been finally removed, the whole sorry saga was best consigned to history. They all believed that no good could come from the publication of the killer's name. They also felt there was little point in disclosing the miserable failure of the police to identify the problem so close to, and actually within, their organisation. Doyle and Bell felt that the police would do well to adopt a training programme for detectives, based on the observation and deduction skills of Sherlock Holmes. After all, it had been the creation of Holmes that had inspired the pair of them to investigate and solve the mystery of the Whitechapel murderer in the first place.

The following day, Joseph Bell boarded his train to Edinburgh, Doyle accompanying him as far as the station. They made their goodbyes and the younger man watched as white steam billowed up to the station canopy before the train slowly got under way. The sound of the steam hissing and the clank of the machinery filled the platform area, giving fierce warning of the tremendous pressures and power harnessed in the engine.

Doyle watched until the train was out of sight then slowly turned away. True to his nature his inventive and energetic mind was already working out how best he might leave his hidden legacy to the world that would follow. He decided to leave it for a while, he was fit and healthy and had years of writing ahead of him. But, he resolved, the solution to the mystery of Jack the Ripper would definitely be concealed somehow in a book he had yet to write. There would be no hurry, the wounds were still too raw and he hoped for years of writing to come. The clues would then be left for anyone smart enough to find them. The thought made him smile.

As he did so he felt for his pocketbook, in which he would make a few notes.

What had Bell called it? *A Ripping Yarn?* ...Or some such title.

He smiled again. Consulting his pocket watch, Doyle planned his own train home to Undershaw and walked away.

The following year his first wife Louise died, leaving the way free for him to marry Jean Leckie and to start raising his second family. Doyle was active locally founding a rifle club and getting involved in all sorts of causes. The Great War came and went. Life in Britain was destined never to be the same again. Sir Arthur Conan Doyle lost his beloved son Kingsley who contracted influenza after being wounded in action. His younger brother Innes, who had been his faithful companion in Portsmouth all those years ago, also died.

With Jean, he had purchased and then extended Windlesham, their house in Crowborough, while Undershaw, the home he had once thought Kingsley would live in was eventually sold off. It was only much later in the 1920s that he finally and belatedly put the plan agreed with Bell into action.

After purchasing Bignell Wood in Hampshire as a second home, Doyle spent many happy times there; it was rural retreat, not easy to get to, standing well back from the road in substantial grounds. It was ideal for a relaxing lifestyle in the summer months and also a good venue for the seances that he and Jean participated in. He still wrote both here and at Windlesham, prolific in his outpourings, and though having finished with Holmes for the umpteenth time he was finally persuaded to give the super sleuth and Watson their one last outing. This was to be in a series of stories entitled *The Case-Book of Sherlock Holmes*. Whether this persuasion was financial or pressure from publishers and his public was a moot point. The money would always be welcome, but Doyle's integrity meant he worried that the stories might not prove to be of the calibre they had once been.

In 1927, once *The Case-Book* was published, Doyle was starting to tire a little, no longer the strong man he had once been. One day the following year the Ripper enigma came back to his memory with a vengeance. Looking back at the notes he had made all those years ago, he realised he had missed a golden opportunity with *The Case-Book* to leave clues to the identity of the killer. Sadly, Joseph Bell had died in 1911 and there had been no-one to remind him, no-one to review things with, no-one to share the gruesome and incredible secret they had uncovered.

Pulling a pristine publisher's copy from his bookshelf, he scanned *The Case-Book* to find the lines he needed, realising that had the stories actually been in a certain preferred sequence he would have had little more to do, but unfortunately they weren't.

Damn the thing, he had missed the perfect chance, could that now be changed? Why not? He was the author, a Knight of the realm, and a powerful man after all. Pulling some paper toward him he started to draft a memo to his publisher.

Once he had finished that he began to compile the number sheet. Propping *The Case-Book* open in front of him he leafed through the pages, the lines and words, counting and then double checking his work. It was painstaking and tiring to ensure there were no errors, not the sort of task he enjoyed at all.

His heading at the top said: *Bignell Wood* and on the right side, *First and last lines contain a Ripping Yarn*, his usual habit of noting where he was when he wrote anything down.

Following that Doyle composed his brief and enigmatic memo on another piece of paper, using the same headings, then below that:

The message is for he who comes after.
Now I have done my duty.

Arthur Conan Doyle

With a sigh he used a paper clip to fasten the two sheets together then slipped them into the top drawer of his writing desk. Leaning back, Sir Arthur folded his hands behind his head and thought. He reflected that perhaps it didn't really matter about the sequence of the stories, there was no urgency, and years could pass if necessary. Once future editions were published with the stories in the correct order, someone would undoubtedly find the hidden secret one day. It would probably be a member of his family who would be cataloguing his papers for a biography or something similar.

His only commitment to Bell had been that he would put the clues out there for someone to find. Doyle chuckled quietly to himself. He had done that now and if the mystery wasn't solved until after his own demise that would be a good thing. No questions, no reproaches, no criticism would be levelled at him while he was still alive, and a good thing too he thought. Pulling a pocket watch from his waistcoat Doyle checked the time, it really wasn't long to wait before dinner would be served.

As he went to change for dinner he put the matter out of his mind once more. Unfortunately he had forgotten something. In his inimitable way he had failed to realise that the pages, lines, words and letters would inevitably change from the first edition that sat comfortably on his bookshelf. It was a classic Doylism, the sort of thing his aficionados and biographers would fasten upon much later. His research was often poor, or badly followed through. Perhaps he couldn't be bothered, or perhaps because it was usually some fiction he was writing, it just didn't matter anyway. At this point in his life he was tired, his health was failing and what was really important was spending time with his beloved Jean.

But with this little code it actually had been important, and with the eventual haphazard distribution of his personal papers, the secret was to remain buried for much longer than he could ever have imagined.

Chapter 54

A Policeman's Lot

Victoria Street, London – Present Day

The twenty-first century demands on Sir John Edwards were considerable, but he had learned to be a ruthless time manager during his slow but relentless career climb. It was a climb to what was recognised as the pinnacle of the policing tree in Great Britain. The hardest thing, he reflected, had always been doing the politics, which became trickier as he rose through the ranks. John Edwards was a vocational policeman, there had been no real fast track for him and he was one of the latest few at his level who had walked the beat in London as a young PC. He imagined the politics must have been as bad for Sir Charles Warren, one of his predecessors at the time of the Whitechapel murders. The crimes had been unprecedented and the Home Secretary, Henry Mathews, would have been breathing down Warren's neck. The political pressure would have been immense and he knew that those pressures never really went away.

Today he had a difficult meeting to deal with. The two young people he was going to see had been followed and harassed by members of the National Public Order Intelligence Unit, for whom he was now obliged to answer. The NPOIU had been a unit belonging to the Association of Chief Police Officers, and theoretically unaccountable, but as it was now in transition back to the Metropolitan Police, Sir John already took responsibility for its activities. Anna Moretti and Sam Taylor had got to the bottom of a mystery which had plagued London and the whole of the developed world for more than one hundred and twenty years, and it was to their credit. They had committed no wrong and yet had been intimidated every step of the way during their quest. He had discussed the matter with a couple of trusted senior people in the Home Office, but he was very aware that others there would take a very different view of what he was about to do and might counsel a different approach. For once, the Commissioner would not be curtailing his time today, his legendary speed and incisiveness in meetings would be slowed. The meeting was going to be delicate and could easily have an effect on his future, as well as that of the organisation he headed up.

It was a strange meeting, Sam thought afterwards, even slightly surreal. He and Anna had kept their appointment with the Metropolitan Police Commissioner in his office at New Scotland Yard. They had been treated deferentially and were shown in without being kept waiting. A small thing, but even that seemed telling. Gesturing to a coffee table in his office Sir John joined them with no attempt to keep his large and imposing desk between them. He shook their hands and a young man offered and brought coffee for them all, then departed with a smile.

Even as they had entered the building Sam had wondered whether they should be there, Anna seemed preoccupied and he could only offer a poor quip.

'Into the lion's den eh?' She had looked nervous, but her anger at the way they had been treated was barely concealed. The fight or flight adrenalin was kicking in, but with Anna it was likely to be fight and rarely flight.

For a long minute the Commissioner held them in his gaze and they returned it, Sam with no expression other than the determined jut of his chin, Anna looking distrustful, and Sir John carefully assessing them both.

'Thank you for coming here, I appreciate it,' he offered.

Sam nodded acknowledgement. There was another pause before the Commissioner spoke again.

'I suppose I should congratulate you both if you have really solved a mystery that has defeated people for over a hundred years. That would be quite remarkable.'

'It certainly defeated the Metropolitan Police didn't it? said Anna frostily. She regarded him coldly, as one might a poor inadequate loser.

Sir John gave a tight smile. 'Yes it did. But of course we can't be sure that you have actually solved it, can we?'

'We have, and we can prove it. We now have the whole picture, and the evidence to back it up,' Anna shot back. 'No thanks to your people, that evidence is safe,' she added.

The Commissioner regarded them both again.

Sam decided to enter the conversation. 'Why did you invite us here? What exactly do you want from us?'

'I'd like to hear all about it. The whole story I mean.'

'Why should we tell you anything?' Anna flashed. 'Your people have chased and harassed us, burgled a car and assaulted us, once we get this published, you can read it in the press. After that we'll take action against the police for the way we have been treated.'

Sir John raised his hands. 'I see that you are upset, but you know you won't be able to prove anything against the police. You are smart enough to work that out. I have been looking into recent events as well as those of the 1880s and have got a good feel for what may really have been happening.'

He paused. 'Look, let's start again, tell me the whole story and let me judge how you have been treated for myself... I am genuinely interested,' he added.

Anna looked at Sam who nodded cautiously before speaking out.

'Okay, there's no reason why you shouldn't know the story, on condition that you tell us why your men were following us and threatening us. You owe us that explanation, at the very least.'

'Done,' said the Commissioner promptly. 'You shall have it. I give you my word.'

Slightly surprised, they both felt they could believe him so started to tell it from the beginning. They took it in turns to expand parts of the story; Sam talked about Conan Doyle's investigation into the murders and gave his own assessment of the political and social situation during that terrible period in east London. Anna graphically described their own recent experiences with the police to Sir John and watched his reaction closely. Much of the time he remained inscrutable, listening intently and nodding to encourage them to continue, but once or twice she detected a pained expression in his eyes, particularly when she recounted the punch in the face and the robbery she had been subjected to on the train.

When they explained the Conan Doyle's part in tracking the killers and his memorandum the Commissioner looked extremely interested, asking a lot of questions about the trail of clues they had followed.

They finished the story and Sir John ordered more coffee. Waiting while it was poured, nobody said anything until the courteous young man left the office once again.

Sir John exhaled slowly. 'It really is an amazing story and I thank you for telling me all about it. I must now explain why you were followed in the way that you were.'

Cocking her head Anna looked at him expectantly, not quite hiding the frosty attitude she still held.

'For a long time, probably since the beginning, the Metropolitan Police has jealously guarded its reputation. Like any organisation it has had its successes and failures. It is made up of humans, humans who often do a good job and yet suffer from all the usual human weaknesses. Pride in the organisation has always been a big motivator, particularly amongst the people who head the organisation up, and that filters down to all levels.'

Sir John paused.

'Police officers often get emotionally involved in cases, they are frequently affected by the things they see and do, they hate injustice and are really glad when they can bring murderers and other evil people to the courts. They are also very proud of their successes and of their institution. Sometimes that pride in the reputation of the institution can be carried to extremes. There will have been occasions when people have acted wrongly to maintain public confidence. It has happened many times and I have no doubt it will happen again. You see, when an organisation is open to scrutiny, and yet has to deliver a robust public service, many of its members develop a feeling of almost siege management. They feel their colleagues must be protected at all costs, when they have gone beyond their authority and even when they have gone beyond the law.'

Sir John smiled grimly at them both.

'I am not trying to justify anything, but can you imagine what it was like in the Metropolitan Police at the time of the Whitechapel murders? It wasn't such a professional organisation then, ordinary policemen were often demoralised, poorly paid and sometimes corrupt. On top of that the press were extremely critical, crediting the police with nothing and carping about their performance at every turn. The murders were a godsend for anyone wanting to attack the police. Also, it is true there were divisions and tension amongst the hierarchy which did nothing to help the hunt. For several years the police took a lot of stick and there were sackings and resignations at high levels. The Home Secretary was involved and of course, the murders became a political issue. As you well know, Sir Charles Warren resigned when the job became untenable to him.'

Sir John shook his head gently.

'A cynic might say that nothing has changed, certainly what matters to a politician is their own standing, and the support they give to any department responsible to them also becomes a political decision. If it is expedient, they withdraw that support, if the department is performing well they attach themselves to it in order to enhance their own reputation. It is exactly the same today of course, though I shall deny saying that if you ever quote me.'

He smiled thinly, and then continued.

'Miss Moretti, you were quite right to identify that Sir Charles Macnaghten came under extreme pressure at the time of *The Sun's* campaign and he acted to get the heat off the Metropolitan Police. I believe that is just one example of a defensive strategy by the police, his memorandum went back up the line and succeeded in stopping anyone from investigating Superintendent Charles Cutbush. Whether or not the Superintendent was a guilty man, Macnaghten probably didn't care; he just didn't want anyone looking into it any further. His object was clearly damage limitation and for the Metropolitan Police to be able to move onwards and upwards. I have made my own enquiries into that and I believe you have described his position perfectly.'

Glancing at the black and silver clock on the wall, Sir John rose to his feet and asked if they would excuse him for a few moments as he had to take a scheduled phone call. Promising to return very shortly he left the office.

Anna and Sam's eyes met, his slight shake of the head confirming they shouldn't discuss things, even here, in the Commissioner's office. Sam stood up to stretch himself and looked around. The office was large and well appointed, several family photos in polished black frames stood on a shelf at the side and certificates of service and commendations hung on the wall above them. They were both thinking the same thing. What was the phone call? Was it about them? Who was it with?

After about twenty minutes Anna was getting restless. Suddenly the door opened and Sir John strode back in. He apologised profusely saying that the call had been longer than he had expected.

Seated again around the coffee table they picked up where they had left off. This time he seemed more conciliatory.

'Sir Charles Macnaghten wasn't the only one whose actions might have been questionable. The code of secrecy I spoke about earlier has always existed and I would be foolish to try and deny that it is still around today. There are certain people in this country who take it upon themselves to be the self-appointed guardians of the establishment. Of course they are not all policemen, though I am afraid that some police officers still act in misguided ways. I believe this is what has happened in your case and I sincerely apologise to you both for that. There can be no justification for the way you were treated, which was a disgraceful episode. During the time when the National Public Order Intelligence Unit was not reporting to the Metropolitan Police, it is clear that mistakes were made by some of their officers.

'I will come straight to the point, in addition to apologising I am going to ask you if you can find it in yourselves to remain silent about the information you have discovered, for the sake of everyone concerned.'

He stopped abruptly. Sam's eyebrows raised and Anna's face was a picture, her jaw literally dropping with shock.

'You really think we are going to bury this, the find of the century, just to please the Met? Why the bloody hell should we do that?' She almost spat the words at the Commissioner.

'I realise it is asking a lot of you...'

'A lot?' blasted Anna incredulously, her eyes flashing in the way that Sam had come to know so well.

Sir John nodded. 'Yes, it is a lot, and I realise I can only appeal to you. Ultimately you must do whatever you feel is best and it will be your decision.'

Sam had been taking all this in. Calmly he joined the conversation. 'You said for the sake of everyone, Sir John, who exactly do you mean, and why is it so important?'

'Well, Mr Taylor, earlier you gave a very eloquent and persuasive view of the risks to the Met and the Government if the public suspected a police officer had compromised the investigation, or worse still actually been involved in the murders. That was the case then and I believe it would be the same now. The damage to the Met could be incalculable.

'That could spread to all UK police forces and make both public relations and internal morale even worse than they are now. I think it could actually be catastrophic, and I use the word carefully, for the Metropolitan Police, who are relied upon to spearhead security in these days of international terrorism.'

There was silence in the room. The Commissioner took up the thread again, addressing himself primarily to Anna, and pressing his case gently.

'I share your enthusiasm for getting to the bottom of a mystery and it would be fantastic to lay the ghost of the Ripper once and for all. If only it were possible without damaging this institution, and maybe others as well. I really would fear for the Met, imperfect though it is, and by extension the safety of the public, if either the force or confidence in it collapsed.' The Commissioner gestured around him as if to indicate the Metropolitan Police Service itself. His manner was subdued and empathetic now, with no trace of the slightly patronising, almost superior manner he had started the meeting with.

Sam suddenly realised they had been there for a couple of hours. He felt it was time to bring this to a close, rising from his chair he offered his hand to Sir John.

'Well, you have certainly given us something to consider, Commissioner. I think we had better go now, but we'll think about all you've said.'

Sir John also rose and took Sam's hand automatically. 'Thank you for listening to me, I wish you both well. As I said earlier, I can only ask you to reflect on everything carefully before you decide what to do.'

Anna also shook his hand, making her parting shot. 'I suppose we can expect to be followed when we leave here?' Her dark eyes pointedly fixed the Commissioner, her face tilted up, challenging him. Then the ghost of a smile appeared on her lips.

'Absolutely not, Miss Moretti.' The Commissioner's eyes twinkled, picking up on her half smile and accepting the rebuke. 'I apologise again and can assure you neither of you will be troubled.'

She was a tough cookie this one, and beautiful with it, Sir John thought to himself.

Leaving New Scotland Yard Sam breathed out heavily, he led the way around the block into Victoria Street and looked carefully up and down the road.

'My god, Sam, what are you doing? You don't really think there's anyone following us do you?' Anna said, shocked.

Sam grinned. 'No, no, I was looking for a pub, I don't know about you but I could do with a drink.'

The big smile appeared with great relief, as she tucked her arm through his and squeezed it. 'Mmm, I thought you'd never ask!'

Sam noticed the arm ploy and liked it. It had been a while since anyone had done that and it felt good.

Chapter 55

After the Storm

Southampton – Present Day

Finally, Anna had come down to the New Forest again. A few short weeks had passed in a whirlwind of sensational events. Eventually as things quietened down, after many frantic emails and telephone conversations, Sam had invited her for a long weekend. With slightly mixed memories of previous occasions, they met again at Southampton station.

They went first to Sam's apartment where he carried her overnight bag, dropping it in the lounge.

'No bugs in there I hope!' he said with a laugh.

Anna had found the location device in her wheelie bag when they had eventually picked up their luggage, and she had ceremonially tossed it into the Thames from Blackfriars Bridge near the hotel.

She was curious to see Sam's home; her sensitive antennae nosed carefully around the room while he prepared coffee in the kitchen. Anna took in a couple of prints on the wall, a few travel photographs and some ancient Greek-style pots, whilst she kept one eye on the kitchen door in case he emerged. She looked at some family photos in frames, one of his parents and a young woman. Would that be his ex-girlfriend? No, it must be his sister Paige, the likeness was extraordinary.

The room she had seen so far was an unusual mix of contemporary and traditional styles, with a patterned carpet and odd pieces of furniture that didn't particularly match, though the place felt comfortable and reassuring, albeit with a slightly faded feel about it. A big bay window looked down onto the street below. Just then the noise of coffee making ceased and Sam appeared with two mugs, hooking his foot behind the kitchen door to pull it closed behind him.

'It's a really nice place you have here,' she said.

'Thanks, Anna, yes I love it here, I was very fortunate to get it. It's spacious yet cosy as well, and it's very quiet to work in during the day.'

Sam pushed open another door and pointed through.

'That's my library where I work and there's a couple of spare bedrooms off the hallway, though one of them is full of junk,' he gesticulated back towards the entrance. 'I'll show you later if you like, why don't we go for a drive in the New Forest? The sun's out and we can get lunch somewhere.'

Anna sipped her coffee, sneaking a foil wrapped chocolate Sam had slipped onto the coffee table for her.

'That'll be great,' she said. 'I'm looking forward to seeing some of it properly this time in daylight and without those people chasing us!'

The sleeping arrangements hadn't been mentioned of course, but they both had an air of suppressed excitement about them as they guessed, hoped, wondered what the weekend might bring.

They spent the rest of the day touring the New Forest, more sedately today than on the last occasion, when Sam had pushed the old Cherokee during the chase from Brockenhurst. Mid-afternoon they stopped for tea and Anna surreptitiously produced the inevitable chocolate biscuits. She had cleared a lot of stuff from her shoulder bag, having learnt one lesson, but not the biscuits, which had been replenished.

Dusk was nearly falling by the time they visited All Saints churchyard in Minstead once more. This time they were able to tour the church briefly so that Anna could see the internal galleries, the ancient font and the private pew with its own fireplace.

Outside in the churchyard she sat on Emma-Kathleen's bench with its plaque and its memories, watching as Sam placed a fresh meerschaum style pipe on the famous man's gravestone. As she now understood, there was often a pipe there, sometimes several, placed by Sherlockians as a grateful and sympathetic tribute to Sir Arthur. It had become a bit of a tradition for a pipe to be in residence at any given time. Beside the grave were some flowers, brown and fading now, no doubt left by a well-wisher or a family member.

Anna loved the feeling, and the tradition. She liked the whole area and was rapidly becoming a convert to the beauty and timelessness of the New Forest. It was all such a world away from her busy life in London.

Sam looked up at the stunted oak above her, the branches of which extended out and over Sir Arthur's grave. He remembered his fear at the height they had climbed, then Anna squeezing against him and the heady perfume that she had worn that night. She was wearing it again today, he had noticed when kissing her cheek at the station. It was the very first time they had shared any sort of kiss; strange really, after all they had been through together.

Sam didn't want to leave the churchyard, but the evening shadows lengthened slowly and the slight cooling of the air reminded him it was getting late. The words on the monument jumped out at him as he contemplated the inscription that he knew so well.

'Steel True, Blade Straight'

'If anyone ever was, you were, Sir Arthur,' he murmured as he turned away towards the brilliant smile that awaited him. A shiver went down Anna's spine, as only moments before she had whispered the same words, but in her case it was about the man now standing in front of her.

THE END

Afterword

Our fascination with the crimes of Jack the Ripper is still as strong as it was in 1888. It seems that every few months there is a new theory or a new suspect, and some of them are undoubtedly credible. For anyone interested in the crimes, walking the murder sites in Whitechapel on a dark night can still be a chilling and thought provoking experience. In the hunt for Jack it's easy to lose sight of the fact that around a dozen women lost their lives during that period. Their suffering is worthy of our thoughts and compassion.

Thomas Cutbush has always been a suspect, since being outed by *The Sun* newspaper in 1894, though his candidacy has waxed and waned. His uncle Charles was a Superintendent in the Metropolitan Police *at the time of the murders*. For those who accept that Frances Coles was the final Ripper victim, it is a fact that Thomas Cutbush was detained shortly after her murder in 1891. He was arrested for allegedly stabbing two women. Because he was found to be insane, no trial took place and he was sent to Broadmoor. The hunt for the Whitechapel killer was then wound down almost immediately.

Superintendent Charles Cutbush undoubtedly suffered from mental illness and shot himself after his retirement, clearly a family with mental problems. Did he suspect, or know, that his nephew was guilty? Was Thomas the Ripper? Perhaps we will never find out, though I hope more information may yet emerge to rule him in or out of the crimes. I am convinced that the Macnaghten Memoranda was written solely to deflect attention from Superintendent Charles Cutbush and the police.

The exposure of the link between Charles and Thomas could certainly have brought down the Metropolitan force.

If you are interested in finding out more about Thomas Cutbush, there are two books I can recommend, 'Jack the Myth' by A.P. Wolf and 'The Man Who Would Be Jack' by David Bullock. Both of these are excellent works.

Although the modern story in this book is a complete work of fiction, all the locations used by Sam and Anna really exist. Amongst these are three of Sir Arthur Conan Doyle's houses. Undershaw in Surrey, Windlesham in Sussex, and Bignell Wood in the New Forest. The great man is buried in All Saints Churchyard, Minstead, where the oak tree still overhangs his grave. Unfortunately the home where he commenced his practice as a Doctor in Portsmouth was destroyed by bombing during the Second World War.

I owe enormous gratitude to my wife Melanie Anne for her support and encouragement while working on this project. Also a big thank you to my sons. Ross inspired the original idea and insisted that I write the book. Luke created the artwork and guided me with technology. Further inspiration for the story came from Richard Lancelyn Green's wonderful bequest to the City of Portsmouth. We are all in his debt.

In addition I would like to thank Chella and Sophie at Honeybee Books for their very professional work and advice. Finally, my thanks to Helen Baggott, whose eagle eyes saved me much embarrassment! All remaining errors, (and I'm sure there are some) are mine alone.

Roy Sanderson